Think
of
Me

ALSO BY FRANCES LIARDET

We Must Be Brave

Think
of
Me

❦

FRANCES LIARDET

G. P. PUTNAM'S SONS
New York

PUTNAM
— EST. 1838 —

G. P. PUTNAM'S SONS

Publishers Since 1838

An imprint of Penguin Random House LLC

penguinrandomhouse.com

Library of Congress Cataloging-in-Publication Data

Names: Liardet, Frances, author.
Title: Think of me / Frances Liardet.
Description: New York : G. P. Putnam's Sons, 2022.
Identifiers: LCCN 2021053557 (print) | LCCN 2021053558 (ebook) |
ISBN 9780593191149 (hardcover) | ISBN 9780593191163 (ebook)
Subjects: GSAFD: Historical fiction.
Classification: LCC PR6062.I137 T45 2022 (print) |
LCC PR6062.I137 (ebook) | DDC 823/.914—dc23
LC record available at https://lccn.loc.gov/2021053557
LC ebook record available at https://lccn.loc.gov/2021053558

p.   cm.

Printed in the United States of America
1st Printing

BOOK DESIGN BY KRISTIN DEL ROSARIO
Map Illustration by David Lindroth

To Pippa and her loving family

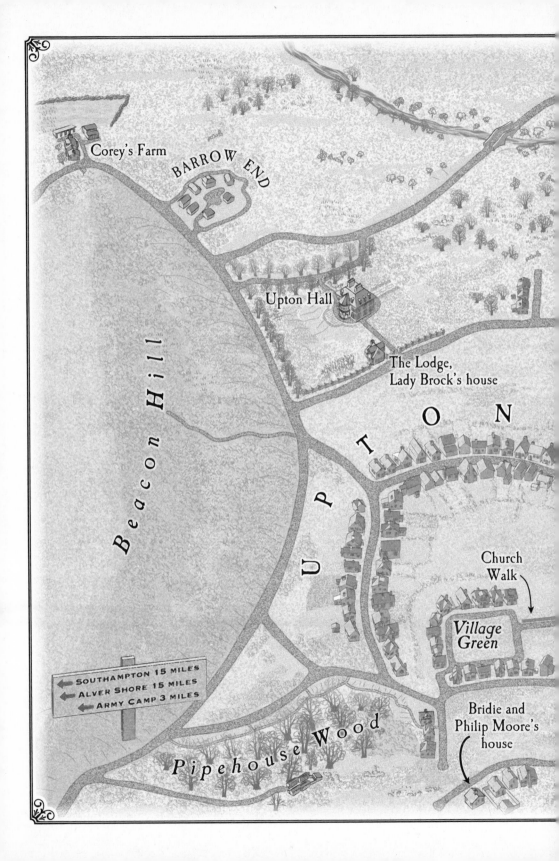

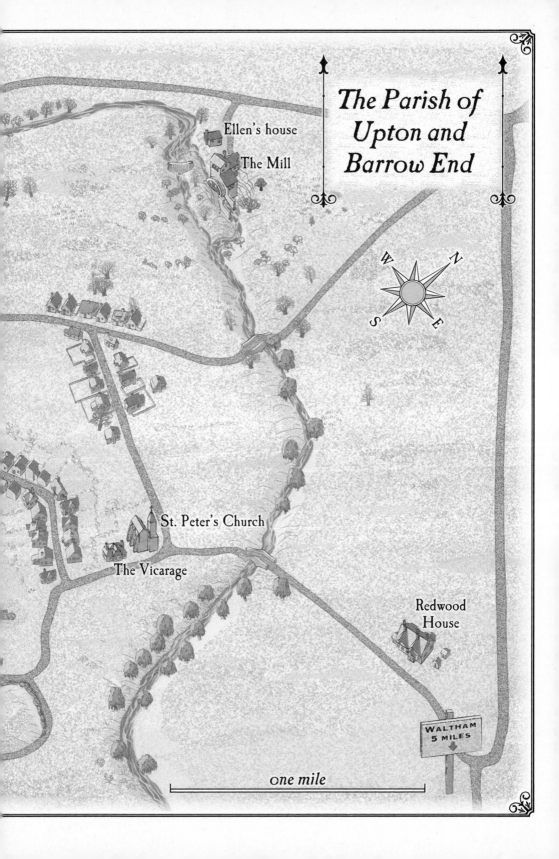

The Parish of
Upton and
Barrow End

Ellen's house

The Mill

St. Peter's Church

The Vicarage

Redwood
House

WALTHAM
5 MILES

one mile

Think
of
Me

PROLOGUE

April 1943, Tunisia

Sunrise, and the encampment is awake. Pans rattle in the cookhouse, grunts and murmurs issue from the rows of tents. Close by, boots crunch over gravel. None of these sounds impinge on the vast silence of the desert.

Two long shadows are flung across the ground. The first is my Hurricane fighter aircraft, motionless and hawklike. The second, approaching with a lanky stride, is myself. A harnessed and helmeted human, twenty-four years old, in love.

The cockpit of a Hurricane is a wooden kennel situated directly behind a fuel tank. There is a firewall, but it lies between fuel tank and engine, not between fuel tank and pilot. On account of this and many other perils, I say a daily prayer before I press the ignition. "Dear Lord, please spare me, James Acton, so that I may return to Egypt and marry Yvette Haddad."

I always use our full names to God, so that He is absolutely clear, through the blizzard of prayers He must receive every morning of this war, exactly who it is I'm talking about.

Yvette is small, lively, Alexandrian. Loyal. Beautiful. Brave. I don't know if I'll live to see her again.

But what a life we will have if I do.

"Amen," I say, as my heart is shaken in my chest by the engine's splattering roar.

July 1974, England

There's only one remaining question, Mr. Acton."

The man who has been interrogating me leans forward with his heavy arms on his knees, big boxer's knuckles on fingers strictly interlinked. As if each hand has been detailed to keep the other out of mischief.

"Which is?"

"Whether you'll go out of your mind."

His tongue appears too large for his mouth; it lumbers from side to side as he speaks, getting in the way of, rather than forming, his words. A man trying to articulate through a mouthful of flannel. When he finishes, the tongue hangs over his bottom teeth, just inside a slack lower lip. His name is Frobisher.

"Go out of my mind? Why?"

I'm slow on the uptake, having been rather mesmerized by Frobisher, his way of speaking, the bulkiness of his limbs. It comes to me that this man, despite his somewhat distracting appearance, has had years of training in winkling out harbored information. He can probably, like a police dog at Customs, simply smell it.

"Why do you think?" Frobisher chortles. "Boredom, man! Look at you, you were an RAF pilot. A prisoner of war."

"That was thirty-odd years ago!" I can't disguise my astonishment. "It's hardly relevant now."

"I beg to disagree." He rocks back in his seat, enjoying himself. "I've seen so many like you. You're one of a whole generation, all ex-services, who signed up for the priesthood at the end of the war, and what were you doing? Arming yourselves to fight another good fight. Think of theological college—all that cold water and discipline and ardent celibacy. Certain similarities to a military training camp, no?"

He's not wrong: both places featured, in varying proportions, muddy cross-country runs and prayer. The prayers shorter and more fervent in the field of battle than in the pew.

"Actually, Archdeacon, I was ordained before the war. And by the end of 1945 I was married."

"Of course you were. Girl you met in Egypt, I believe?"

His beady little eyes track over me. He doesn't "believe": he's learned my file by heart, memorization being a tool of our trade, and so he's simply prodding me now. I can't think of anything I want to say about Yvette. Not now, not to him.

"Yes," I reply. "My late wife was from Alexandria."

There follows a tense silence while the instant coffee cools in the cups, the ginger biscuits soften in the humid late-summer air. From beyond the leaded window a pale sunbeam does what it can to make Frobisher's bald head gleam. As far as I'm aware he hasn't blinked.

"Archdeacon," I say at last, "I've got nothing to hide."

He stretches his lips into a broad grin. They have no shape, these lips, being the same thickness all the way along, and no color to distinguish them from the rest of his face. "My dear man. Nothing was further from my mind. Nevertheless here you are, all set to leave the West Country at rather short notice after, oh, it must be more than twenty years, just when all your work at your current parish is bearing fruit, and come here to Hampshire, to Upton, which for all—"

"Upton and Barrow End. I believe they're quite particular about that."

"—*And* Barrow End"—the grin becomes ferocious—"a community which, for all its good points, is hardly the most challenging environment. For a man of your experience, that is. And you're not yet sixty." He hunches forward, once more a pugilist. "Is it burnout? I mean, from what I've read about Fulbrook—the signs in pub doorways saying *No Knives,* goodness me—"

"In fact they're pictures of knives with an *X* over the top. For the unlettered."

"Well, there you are. I wouldn't blame you for searching out a sleepy village to have a nice quiet breakdown in."

"I assure you I'm not another Blakemore."

The Reverend Charles Blakemore, previous vicar of Upton and Barrow End, collapsed in harness four months ago, mentally unstrung. He's the reason we're all here—myself, and the other short-listed candidates waiting behind the imposing oak door. We've managed to clear the hurdles set in our way, the applications and panel interviews and parish visits. Upton—and Barrow End—was all I hoped it would be, a village and neighboring hamlet settled on the chalk hills before Domesday, the people at long last cautiously prosperous, not given to show, the handshakes friendly but conditional in a way I perfectly understood. And now it's down to this odd, unwieldy man with his clumsy tongue and his direct questions. In all honesty, I can't say it's going well.

"Please continue." Frobisher is suddenly curt. Perhaps he's already thinking about the next candidate. Or his lunch.

"In fact . . ." I clear my throat, take another run at it. "In fact, it was this very situation that attracted me. Mr. Blakemore's illness was gradual, so the parish may have been fairly rudderless for some time. I'd like to help them get back on course. Bring some cheer, comfort. Guidance. When I visited, I came away with the sense that I could win their trust."

Frobisher lifts his chin. The strengthening sunlight catches the solid black frames of his glasses. Desperation spurs me on.

"Archdeacon, I've been a widower for ten years. My son's a student now, on the other side of the country. I've spent over twenty years at Fulbrook, they need someone new. And *I* need a fresh start."

"Ha!" His big hands release each other and each one begins to rub a meaty knee. "We got there in the end."

"Got where?"

"It's all very well saying what you can give to Upton. But what I needed to know was"—his words now emphasized by a pointing forefinger—"what Upton will give to *you*. And now you've told me. A fresh start. Thank you, Mr. Acton. You should expect a letter in a few days."

We both rise to our feet, Frobisher's relief evident in the stretching of his cumbersome frame. I steel myself for the clammy grapple of his handshake. As he releases me he suddenly says, "Remind me, where was your first parish? The one you served immediately after the war?"

He knows perfectly well that my first parish was Alver Shore, a battered port town on the Hampshire coast. I repeat the name to him obediently.

"Ah, yes. No great distance from Upton, is it. Half an hour's drive, hmm? I only mention this in relation to your making a fresh start. Some might suggest it might more aptly be described as going over *old ground*."

Alver Shore. A place of crowded brick terraces cratered by air raids, children swarming over the bomb sites. Waiflike young mothers who scrubbed and baked and carried home the coal, and fell asleep darning socks of an evening. Old men, backs bent under the sea wind, mining the black mud of the harbor for cockles and clams to add to a family diet consisting largely of bread and potatoes and fresh air.

"The Alver Shore of 1946," I say, smiling, "is a far cry from the modern-day Upton of 1974."

"A far cry. Of course." He gives a strange unnerving little chuckle. "I must say, Mr. Acton, that is very well put."

It began one evening in early May, less than three months ago.

The dusk was draining from the sky and I was sitting at my desk writing a sermon in candlelight, something I'd learned to do over the decade since Yvette died, so effectively did the small flame cast the world, even if only for an hour or so, into shadow. A few days previously I'd said goodbye to my son, Tom, who, having completed his first year at university, was off to fruit-pick his way across France until the autumn. I was well used by now to Yvette's absence from my bed, and I was even taking my student son's increasingly sporadic visits in my stride, but that evening the house seemed especially empty. Safe in the candle's soothing glow, pen in hand, I happened to glance at the latest issue of the *Church Times* which lay just within the light's perimeter; my eyes, wandering down the Positions Vacant column, came to rest upon the phrase *rural parish, Hampshire*. It didn't even register properly at the time.

But later that night, as I started my usual prayers before sleeping, I felt a tension inside me, a pulling—or was it a push? Was it coming from outside or was I the one seeking? I couldn't be sure. By the following morning the feeling had formed itself into a statement so urgent that it woke me up.

It's time to go.

Tom and I had been glad to stay in Fulbrook after we lost Yvette. A working Somerset town half an hour from Bristol, it was the only home Tom had ever known. He was ten when his mother died: we both needed to cling to the tossing life raft of familiar surroundings and daily routine. Now he was a tall rucksacking student with his whole life unfolding in Norwich, on the other side of the country, leaping up the steps of the National Express bus. He didn't need Fulbrook anymore. And now, suddenly, in spite of all the memories, the achievements, and the many deep friendships, neither did I. And all because of this startling, almost animal urge that had materialized on that still evening out of the candle flame. I couldn't even explain it properly to myself, let alone to my archdeacon. *You see, sir, I happened to catch sight of the job ad, and, well, that same night I got this feeling . . .*

That would have cut no ice with Frobisher.

A fortnight after my interview, a long white envelope with *The Reverend James Acton* inscribed on it in austere black capitals, arrives.

8th August 1974

Dear Mr. Acton,

I have pleasure in informing you that you have been successful in your application to the post of Vicar of the Anglican Church of St. Peter in the Parish of Upton and Barrow End within the diocese of Winchester.

You will be expected to take up your post on or before the 1st October of this year.

All pertinent documents will be sent under separate cover in the next week.

Yours sincerely,
Ronald Frobisher, ArchD.

I am, as my curate Rick puts it, "gobsmacked."

A month later, Fulbrook has found a new vicar. He's young, extremely cheery, plays the guitar during his services, and enjoys rock climbing. The people involved in this choice are all awfully pleased with themselves. I sense a certain embarrassment: now it's happened, in spite of all their kind words, they quite want me to be gone.

One day in mid-September I'm packing hand over fist when another significant piece of mail arrives. It's a postcard of the city of Cahors: the arches of a medieval bridge skimming a wide river under the sunshine of southern France. The stamp, however, is English.

Hi Dad. Back in the UK. Just moved into house in Norwich. 12 minutes from uni on bike. Vines were hard labor but got some dough plus a cool tan! And now have phone but old tenants left without paying bill >> might get cut off soon. So ring me asap!!

A phone number, and then *Love, Tom.*

Immediately I dial the number. I should be thinking about the Bible study group that I'm due to host in a matter of minutes, but I can't help myself.

The ringing stops. *"Allô?"* The voice is young, French, and female. "May I help you?"

"Yes," I reply, startled. "May I speak to Tom Acton?"

"One moment. I will fetch him."

A creaking, rumpling sort of sound, and a lot of gruff throat clearing. It doesn't sound as if the young woman has to go very far to find him.

"Hello?" says my son, deeper, hoarser, but recognizably him.

"Tom, dear boy!" I burst out. "You're back!"

"Dad!"

A shout of delight. My heart sings.

"Is this a convenient time?" I say, still smiling.

"That was Florence," says this husky young man of mine. "She's . . . she's with me."

"She has an excellent telephone manner."

"Yes. That was the first thing that struck me."

"Tom . . ." I can hear my front door opening, a hubbub in the hallway. Rick my curate is admitting the Bible study crowd. "While you were away, I . . . I decided to leave Fulbrook."

"Leave—Dad, is everything okay? They haven't defrocked you for stealing the silver?"

"No, I've got a new parish. A village called Upton, in Hampshire."

He whooshes a long breath of surprise into the receiver. "Hampshire, that's miles . . . that's a different whatchamacallit, isn't it?"

"Diocese, yes. I'm moving in a couple of weeks."

A pause. Behind him I hear the muffled, beseeching tones of Florence.

"Look," he says finally. "We've got to split . . . Tell you what. Term doesn't start till October. I can help you. Pick me up at Southampton and we'll go to your new place together. You helped me, after all."

He means when we drove to the University of East Anglia a year ago, at the beginning of his first term. Two hundred and fifty miles eastward with a shiny kettle and crisp new duvet in the back of the car. I was all for blankets but he insisted on a duvet. Nobody had blankets anymore, apparently.

"That's very kind, Tom . . ."

"Come on, Dad. It's the least I can do."

Suddenly magnanimous. We're two men now, I understand. Equals.

Toward the end of my time in Fulbrook I gather my friends and colleagues together, open many bottles of wine. They leave late, a little tipsy, with torrents of kind words and embraces. "You are a rotter, James," says one dear, wild-haired female friend, hitting me softly in the chest with a jingle of bracelets. "An absolute rotter, to leave us all in the lurch."

"There's no lurch about it, Maureen," I reply, laughing, because the parish is in such safe hands.

"Oh, yes there is," she says, and wanders unsteadily away down the path.

On the eve of my meeting with Tom in Southampton, I load up a hired removal lorry with the help of the curate Rick and a couple of burly parishioners. We set about our task, starting with the most cumbersome objects. It's a job and a half.

"Bloody thing," I say to Rick as we push the sofa across the floor of the van. "I don't remember it being so heavy when I moved in."

He grins. "Sofas do get heavier over the years. It's well-known."

The last to go into the van is a giant leather armchair. Rick's eyes are red behind his glasses.

"I remember how she used to have a snooze in that chair," he says. "Before she took to her bed, God bless her."

I close my eyes and am visited by a sudden vision of hot desert sky and a woman, very young, walking toward me over stony sand.

"God bless *you*, Rick," I say.

Yvette
8 January 1964

He held my hand in the dust. That was the first time he touched me. Every time the building shook, more ceiling plaster came down. I had one hand on my sister's shoulder and James was holding my other hand. His grip tightened with each bomb that fell.

He wasn't meant to be there at all.

Of course, James and I had already met. But this holding of hands, in fear and darkness, has to come first. Such an impression it made! As I write, I taste the dust on my lips all this time later.

I said that James wasn't meant to be there. But it was April 1942, and precious few people were where they should have been. Half of Alexandria had fled to the countryside, unable to bear any more bombing, to be replaced by crowds of foreigners of every conceivable stripe both military and civilian. My mother used to wring her hands. "I can put up with a lot," she was given to exclaim, "but this *jumbling* of people is quite intolerable!" She made me laugh. As if social displacement were the worst consequence of the fighting.

My mockery didn't bother Maman. Without the war, she asserted, my sister Célia would have settled down with a nice, familiar, French-speaking young man from a Levantine commercial family like ours, preferably in a villa in Cleopatra, the same leafy quarter of Alexandria as our parents' house, so she—Maman—could trot around the corner and visit. Célia would call her children Maurice and Philippe and Lucette and they'd all go to hear Mass together and everything would go on forever.

But Célia had spoiled this scenario. In 1940 she'd fallen in love, heavily and irretrievably, with Flying Officer Peter Ingram, a Hurricane pilot of 274 Squadron, RAF. Now, two years later, Peter having survived the war thus far, she was going to marry him.

The strain on my parents was enormous. Maman couldn't get through a day without weeping and my father chain-smoked all evening, a thick, worrying vein pulsing down the middle of his forehead. They had come to love Peter, you see, after the initial shock. Maman wept because she dreamed of his death every night, a far from fantastic scenario but thoroughly unhelpful in the circumstances. Papa smoked for the same reason. However, Papa felt that Célia's choice of husband, provided he stayed alive of course, was anything but disastrous. Maman's family had been in Egypt for centuries but Papa's had arrived only eighty years previous from Sidon, and he had a sense of the changeability of things. "You think life will go on forever like this, for people like us," he used to say to her when I was a child. "As if Alexandria is an old auntie, turning up every spring at Sham el Nessim with trays of eggs for the picnic, wagging her finger at the youngsters, saying, *Haha, bet you thought I was dead.* But it will come to an end. Mark my words."

And Papa's been proved right. It did all come to an end. Alexandria, *Alexandrie*, by which I mean the city of my youth, exists only in the past. Célia and Peter went to Australia, James and I to England, Maman and Papa to Nice. All of us gone by 1952, taking our lives (and our money: let's not forget the money) in our hands and making the leap. Landing in foreign lands, rooting down, loving each other, the young having children.

Love, and children. Those are the important things. And keeping going.

As our parents had given themselves over to weeping and smoking respectively, Célia and I took it upon ourselves to arrange her wedding. Having flown and fought themselves to absolute shreds during this latest retreat, 274 Squadron had been put on rest for the whole month, *quelle miracle*, so Célia and Peter had jumped at the chance. I had managed to squeeze the happy couple in at St. Mark's Anglican for the ceremony, and booked the tea lounge at the Metropole for the reception. All that remained, on the eve of the great day, was to get dressed to the nines and go to a lovely calming piano recital.

Accompanying us to the concert was Peter's best man, Alastair Pearce. I was very fond of Alastair. My parents had decreed from the beginning that Célia and Peter needed to be chaperoned at all times, and Alastair and I had made up the foursome. Célia, an ex-pupil of the English Girls' College, was a competent anglophone (although you wouldn't think it, the amount of time she and Peter spent in the dumbstruck golden silence of infatuation). But Maman, to keep us from killing each other, had sent me to the Lycée Français, where English was taught through the lens of the absolute supremacy of French culture: grammar perfect, devoid of idioms, uninterested in the sounds *h* and *th*, and accompanied by a strong, guttural French *r*. (Try, as a French speaker, the phrase *thoroughly horrid* at speed.) Anyway, Alastair soon put paid to that: he didn't have a word of French so I had to make all the running in English, and soon I was familiar, or rather *at home*, with marvelous words like *scrounge* and *wizard* as well as phrases such as *use your loaf* and *piece of cake*, which I found quite irresistible. Alastair, furthermore, was married, which made life easy since he was a sandy beanpole of a man, sweet tempered and genial and not remotely my type, and when the boys were on leave we had—within the strict parameters of the Haddad family moral code—what I learned to call a *whale* of a time.

So there we were, waiting in the drawing room for Alastair to call and escort us to a relaxing evening of music. Célia in a charming two-piece, glancing regularly at her new tiny watch (which came in a box with six different-colored straps including a white one for tomorrow). Me, smartly attired in a navy shift, repeating, "Darling, it's not seven yet and I'm sure he won't be late," every time she did so.

Sure enough the bell rang on the dot and I ran to the door. Saying, "See? I knew he wouldn't let you down!"

Standing on the step was a medium-height black-haired somber-looking stranger, pressed and starched in an RAF uniform, holding his hat in his hand.

"I'm terribly sorry," he said without preamble. "Alastair's been held up at Growler. So it's my honor to come here on his behalf and take you to the concert."

Such was my surprise, I caught half of this information at best, and ushered him wordlessly inside where he repeated his announcement, sounding remarkably as if he were issuing a bulletin to the assembled 274 Squadron instead of two women in a drawing room. "Oh—my name is James Acton," he concluded this time, and we all shook hands.

I didn't care what his name was. I thought, honestly, Peter, you could at least have got someone a bit like Alastair. It was idiotic of me but seriously, lighthearted blond pilots were ten a penny, weren't they?

I so wanted everything to be nice for Célia that I nearly rang up the club, to get Peter over here to save the evening, but he was superstitious about seeing her on the night before the wedding.

"Oh, blow," Célia was saying, on receiving this news. "Is he training again? He has the most awful luck."

It was true. Alastair seemed to be kept back at the last minute, or called away early from leave, far more often than Peter. But at least we had Peter. Célia knew a girl whose wedding had been postponed three times.

"What is Growler?" I dared to ask.

"Gerawala," Célia said, with a slight lift of her chin. "It's an airfield, Yvette."

I allowed her this pride she had, in her knowledge of airfields.

"Not far from Marsa Matrouh," added James Acton, without smiling.

"Thank you," I said, absurdly.

Maman and Papa came downstairs at that point and the news was repeated a third time. Papa was tremendously charming and kind as always. Maman pouted and peered around, saying, *"Mais où est Alastaire?"* as if he might be hiding mischievously behind the couch. I was furious with her but Célia just turned the full power of her beauty onto James and thanked him with a dazzling smile.

A note on Célia's beauty

Célia looks nothing like the rest of us. You'd think she was a changeling were it not that her face turns up like a new-minted coin somewhere in every generation of my mother's family. In our time, apart from Célia, there was Aunt Monique who lived in Cairo—I say Aunt, but she was really a cousin of Maman's. When I was a child Aunt Monique came to Alexandria in the summer expressly, it seemed, to show me how beautiful Célia would be when she was grown up. By contrast I was—and am—a fawn-colored, skimpy personage with pitiful legs and arms—vexing, since I'm actually quite strong—and my bust has never really needed a brassiere; hair an unremarkable dark brown, eyes the same without any kind of lustrous allure, and believe you me I knew what lustrous allure was. When I was a child I used to vent my jealousy in ugly comparisons—*my sister's hair is as black as Quink ink; her eyes, two bowls of chocolate torte mix; her lips the exact shade of a raspberry stamped all over the floor.* But Célia didn't care, she just sailed on like a figurehead with her fine-cut profile and gracious neck while her bust and her bum got steadily more ample and sumptuous and molded with every passing year. The wealthier echelons of our little society, people with far more social cachet than us, liked to remark that only ugly girls married RAF pilots because nobody else would have them. Ha! They couldn't say that anymore. I've got a photo of Célia on my dressing table, she sent it a couple of months ago. She's with Peter and the boys in their garden—or *backyaad,* as the boys call it—and she's wearing sunglasses and sugar-almond lipstick with her hair in a curvy bob like poor Jackie Kennedy, and she looks just heavenly. She and Peter are planning to visit but it's such a long way from Adelaide and I'm rather unwell at the moment. I want to be fit again by the time they come.

Anyway. After Célia had thoroughly banished Maman's rudeness, we went out to the car. The jasmine vine covered half the front of the house these days and the very first flowers were out. The jasmine didn't care about the war. It just kept on flowering.

Our streetlamps had been covered with so much blue paint that they barely lit themselves, but there was a glow in the sky from the moon rising behind the houses, and a palm tree stood like a signpost at the junction. Célia got into the back, James sat next to me in front. I started the engine and idled, foot hovering over the gas.

"Is this a Citroën?" James asked.

"Yes, a Fifteen," I said, as casually as I could. "Papa trusts me with it, you know, even in the blackout." I used to go to the *mekaniki* with Papa; he sat me on his knee so I could steer his old car out of the repair yard—I must have been eight—with the engine thundering. I felt like a mahout on a war elephant shouldering its way through ranks of beating drums.

"Ready," Célia said, peering at her watch in the glow from her cigarette. "Go."

I stamped on the gas and we screeched away from the curb. The needle bounced up to fifty, eighty, ninety. "Now!" I cried, as we reached a hundred kilometers an hour.

"Twenty-seven," Célia said mournfully.

"Damn this war petrol." I slowed the car to arrive at the junction with another milder screech of tires. The Citroën was meant to reach a hundred in twenty seconds, but it was ages since I'd done it. I pulled out onto the main street. A tram passed on the seafront road ahead. I glanced at James. His jaw was clenched and one hand was braced against the dashboard.

"Oh, no." I put my hand to my mouth. "We didn't warn you."

"We were trying to beat the clock," Célia said. "How *awful* we are."

"Not at all," James managed to say, tight-lipped. Which made us both, horrid, silly girls that we were, burst into hysterical laughter.

By way of apology I went along the Corniche at the speed of a hearse. I was overtaken by a gharry, for goodness' sake, the horse going at a fast-shambling trot, head up, blinkered, the carriage full of Australians who whistled and clapped in derision—*lady driver*—as they passed us. The promenade cafés lay in shadow under a great big searchlight of a moon that was turning the sea into chain mail. I was glad of the roar of the Citroën. You needed something jarring, otherwise the beauty got ridiculous. On summer dawns when the water seemed weightless, rippling, smeared in golden mist, you needed a bit of a stink of fish.

Out of remorse at my thoughtless behavior and jackass-like mirth at his expense, I made an effort with James Acton.

"The pianist is Edouard Shama," I said. "One of our oldest friends and the . . . Célia, what is *entremetteur*?"

"Matchmaker."

"Matchmaker for Célia and Peter. Not knowingly, of course. But if Peter and Alastair hadn't gone to the Parisiana that night to hear Edouard play, Peter would never have set eyes on Célia. We hardly ever go to nightclubs, you see. But Edouard invited us, and look what happened! Do you like the piano, James?"

Indeed he did. "I go whenever I can to hear Gina Bachauer play at the Rue Rassafa."

"Ah, Madame Gina!" I cried. "She is superb, isn't she? And did you hear Monsieur de Menasce? He duets with Madame Gina sometimes. Some might say they prefer to listen to Madame Gina on her own, but, after all, it is his house. Or palace, really. Did you get a peek at the tapestries? And oh, heavens, the teas afterward! Célia and I look at the mille-feuilles and sit on our hands. A contest between greed and vanity, you see. Do you play the piano?"

"I used to be quite good. But the more I practice, the worse I get."

"Oh, that can't be true."

"It is. I'm going to have to stop before I lose my gifts entirely."

"James, how ridiculous!"

I burst into giggles. I was so relieved to be amused by him. Perhaps the evening might go well after all.

The recital room, part of a very ancient, very musical institute, was on the first floor up a winding marble staircase, the grand piano so burnished and glowing that the cabinet looked almost red in the low lighting. I sat down between Célia and James. While we waited for the performance to begin I stole surreptitious glances at him. He gazed quietly ahead, his face serious, contained: I could imagine him studying. The books would be thick, leather-bound. He was black-haired where Peter was fair. His eyes were blue like Peter's but I had already noticed how dark they were, a different, Delft blue, beneath black brows.

Just then a hush descended. Edouard sat down at the piano and launched into the recital.

Debussy, then Chopin—what a romantic effusion this was, perfect for Célia's last night. Next, without an interval, came Khachaturian's *Poeme*. Swiftly Edouard conjured up the moonlight on the water, smashed it to bits with a hard flood of major chords, brought it back again in little glims of white that floated on the ripples of a deep, dark lake. (I can't help it. I adore that piece.) It was toward the end, when I was utterly entranced, that the piano began to emit a strange buzzing. Was it a broken string in the lower register? The buzz became a whine. No, it wasn't coming from the piano. The whine rose and swelled into the wail of an air-raid siren. Edouard said, *"Ah, c'est pas possible,"* and took his hands from the keyboard.

There was nothing to be done. The director of the institute and his ushers insisted we take cover. Edouard, furious, strode out saying, "Damn the planes, I'm going home," brushing off all restraining arms and pleas to stay. I didn't blame him.

The rest of us, about thirty or forty people, left our seats and trooped down to the basement. We sat on the floor, with our backs against the rough plaster of the wall. People got out their newspapers, books, cushions: I hadn't thought to bring anything. It was the eve of Célia's wedding, after all, and I simply hadn't allowed for air raids. Once more I sat between Célia and James. He had tilted his head to stare at the ceiling. I didn't like it when people did that. If you took no notice of ceilings, I maintained, they were less likely to come down on you.

Around us, the crowd got restive. I began to think we might as well go home like Edouard. Ten to one he was back at his flat, fuming. He could have finished the *Poème* by now. He could have played the whole thing over again. How I would have loved that. "Here they come at last," someone said, and the room fell quiet.

"Italian," James murmured. "Maybe a Kingfisher." I didn't like it when people tried to identify aircraft, either.

I listened, waiting for the engine noise to rise and fall away again as it did when the planes passed to the north on their way to the harbor. But the roar grew harder and flatter. It had appetite.

The noise mounted up on itself. One, two seconds and it was overhead. Now another sound, this one too big to hear. Only to feel.

The blast hit the inside and the outside of my head simultaneously. The pressure was unsurvivable. I pulled Célia against me but had no time to tell her I was dying before the floor bounced under the next bomb and we screamed into each other's ears.

The planes followed one by one. Another bomb and another. Pieces of my life started to peel off and float loose. I reached up aged ten to pick an apricot from the tree in the garden at Muntaza. Simultaneously a wasp stung my finger, and my old dress, the only one I loved, tore from the armpit to the waist. Another bomb, and I lay on my side aged fourteen with the muscles of my innards clutching in spasm at my fresh appendectomy wound, yelling, *Dieu, aie pitié de moi*, God have mercy on me, as each convulsion nearly tore my stitches out. Again and again they came. Oh, I screamed then and now, *Dieu, aie pitié de nous*, God have mercy on us.

And all this time James was holding my hand, his fingers squeezing mine.

It finished at last. Our ceiling was still holding. I sensed that, in spite of all the noise, the building had been spared a direct hit. Temporarily deafened, I shook my head and swallowed. As my ears cleared I heard outbursts of coughing and crying. Faces flickered here and there, underlit by match flames and lighters. They could have been Goya's people, gurning and grimacing at the disasters of war. My lips were caked in dirt. I tried to wipe my mouth but my hands were also filthy.

Célia stirred beside me and put her hands to her head. She said, "Oh, damn, I'll have to wash my hair again."

In a loud, singsong, only mildly cross voice, as if she were lounging in her bedroom, calling to me across the passageway.

"Darling," I croaked. "Don't worry about your hair."

"And it'll never be dry in time," she declared, as if I hadn't spoken.

"Lie down, sweetheart, put your head in my lap," I said, and she obeyed me without a word, and went to sleep.

"She's in shock," James said.

"I know."

The crying had subsided into murmurs and groans. People were starting to talk. Somebody said, "Not long till the all-clear," and other voices agreed.

"Are you all right, Yvette?" I heard James say.

"Yes," I said. "I think so. Are you?"

"Yes."

He wasn't holding my hand anymore. I wasn't sure when he'd let go. I wanted to thank him for it. But the hand-holding had belonged to the bombing, and that was over now.

So I said, "Good."

I suddenly pictured St. Mark's Church ruined, that lovely stone frieze, that always reminded me of a row of *palmiers*, crashed down from the tops of the broken walls. Suddenly I wanted to eat a *palmier*, which was strange because I didn't even like them, the way the pastry was simultaneously flaky and hard. It gummed up my teeth. Next I imagined a rubble-filled cavern in the middle of the Metropole. Then, worst of all, a sheet of smoke hanging over Peter's club.

"James," I said in desperation, "talk to me. Tell me about—about Hurricanes. You fly a Hurricane too, like Peter and Alastair? Tell me about them."

If he was surprised, he didn't show it.

"Well," he said. "Hurricanes are very sturdy planes. Workhorses, you could say. They've all done four thousand miles before we even set eyes on them. We can't bring them across the Med, you see, or the Germans will get them, so they get shipped to Takoradi in West Africa and flown all the way to Egypt. Some of the pilots get lost en route and run out of fuel. Others just crash. But most of the planes reach Heliopolis more or less intact."

That was fairly awe-inspiring.

"What else?"

"We call the cockpit the dog kennel. Because it's a sort of wooden box. In fact the outer frame of the airplane is made mostly of wood."

"Wood? Now you're *having me on*." That phrase was one of Alastair's.

"Nope. Wood, covered in Irish linen, which is stretched and doped and painted."

"Really, James. Irish linen, indeed. For a theatrical production, yes, but a real plane?" I chortled at this rank attempt at deception. "I wasn't *born yesterday.*"

"The shells go straight through without exploding." I could hear the smile in his voice. "And it's quick and easy to repair. I'm not making it up, I swear."

"Good heavens," I said, as it sank in. "Wait till I tell Célia . . . Actually, no, I won't."

"No. It doesn't inspire confidence in the civilian."

The chatter around us was now at the level of a promenade café. Sweets and cigarettes were being handed, or rather fumbled, around, new friends were being made. Soon, I thought, we won't be able to hear the all-clear.

"What do you do in the desert, when you're not in your Hurricane?"

My misery had quite gone.

"What do we do? Let me see . . . Oh, yes. Last year my squadron leader commandeered an abandoned Italian tank. He drove it around, crashing into the other wrecks."

I gasped. "Why on earth?"

"For fun!"

"Insane," I said in admiration.

"The game was called bumpers."

"I bet I could handle a tank."

"No, no, Yvette." He started laughing. "You'd never be happy driving a tank. They do sixteen miles an hour flat out."

I was covered in shame. "I am sincerely sorry about our speed trial. We should have prepared you."

"Yes, you should have!" He was still laughing. "I thought that was how you drove all the time!"

We fell silent again. Apart from the glimmers from little flames here and there, it was completely dark. Célia lay dead to the world, her head heavy on my legs. I stroked her hair, picturing her ascending the marbled staircase of matrimony, the heavy hem of her dress following her, an ebbing silken tide, through soundlessly closing double doors into an unseen chamber where Mademoiselle would become Madame. She had remained utterly innocent of the act in question, a pretty impressive feat in a girls' school. Anyone who thinks it's men who are preoccupied with sex should eavesdrop on the private conversations of any random group of well-brought-up young women. Their facts might not always be quite straight, but their interest is unparalleled. Célia, however, would place her hand, palm outward, in front of her averted face, saying, *Please, I prefer not to know. When the time comes, I will pray to Sainte Julienne de Norwich.* Although it caused her friends at the English Girls' College to yelp like seals at feeding time, this remark moved me. *Tout finira bien,* Sainte Julienne had famously said. Everything will be all right in the end.

"James, do you know Sainte Julienne de Norwich?"

"Saint Julian of Norwich? Yes, I think so." He pronounced it *Norritch.* "Didn't she say, *All shall be well, and all shall be well, and all manner of thing shall be well* . . . Why do you ask?"

"Célia." I spoke automatically. "She's not remotely prepared."

"There'll be plenty of time. The wedding's not until three. And we'll be out of here before dawn, I bet you."

"Yes, of course. Of course." In the darkness I blushed and blushed.

A soft, awkward silence. Filled, very slowly, by his understanding. Expressed by a small intake of breath. I was terribly embarrassed.

"Yvette, don't worry." He touched my elbow. "Peter's not an idiot. He'll look after her."

I remember the gentle cup of his palm against my bare skin. When he took his hand away I still felt it.

THREE

A tall, tanned stranger is lying asleep on a bench outside the entrance to Southampton railway station. His head is pillowed on one arm, and both feet are stuck out over the end of the seat. His shirt is threadbare, his jeans ragged. He's got his mother's hair—dark brown curls, now almost shoulder-length. Thank goodness he's sleeping, because I'm suddenly blinking my wet eyes like an old fool.

"Am I late?" I ask a few moments later, after rousing him with a touch on the shoulder.

Tom stands up, smiling. "I hitched. Been here since eight." He envelops me in a bear hug.

"You look like John the Baptist," I tell him when he releases me.

He grins, stretches his arms out. *"Pre-ee-pare ye the way of the Lord,"* he sings, a line from a new musical about the life of Jesus. Along with the mass of hair—complete with sideburns—and the general rangy demeanor, there's a new fine line under each eye. That touches me the most.

We drive north out of the city. Tom map-reads. A thing from when he was very young, his yen for navigation. Marsh, railway, church with a tower, church with a spire. Youth hostel, footpath. Comfortingly distinct shapes and colors, each one endowed with a single unequivocal meaning. Balm to an orphaned young male mind.

"So," I say, "are you looking forward to your second year? Will you miss your cell in the Swedish prison?" Rumor has it that the university's famous architecture is modeled on one such establishment, and Tom spent his first year living on campus.

He smiles. "Yes I am, and no I won't. This year's going to be out of sight. The house is a dump but we don't care . . ."

So it's not university that is the source of this slight reticence, this clouded mood that I've detected since we've been on the road.

"Tell me about Florence," I venture.

"She went back to France yesterday." His voice is tight with misery.

"Oh, dear."

He tells me how they met in a vineyard in the vicinity of Bordeaux, how her father managed the place—"massive great bloke, never off his tractor"—and how she ran away with Tom to England. "I wanted to smuggle her into number twenty-three with us. The bedroom's big enough." He sighs.

I try not to smile. "But she wouldn't be smuggled?"

"Too sensible," he says in despair. "She rang her mum, all is forgiven. She's back doing political science at Bordeaux."

"Clever girl, then. Are you writing to her?"

"Every day. We're really, really sold on each other. Actually I'm hitching down in the holidays." It is almost comical, the way his mood rises again so quickly. "She's just beautiful, Dad. Turn left here."

I do as he says, swing off the main road too fast, the brakes are spongy. The road dives between embankments dark with wet foliage, pulls its shoulders in to duck under a railway bridge and doesn't widen again afterward. Any minute I expect to find grass growing in the middle. I've driven a lorry this size before but I was younger then, and the visibility is poor, and the hire company's damage deposit is enormous.

"Tom, I didn't come this way last time . . ."

"Stay calm," he intones. "This is the shortcut to Waltham. Beyond Waltham lies our destination, the Parish of Upton and Barrow End."

"In the land of Mordor."

It was meant as a joke, but I sound too apprehensive.

"Courage, mon vieux," says my son.

In Waltham rain covers the windscreen in sheets that are beaten back only for a second or two by the wipers. Because of the shortcut we've come into the town from an unfamiliar direction and I don't recognize the buildings. "A Fine Fare, look," says Tom as we cross a square, the tires slapping over cobbles. "We could stop and get some stuff—"

"I can't look. I can't even see where I'm going." A signpost appears between torrents of rainwater. *Southampton.* "That's not right—"

"We're fine. Don't panic, Dad."

"I'm not *panicking.*" Everyone uses this word now.

"Take the Southampton road, then."

"No," I say. "That's back the way we came!"

Disobeying him I bear left and head, for want of anywhere else, toward a narrow alley leading off the square. To my alarm, I find I'm overtaking a moving bus. For a paralyzing second we jockey neck and neck for the same tight little exit. The bay window of a florist's shop bulges into the road, bringing me to my senses. Three yards from the plate glass the sluggish brakes bite at last, and Tom and I are flung forward against our seat belts. We both shout loud curses, and the engine stalls.

No impact from behind or sides, only the blare of horns as the bus shoots past in a stream of electrically lit windows, followed by an irate camper van, a V sign held up against the misty windscreen. I realize Tom's got his hand on my hand which is on the gear stick and shaking.

"Shit," he says. "No harm done. Shit."

"I have not heard such language . . . ," I recite.

"Since the Battle of Bréville," he concludes, with an uncertain grin. "Why do we always say that when we swear? Nobody else does."

"I'll tell you later. Help me find a parking space and we'll go to the supermarket. You were right, by the way."

"What?"

"I *was* panicking."

We cross the square, collars up against the rain. Above me a weathercock, high on an imposing municipal building, backs his green rump into the wind. Tom swings the shop door open and I make for the frozen aisles, throw cardboard cartons into the trolley. Sausages, fish in bread crumbs. Then tins—carrots, potatoes, peas, soup.

"Seriously, Dad? You can't peel a potato?"

"I haven't got time."

"I don't think you're eating properly these days."

I snort. "Mind your own business."

He lopes off toward Fresh Produce.

Tom takes the wheel for the last five miles. The road is now a tunnel through lashing beeches and high banks, the edges lapped by rockfalls of lumpy chalk. Tom takes no notice of the obstacles, pushing on over them, bumping us in our seats. Can he handle this road? Of course he can. Yvette drove lorries during the war with practically no training at all. I look at his hands, so much bigger and stronger than his mother's, but his fingers are alive on the wheel like hers used to be.

Abruptly the beeches clear, the road levels, and we begin to travel between dank hedges. We're crossing the boundary of Upton. The church heaves into view—a square flint tower above a dripping monster of a yew. "A hundred yards down on the right," I say, as the hedge spins past in the wet. "Slow down. Here, Tom. *Here.*"

Tom swings in between two crumbling stone gateposts and brings the vehicle to a lurching halt. In the back of the van, something crashes to the floor.

"Ah, *zut*," he says. "The Venetian chandelier."

"Haha."

We get out into the kind of solid, drenching, vertical rain reserved especially for people moving house. Tom opens up the back of the lorry while I wrestle with the front door key. On the floor of the hall is a letter addressed to me. I recognize that elegant hand. Tearing it open I learn that Archdeacon Frobisher wishes to visit at my earliest convenience. Those two things, convenience and Ronald Frobisher, don't go together at all well.

We enter the vast bare cube of the kitchen. It contains a stone sink, a cold black solid-fuel Rayburn stove mantled in dust, a fridge from the atom bomb era. The fridge is plugged into the only electric socket.

"Whoa," Tom says. "I thought *my* place was grotty!"

"It'll do."

"For what?" He folds his arms against the encroaching chill. "I wouldn't put Borstal kids in here."

He has a point. The house looks much more forbidding than it did in the summer when I was taken around it. The sitting room has turned into a cavern where absent pictures have left pale rectangles on the otherwise tobacco-browned walls. The smell of nicotine I noticed before is now competing, for the place of dominant odor, with damp: I'd better check the gutters. The dining room differs from the sitting room only in that as well as the odors it contains two items—a large dining table with bulging calves, and a telephone. I place Archdeacon Frobisher's letter on the dining room table and lift the receiver. The line has been connected, for which I suppose I must thank him, but I wonder why the phone hasn't been installed in the study. The study had been locked on my last visit and no one could find the key. It had been mislaid by the previous incumbent, the unhappy Charles Blakemore.

But the key, I discover, has been found, and left for me in the lock of the study door. I open the door, and instantly understand why they didn't put the phone in here.

Not only has the room not been cleared, I wonder if it's been touched in years. A thick fuzz of cobwebs covers the single high window and the bookshelves are still loaded with dusty dilapidated volumes. The most outstanding feature of the room, however, is the collection of old newspapers. Bales of them, tied up with string, stacked one on the other everywhere on the floor. The stacks stand at varying heights, rather like a city of high-rises, nearly obscuring the heavy hardwood desk and table, which are both heaped with a mountain of unopened mail. I turn on the light—a weakling thirty-watt bulb. I can't see into the corners of this room.

I don't want to see into the corners of this room.

Poor Blakemore. Surely they could see he was losing his grip. Why didn't anybody help him?

Tom has got very fit laboring in the vineyards. It takes us one hour to unload and distribute the lorry's contents. In the sitting room I survey the altered surroundings. The armchair that my curate Rick mentioned is by the fireplace. Such a mistake, we thought, when we bought it. Yvette, a small person, feared it might corner her like a rhino. She used to claim that it moved during the night. In bed she whispered to me, giggling: *James,* she said, *I swear, we should leave the back door open. Give it its freedom.* But when Tom was born it proved to be the perfect shape for nursing an infant and then later, as Rick remembered, for cradling her aching limbs. Now the rhino's hide is rubbed raw, its back and seat welted and torn. My gaze moves on, over the swaybacked chintz sofa, the coffee table scarred by cup rings and felt-pen doodles. The gnawed legs of the rickety wooden chairs, victims of Roger, the long-passed collie dog of Tom's childhood.

Tom's standing behind me, in the doorway.

"Oh, Dad," he says. "These things . . . they're bloody tragic."

Immediately I bristle. "They're not tragic, just old."

"We should have got rid of them years ago."

I turn around. "I kept them for *you.* So you'd feel at home here."

Thirty years ago, as a fugitive prisoner of war in Silesia, I scrambled up a scree slope with nothing between me and my pursuers but a stand of thin young pines. I was tracking across the slope trying to keep behind the pines. But then the scree dislodged below me and the whole face of the slope began to move downward, bearing me into the guards' line of sight however fast I climbed. Just as I couldn't help being seen by them, so am I unable to escape my son's piercing stare.

"It all happened so quickly," I plead. "The move, the job. I didn't have time to think about the furniture . . ."

His only response is to fold his arms.

"Okay," I say in capitulation. "So I want to keep it. Is that so bad?"

"Yes. No." He sighs. "I haven't a clue." He falls silent and I say nothing. Presently he speaks again. "God, I'm starving. Aren't you?"

"Not sure. I never really know until I see food."

"I cooked too often, that's the trouble. And now you're as helpless as a baby."

When she knew she was dying Yvette made us a cookery book, the plain facts, down to boiling vegetables. (*Those that grow belowground*

are put in cold water. Aboveground, hot.) Over the years I left more and
more of the catering to Tom.

"At least babies know when they're hungry," I say. "Let's see what
we can do with my camping stove."

In the kitchen we heat tomato soup on the gas ring, eat it with toasted
slices of white bread from a packet. Bicker briefly about this bread,
how it's a nasty cheap dough inflated by steam—Tom's view—and
makes jolly nice toast—mine. The two opinions aren't incompatible.

"I dunno," he says finally, after taking the edge off his appetite. "I
can't work out what you're doing. With your life, I mean."

I aim for a reasonable tone. "You don't have to. That's my concern."

"Weren't you happy at Fulbrook?"

"I was perfectly happy. I simply needed something new."

He laughs. "Says Steptoe. You know, *Steptoe and Son*? With the
junk shop full of the most amazing ancient crap?"

"Where? I don't remember them."

He rolls his eyes. "It's a TV show."

"I'm sorry I haven't watched enough television to be able to follow
your conversation. Perhaps you never noticed that I spent every evening working—"

"Oh, here we go—"

"After helping you with homework, tidying the house, doing the
dishes—"

"Begging your pardon?"

He's pointing a spoon at me. It's not a very accusatory sort of
thing, a soup spoon. I can't remain affronted.

"Okay, I grant you the dishes." I look at him fondly. "You were a
good boy."

"Where are you going to put Mum's urn?"

Of course he'd want to know. He sounds wary and I don't blame him. The house is so bleak.

"I'm sure we can find somewhere. Let's go upstairs."

The box we need is in the room I've chosen for my bedroom. I pull away the packing tape and lift out the urn. A cylindrical jar of chased silver, six inches high, handed down from her father. Always a bit lighter than I think it's going to be. She brought it with her from Alexandria, a pretty thing to grace her dressing table. Toward the end she talked about her ashes being scattered somewhere, but she never named a place. So for ten years we've kept her with us.

I pass it to Tom, who takes it in both hands. He casts his eyes around the bedroom before making his way to the fireplace, a small clean black-leaded grate. He places the urn on the mantelshelf above it. He stands back, eyeing the jar, and then nudges it just a touch to the right. When he's satisfied that it is sitting in the exact middle of the shelf, he kisses his fingers and strokes the kiss onto the lid.

"Where's that tiny little wooden chest?" he asks.

"What?" I'm still recovering from the impact of my son's gestures, their grace and tenderness in this dark, cheerless room.

"You know. The one with the sand in." He goes back to the packing box. "The sand from her favorite beach in Alexandria, what did you say it was called?"

"Stanley."

"No, it wasn't Stanley." He darts a look at me. "I remember you said, Sidi something—"

"Sidi Bishr, yes. I haven't seen that chest for years, Tom, there's no point rummaging . . ."

But he is, he's rummaging with gusto. He lifts out a lampshade, a

single canvas sneaker, and a cardboard folder labeled *Sermons, 1956.*
"Honestly, Dad. This could have been packed by a burglar."

"There was so much to do, I just chucked everything in. Leave it,
Tom. I've no idea where it's got to."

Too late, he's holding the chest in his hand.

It's made of cedarwood, with a barrel lid and brass hasp and
hinges. Perhaps two inches by three. It looks even smaller, sitting on
Tom's open palm. Before I realize what I've done, I've reached out and
taken it in my hand. He blinks in surprise.

"I was going to ask if I could have it," he says mildly.

"Really?" I rack my brains for something I could give him instead.
"Why don't you take the photo albums? They're much more interesting."

"And a lot harder to carry."

I struggle to speak, clutching the chest in my fingers, holding it
close against my body.

"I feel this should stay next to Mum."

"It was never next to her before. I remember. It was always on your
bookshelf, in among all the clutter—"

"Tom . . ." I'm shaking my head. "I'm sorry—I don't know what to
say . . ."

"It's okay, Dad." He touches my arm, his eyes wide, full of baffle-
ment. "It doesn't matter that much. You're right, the photos are more
interesting."

I set the little container on the mantelshelf. It's true, it never used
to sit beside Yvette, and now the arrangement isn't symmetrical anymore. I'm seized by the urge to get these awkward boxes and their
jumbled contents out of my sight. "Tom, can you help me put all this
stuff in the attic? There's nothing I need. I'll sort it out later when I've
got more time."

Tom has found the photograph albums. Three heavy leather-bound books, containing Yvette's childhood, youth, and our family life. "Is there an attic?" he says.

"Bound to be."

On the landing we find a ladder propped against the wall. Above the ladder, a ceiling hatch. Tom climbs up, pushes the hatch upward with a clatter. "Bloody hell," he splutters, coughing from the dust as he takes each box in turn from me and manhandles them into their new stowage. "No one's been up here for a hundred years. And I can see a couple of holes in the roof. Broad daylight, Dad, showing through."

"I'll deal with them." For the first time today I'm starting to feel tired.

It's still raining hard when I pull up outside the station. "Well, good-bye," Tom says, with the almost baleful stare he gives me when he has a lot more to say.

"What?" I prompt him.

"Oh, I don't know. I wish I knew what you were doing, Dad."

I laugh. "Don't worry about me, dearest Tom. Get on with year two. Have fun."

He gives me a mock salute, gets out of the lorry, and makes for the station entrance. I watch him dodge the puddles, the photo albums crammed into his rucksack. I could have given him more reassurance, told him how much I was looking forward to this new post, but honestly, on a wet evening with five hours' driving ahead of me, I hadn't the energy. I leave the station and work my way through the traffic toward the West Country, reach Fulbrook, swap the lorry for my car, and drive all the way back to Upton.

As so often, I get a second wind on the journey home. I'm wide awake by the time I reach the vicarage.

I find a torch and an umbrella and set off down the lane to the church. My torch beam sweeps through the rain to light up the wet verges, the hazel trees on the bank, the startled striped face of a badger.

The church door opens with a scrape of wood across stone. I've been here several times over the course of the summer and the feel of the flagstones, the way they dip in the middle under the tread of parishioners across the centuries, is starting to feel familiar. But I've never yet visited after sunset. I switch on the main lights. A clear brownish glow rises to the roof and fades into dimness only at the very highest point. The font is formidable in the low light, a huge piece of limestone bare of decoration, made functional by the hewing of a circular hollow in the top. I am to use this font on Sunday morning, the day after tomorrow, to christen a child. So far, all I know is that the family are called Sutton.

Running my hand across the bowl I become aware for the first time of eons of fossil shells, and wonder where this great block of stone comes from.

In a church, time is hard to see. The decades flick by in tiny shifts and alterations, mostly bits and pieces breaking and falling off; occasionally something massive occurs, like the punch of a vaulted arch, a curtain of whitewash sweeping over the saffron and rose of a fresco. It happened here, I know: the fresco, of Saint Peter bearing keys, has been uncovered. The priests of this parish are listed at the door, and the total is sixteen. Sixteen names since 1389. We'd fit nicely into a minibus. What a journey that would be.

I go and sit in a pew. Glance up at the flowers, ready for the day after tomorrow. Suddenly think of Tom, how sometimes, at bedtime, he used to pull the blankets over his head. Then a hand would appear with an open palm: the signal for transmission. I would grasp this hand and, hidden beneath his blanket, in the darkness or semi-darkness, my son would disclose his fears and pains. *Harry Hopkins stole my protractor. Mr. Bates says I'm too short to play Henry Vee. What will happen to me if you die as well as Mum?* It was soft and warm, that small boy's hand, and I held it many times as the fingers lengthened over the years and the palm grew stronger and the grip harder.

When I was called out in the evening a neighbor, a Mrs. Marshall, used to come and sit with Tom. She taught him to knit. I remember Tom at the kitchen table, working on a long, increasingly grubby scarf while Mrs. Marshall heated up his favorite tea of tinned ravioli; I remember looking at him and being seized with the certainty that nothing lay between him and the dolor of the world except a layer thin as eggshell or even thinner, thin as the white membrane that peels off the egg, and this layer was made out of Mrs. Marshall, a ball of wool, a tin of ravioli, my love and my fear, and chief among those was my fear, my irreducible, granular conviction that anything could happen to him. I close my eyes and give thanks for the fact that as time went on my fear dwindled away, that Tom flourished, that we lived together in peace. That we found each other good company.

I'm sorry I upset him about the little wooden chest. I responded instinctively. He was set back, puzzled, that I couldn't let him have that tiny thing. But he seemed to recover. Perhaps it didn't mean that much to him, after all.

I hope not.

As I rise to my feet, I catch sight of a dark shape on the edge of the pew under the window. I stretch my arm toward it, but at the barest touch of my fingers it slithers off the pew onto the floor. Switching on my torch, I stoop down into the narrow space between the pews and retrieve it. The fabric is very fine and light—silk, at a guess. A woman's headscarf. Perhaps one of the flower arrangers left it behind. I lay it down on the pew and rummage in my pockets for the church key.

The beam of light from my torch strikes the colors, catches my eye. Blue and orange on a cream background, the blue Mediterranean, the orange hot and burned.

My heart thumps, a slow counterpoint to the lightning of my mind that tells me, before my eyes have made sense of the image, that the design on the scarf will be of a train. Yes: the beam of torchlight plays over a jumble of carriages rollicking through mountain meadows behind a puffing engine. And a farmer's wife will be waving at the train. Look, a peg-top woman with round face and blob of a blue hat and blue clogs. She'll have a cow. There she is, the merry cow, tail switching, laughing like the cow on the cheese box.

Daubed over the sky, a banner of cheerful orange capitals that I know, a split second before I read them, will make the words *LE PE-TIT TRAIN DÉPARTEMENTAL.*

The little local train.

Adrenaline sweeps through me, darkens my vision, shrinks the world. I stand for a minute, one hand at my mouth. I could swear I've never seen this scarf before. But I knew it. When I saw those colors, I knew the shapes and words they were going to form. As if I've held it in my hands before. As if it's been next to Yvette's skin.

I'm being ridiculous. I imagine Tom saying, *Get a grip, Dad.*

"Get a grip, Dad," I echo him aloud. I pick the scarf up and head for the door. On my way out I leave a scribbled message pinned to the noticeboard. *Found in church: one silk headsquare. Please apply to the vicarage.*

By the time I go to bed I've nearly convinced myself it's a case of déjà vu. I've driven for hours, I tell myself. My tired eyes and brain fell out of sync for a moment. I have left the scarf downstairs on the kitchen table, the bright design safely extinguished in darkness. In the morning I bet it'll mean nothing to me.

I wind up my tin alarm clock. The rain stopped on my way back from the church, but the dripping from the trees is as loud and steady as the downpour.

FOUR

Yvette
12 February 1964

Yes. As I write all these years later I taste the dust on my lips.
And I think of those young bomber crews above us that night, trapped in their tin cylinders, netted by searchlights as the big anti-aircraft gun at Kom el-Dikka opened up underneath them. They must have screamed as loud as Célia and I did. I pray that when Tom falls in love—it's hard to imagine now, he's still such a small boy, only ten—I pray that it will be in peacetime, so that lovely warm feelings can grow at their leisure, and sparkling glances can be exchanged until the moment comes for their fingers, his and his lover's, to gently inter-link. Let there be no more clutching of strangers' hands in terror. Let no more young people scream in the air and on the ground.

The all-clear sounded. We had become strangely used to the basement. We got to our feet sluggishly, and joined the crowd trudging up the stairs to the ground floor. All the doors and windows had been blown in. We crunched across the tiles and out down the steps to see two vast craters in the street. We might have been on the moon had not the moon been up there above us, as bright and bold as before and even higher in the sky. We picked our way in single file past hills and valleys of rubble. In between them stood undamaged buildings with not so much as a dent in the wrought-iron grilles of their balconies. I will never get used to this. I mean, the simple reality that bombs fall in one place and not another. It's sickening.

We looked absolute frights. Célia seemed to be wearing a disheveled ashy wig and James had gone gray overnight. I put a hand to my head, felt my hair matted with dust and plaster.

"Where's the Fifteen?" said Célia, wiping her nose.

"Oh Lord. If they bombed the car, Papa will kill me . . ."

But we found the Citroën at the end of the street, completely untouched. Driving is a reflex action, thank goodness. I left James outside the club where he would rejoin Peter. When we got back to Cleopatra my parents were standing out on the street in their robes. They were hoarse like us but from crying, and their eyes were red.

They had bombed my hat shop. I'd left it until the last minute to collect my hat for the wedding. I arrived there later that morning, and found the entire interior gutted and black with soot. My little lemon pillbox with its equally lemony wisp of a veil, the prettiest thing I'd ever bought, was no more. I went home and found a cream felt cloche I'd bought in a hurry from Hannaux. It was the only thing in my wardrobe that went with my outfit. I felt like an off-duty nurse from the Queen Alexandra, and told Célia so. "But I'm ever mindful of my calling," I added. "I will be taking your blood pressure hourly."

She stood by the mirror in her wedding dress. It was a column of starch-white silk with a furled neckline. She might have been rising head and shoulders out of an arum lily.

Papa drove us to St. Mark's. I sat in the back with Célia. All this waiting and now time was rolling up so smoothly, leading us to the church, through the doors, and up the aisle. There was Peter, solemn with joy, at the altar. Standing to one side, James. Dark, serious, wiry compared to Peter, not as tall. My father, crying rivers of tears, led Célia up the aisle.

The ceremony unfolded, the priest asked for the rings. James put his hand in his pocket and held out the two rings in a steady open palm, nothing showy, no theatrical proffering, and when Peter's fingers fumbled the smaller ring, James's other hand closed on Peter's for a second, just a second, to stop the ring falling. I heard a brief English whispering in the happiness-charged sunlight, perhaps something like "Steady," and a small quiet laugh, and Peter put the ring on Célia's finger. There was no clumsiness with her, rather a satisfied ripple from the congregation as she plucked Peter's ring deftly from James's palm and claimed Peter in a trice. But I didn't laugh or murmur with the others because the brotherliness of that gesture, of James's hand on Peter's, had moved me so much.

Peter and Célia were borne around the lounge at the Metropole, a bridal couple sucked into whirlpools of family and friends, and James and I were towed behind on the current. James looked at his watch: he had to go, he had a train to catch. "Please," I said, "let's say goodbye together, all of us," so we managed to gather in relative space and solitude, Célia and Peter and James and me. We wished James *bon voyage*.

Célia was shining like a lighthouse, a very elegant lighthouse, showering love and joy.

"Oh, Célia," I said, "I wish Alastair could see you!"

"Peter and I will bore him stiff with the photos," she said. "Won't we, Peter?"

Peter looked down into his glass and for a moment I was puzzled, because I really thought that he was considering the question, of whether his friend would find his wedding photographs tedious to look at. But then my confusion began to fall away. I glanced in desperation at James but he had nothing for me, he was also standing with his head bowed.

We all stood immobilized in a long silence, broken in the end by Célia saying, on a sighing breath, *"Ah, non. Ah, non."*

"When?" I blurted.

"Tuesday afternoon," said James.

Today was Saturday. All these past days I'd been thinking of Alastair, expecting him. But he would never come now.

Peter said, "They don't think he suffered—"

"No." Célia raised her hand, shaking fingers splayed. "Don't tell me, Peter. Not today. Today we'll drink to him. Yes." She snatched up a slopping glass. "Let's drink to him."

Obediently the men raised their glasses to touch hers. Peter said, "To Alastair Pearce."

"Alastair," said James, and both men drank.

"To Alastair!" cried Célia, her eyes brimming. *"Allons, Yvette!"*

I drank, having choked out his name, as Célia, her face crumpling, was enfolded in Peter's arms. I turned away blindly to James.

"Come," he said, "let's get some fresh air," and I found myself being led by him out into the lobby and then through the revolving doors to the street.

"You must tell me what happened," I said, as soon as I was able.

Alastair had been out on a sweep over Gazala when two Me 109s found him. These German fighters were the most dangerous. He didn't manage to shake them off. It was likely that Alastair had been shot in the plane, wounded or killed they couldn't tell, because he didn't bail out. His plane carried on flying and crashed in the sea.

"Alastair." I burst into noisy weeping. "Oh, *Alastair*."

We crossed the road to the seafront. I walked with my shoes scraping on the ground. The salty air buffeted my tears as they flowed.

"I didn't want to lie," James said. "But Peter convinced me it was for the best. He was going to tell Célia tomorrow."

"How could we be so stupid?" I sobbed. "We should never have believed you."

"You weren't stupid."

I wiped my face. "Yes, we were. Actually, I'm the idiot. Célia's forgiven. She can't even contemplate the idea of pilots getting killed. She has banished it from her mind."

"Is that true?"

"Obviously." I stared at him. "How else could she possibly marry Peter?" I sniffed and wiped my eyes. "I don't know how she'll carry on now. Day after day, hoping for good news from Peter. Thinking of Alastair's wife . . ."

The notion made me even more desperate.

"Célia will manage," James said in the end. "She's got you."

"Oh, James." I sighed. "I've hardly enough courage for myself, let alone her. If I was her, and Peter died, I'd throw myself into the sea."

We both looked down at the playful wavelets slapping against the seawall. You could see the bottom quite clearly. It was perhaps a meter deep.

"Well," I added, "perhaps not here."

"No. You'd sprain your ankle at most, I should think."

I gave him a sad smile and then we both gazed out over the bay, at the water that was dazzling under the stiff breeze. I thought of Alastair flying unknowingly onward, mile after mile over the sea. Had he suffered? Please, let him not have suffered. I glanced at James; he was leaning against the railing, seemingly absorbed in the view. He must have thought about it, the suffering, but I wasn't going to ask him. For his sake and mine.

"Where are you going on your train, James?"

"To the South." He turned toward me. "The temples, the Valley of the Kings. I haven't been there since I was a boy. I remember looking out of the train window. All the fields were flooded, egrets flying over them."

"You know Egypt, then!"

"I lived here. Very briefly—my father worked on a project at Suez. Widening the canal."

My eyes stung, I shielded them from the sun to look at him. "Have you got a Baedeker?"

"Yes."

"My father has Georges Bénédite's *Le Temple de Philae*, the first edition. I wish I could lend it to you but it's too precious . . ."

"I've heard of it! How wonderful."

There. I knew leather-bound books would suit him. I pictured him turning the pages, enthralled.

"Thank you for being the best man, James," I said after a pause. "Alastair would have been proud of you. But now you must get to the station."

"I don't like to leave you alone out here."

But I had to be alone, at least for a moment. I told him so and he said, "If you're sure."

We shook hands, which was a relief to both of us. It was apt: it restored everything. We were the bridesmaid and the best man. He'd performed impeccably; I, perhaps not quite so well, but I could make amends. We said goodbye and I watched him make his way over the square toward the tram station. There were so many people around. Men, principally. Men in long tunics and turbans, in suits and tarbooshes, in every kind of uniform, and James, another man in uniform, threaded his way among them to be lost from sight, and the crowd continued to gather and talk and gesticulate, to make business and war.

The warm breeze started to dry my face. I licked my lips, tasted salt, remembered the dust of the air raid. The night seemed like another world.

A gharry drew up, harness jingling, on the promenade. A man got out, carelessly tipped the driver, and strolled toward me, his tie flapping in the sea breeze. I realized I knew him. It was Sébastien Khoury, a family friend. He'd been invited to the wedding but urgent business in Port Said had kept him away.

"Yvette," he called. "Yvette Haddad, what are you doing out here when your sister's in all her glory? You've abandoned your post!"

"Sébastien," I said after a moment, when I had gathered my wits. "You're back."

He was older than me. The type of man who came with warnings, according to Célia. A phrase that had amused me highly, the first time I heard it.

"Yvette." He came closer. "You've been crying."

I shook my head. "Don't worry about me. I must go back inside . . ."

"Darling, you look a mess. Come, walk with me and get some air, and then you can do your face and we'll go in together."

He took my arm. We walked together into the square, sat down on a bench under a stiff, sturdy palm tree that gave no shade. A roast corncob seller was doing a roaring trade nearby, little clouds of smoke puffing off his charcoal grill while children appeared from nowhere and thronged around him, some presenting their piastres carefully with both hands, others, slightly older, tossing the coins insouciantly into a clay dish. The smell of the corn made me ravenous. I took out my compact, renewed my powder and lipstick and did the best I could with my eyes. Actually Célia looked worse than I did after crying: she was so creamy and dewy, her eyes and nose turned the pink of crushed rose petals. By contrast my complexion was olive, my skin tough.

I was a tough, olive-skinned girl.

Sébastien took out a cigarette but didn't light it, instead gazed out at the water, his eyes narrowed against the glare. "Look," he said, "the king's yacht."

I glanced toward the sea. The boat was barely visible, a blazing wedge of silver in the spring sun. It was nice of him not to look at me, to speak of something inconsequential while I attended to my face.

Sébastien had extremely short hair, the color that I now know in English as *mouse,* but that would never do for Sébastien. How would he like it to be described? The color of the desert at its brief dusk, perhaps. It was cut short, I realized, expressly to show off his beautifully shaped head. His jaw was angular, his eyes a dark amber. He had a rather flat, pugilistic nose and an amused, thin-lipped, intelligent mouth.

He felt me looking at him and turned his head. "That's better," he said, smiling.

"I'm glad. There was an air raid last night, you know. Célia and I went to a concert and the bombing started halfway through. We had a ghastly time in the basement, they hit the street right next to us, and when we came out there was my papa's car without a mark on it."

"My God!" Sébastien cried. "No wonder it all got too much for you in there." He jerked his head toward the hotel. "You must be exhausted. Oh, you poor girls!"

That was the way to do it. Skip the things that really give you pain, and make a ripping yarn out of the rest. My eyes were so dry I thought I'd never cry again. I regarded Sébastien, his crinkled-up eyelids, his carelessly knotted tie, the unlit cigarette between his tanned fingers.

I'd never met a man—even when expressing genuine dismay, because I could see he was properly shocked—more aware of his own good looks.

"Yes. Us poor girls. But we bounce back."

"I'll say you do." He was shaking his head. "The Haddad sisters. You've got a reputation, you know."

I sat up straight. "Sébastien, you know we live like absolute nuns. I never go anywhere without Célia."

"No, I don't mean that. I refer to your exceptional qualities. There's Célia, who could be on the cover of *Vogue*, and you? From what I've heard, you're a racing driver in the making."

"Oh, how absurd."

"Far from absurd," Sébastien insisted. "You did Alexandria to Marsa Matrouh in . . . how long was it? Nicky Barba told me. He thought he was in for a leisurely drive and a picnic. Ha!"

"That was two years ago. I've matured. I'm much more sedate now."

He was looking straight at me, the amber in his eyes glinting. He was making his eyes glint on purpose. What sort of imbecile would you have to be, to fall for that? I began to smile. "Come now, Sébastien. Enough languishing. They'll be wondering where on earth I am."

Obediently he rose to his feet. I waited while he lit his cigarette at last and we strolled back in the direction of the hotel.

"Have you ever driven a lorry?" he asked me, as we reached the steps.

I turned in surprise. "When would I ever get the chance?"

"You know I spend my whole time carting goods around to the soldiers and airmen. Eggs, shoes, mattresses, whatever they want." He threw his cigarette down and ground it under his heel. He didn't smoke them, I realized, as much as hold them, so that people would look at his beautiful hands. "You could come with me one time. It's a Bedford, somewhat cannibalized. Think what fun it would be."

I could tell his English was far worse than mine. Just the way he said, Bed*forr.*

We went into the hotel and crossed the lobby. We could hear music: in the lounge, the wedding party had started dancing. I glimpsed Célia and Peter through the glass doors, his arm around her waist. The glass mottled everything but I could tell it was them from the colors. The white and the air-force blue, the black hair and the golden.

"That's an awful idea," I said, smiling.

"I knew you'd like it."

I opened the doors. The music stopped and the air filled with applause and laughter. Célia saw me and waved. Her eyes were still wet but there was determination in them. No enemy was going to take the joy of her wedding day from her. I had misjudged her—misjudged her potential, at least. If she didn't have the courage now, she would find it.

I drew Sébastien behind me through the crowd so that he could congratulate her. *Look who I found outside*, I would say. Sébastien followed me with a long leisurely stride. I led him onward like a leopard on a chain.

FIVE

I am traveling at sunset over a strange land. Beneath me lies a vast continent of dried lakes, bare riverbeds, empty canals that flick by so quickly that I know I must be flying at immense speed. The sun, haloed by the storm of scratches on my windshield, hangs above the horizon and casts a black shadow over the near side of every prominence, the far side of every concavity. I race on over the plateaued mountains and towered cities of this enchanting landscape which is as alien as Mars but which I know, on some deep level, is North Africa. At this extraordinary velocity I shall be out of Egypt in minutes, through Libya, Tunisia, Algeria in an hour or so. Before the sun sets I'll reach Morocco. Fly on out over the Atlantic breakers into the dusk.

I check my fuel. After all these hundreds of miles, I still have eighty of my ninety-seven gallons. Impossible. Even more puzzling is my altimeter. It seems to be stuck, or simply broken. Both the fat "hour" hand, which measures thousands of feet, and the thin "minute" hand, which marks off the hundreds, are nudging the zero at the top of the dial.

Very slowly, I blink. My eyelids descend and lift again.

The continent was a trick of the light. Troughs, hillocks, drought-ed channels, single stones spin toward me just under my aircraft.

I'm flying ten feet off the ground.

A bell starts to ring in the cockpit, one I've never heard before. It must be some kind of warning height alarm. Where is the switch? I can't turn—

"—the damn thing off," I say aloud.

My alarm clock is shrilling. I fling out one arm, only to sweep it onto the floor. A buzzing noise now accompanies the bell. I peer over the edge of the bed and see it rotating in a frenzy on its back. Alarm clocks respond poorly to invective but that doesn't stop me giving it a piece of my mind as I capture and disable it.

Peter Ingram, blast him, doesn't have any dreams. Obviously I don't really mean *blast him*. Considering how badly he was injured in the end, I'm glad for him. "Those days are nicely buried, thank you very much," he likes to say. "Triple padlock on the old subconscious. It's all that mental self-examination you priests get up to, James. Not good for a chap."

But *Peter,* I want to say. *You never flew with 6 Squadron.*

I had been told how low they had to fly, the Hurricanes of 6 Squadron. But I didn't understand it until I saw them.

It was July 1942 and the panzer tanks were forging their way east-ward across Egypt, each tank dragging what looked like a forest fire in its wake, but it was actually a pall of dust and smoke so high it turned the sun brown. A terrifying sight, even at eight thousand feet, where Peter and I and some others from 274 Squadron were protecting 6 as they worked below us, laden with anti-tank cannons, trying to pierce the armor of the panzers. An Me 109 would make short work of a heavy Hurricane. I was doing my job, keeping an eye out for 109s, but I happened to look down as the sun broke through the thinning smoke and I saw one of 6 Squadron on the attack. He skimmed like a skipping stone toward a tank, his shadow fleeting beneath him. And then I couldn't stop looking, because shadow and fuselage were so close to kissing, it made my mouth dry.

This was three months after Peter's wedding.

I hadn't bargained for Yvette. My only concern as Peter's best man had been to do my duty by poor Alastair Pearce. But there she was, with her round-eyed gaze, her sudden gleeful grin. Hair that curled up from her forehead, not black but almost. Eyebrows beautiful semicircles that made her look—not surprised, exactly, but alert, curious. Beside the stately beauty of Célia, on whom all eyes rested except mine, she was as slight and dainty as a deer. Instinctive in the way she handled a car. Lively when she listened to Khachaturian, which she couldn't do without swaying in her seat, and each time she swayed toward me her bare shoulder brushed my arm.

And the way she talked, direct and disarming with sudden bursts of slang—I swear she said *ripping*—it gave me a pang because it was one of Alastair's words, and she had known him so well.

When I told her about Alastair she wept for him. Said she would never consider a fighter pilot. So yes, on that day in July '42, although I was smitten with Yvette, I didn't think I had any chance at all. Granted, I had plenty, in the form of the First Battle of El-Alamein, to take my mind off my plight. And I was glad at least, seeing 6 down there below me, that I was in 274 Squadron. Because 6 Squadron looked like a very quick way to die.

Ha. There must be a mischievous demon of war who listens in to the thoughts of pilots. It didn't take this demon long to act: I was in 6 by December of that year. And destined to dream of 6, it seemed, forever after.

I roll out of bed and make my way downstairs, unfamiliar with this barrack of a house. I find the kitchen, fill the kettle—and turn around to see the scarf lying on the table where I had left it last night.

The orange and blue, the train, the script. *LE PETIT TRAIN DÉPARTEMENTAL*. Once again a sense of knowing seizes me, knowing before seeing, like a repeated dream.

Just then, the telephone rings, startling me nearly out of my skin. I hurry to the dining room.

"Hello, Dad. Sorry to call so early. I've been out all night, cataloging owl calls. I just wanted to check that you're okay. Are you okay?"

"Oh, Tom." I'm so relieved to hear his familiar voice in all this strangeness. "Do they catalog easily? Owl calls?"

A long sigh escapes the flatlands of East Anglia.

"I'm genuinely interested," I protest.

"I can't stop thinking about you in that horrible house."

"Tom"—I try to sound bright and forceful—"I wanted to come here. Please trust me to get on with it."

He pauses, digests this. The stone floor leaches cold into the soles of my feet.

"I'm knitting again," he says suddenly. "Shall I do you a jumper? You're gonna need one in there."

It's so unexpected that I take a step backward. "I'd like that very much indeed. You could bring it to me. When's your, not half term, what do they call it?"

"Reading week," Tom replies. "I'll see if I can."

"The house'll be less grim by then, I promise you—"

A tumult erupts on the far end of the line—thundering feet, urgent shouting, as if the other occupants of the house were fleeing a fire.

"Ade and Jase, off for their training run," Tom says. "That means it's seven o'clock. Got to go, Dad. Send me your measurements. Bye."

"When is reading week?" I say, but he's hung up.

If he does make the sweater, I'll gladly wear it. Tom carried on knitting after his early lessons with Mrs. Marshall, and he's an expert now.

I put down the phone, catch sight of Archdeacon Frobisher's letter on the table, remember his promise to visit at my *earliest convenience*. I can't have him shuddering at this squalor. Suddenly persuaded that physical activity will do me the world of good, I get dressed in old clothes and set to work with hot water, detergent, and rags on the dining room's nicotine-stained walls. Before long a licorice-colored tide is dribbling down over paintwork that turns out to be cream. Shafts of pale sunlight strike the cleaned patch. I find myself whistling.

Maybe I should have started with the study, that odious layer of cobwebs and those strange stacks of newspapers. But I honestly can't face it.

At eight o'clock Clive Perry, my new curate, turns up. He's a shining, reddish-blond young man a few years older than Tom, fond of golf, just as mild and easy this morning as he was on my previous visits here when I was merely a candidate for the job. He's come to tell me about the Sutton family, whose child—a daughter, I learn, called Meg—I am to christen tomorrow. "Meg's already nearly two," Clive says, "and she's a well-made child. But they want her done at the font, headfirst, the whole works. I warn you, she's got a mind of her own."

I smile. "I'll speak to her parents."

"Their phone number's there." He nods at the piece of paper he's brought with him. "Now, here's your visiting list."

Underneath the list is a sketch map of Upton. I've already got the lie of the land, having done my own reconnaissance over the summer, but this map has been marked with the names of the people I am to see. Clive takes me through them in short order, describing succinctly the predicaments—a combination of age and ailments—that keep them housebound. Each visitee, I notice, has a number: Clive has constructed the shortest route between them. My old curate, Rick, though I was extremely fond of him, would make heavy weather of this task.

"I can see why Archdeacon Frobisher spoke so highly of you, Clive."

He gives me a tense smile. "To be honest, it's been ghastly. Mr. Blakemore . . . well, let's say a lot of people have given up on church." A haunted look passes across his face. "You know he was chaining the door shut? To keep out the evil spirits."

"We'll tackle it together."

He glances up at me, and at the freshly cleaned area of wall, and suddenly smiles. "Yes. Yes, I'm sure we will."

I change into clerical attire and say a brief prayer for the day, my first in this ministry, that it should go without mishap. The rain seems to be holding off this morning, so I search out bicycle clips. I can't afford to fill up my car until the end of the month, and the little fuel I have needs to be kept for emergencies. These are often hospital visits at unsociable hours, where tearstained relatives sometimes tell me, dumbfounded, *I don't understand why he's calling for you, Vicar. He never mentioned God his whole life long . . .*

The first name on my list is a Lady Althea Brock, latterly resident of the big house of the village, Upton Hall. The hall has been turned into a girls' boarding school and Lady Brock has retired to the lodge of that same house. As I have half an hour to spare, I make a circuit of the village, enjoying the peace of the lanes and dismounting to wheel my bicycle along the lowest path of a glorious beech wood, marked *Pipehouse Wood* on Clive's map, rising uphill from one side of the road. It is a blessing to be in the rushing quiet of the woodland: the beeches are beautiful, their trunks gray and smooth except for where the roots and limbs meet the trunk. At these places there are fine wrinkles that remind me more of skin than bark.

The air is mild, the soughing of the wind the only sound. I doubt I would hear a car if it passed along the road. I pause and breathe in. The nearest beech is elephantine with age, the roots spreading, bunioned. A grandmotherly tree. Was this the sort of place Yvette had in mind for her ashes? We never talked about it properly. For all I know she could have changed her mind. Preferred to stay close to us in her urn.

I put my hand on the tree trunk. It is cool and damp. Above me I hear the familiar patter of rain on leaves.

Emerging from the shelter of Pipehouse Wood, I bicycle, anorak flapping, along under a great slope of bare downland toward Upton Hall. The rain increases as I approach my destination. In my haste I miss the turn, so I dismount again and make a shortcut through stands of coppiced hazel trees, very old, with thickets of thin, upright branches springing from the base. I'm within sight of the lodge when a small brownish terrier bursts out of the undergrowth. Teeth bared under a wet mustache, it rushes toward me and stops about a foot away, emitting a single, long, quarreling bark.

"Go away," I say, as many have before me when confronted by small dogs with their hackles raised, and just as uselessly. "Push off, you horrible little animal."

"He is, isn't he," says a woman's voice, laughing. "I can say so because he's not mine. Stuart, do come here."

The woman herself is no more than three yards away but hidden—no, not hidden exactly, but standing behind a coppiced hazel tree so she's visible only in narrow slips and sections. I make out a slice of mackintosh, slick with rain, a swirl of blond hair. The dog hasn't taken any notice of her. Not surprisingly, since her voice is good-humored, almost indulgent. In fact, her coaxing tone seems to encourage him into a deeper, more threatening bout of growling.

I take a few steps backward. Priests, like postmen, are twice shy.

"Don't worry—he won't bite."

I glimpse a pair of laughing blue eyes through the leaves. She's not taking this at all seriously.

"That's what people always say!" I exclaim, rather more heatedly than I intended.

But she doesn't respond. When she speaks again her voice is farther off, as if she's calling back to me over her shoulder. "Don't worry—Althea's coming!" she calls blithely through the greenery. And then she disappears, a shadow moving through the trees with a long stride.

"Stuart! Stuart!"

Another voice penetrates the coppice, also female but this time elderly, hoarse, and carrying an unmistakable note of command. A tall, cadaverous being is working her way toward me on two canes, her legs encased in a pair of muddy scarlet flared trousers and her bony forearms escaping the unraveling sleeves of a man's cardigan. The clothes alone tell me this is Lady Brock. The poorest women in Fulbrook darned their stockings and sleeves, cleaned their clothes of dirt, and I'm sure it's the same here. It is simply that people of Lady Brock's class know that their superiority is beyond question and so they don't bother, preferring to flaunt their social prestige in every mud stain and fraying woolen hem. However I can also see she's very old, underweight without a doubt, and leaning from the vertical in a way I recognize among many elderly whose spinal columns begin to erode in the sandstorms of age.

"Lady Brock? I'm James Acton. The new vicar."

"Good Lord!" She limps a little closer. "The absolutely *drenched* new vicar. My dear man, why are you not in your car?" Without waiting for an answer she flings out a hand. "Althea Brock."

The hand is thin-skinned, grape-hued here and there with minor bruises, and spotted with age. I take hold of it very gently.

"James Acton. How do you do."

"Stuart, for the love of *Christ*, cease fire!" The dog is immediately mute. "Such a little monster," Lady Brock says, into the dripping quiet. "Belonged to a friend of mine. Colonel Daventry, you'll meet him soon enough. He can't walk out anymore."

"Ah." I know this name. "He's next on my list after you."

Lady Brock gives me a glare of rank incredulity. "I'm on Perry's blasted *visiting* list? The absolute cheek of the man. And there I was, thinking you wanted a word about the church flowers!" The glare disappears—she guffaws, her teeth large, stony with age, held in place by a picket fence of gold wiring. "There's only one way off that list if you're over eighty. It's the kiss of death. Kindly remove my name at the earliest opportunity. But I'm being fearfully rude, making you stand out here. Come with me."

She scrapes her Wellingtons on the metal rack by her back door. When she steps out of them I see that they are cut down to the level of ankle boots. The dark hallway smells of tinned dog meat and damp coats.

But the impacted odor of neglected old person, that I've come to dread as I walk in through my own front door, is absent here.

"I'm awfully sorry but I've only got ten minutes," she announces. "My friend Mr. Kennet is taking me to look at some Sussex trugs. I can't abide *plastic* baskets when I'm gardening, and they're pretty thin on the ground these days, proper wooden trugs. You won't find the church flowers up to much, I'm afraid. This time of year we have to fall back on chrysanths, a bit of monkey grass, and lots and lots of leaves."

"I saw the flowers last night. Admittedly it was about one in the morning, so the lighting was rather dim, but I thought they looked very nice."

"What on earth were you doing in the church at that hour?"

"I'd just driven back from my old home." I explain my move, the events of the previous day.

"My word. Only just landed, and you're up against Meg Sutton tomorrow. Well, perhaps that's for the best. There are some ordeals it's better not to *dwell on* beforehand." She leads me into her sitting room. The sofa, armchairs, and tables are covered in pieces of armor, some misted with polish, others a brilliant silver. Lady Brock picks up a breastplate and dumps it on the floor. "I'm about halfway through." She nods toward a wooden armor stand in the corner of the room, which is topped with a shining silver knight's helmet. "Sir Gregory usually stands guard over there, you see. Goodness, he was getting dull. I can't stand dull men. Your archdeacon, now. Ronald Frobisher. What an absolute crasher. Tried to buttonhole me about pectoral crosses, my *view* on same. As if it could possibly matter, when poor Charles Blakemore was going off his rocker."

"I find him rather fascinating," I say.

"Who? Blakemore?"

I shake my head. "I meant Frobisher. Though I'd love to have met

Mr. Blakemore. His story is really quite . . ." I can't think of an adjective, and in the pause decide I don't want one. It's not fair on Blakemore.

Lady Brock is sighing. "Of course. Your trade. *Everyone's* worthy of your attention, all the time. I don't know how you do it, any of you." She motions toward the rather cramped space she's made on the sofa, incorporating into this ushering gesture a flourish of mild exasperation, a sort of benign despair at—what? Clergymen in general, perhaps.

"It's true that we persist." I sit down. "Often persistence is all we've got."

"Oh, for heaven's sake. Let's have some tea. And turn that fire on. One bar, mind. I'm not made of cash."

Rejecting help, she brings two mugs of tea, one in each knotty hand. "Aren't mugs super? All those years of cups teetering on saucers. I'd never manage now."

When we're seated I say, "I'm aware that you haven't got much time . . ."

"Oh, don't worry about that."

"I thought you were going out to look at some wooden baskets."

"That was just to get rid of you, if you turned out to be—"

"A crasher."

A frieze of riveted dentition. The work that has gone into preserving those old teeth. In a way I admire her, refusing to give in to porcelain. "So." She leans forward. "How are you finding the place? When will the light of civilization shine once more upon that ghastly old heap of a vicarage?"

I give an uneasy laugh. "Not for a while yet. It's freezing and the ground floor is kippered with pipe smoke. But I've made a start. And my son's going to knit me a sweater, which should help against the cold."

Lady Brock smiles. Her top lip is oddly protuberant, reminding me of some kind of fish. "How absolutely marvelous!"

"Tom's been knitting since he was a boy. His mother died, you see, and the woman I employed to look after him if I was called out in the evenings—she taught him."

"How did she die, his mother?"

"Leukemia."

She hisses, shaking her head. "Ah, that is hard."

"Yes. Well, he's twenty now, Tom. Quite old enough to boss me around. He's told me to get rid of our furniture. I brought it all from the old house, you see. I can see his point. My sofa's a wreck, the cushions have lost half their stuffing. My wife used them to play catch with Tom when he was very small . . ."

Only Tom didn't know how to catch yet. He opened his arms and the cushion collided softly with his chest and he'd sit down with a bump and a rattle of giggles. Yvette would say, *Houp-là!* Then she'd throw the cushion again, and once more Tom would bump down onto his bottom with another gale of delight. Toss, bump, giggle, *houp-là.* Five, six, a dozen times. I lace my fingers together and stare hard at Sir Gregory, try to armor myself with his bright breastplate but this memory is a heavy spear and I didn't see it coming.

It must be years since I was last ambushed like this.

Silently—or rather, without speaking, since the action has a soundtrack of gasps and grunts—Lady Brock rises to her feet and crosses the room. There is a clink of glass, and then a small neat whiskey is placed on the table near my knee. She fusses with the curtains, drawing them wider, allowing me to drink it without an audience. I bind my fingers around the glass and bring it to my lips. The alcohol lights a familiar path down into my chest, unifying this time with all the other times a stiff drink has brought me to my senses, making me feel old. Making me feel better.

Lady Brock leaves the curtains, collapses herself carefully back into her seat opposite me. Her face is ancient in the brightening daylight, her eyes hooded.

"Oh, what do they know, the young," she barks suddenly. "My goodness, when I moved here, it was like being eviscerated. Things I hadn't noticed for decades, a pair of Michael's riding boots, for example—brought him back as if he was standing in the room wearing them. He died in '39, a week before war broke out. We had no children. He'd been gassed on the Western Front in 1917 and his lungs slowly filled up."

This, I think, is suffering of a different order.

"A very long war," I say after a moment.

"Exactly. Seeing a life like Michael's—witnessing it at close hand: he drowned, essentially—means that I come to church for form's sake only. I believe in form, you see, but not God. I don't have any truck with Him."

I sip my drink. "That strikes me as an entirely understandable attitude."

Her eyes sharpen. "No guff, then?"

"What?"

"Spiritual guff. You haven't tried to persuade me of the reward in heaven and so on."

"I wouldn't dream of it."

"Good. No conceivable afterlife is worth what he went through. Now." She brings her bony knees together, clasps her fingers around her now empty mug. "Morale. You'll be busy enough, which is good. Keep busy, and fill up those little empty corners with Scotch. Or golf, like your smooth young curate." A glimmer of a grin. "Are you feeding well? Doesn't look like it."

"Tom used to take care of the food." I feel idiotic, admitting this.

"Deirdre Harper does nice little meals at the Women's Institute market. In special tinfoil dishes. Stews and so on, and very reasonably priced. She feeds half the elderly in Upton, those who can afford it, anyway."

I scratch my head. "*I* can't afford to think of myself as elderly."

"Then teach yourself to cook, man. All you have to do is read instructions. D'you like dogs?"

"Er . . . some dogs." I start to smile. "Why?"

Lady Brock snorts. "I apologize unreservedly for Stuart. I'm entirely aware of his defects. No—I asked you because there's a hound pup going spare at the kennels. You can have him for nothing. Perfect for you, I'd have thought. Keep you company in that awful barn."

"Oh, I see. That's very kind, Lady Brock, but a dog . . . I'd have to take it for walks, and I haven't got time."

"Oh, don't worry about exercise. The puppy's a runt, that's why he's not wanted. The well-grown ones run thirty miles in an afternoon, I admit, but this one'll be content with a trot around the garden and a cushion by the fire. I can get my friend Lucy Horne to give you a ring. She and her father look after the hounds."

"Well . . ." I glance at the clock. An alarming amount of time has passed. "I'm so sorry, Lady Brock, I must go."

"Of course! Visiting the *old crocks.*"

I find myself laughing. "Be assured, Lady Brock, that your name will be struck from the visiting list."

"Good. If you come back—and I hope you will, for the odd glass— it'll have to be in your own right."

"I'd be very glad to."

I rise to my feet in a leisurely way, so as not to force her to hurry and struggle. When she's upright I shake her hand, feeling immensely cheered. "Goodbye, Lady Brock. I'll be sure to take *all* your advice."

"Oh, dear, I've gone too far," she says without a shred of remorse. "I often do."

On her doorstep I remember the woman I glimpsed earlier.

"Oh—I met a dryad on my way in," I say. "Some kind of nymph of the woods, anyway. She called off Stuart—tried to, at least."

Not overly hard, I remember.

"Nymph! I'll tell her that! It was Ellen. Ellen Parr, a dear friend of mine. She was just leaving when you came through the coppice." A small smile plays over Lady Brock's face, a glint of sunlight on the crags. "It'll be a rare sighting for you, I'm afraid. She's even worse than me. I don't think she's ever really acknowledged the existence of a god."

Following my curate's map I make the rest of my calls. One old man is stuck in the bath: he implores me to fetch his daughter from three doors down. At another house I'm greeted by a six-year-old boy who, when I introduce myself, shouts, "You're not the vicar! The real vicar's a loony!" and slams the door shut again. My last call is to Colonel Daventry, erstwhile owner of Stuart. He's an aged gentleman whose door is answered by a housekeeper. He converses for ten minutes with great courtesy, and then I'm ushered out by the housekeeper. "Little and often, Mr. Acton," she murmurs. "He gets very tired."

That's fine by me.

I spend the evening on essential unpacking and preparations for tomorrow's service. I'm ironing my surplice when the phone rings. It's Mr. Alan Sutton, father to Meg, the child to be christened. He's sorry she's got so big, but they didn't want to get her done while Mr. Blakemore was in charge, because he kept forgetting the babies' names. "I'll be standing by," he tells me, "if she tries to make a break for it."

I'm an experienced wrangler of small children, but I appreciate the reassurance.

I eat my supper staring at the scarf on the kitchen table. The day's encounters have drained it of some of its power. If I gaze long enough at the picture, it starts to seem so unfamiliar that I'm able to believe I've never seen it before. But then, when I look away, it glows in my mind's eye.

I fold the scarf up and slip it into a drawer in the kitchen table. Out of harm's way.

SIX

Yvette
3 March 1964

Last week I went out for a walk with James. We like to stroll along a tree-lined lane that runs behind Tom's school playground, a little bit of country in the middle of Fulbrook, and at this time of year the bank is covered with masses and masses of primroses. I was reminded of my beautiful lemon hat, the one that was destroyed when they bombed the milliner's during the air raid. I realized it hadn't been lemon at all but the color *known* as lemon. Lemons are actually a bright solid yellow, like daffodils. My hat had been primrose all along. I shared this realization at some length with James as we walked.

He said, "Mm, yes, it was very pretty."

I came to a stop. "James. You never saw that hat. It was blown to pieces."

He laughed, very sheepish. "I'm sorry. I might have let my mind wander, the last few minutes."

"It's just background noise to you, isn't it. A woman, prattling about hats and colors and flowers. La, la, la. Like birdsong."

He pleaded for forgiveness, I harshly withheld it, he embraced me.

What I was actually wearing that day, of course, was that disastrous cream felt cloche that I'd bought from Hannaux. I say cloche—it wasn't at all like Maman's cloche, which was a good ten years old and came down over her eyebrows giving her the air of a retiring tortoise. Mine was worn back off the face so the brim framed the hairline. I had thought this style was made for women with high saintly foreheads, but when I put it on I realized it was the hat that made the wearer's forehead high and saintly. My eyes seemed farther apart too. In fact my whole face appeared flatter, more placid, more readable. When I was trying not to laugh my lips tended to go in at the corners, in and up, in a way that Célia called impish sometimes or cheeky or even flirtatious. Not in this hat. My lips were virtuous.

I'd bought it at the end of the day, I remember. You should never do this in a department store. The assistant is bound to be tired and, at Hannaux, will start murmuring under her breath in Greek.

It definitely wasn't me.

I wasn't sure if I was going to say anything about Sébastien at all. But look what happened. He sneaked in on the tail end of the previous chapter, which was meant to be about James and only James. Strolling into the scene with a cigarette in his hand as if he had every right to be there. Nobody approved of Sébastien, for all sorts of reasons. I didn't approve of him myself, precisely because of the way he insinuated himself into my life.

He did it completely openly. That was what was so underhanded.

"Come for a spin," he said, a couple of weeks after the wedding, like the family friend he was, and so I did. He turned up every month or so in the Bedford and I jumped on board and we took supplies out to the army and air force bases. There was no funny business. He was careful that I stayed in the lorry when we reached the camps, so as to prevent fifty lonely servicemen ogling my backside. The only time he touched me was when he took my hand as I jumped out of the cab at the end of the trip.

That Bedford. Even empty it was a mule. The steering was brutal. He was a good driving teacher, unflappable, patient. That was unexpected. "Hang on tight and heave," he would say as we thundered toward a bend and the wheel slipped under my sweaty palms. God, it was wonderful. This was 1942, remember. May was terrifying, June was worse, with German tanks at Marsa Matrouh. Marsa Matrouh, for heaven's sake, where I'd driven Célia and our friend Nicky Barba at top speed for fun. If screaming at the bitch steering of a two-ton lorry took my mind off the war, then who could object?

Célia could, as it turned out. After the first trip, she told me to be careful.

"But he's so natural," I said. "So much fun."

"You idiot," she said. "That's how they do it."

We were on the beach at Sidi Bishr. Smoke was rising from the harbor. There had been another big raid two days ago and a cotton warehouse was still on fire. They had bombed the synagogue as well. Edouard Shama told us that Rommel had been looking for it for a long time.

I looked out at the sea that hardly moved, heavy as it was with milky light. No waves, just the odd slap at the shoreline. It was early in the morning. Maman allowed sea bathing on the grounds of healthy exercise, but only before nine o'clock. Lolling on a busy beach in one's costume, being stared at by all comers, wouldn't be remotely correct. We had been for our swim and now reclined, slightly damp, slightly sandy, tasting the salt on our lips as the sun rose higher.

"Do you know we're not supposed to say *Rommel* anymore?" I said. "General Auchinleck has forbidden it. We have to say *the German general* instead."

"Yes. It's to bolster morale. You're changing the subject."

Mrs. Ingram had returned from her honeymoon quite glowing. Glowing, and somewhat censorious, it seemed.

"Ah, the married state," I said. "It affords so many prerogatives. The right to inquire into a sister's business, for example, as if it were actually the questioner's concern. Give me some credit, Célia. Sébastien Khoury, for heaven's sake. Everyone knows what he's like. I'm not that much of a fool." I sniffed the sea breeze. "Nothing will happen."

"It's not what will or won't *happen*. It's what will be *assumed* to have happened. We can't get away with it, Yvette, families like ours. We behave properly. Maman and Papa are greatly admired for precisely that reason. You know this full well."

Did I think of James at all? Yes, I did. As that terrible year went on I thought of his voice from time to time, how he spoke to me that night in the cellar after the bombing. *Are you all right, Yvette?* One evening when I got home I overheard Célia in her room saying some prayers. The door was open. She broke off when she heard my footsteps.

"Did you have a nice time?"

"Yes. I got into top gear on the way home."

Célia had said nothing more to me about Sébastien since the day on the beach. She had other, heavier things on her mind. Now she merely smiled, indulging my childish triumph, and turned back to her prayers. *"O Seigneur, O Dieu tout-puissant, dans ta bonté, épargne la vie de mon époux Peter et de son ami James . . ."*

I didn't know until then that she also prayed for James. And I felt a kind of sore longing for that time when we were companions in the dark and the dust.

Are you all right, Yvette?

Was he all right?

One day we stopped, Sébastien and I, on the edge of a plantation of date palms. The engine was overheating—it really was. No ruse on his part.

The palm leaves caught the least breath of wind. The rustle alone was refreshing. Sébastien handed me a canteen of water as he often did.

"Yvette, why do you always look as if you've just been kissed?"

I took my time swallowing down the water. Listened to the engine tick as it slowly cooled.

"Sébastien," I said at last. "I never heard such nonsense. Has the sun gone to your head?"

He carried on as if I hadn't spoken. As if he was talking to himself. "Maybe it's the way your mouth is always slightly open." He put out his hand and brushed the middle of my lips with his thumb. "Just there."

I didn't think it was true but I felt my lips were parted just the same, even though I had no words.

"And there's a kind of heat in your cheeks, the tops of your cheeks," he went on. "Not a blush. Just a sort of glow. And in your gaze, the same heat."

He had turned toward me so that his shoulders and hips and knees were facing me. I saw the sweat at his temples, how dark it had turned his hair there. His eyes were dull tawny, like a lion's. Or how I imagined a lion's to be.

"I've tried so hard not to say anything," he said. "But I can't help it."

There was a note in his voice, deep, hard and dry, like the bass string of an oud.

Yes. A flat, tense, imperious note, older than the human race.

It bypassed my brain entirely.

There was no compunction or urgency. Sébastien and I whiled away hot hours kissing each other's hands, mouths, necks. There was a small arrowhead of a scar on his thumb, an accident with a fishhook on Lake Mareotis when he was a boy. Just one of his hands was more beautiful than my entire body.

I told him so one afternoon and he said, "Ah, beauty's overrated. Look at Celia. She's like an Alp in one of those pictures at the Swiss Club. A snowy peak. You admire her from all sides, give her ten out of ten, tick her off in your guidebook. La Célia."

"Sébastien, t'es affreux." Sébastien, you're terrible. "Do you think of me when we're apart?"

He smiled. "Every waking moment, *chérie.* You know that."

Then he reached for me and once more I slid into a hot original world that was still new to me, where continents and islands were forged in the heat haze out of salt water and magma.

Not long after he suggested spreading a blanket out in the rustling depths of the plantation, where the sun flared between the palm fronds.

"No, Sébastien. We would be seen."

He laughed. "Who by?"

"The boy that drives the buffalo." This boy, who couldn't have been older than nine, had taken to leering up at the open window of the cab. Even the buffalo gave us a stare.

"I'll pay him to go the long way round."

Still I demurred.

Autumn came, and the Second Battle of El-Alamein. When they opened the bombardment, the sea jumped in the bay. Célia and I stood weeping at the noise and the unholy glare to the west, a dawn rising on the wrong side of the earth. The enemy lost its footing in Egypt at last, fell back, and the town went mad. The streets were lit up for a gala every night, gharries galloped along the promenade. December came, then the New Year, and Sébastien told me he had a little apartment, very simple, very tucked away.

"There's no obligation, darling," he said, the next time we drove out in the lorry together. "Although it goes without saying that I'm dying a slow death for you."

I'd never seen a man less in danger of dying any kind of death, let alone a slow one, than Sébastien Khoury.

At the end of January the blow fell. The phone rang, Célia answered, and began to scream. I took the receiver from her. "Please try to keep calm, Mrs. Ingram," a male voice was saying in English. "We have every hope of saving the left eye." Peter was in a hospital in Cairo, I managed to establish, scribbling the address as Célia continued shrieking. *The Fifteenth Scottish General,* I wrote, pressing so hard that I broke the pencil point halfway through the word *General.*

We traveled down to Cairo that same day. Aunt Monique met us at the station and took us to her apartment.

Peter's right cheek was hard, shiny and crimson, hatched with chisel marks of such a deep purple that they were almost black. White bandages spread from his nose to his forehead. Over his right eye socket, now empty, a round pad that made a lump under the bandage. On his left a bulge. A small cage the shape of half an egg was protecting his precious remaining eye.

A shell had done this, exploding just outside his cockpit, shattering the hood, driving shards of Perspex into his face. He had taken off his goggles to see better while he chased a 109 into the clouds above Misrata. Another 109 had followed him, fired, and missed. Missed killing him, I mean.

Aunt Monique ran lavender baths for Célia and cooked her bowls of broth with vermicelli. Aunt Monique was glorious still, her lips covered in a rich wine-red sheen. I spent a lot of time wondering how much her makeup cost. It was better than thinking about Peter.

I wanted to give him and Célia their privacy but they liked me to be with them. I think they were scared to sit together alone. I would take a chair by the window and look down at the nurses. They lived on a houseboat on the bank of the Nile right next to the hospital, and on their free afternoons they'd have tea on deck. One nurse had a neat nunlike bun and poured her tea from an English china teapot and sat with her knees pressed together. Another one used to recline with her shoes off, smoking, running her hands through her short shock of hair.

About three weeks after we arrived in Cairo, I saw James again.

The light off the river silhouetted everyone who came in through the hospital doorway, so it was just another shadow of a man I saw pausing on the threshold. Many first-timers stopped there, momentarily persuaded by the spacious lobby, the comfortable seating, and the tray-bearing waiters—all Sudanese, all in white tunic, red tarboosh, and red sash—into thinking they had walked by mistake into a first-class hotel.

He paused for a second, and then came forward. I was watching him idly, chin on hand. I spent a lot of time there waiting for Célia. When I recognized him I sprang to my feet. "James!"

He saw me, broke into a smile, and strode toward me. He was taller, browner. Of course he wasn't really taller, just thinner. I didn't remember those lines in his cheeks and around his eyes. Everything, his uniform, his body and face, looked equally scrubbed and scaled away as if he'd been blasted all over by sand. He probably had. "Yvette!" he exclaimed, and then laughed. "I don't know why I'm surprised. Where else would you be but with Célia. You look very well!"

His teeth were white against his tan. It was lovely to see him laughing and it spread to me, it was such a relief to be jolly.

"I do not!" I ran one finger under my eye. "I have circles like a panda!"

"A panda who's very well, then." He became serious. "What happened, Yvette? I wasn't told much . . ."

I related the story, the 109 and the cannon shell and the Perspex. When I got to the bit about no goggles, he gasped.

"I don't understand why you didn't know, James."

"I'm in a different squadron now. I only found out about Peter last week." He rubbed his hand over his head, a tidying gesture, although his hair was too short to need it. "I'm on my way to collect a plane from Heliopolis. It'll be ready tomorrow. So I seized the chance."

Unlike me, he really did look well. Livelier in the way he moved and more bright-eyed. He had seemed such a somber starched person at the beginning. Of course, the pretense about Alastair had constrained him. Even then he had been kind, and made me laugh. With a soft intimate flash I realized that those were not glimpses of some occasional mood, but how he was essentially.

"Célia's with the surgeon," I said. "But we can probably go in." I pointed toward the corridor that led to the wards.

Together we entered the green-tiled interior of the building. We were properly inside the hospital now, and we both fell silent. I searched for something to say to James.

"So what have you been doing since I last saw you?"

"Some bombing," he said. "A little strafing."

My face flamed. "I'm sorry, what a silly question."

"Not at all. Very few people ask. Apart from that, it's mainly been anti-tank practice."

Behind us I heard the rattle of a trolley. We stopped to let it pass, the orderly moving at an efficient trot, the patient curled on his side under a sheeted frame. As they went by a young male voice burst into heavy groans from beneath the sheet. James turned his head away.

I brushed his arm. "Come on. We're nearly there."

Célia was standing outside Peter's door, parting company with a tall, lean, white-coated Englishman who was striding away with a cheerful wave. This man's chief obsession was the removal of foreign objects from the human eyeball while preserving as much as he could of the eyeball's function—and, as if that were not enough, experimenting with ever more delicate and ingenious ways of doing so. Célia and I, indeed the whole Haddad family, revered him as a minor god.

Célia was pasty, her hair like soot. She was breathless, smiling, so focused on me that she didn't even notice James. "Mr. Stallard is terribly pleased with the eye!"

The eye, that's how we referred to it. The eye was small and gray and shy, sunk between mauve folds of lid. Reluctant to show Peter anything but clouds. "It was bloody clouds that got me into trouble in the first place," Peter would say, in a light voice that did not fool us.

I indicated James. "Look who's here!"

Delighted exclamations: "Oh, Peter will be so pleased to see you!

He'll actually be able to—a bit. He can definitely see the window to-day. Just a white square, but he can see it!"

The tears leaked from my eyes. She'd been crying too. Any tiny bit of progress and she cried, and I cried with her. We all went into Peter's room.

Peter got tired after half an hour. The eye needed to shut down. Célia and I had not been able to understand much of what he and James said to each other. "It must be a special airmen's argot," Célia whispered, mystified. There was a joke about "tin openers" that they both seemed to find very funny. Then Peter called James a "sky pilot."

"What other kind is there?" I murmured.

Célia didn't know.

When Peter fell into a doze, Célia got out her sewing. She was just about to settle into the chair next to the bed when James spoke.

"Come along, Célia," he said in a low voice. "We're going to Will-cocks for tea. It's just across the river."

It was the first I'd heard of the plan, but that didn't matter. Reluc-tantly Célia abandoned her sewing and left the room with us. "What if he wakes up and I'm not there?" she said when we were in the corridor.

"He's a big boy," said James.

We could stand to hear this from him. What with the sun and breeze and health that James had brought in, not to mention the code words and jargon, Peter's whole face had started to move normally, visited for the first time by proper expressions instead of the rigid lips that emitted only clipped chipper remarks.

We crossed the river blinking in the sunshine, strangers to the open air, glad to be in a boat on the water. The boatman heaved on his oars with calloused hands, the oars bound with canvas where they worked in the oarlocks. He threaded his way between barges and feluccas, their slanting sails filling with the breeze. James was sitting in the bow behind the boatman, so I couldn't talk to him. Besides, the noise of Cairo drove all thoughts from my head. The city roared in a way that Alexandria didn't: the traffic was louder, the squares more bustling, the grand buildings more broad-shouldered and imposing. They called Cairo *umm ad-dunya,* mother of the world, but these days the city seemed more like a man to me, a bumptious, hurrying fellow in a double-breasted suit, pushing his way through life. Suddenly the stamping blare of a dance band swelled above the roar: a paddle-steamer appeared out of the haze. Our boatman backed away, delivering a long and impious protest as the big boat swept past, the wheel making a wash that rocked us from side to side. Soldiers and airmen waved down at us from the stern. I waved back and so did James. Many of them had bandaged faces, and some of those faces were badly lopsided.

Célia was gazing downriver, away from the boat.

"Who's for a game of croquet?" James said, as he paid the boatman.

Célia looked rather wildly at him.

"Didn't you play croquet at the English Girls' College, Célia?" I asked her. "My word. What a gap in your education."

"You haven't played before either," Célia said snootily.

"Yes, but I pick these things up so easily."

It had been ages since I'd teased my sister.

"I'm afraid you'll have to let Yvette win," she said to James. "Otherwise she gets quite unhinged."

Croquet, we discovered, was a game of the utmost finessing

malice. As such, it suited me and Célia very well. Within half an hour we were reduced once more to a pair of snarling teenagers, both our croquet balls whacked, each by the other, out of play into the dust.

"*Espèce de coquine*," Célia said to me.

"*Scélérate*," I replied. "*Vipère*."

James, who had reached the end of the course some time ago, said, "Time for tea," with a broad grin.

Célia did not stay. She couldn't leave Peter alone any longer. We deposited her, pink and sparkling-eyed from pique, into the boat.

"Well done," I said, as we went back to the club ground. "I didn't think anything could take her mind off him."

"It was a pleasure to play with such worthy and fair-minded opponents."

We sat down at a rickety iron table and ordered tea. James leaned back in his chair and sighed. "Oh, Peter. What a mess."

"I *hate* 109s."

It was a 109 that had done for Alastair too.

He shrugged. "They can climb faster and higher than a Hurricane. Look into the sun and you'll find a 109, sizing you up. What's the prognosis?"

"We go day by day."

"Bloody fool."

Yes, but Peter was safe. The gap was narrow but he had scraped through. If he'd lost an eye along the way, even an eye and a half, what did it matter? Nothing could harm him now.

"I have great faith in the surgeon," I said aloud. "And whatever happens, Peter will have Célia."

He nodded slowly, stirred his tea.

"Where will you go to, James, with your plane?"

"Libya." He pointed westward.

"I know where it is."

That made him laugh. "It'll be the spring this time," he said. "Last year we were there in the broiling heat, with dust storms. And the year before. It certainly didn't improve upon acquaintance."

"So many times you've gone back and forth!"

The horror of it, and the waste: it chilled me.

"I know," he said. "We're like two dogs on chains. We fight to the end of our chain, get choked back, then the enemy dog advances on us, fights us all the way to the end of *his* chain. Now it's our turn again." He rubbed his face. "But this time we've got the Americans to help us. This should be the end of it."

"Thank God for them."

I sipped my tea. The winter sky was clear above us, blue, the breeze fresh, not as strong as it had been on the water.

"So tell me," he said after a moment. "How has life been, for you?"

"Oh!" I said. "Guess what. I've been learning to drive a lorry. A friend—a family friend has been teaching me. James, you're supposed to look amazed."

I felt suddenly flustered, as if I'd stumbled over a trip wire. Why had I mentioned the lorry driving?

"I can't think of any woman more likely to. Good for you," James said, smiling. "You could join the WAAF."

"Could I? I thought they were all British."

"They're recruiting locally now."

"Oh."

There was a silence.

James cleared his throat. "How about music?" he asked. "That tremendous pianist, friend of yours—is he still playing?"

I shook my head. "He left last June. They're all in Cape Town now, the Shamas. Two hundred years in Alexandria and they were gone by the First Alamein. Along with half the Jewish families we know."

"Will they come back?"

I made a moue. "Some of them, maybe. Not the Shamas."

"So it isn't the same anymore."

"Nothing's the same. I'm not the same."

"No, I can see that. You've met someone, I think. Is he teaching you to drive a lorry, by any chance?"

Bang bang bang. A waiter was dusting off his tin tray. A small flock of sparrows alighted at his feet to peck among the gravel for fresh crumbs. A deep sadness swept over me. Célia and Peter had a life together. They had stood up in front of fifty people and given their hearts to each other, come what may. Peter would never have sneaked a girl off to a flat, and neither would James. He wouldn't sneak anyone anywhere.

Sébastien wasn't a bad man but my God, he didn't love me. And I didn't love him. I couldn't even mention him by name, because . . . because I was ashamed. It was as simple as that. I was ashamed of my conduct. I closed my eyes, and tears scalded the inside of my eyelids.

"Yvette, I've upset you." James's voice was gentle. "I'm sorry, I was being nosy. It's clear that I've completely forgotten how to talk to people."

I opened my eyes wide to stop the tears falling, tried to laugh. "No, no. I'm being silly, I . . ."

"You don't have to explain. Forget I said anything."

More croquet players had arrived. They weren't doing it properly, just hitting the balls around the course. The air was full of the clack of mallets, of braying laughter. James was looking at me, watchful and concerned. I would remember this afternoon for a long time, I realized. Just as I had remembered the air raid and the day after. They were precious, these hours and minutes we had spent together. I would treasure them, holding them as tightly as he had held my hand.

We would sit there for a few moments longer. The sun would move a little lower, and then James would leave. I might never see him again.

The thought nearly choked me.

Slowly I sat up straight, took a deep breath. "James, are you hungry, by any chance?"

He grinned. "Starving."

"Shall we go to my aunt Monique's flat?" I said, pushing my chair back. "We can buy something filling on the way. Célia will join us. You've got time, haven't you?"

"I'm meeting someone at the Osborne House Club at nine. That's where I'm staying."

I smiled at him. "Well then, you have no excuse."

I was desperately hungry too. We went to Abu Magdi's in Zamalek. Any time Aunt Monique felt a taste for *baladi*—local—food, she went there. Abu Magdi had zinc tables and a shining tiled floor. On the counter were brass jugs of tangy drinkable *laban* made from buffalo milk, bowls of *foul* beans, piles of bean patties, heaps of hot leathery *kobeiba* shaped like two cones joined together, rich inside with ground lamb and spices. And pyramids of tomatoes, large and a bit wrinkled, absolutely bursting with juice and ready to be cut into meaty slices. And turnip pickles, and sesame sauce, and mint. I ordered everything, along with some soft white flatbreads to wrap it in. We had the food packed into a warm parcel that we carried over the road into Aunt Monique's building. Her lift was a wrought-iron cage with an outer grille that shut with an oily click and an inner door made of a metal trellis that I pulled across. We creaked and swayed upward, the dusty cable above our heads winding jerkily onto a wobbling iron pulley.

James glanced upward. "I'm safer in the air."

"James, do you fly at very high altitude?"

"No—the opposite, in fact." He looked down at me, puzzled. "Why do you ask?"

"Peter said you were a sky pilot." I made a foolish, upward flap with my arm.

"Oh!" He smiled, his teeth white in the shadow of the lift shaft. "That's slang for a priest. I finished my ordination before the war. When I go home I'll be a curate in the Church of England."

"A curate!"

"Well, a vicar soon afterward. Hopefully."

"My goodness!"

"Oh, Yvette." His laugh was lovely, masculine and clear. It echoed in the stairwells. "Your face."

"I'm just surprised . . ."

"No. That was a look of horror. Now I've got two counts against me."

We came to Aunt Monique's floor. I pulled the trellis aside and pushed open the outer door. "What's the first count?" I said, as we went into the apartment.

"I'm a pilot, of course." He followed me down the passage into the kitchen. "The sort of man who would make you go mad if you married."

"What?"

"You said so, straight after the wedding. When we left the hotel and went down to the seafront. You were crying because of poor Alastair. Anyway, you said you couldn't marry a pilot because you'd have to drown yourself if he was killed. Or words to that effect."

Footsteps sounded in the hall. Aunt Monique came into the kitchen in a cloud of perfume and hairspray. *"Bonsoir!"* she cried. "I thought I heard voices." I introduced James and she turned a brilliant smile on him. "Of course! I remember you from the wedding! You were the best man! Have you visited Peter? Of course you have. Darling Yvette, such a shame: I have to go to Maadi to visit a friend, she's dreadfully unwell, I hope you don't mind me being so rude." This with a mournful glance at James and then a glint for me from between smoky eyelids, and then she was gone with no further blandishments.

Aunt Monique was extremely good at things like this but somehow her expertise made the ensuing silence more awkward. I filled it with the clatter of plates and cutlery.

"I spoke without thinking," I said as I unwrapped the food. "I was just a silly girl."

"It was only ten months ago."

"Enough time to grow up."

I served out the *kobeiba* and accompaniments. We were both young, we ate like wolves. He approved of the huge heap on my plate, said he liked girls who didn't pick at their meals. I shunned cutlery for this kind of food and was gratified to see he did the same. Soon the crumpled papers were empty of everything but crumbs.

"We've eaten Célia's helping," I said in dismay.

"I'm mortified!"

"It's not your fault, it's mine." I searched in the cupboard for eggs, found three. "She can have an omelet. Go into the sitting room, James, I'll bring coffee."

When I did so he was standing looking out of the window. The sun was low and it lit him up. He was lean, strong, quick-looking even when he was still. I put the tray on the low table. He sat down, and I sat next to him. We sipped our coffee.

"Do you like it like this?" I asked, because the coffee was black and sweet and scented with cardamom.

"Very much."

We looked each other over. I could see the marks of the desert on him, the white lines radiating from the outer corners of his eyes. I dropped my gaze.

"The chap I'm meeting tonight," James said into the silence that had suddenly formed.

"Yes?"

"He bent the airscrew on my plane, the one I'm waiting to collect. That's why it wasn't ready. He was firing at a tank, a practice target, and he didn't pull up in time."

"You mean he hit the tank?"

James nodded. "It's very easy to do."

"Is it?" I frowned. "Surely it's a terrible mistake, to fly so low."

"We have to fly that low to get the tanks. It's a specialty of my new squadron, you see. We approach at a height of about fifteen feet"—he swept his hand in a slow horizontal line over the table—"fire the gun, which is a special anti-tank cannon, and then climb as fast as we can." His hand rose up, finished the demonstration, and came to rest on the table. "If we fire too soon, we don't penetrate the tank. If we fire too late, we fly into it. I'm sorry," he said with a forced laugh. "This is a most unsuitable topic of conversation."

"Of course it's not," I said. "I expect you think of that cannon all the time."

"Yes," he said, his face clearing. "Yes, I do."

I met his eyes. I remembered from before how dark blue they were and how open and watchful. I understood it now. He couldn't afford to miss anything.

"I'm glad." I smiled. "It will keep you safe."

Another moment of silence passed. I didn't want to be anywhere else but there, with him.

"James, you're going to think I'm strange, but sometimes I miss that air raid."

"I've missed it dreadfully."

I looked up, struck. He was smiling but his eyes were very serious.

"I remember everything we talked about that night, and the next day." He shook his head. "I left you crying, and went off to my train to Luxor—unforgivable. I kicked myself all the way down the Nile, wishing I'd said something to you. Never mind what you thought of me. I should have told you how lovely you were. I wanted to take you in my arms."

And I would have stopped thinking and simply been held, by the man who had spoken to me in the dark. Yes, of course. That should have happened.

"Yvette." He leaned forward. "Is it too late?"

One simple word. All I had to do was get it out. I found I couldn't stop blinking. My eyes were wet but I wasn't remotely weeping.

"No," I managed to say.

He took hold of my hand. His hand was warm, dry, sunbrowned except for splashes of pink over the knuckles.

"What is that?" I said, stroking his knuckles with my other hand.

"Glycol burns. But they're old."

I remembered his touches, his fingers linked with mine, then cupping my elbow in a gentle clasp. Now he was cradling my hand tenderly. I put my free hand over the back of his, so that I was holding him as well as being held. His palm and fingers were rough, his hands square, strong. They had not the Olympian beauty of Sébastien's hands. But Sébastien's hands were always so languid. There was no feeling in them. There was no feeling in Sébastien, beyond certain lionlike urges.

All in a rush, James took his hands out of mine and put his arms around me.

Célia appeared in the doorway of the room and looked at us.

I let go of James and sat up straight. "Oh, Célia," I said, "there are three eggs."

She burst out laughing.

I met Sébastien at a café by the beach. Explained why we had to stop.

"I shall miss you." He sighed. "I shall be sad for days."

"Days." I laughed. "Goodbye, Sébastien, darling."

He said, *"Au revoir, ma chérie, et bonne chance."*

Goodbye, darling, and good luck. We parted without rancor. We had driven hundreds of miles together. We were comrades.

Out of the two nurses on the houseboat, it was the smoking nurse, not the nunlike one, who attended to Peter. The smoking nurse was a genius with dressings, unfailingly deft and gentle with him. It was she who fitted the eyepatch, the black, rakish eyepatch, when he was healed and when his good eye glowed a bright light blue again even in the strongest sunlight.

"Dear Yvette," he said, "you don't have to," when I told him of my intention to join the WAAF.

Célia said, "James won't think less of you if you don't."

"Don't worry," I said. "I'm doing it for me."

The uniform came crumpled it seemed, so there was no shame in looking like a bag of laundry. On my first day they ordered us to *dress up a line!*, which, I speedily learned, was to stand in a row and shuffle until our extended right arms barely touched our neighbor's shoulder.

I formed a rank under the beating sun alongside girls called Nadia and Ginette and Miriam with heads turned smartly to the right. Serious girls with serious eyes narrowed in the sun in spite of our peaked caps because the light glared so hard off the desert. I turned my head to the right with all the others as the light nearly blinded me, and I almost fainted there from the apprehension, from the heat, from suddenly being this close to the war.

Last week James and I went for our walk down the lane past the playground. This week, no.

"Why not?" asked Tom. "The primroses are still there."

James heard him and after a murmured conversation, Tom left the house on his bicycle, returning flushed a quarter of an hour later with a straggling bunch of primroses. He put them in a water glass on my bedside table. So I look at them and think of the hat that left behind nothing but its color in their petals. Remembering how they moved under the patches of low spring sun, as if it were the light and not the breeze that fluttered them.

SEVEN

On Sunday morning I stand up in church before the whole of Upton and Barrow End or near enough, all in their best coats and hats, folding their umbrellas and herding their children into pews as if they were penning sheep, and then, once they are seated in silence, offering me one unified, watchful, level stare. The kind of stare that asks a man what he is made of. In the event it is Meg Sutton who comes to my rescue: the child is hardly baptized before she's raring to be released, preferably into the font, and laughter and joyfulness breaks out in the Sutton family and spreads down the aisles. We celebrate Meg—Meg, and all the other children who will take us onward into a future we can't imagine. *O God our strength in ages past, our hope in years to come:* this hymn is roared out, three basses in the choir making a fine drone, underpinned by an organist who can keep time. Not bad, not bad at all. At the door, smiles and wringing handshakes and "Fine job, Mr. Acton."

Mr. Acton, it is fair to say, is thoroughly bucked up.

The following morning, guilt propels me to my typewriter. Frobisher's letter is still unanswered. I get as far as typing *Dear Archdeacon* when I hear a vehicle draw up outside.

A van has been maneuvered expertly into the narrow slot between my heap of a car and the low wall by the road. The driver gets out. She's a diminutive, high-shouldered, energetic-looking woman with dark hair and equally dark, unsmiling eyes.

"Mr. Acton? I'm Lucy Horne," she says, wiping her hands down the front of a dilapidated canvas jerkin. "I work up at the kennels with my dad."

There's a hound pup going spare at the kennels, Lady Brock had said. *I can get my friend Lucy Horne to give you a ring.* My heart begins to sink.

"How do you do, Miss Horne." I shake her proffered hand. "Lady Brock said you might telephone."

Instead of turning up without a by-your-leave. If she knows what I'm thinking, she doesn't show it. In fact, she's already opening the back doors of her van and lifting out a cardboard box with the words *TOP DECK CIDER SHANDY* emblazoned on the side.

If only it did contain Top Deck cider shandy.

The puppy is sitting on his bottom in the darkness of the high-sided box. His stubby legs are white, his body patched with black and brown. His face is black except for ginger eyebrows and a white muzzle. As I watch, his head droops as if he can barely hold it up under the weight of his sumptuous, velvety ears. These ears are the only abundant thing about him. The rest of him is diminutive, skimpy, his ribs staring: he takes up far less room than his food supplies, two pints of milk and a biscuit tin with *BABY RUSK* scrawled on the lid, which are packed in beside him.

"Dad and me, we thought you might as well have a look at him. He's called Bailey."

Miss Horne's speaking voice is flat, piped. I think she might be asthmatic. I look up at her. "So you brought two weeks' food, just in case."

"I've asked and asked," she says. "But there isn't a soul in Upton or Barrow End who'll have him. Lady Brock, she said—"

"She said, 'Try the vicar. He's a soft touch.'" I can't help smiling.

"You're my last hope, Mr. Acton."

She states it flatly. She doesn't ingratiate herself in any way. There's an almost flinty look about her, the directness of her dark eyes. I'd call this blackmail if she were a more importunate person. But I sense that importuning has never been her style. I sense that Lucy Horne's aim in life is to make a good fist of things, and if that means, as in this case, finding a home for a dog she'll otherwise have to put down, she will go to great lengths.

"Miss Horne—"

"He's had all his jabs. No fleas or worms. And you can call me Lucy, Vicar."

"Lucy. I was going to ask if you'd like to come in."

Once in the kitchen Lucy takes off her battered jerkin, looking even smaller without the bulky garment. She could wear the clothes of an eleven-year-old child. She lifts the puppy out of the box and he hangs from her hands, swaddled in empty folds of skin, his mouth drawing back to show small needles of white teeth.

"His mum had no interest in him," she says. "She had her work cut out feeding the other six, and the big ones squeezed him out like a pip. He never got a look-in. Would you please heat some of this milk for me, Vicar?"

I do as she says, firing up a ring of my gas camping stove. It's a bit like having a baby to visit. Except this particular baby has been foisted on me forever after.

"How old is Bailey, Lucy?"

"Eight weeks. Not got your range started yet, I see. I know that stove of old, when we used to do Christmas carols. Such a bugger, it was. We used to end up with lukewarm tea."

She gives me a grin and I realize that her teeth are false. I'm reminded of a young armorer of 6 Squadron who'd had all his teeth pulled before he was posted; they were already more trouble than they were worth. During dust storms he used to take his dentures out and button them into the front pocket of his overalls. Neither he nor Lucy, I suspect, saw a dentist in all their childhood.

The milk comes to the boil. Lucy mashes some baby rusk into the milk and dabs tiny gobs of this mixture onto the edge of the puppy's mouth. This tempts his tongue out, and he feebly licks his lips. "I doubt you'll have to spoon-feed him more than a few days. Look." Lucy stands the puppy over the bowl so his front paws are astride it. He blinks, looking around him with misty eyes, comprehending nothing. Lucy pushes the spoon under his chin before lowering it into the bowl. His nose follows the spoon down into the pap. "Just sniffing for now but soon he'll be licking it up himself. He'll need four meals a day, mind, spoon or not. Won't you, you little brute."

I've never heard such affection behind the word *brute*.

"Four meals," I echo. "How on earth am I going to manage that?"

"I'm sure you'll find a way, Vicar. Oh—have you spotted your ancient relics yet?" Lucy puts down the bowl and spoon and carries the puppy toward a corner of the room. She kneels down and runs a finger over one of the filthy terra-cotta tiles that pave the floor. "Here's one."

Lucy's freestyle mode of conversation, the way she hops from one subject to the next, is keeping me on my toes. I go and join her, intrigued. The shape on the tile can hardly be seen through the impasto of grease and dirt. It's an inch and a half long, the color of butter against the terra-cotta ground. An animal, running? A curved back, perhaps? Are those legs, below?

"Look at his ears," Lucy prompts. "And his mouth, open like that. The way he's leaping. There's three, four more on this tile alone. A pack of them. *Hounds*."

"Oh yes!" Now she says it, I see them. Eager, lop-eared, high-tailed, they leap all over the tile she shows me and the neighboring ones too. Excitement rises inside me. I'm no expert but I've trodden the floors of many of our oldest cathedrals.

"But these are ancient, Lucy!"

"I know they are, Vicar, I just told you so. Robbed from the priory in Waltham, people say. When I was young they stood out properly. But the Reverend Blakemore, he wouldn't allow anyone to come and clean and, well . . ." She shakes her head, then smiles again. "You did a terrific job in church yesterday. Goodness, that child can roar. The Suttons were ever so pleased, and so was I. You've kicked it off to a good start, I reckon. Now, poor Bailey's still hungry." She points at the bowl and spoon. "Go on, jump in the deep end while I have a look at your range. You got coal, I see."

Bailey will eat from the spoon, his pink tongue darting cautiously in and out, but when I lower the spoon to the bowl he stares hopelessly at me without moving. It takes Lucy a couple of minutes to set a small fire in the firebox of the range. She shuts the firebox door, listens, opens it again. A cloud of smoke billows out. "Not drawing," she says almost triumphantly, standing up and tugging at a lever at the base of the chimney. "Flue damper's stuck, or broken. You might need a new one from Waltham Spares."

"Seems a lot of trouble to heat a can of soup."

Lucy agrees. "I remember my nan on her knees on a winter

morning, feeding in bits of kindling and turning the air blue. I didn't realize she even knew those words. When we went over to electric she thought she'd died and gone to heaven." She laughs, and the laugh turns into a splutter. She coughs hoarsely for a moment or two. "I think it's just Ellen and you left, now," she adds when she can next speak.

"Ell—Ellen and I?" I clear my throat.

"In the village," Lucy elaborates. "Still hanging on to your ranges. Ellen Parr, at Parr's Mill. She's wedded to that stove, anyway, swears by it for stewing apples and baking bread."

"We met the other day," I tell her. "Well, almost." I explain my encounter outside Lady Brock's lodge. "Lady Brock said it would be a . . . a rare sighting."

"Yes." Lucy Horne sighs. "She's no churchgoer, not anymore. You can lead a horse to water, Vicar, but you cannot make her drink, is all I'll say."

I remember the figure I glimpsed that day. Tall, fair-haired, vanishing among the hazel trees. "I can't imagine leading her anywhere she didn't want to go."

"Ha! You've got her in one. Top marks, Bailey." She gives a nod of approval at the dog, who has been butting his small muzzle against the spoon and licking off the contents with a sudden surprising vigor. "Change of scene, you see. Just what he needed. Now he'll want to do his business. If you put newspaper nearer the back door each day, he'll soon get the hang of going outside. Well, I must go to work." She regards me, eyes narrowed in appreciation, lips tightening on a smile. "I must say, Vicar, you've saved my bacon. And Bailey's too."

After Lucy leaves, I go back into the kitchen and stare at Bailey. He meets my gaze, a patient, long-suffering look in his eyes. I scratch my head. "Well, Bailey, here we are," I tell him. "We have both been thoroughly finessed."

Thanks to Blakemore's study, I'm well supplied with newspaper. I haven't touched the room since my first inspection. It's just as appalling on a second viewing. I drag out a bale of ancient, yellowing editions of the *Hampshire Chronicle,* which I carry to the kitchen and set down next to the puppy's cardboard box. Newspapers are never so fascinating as when they're spread out on the floor for purposes other than reading. My eyes are drawn to a column enticingly headed News from the Districts, which informs me that two hundred dozen eggs in total, goose, duck, and hen (including bantam), were sold the previous Wednesday at Waltham Market. I peer at the date at the top of the page. It's 27th September 1950.

We were at Alver Shore back then, Yvette and I, our first parish. Half an hour away on the coast. We'd been there nearly four years. Most of them Yvette was happy, but not that September.

I went out, on one of those September days, to pick some apples from our tree. There were so many and they were so delicious and red. I gathered them in my arms, awkwardly, and brought them into the house. *Look what I've got for you,* I said to Yvette, but she turned her head away. She didn't even want to see them.

I didn't understand. I wanted to distract her if only for a moment.

Bloody Blakemore. Curse him and all uncared-for, uselessly hoarding old men. I sweep the newspaper from the floor and take it back to the study, returning with an edition safely dated 30th June 1973. Just as I'm finishing the task, the telephone starts to ring.

It's Althea Brock. I speak to her forthrightly, but then, I feel fairly forthright. "I'm now, for better or worse, the owner of a small, sickly hound pup, Lady Brock. A state of affairs which I lay wholly at your door."

She crows with mirth. I'm so glad to hear laughter, even if it is directed at me.

"You'll get used to each other," she says. "And you never know. Someone might come along and fall in love with him."

"While we're on the subject of dogs, Lady Brock, is there anyone local who knows about medieval floor tiles? Lucy's shown me the hounds from Waltham Priory. They're in a sad state."

"Oh yes, the hounds! I remember sun designs, and flowers as well, in the distant past. Don't suppose you can see a glimpse of them now. No, I haven't got a clue what to do about them. Though I'll tell you if anything surfaces. My memory's rather a muddy pond, you see. Now, the reason I rang—memory a case in point, actually. My scarf. I realize I must have left it in church after we did the flowers. Silly thing with a picture of a train on it, yes?"

"Yes, that's the one."

I'm suddenly aware of my heart beating solidly in my chest.

"I went back for it but it was gone. Then I saw your note in the porch, so I *applied*, as you directed, to the vicarage but you were out."

"I'm sorry to bring you out of your way. I thought it would be safer in the vicarage. In my old parish we had to keep our eyes peeled, you see. I'm no expert but it looks . . ." What do I need to say? "It looks quite special."

"Heavens no, I got it from the jumble sale. I think it belonged to old Edith Phelps. She went into the nursing home and her family had to clear the house. She had heaps of ghastly jewelry, jet earrings and brooches and frightful mourning bracelets made of hair, absolutely unsalable now, but her son Mottram took it all to Waltham for valuing, to that crook Freddie Spall who diddled his own aunt out of all her savings, and do you know, Freddie gave Mottram Phelps fifty pounds . . . Where was I?"

"The scarf."

"Oh, yes. It makes me think of those marvelous designs from the thirties. What was he called, that fellow. Hermès. I'd never have been able to afford that sort of thing at the time . . . Oh Lord, supposing it's actually antique? Supposing the Phelpses put it in the jumble sale by mistake? It really ought to go back to Edith, if that's the case."

"I don't know," I say. "It's possible."

"Well, let me pop round anyway and fetch it. I could show it to Edith one of these days, see what she thinks. I don't want to snaffle up one of her beloved treasures for a few pence, it would be quite wrong."

"Would the nursing home be Redwood House? The one on the edge of the village?"

"Indeed, Redwood."

"Let me take it, then. I'm due to visit them. If she doesn't want it, I'll bring it back to you."

"That would be most kind. My left hip is currently . . . what are people saying at the moment? *Working to rule.* Oh—well done with Meg Sutton on Sunday, by the way. Are you sure you've never done any shearing?"

"No, but her father has," I tell Lady Brock. "He told me to get a good purchase on her."

I haven't looked at the scarf since I put it away. It's disturbing, and I'm very keen, at this busy time, not to feel disturbed. Even so, it has insinuated itself into my thoughts, at odd moments of idleness or before sleep. I have been wondering where it came from, what circumstances could have infused it with this odd power. I didn't lie to Lady Brock: I *am* due to visit Redwood House. But not until next week, when I will conduct Holy Communion for those unable to leave the home.

All the same, it might be polite to pass by beforehand. Let the staff put a face to the name before my official visit. And this morning seems as good a time as any.

It is disgraceful, how quickly I persuade myself of this.

In the kitchen Bailey has overturned his box, pulled out his bedding, and availed himself of the newspaper. I replace the paper and search for my bicycle clips. For a wild moment I forget where I've put the scarf. Then I remember the drawer in the kitchen table. I slide the scarf into a paper bag and set off for Redwood House.

On the way I post my letter to Tom. Among other things, including my measurements for the sweater, the letter contains a request. I've asked him to look through the photo albums, see if he can find any pictures of his mother wearing a scarf. I wrote, *I know it sounds rather odd, but,* and then came to a halt, unable to think what to write next. So I crossed out the *but* and left it at that. The sentence still makes sense. And it certainly does sound rather odd.

The nursing home was a military hospital during both World Wars when, no doubt, the staff struggled as they do now with the heavy oak doors and the windows made of leaded lights that creak open only with a judicious blow of the fist. "It's all too bloomin' well-made to get rid of," says an orderly as he takes me to meet the director. "And as for the water . . ."

"What water?"

"River's bank high, Reverend. Haven't you seen it?"

"No." I had no idea, preoccupied as I've been.

"If this keeps up we'll be awash. Mrs. Shaw's sending us all out to do the sandbags after lunch."

He leaves me outside the director's office, where the sign on the door proclaims that Mrs. Theresa Shaw is *In*. But just about to go *Out*, as I see from the pleated transparent plastic headscarf she's tying under her chin as I enter at her summons.

"Oh, God," she blurts, with a stricken expression. "It's not today, is it?"

"No, it's not." I extend my hand. "I thought I'd drop by and say hello, that's all, before our service." Her handshake is hot and agitated. I feel doubly awkward now. There she is, grabbing some free time and I've come along unannounced to fill it up in a most unwelcome fashion. "I'm sorry, Mrs. Shaw. I should have rung, especially when you've got the river to deal with. I didn't know a flood was coming."

"Well, we don't know as such. We look at the river and *feel* it. Something about the color, and the speed. Boiling tea with not enough milk. And do call me Terry." Recovering herself, she pulls off her plastic head wrapper. "Thank God the service isn't today, though. There, I've said it again. Something about the sight of a vicar and I immediately take the Lord's name in vain." She gives a musical little laugh. "Now, I'll take you to the dayroom. It's coffee time. We can remind everyone about the service." She leads me out of her office and, at a brisk pace, down a corridor. "You know we bring a minibus to the church every month," she continues, her heels rapping over the linoleum. "I'd love to make it more often, but the cost. I'm so glad you're able to do this for them. Mr. Blakemore used to, but then, well . . ."

"Actually," I say, "I'm also on a mission from Lady Brock."

"Oh." Mrs. Shaw comes to a halt.

"A scarf belonging to Mrs. Phelps found its way into a jumble sale. Lady Brock bought it, and now she's not sure if she should have. I mean, the scarf is quite antique, and the family may not have realized, or noticed it, even."

I pull the paper bag from my pocket and liberate the scarf. The colors look dark, the blue like a bruise, in the dimness of the corridor.

Terry Shaw takes it. "Goodness me. I see what you mean." She holds it up in the gloom, as if about to pin it to a clothesline. "Might be *Hermès*," she says after a second or two. Unlike Lady Brock, she pronounces the name correctly, in the French manner. "I studied art and design when I was young, before I got into this game. Textiles." She eyes me, her lids heavy; a speculative, suggestive gleam appears. I've seen this gleam before in the eyes of female parishioners and as always I meet it with an expression of benign impassivity. The gleam fades, *oh well.* She returns her attention to the scarf. "Let's ask Edith."

Coffee time is in full swing in the dayroom, the chatter loud. Here is Mrs. Phelps, breathless, her cheeks flushed to match her pink cardigan. "Dear me, Terry," she puffs as she sits down. "I shall never get used to this central heating." She tries to unbutton the cardigan, but can't manage it. Her fingers are blue at the tips and as bent and thin as twigs. Terry Shaw sits down beside her. "What a lovely Fair Isle pattern, Edith. Let me help you."

"Go on, then, Terry, my dear." Mrs. Phelps turns to me. "It's being helpless I can't bear. There's so many things beyond me now. Do you know, I drink my tea through a straw? Who wants to drink tea through a straw?"

"It can't be much fun," I say.

"This is the new vicar," Terry says, as she attends to Mrs. Phelps's buttons. "Mr. Acton. He's brought something of yours from the jumble sale, something that you might have wanted to keep?"

Mrs. Phelps, extricating herself from her cardigan, peers at the scarf. "Not mine, dear," she says. "I'm sorry I can't help you. Somebody lost it?"

"We're not sure," Terry says. "Let's hope it was put in the jumble on purpose." Hurriedly she rises to her feet. "I must get on. I've got so many phone calls to make." She hands me the scarf. I stand up too and we shake hands and say goodbye, and she makes her way carefully across the lounge, picking her way past the canes, crutches, walking frames, and wheelchairs, the paraphernalia of old age. A whole generation is here, washed up on a high tide, too light and inconsequential to be carried back with the rest of us into the tumbling sea. It's not right. But I can't find an answer.

I'm about to return the scarf to its paper bag when, a few yards away, a woman in a wheelchair announces, "Yes. Yes. *Yes.*"

A stroke has dragged half of her face downward and one arm lies useless on her lap. The other arm, however, is raised. She's pointing at my hands.

"Does this belong to you, madam?"

"Yes," she says again, but less certainly. Her good hand is now beckoning. Ah—she needs a better look at the scarf. I spread it out over a small table and pull the table in front of her. No big thumps this time but all the same my heartbeat picks up a fraction. Enough to notice.

She stares, frowns, cocks her head. But the next yes is even more cautious.

"I hope you don't mind me asking," I say, "but can you only say yes?"

"Yes." Very firm, and her mobile eyebrow frowns. *And I'm absolutely fed up with it.*

She peers closer. Abruptly the light leaves her eyes. "Yes." She sighs, her tone now utterly dismissive, as if she can't believe what silly nonsense I've presented her with. For good measure, she flicks the back of her good hand at the scarf and at me together.

"It's not yours, then?"

Another deep, cross sigh. "Yes yes yes!" she says, with an irritable little shake of the head. *Of course it's not,* she means. *Haven't I made myself clear?*

"Never mind. I'm sorry to have bothered you. Goodbye."

She stares away at the window, avoiding my gaze, her eyes hot. Expecting no further response, I reclaim the scarf and make my way out of the room. The corridor is deserted, Terry Shaw's door closed. I can hear her voice on the phone, only the rise and fall, no words.

The front doors of Redwood House have opened to the overcast sky and a metallic light comes in, blazing around and blurring the outline of a tall man in a black mackintosh who is coming over the threshold, his shoulders spangled with raindrops. I let him pass and make my way outside.

The woman in the wheelchair thought she had glimpsed something, but it wasn't really there. It must have been another figure or pattern she had in mind, part of the lost fabric of her own life. These things trick and tease the eye and the heart and there's always a disappointment, as when you half recognize a face in a crowd and then a clearer light or closer look reveals it to be nothing like the face you love. And you wonder how you could have been so deceived.

EIGHT

❦

Yvette
18 March 1964

I swore I'd never forget how to pack a parachute. I was hoping to be able to begin today by writing down the numbered list of steps I used to know by heart. But to my horror—is this what happens when you're *middle aged*?—I can only remember the essence of the task. Which is, in brief, to reduce thirty feet of white silk tendril-trailing jellyfish to a parcel the size of a cushion. It was my first job in the WAAF and my trainer was a girl from a city in England I understood to be called New Kassel. On my first day she abused me for arriving at work with my hair tied in a black muslin wrap.

"But I've put a treatment on," I protested. I thought the muslin would be hidden by my WAAF cap. "The desert air is so harsh on the hair, no?"

"It's not regulation, pet," she said, softening, since I was clearly another of those local recruits who didn't have a clue.

To pack a parachute is to become a master in the arts of folding and tucking. In the corralling of cords. My teacher—Pam—was dogged. Under her somber eye I tussled and yanked and perspired. I dreamed of my 'chutes snagging, bundling in the air, spinning the cords into a rope on the end of which a writhing airman plummeted to earth. But Pam would never have permitted that. I packed with her breath on my neck—hot, slightly onion-smelling at all times. *Again, dear. Again. And once more, pet.* I don't know how many times I packed the same parachute. After three weeks I was beginning to comprehend the true meaning of patience and precision. It was a belief, parachute packing. A one true way. And there is something miraculous about a 'chute blooming in the sky, every cord flitting out of its binding without a hitch, the canopy plumping open into a perfect dome. Almost, I would say, holy.

After five weeks, I learned that James had been shot down and reported missing.

It was Peter who told me. He tried to protect me by saying, "Everyone's being picked up by the New Zealanders, Yvette. I bet you he'll be back with his squadron in a couple of days . . ." But by this time I was sobbing and snarling in Célia's arms.

I was taken off my lovely parachutes. The precious procedures had been driven quite out of my head. Pam told me to go home. I was just about to when some visitors arrived from Heliopolis, a couple of genial top brass. While they inspected us, their driver, an army girl, fainted. Before I knew it, my hand was in the air. "I can drive you to Heliopolis."

They were fairly taken aback. I told them about the Bedford two-tonner and the Citroën Fifteen. I didn't say, *Oh, please*, like a schoolgirl, but my face must have conveyed the message.

The car was a Humber Pullman. Nothing on the Citroën, of course, but comfy for the brass and for the wilting driver who I belted tightly into the front seat. After I'd ferried them all back to Heliopolis I begged to be put into the driving pool but nothing doing, it was army girls only. I got a lift back to Alexandria, dreadfully low. All the time I was behind the wheel I hadn't worried about James for a single second.

A week later I went back to the parachutes. I simply could not do nothing, and I had learned in the meantime that James had parachuted from his plane. I packed with a cold precision, for the sake of all the other airmen, and saved my tears for the evening. Célia and I prayed together, her voice continuing steady when mine broke off.

A month later I received a letter from a Mrs. Iris Acton.

His widow. I swear, I was so deranged those words went through my mind. He was dead, and—almost worse—he'd been married all along.

Stupid. He was true to me. And how would his widow know about me anyway? I ripped the envelope apart. Yes, Mrs. Iris was his mother. But he could still be dead. Please let him not be dead.

She was writing at his request. He was in a prisoner-of-war camp at Sagan in Silesia.

I burst into awful choking brays of joy that brought Célia, violently alarmed, from the other end of the house.

Later that day I leafed through Papa's atlas looking for Silesia. Found it, a patch of territory on the double page marked *Allemagne-Pologne.* "Lower Silesia," I said, looking up at Peter. "Germany."

He gave a pale smile. "I think it depends on your point of view," he said.

The camp was a Stalagluft, Peter explained. A prison for airmen. They got parcels from the Red Cross but not all the time. When there were no parcels it was cabbage soup. "But he'll meet old friends there," Peter told me. "They play cricket, and learn languages."

"Sounds quite jolly," I said without conviction.

James and I began to write to each other. Small questions: how my uniform looked awful however much I ironed it. At the end of a page of scribbled trivia I apologized for my nonsense. He wrote, *Your nonsense is keeping me going.*

Big questions: he was beginning to wonder how, after all that killing, he could serve God. The padre in the camp had reassured him that (1) the killing was not murder, since the church ruled that it was justified in war. And (2) God had saved James to serve Him. *I don't know how the padre can be so certain,* James wrote. *God might have saved me so I can be a plumber. And I'm still not sure about the killing. Our guards are all old airmen, they're not Nazis, they hate the Nazis. They're decent. Makes me think how many other decent men I put to death.*

Do you want to be a plumber? I wrote.

Six weeks later: *No, I want to be a priest.*

In that case, I replied, *the question is as follows: After all that killing, how can you not serve God?*

In early 1944 he told me that because he was going into the church there wouldn't be any money ever. That England was cold and poor, and I would be the one doing the housework and bringing up the children. *This is by way of asking, dear Yvette, I cannot promise you much more than my heart but, darling, will you marry me?*

I accepted.

Adding that, given the situation, I would make sure I came with a substantial dowry.

Then, in March '44, he was moved to a place called Belaria. I found this out afterward. At the time, all I knew was that the letters were fewer. After Christmas there were none at all. In January 1945 the news bulletins told of Russians advancing, prison camps being emptied out by the Germans, prisoners being marched westward. I looked again at the map. It was a long way to the Allied lines. His mother, who I addressed as Iris now, assured me that it was the same for everyone. We were all as ignorant as each other. But in May 1945 Iris wrote again. *In case his own letter gets lost, James would like me to tell you that he left the camp in January of this year. They were forced to march eighty kilometers in the snow to Luckenwalde, from which place the Russians finally liberated them.*

James was lucky as there were a number of deaths on the march.

His squadron will soon go to Palestine but James will spend the rest of his service on leave for recuperation, so he will not fly again. He plans to be with you in Egypt by the end of May.

I hope that we will meet one day soon, dear Yvette.

I received James's letter the next day. It was brief, and contained none of those details apart from his estimated date of arrival. The writing was very small.

That May was hot and restless. Great joy succeeded the victory over Germany but we would not be released from our service until the end of the summer. The driving pool was very shorthanded so they finally let me behind the wheel of a two-ton lorry. One afternoon I took some airmen from Heliopolis to the RAF base at Amiriya. The airmen slept all the way and bundled out in a hurry. I stood there in the slaying-hot wind at Amiriya, my skirt flapping over my legs and whipping sand in my eyes. Swearing at the sand, thinking I wouldn't be overheard in the wind.

"Yvette?"

I stared wildly around.

"Yvette!"

A thin, pale, boy-like person was calling my name.

At first he hadn't recognized me either. We found each other as if in the dark by voice and then by touch.

Oy, break it up, somebody said, braying, but we took no notice. He was nothing in my arms, he didn't feel like him.

I was blinking from the sand. He was blurring in front of me.

Peter and Célia were at home. We didn't have anything ready, we scurried around preparing a scrappy meal, but it didn't matter, he only picked at it. "I'm sorry," he said. "I can't eat very much at one time." His voice was the only thing that was the same, so I started to look away when he talked, to steady myself. Célia saw me do this and squeezed my hand.

At the end of the meal my mother made him up a little plate and left it on the side table with a fork. For once she did something matter-of-factly without fuss. "Tell him it's so he can take a morsel when he wants to," she said to me, and he said, "Tell your mother she's very kind."

"You can tell each other yourselves," I said, smiling at both of them. "You'll understand well enough."

We sat with the blinds drawn against the heat, drinking hibiscus. The ice cubes clinked in the silence. Peter and Célia knew what was happening. So did I. Even in the warmth of the afternoon we could see the journey running like a film behind his eyes, the snow, the biting cold and hunger. We knew that every day he saw it again, and his friends died afresh. He had told us, "We didn't have far to go, compared with some." Another time he said, "Once I slept in three foot of hay. Never had a better night!" But it was unconvincing.

Célia gave me a significant look. She stood up and so did I. We took the cups down to the kitchen.

"Can you do it?" she asked me.

Célia still had that blankness sometimes, the look of someone colliding over and over with the enormity of what might have happened. Peter could have died, been burned, blinded. Each improvement in his sight—the gray blur, the sliver of white, the square of light from the window—could have been the last. Only someone who knew what that was like, had the right to ask me this.

"Yes, I can."

But I did not *feel* that I could. I only hoped.

I quickly learned that he did better with small amounts of everything, not just food. A lengthy conversation, no matter how light the subject, was too much. Even, or especially, this was true with kisses and embraces. They had to be supplied like everything else, in little spoonfuls.

My father, noticing this, took down from his shelves all his archaeological and architectural works on the Middle East, laid them on the table in his study. His Bénédite, that I had told James about, his Bonfils. James's eyes brightened at the sight. He spent a lot of the day in there while my father was out at the office and then, when he came back, they would sit there together, reading without disturbing each other beyond the occasional comment. Over the weeks, James told my father about his father, Findlay. I learned from Papa how the family had lived in Rosyth, a place in Scotland, where Findlay spent years building the dockyard and then later, after the Great War, lifting the wrecks of battleships from Scapa Flow. Then they went to Egypt: James had told me about that, I remembered, to Suez, where his father widened the canal. And then it was Singapore—a naval base to be built at Sembawang—but James was almost grown up by then. "A fascinating life," said Papa, musing, as I imagined this Findlay as a Titan dragging warships from the water with his huge bare hands. Pushing the sides of the Suez Canal apart. James had said much more to my father than he had to me.

But I was glad he was talking.

By and by we started going out. Just to play cards at a beachside café or to walk along the sand. Sea bathing as James got stronger. We went to a different beach every day for variety. Peter's injury and James's ordeal had given Maman some perspective on life: now she couldn't care less what time we went swimming. So James floated in the shallows at Stanley, Sidi Bishr No. 1, Sidi Bishr No. 2, in the late afternoon when the sea was at its warmest, while Célia and I did our hundreds of strokes. We would come across him as we pulled our caps from our heads, shaking out our hair and puffing, and there he was, thin and white, his eyes closed, like a piece of flotsam. Once I kissed him. He went under in surprise, came up spluttering, laughing, and when he recovered he kissed me back, a smacking salty kiss on my lips.

We began to play tennis, as Peter and Célia and Alastair and I had done at the beginning of the war. It was easy to get a court at the Sporting now. Many people we knew had gone, and it was quiet. The boys were glad no one was milling around because they disgraced themselves, or that's what they thought. Peter, with his one eye, thumped his serve onto the baseline and James, with no strength in his legs, flailed at an outlying backhand of Célia's. The air became quite blue. Célia and I started patting gentle balls directly to them, which infuriated them even more. We tried to call it a day, but they both insisted crossly on a second set.

We spent a lot of time together, the four of us. So much time, in fact, that in the end Célia made an announcement.

"You two simply *must* go for one last visit to Cairo. Tea at Groppi, a trip out to Mena House and a last look at the Pyramids. Go on. Aunt Monique will never forgive you, Yvette, if she doesn't see you before you leave."

We took Aunt Monique out to dinner. In the powder room she gave me the key to her apartment and kissed me. "Take care," she said.

At the apartment I put on some coffee to brew. The window was open and a strong smell of jasmine filled the sitting room. "I always smell jasmine at Boulaq Bridge," James said.

"Yes, it grows there."

He was standing by the window with his hands in his pockets. I put down my bag and took off my light jacket. The only sound was the rustling of my clothes and then the bubbling of the coffee in the kitchen. I went and set the tray and brought the coffee into the sitting room. He sniffed, smelling the aroma, and turned his head away. By this time I was convinced that this had been a mistake. He didn't want to be here, in this apartment. Everything about the place, even the coffee, was reminding him of how he used to be, how he had been when we met here the last time, before his capture and the camp and the march.

He picked up his coffee cup, his hand trembled, he set the cup down. "Look at me." He tried to laugh. "The man you agreed to marry. I won't always be like this, I promise. I'll soon get back to my old self again."

"There is no hurry," I said. "You won't be your old self, anyway. You'll be different."

"I expect so. I can't imagine it." He looked up at me. "I should have stayed longer in England. Some of us went to these rest homes. You know, to recuperate. Maybe I should have done that."

That was what his mouth said. But his eyes were asking me a question.

They were asking if I still wanted him.

"I cannot think of a better place for you to be," I said, "than with the woman who will be your wife."

I found myself stammering over all those *w*'s. English suddenly felt very foreign to me.

Sometime later I said, "Darling, we don't have to." Which was, of course, the worst thing to say.

I undressed shyly. When I turned around he was sitting with his back to me on the bed. His ribs showed. His shoulder blades moved under his skin like a stripling lad.

My whole idea of what is beautiful changed in that instant.

Even though it was a hot evening we acted as if we were in a chilly English autumn, almost shivering as we arranged ourselves, rumpling the sheets and pulling them away from our bodies. His foot struck my calf. "Oh! I'm sorry," he said.

"It doesn't matter." I knew I would have a bruise.

It was a tender, terrible disaster. We were, each of us in different ways, too hasty, too tardy, too frantic, too cold. Clumsily we put out each other's fires and blew on the coals with no flint to strike it seemed. It had to be my fault. I was such a novice: clearly I'd done something wrong.

Presently James sat up.

"It'll be better next time, darling, I promise." He sounded stronger now. Not so lost or afraid. More straightforwardly embarrassed. "If I hadn't—"

"No, no, it was me, I—"

"Really a complete idiot—"

"Simply can't blame yourself—"

By now we were laughing. He was laughing. I remembered this same laugh echoing in the stairwell of this building. Suddenly this mishap was nothing to us. We sat up in bed, side by side with our knees up. We were at the top of a mountain pass, companions after a cruel climb, looking down on our future lying spread out below us. I knew there would be slips and stumbles ahead. But I could see the way forward.

Before the wedding I got confirmed into the Church of England. My father said, *"Paris vaut bien une messe,"* Paris is well worth a Mass. The Protestant Henri III of Navarre had uttered these words in 1593, Papa reminded me, on learning that if he, Henri, converted to Catholicism he could make peace with his enemies and rule all France as Henri IV. "And now *you*, Yvette, are converting the other way!" Papa slapped his knee. "For England, and James! Do you see why it's so funny?" Then he sighed a long sigh, pushed his spectacles up on his head, his eyes suddenly blurry. "I've got plans too."

I knew what he meant. So many of our friends were gathering themselves.

"Where will you go?" I said, my heart beating fast.

"Nice, I think. But slowly." He put his finger to his lips. "Not a word yet to Maman."

We married at St. Mark's. No fuss—definitely no hats. The black-and-white photos show Maman and Papa with teary smiles. Célia, beaming, her skin like alabaster. Peter, the black patch over his missing eye already starting to seem familiar. You can't see James's eyes, the midday sun has made shadows of them—of his eyes, and of the hollows in his cheeks. I have a sort of spray of white flowers in my hair—Célia's idea. In one of the photos I am looking up openmouthed, as if in surprise at these flowers bouncing on top of my head. Tom can hardly bear to look at our wedding photographs because of the unacceptably high incidence of soppiness, but he makes an exception for this one.

Saying goodbye at the port would bring on Papa's angina, he said, so I parted from my parents at home in Cleopatra. But Célia and Peter came to wave us off. In a few months they too would leave, for Adelaide.

Alexandria shrank into a thin white line on the horizon. At the last second it jumped above the sea as if floating in the air, and then *pouf*, it was gone. It was just a city rimming a bay. There were other harbors to discover, and other darker, deeper seas.

NINE

✤

The morning after my visit to Redwood House, I wake to a silence that is quite different from the rural quiet I have been getting used to over the past few days. There's no birdsong, no murmur of traffic on the distant main road. No tractors plowing. It's rather like the silence of a snowfall.

Of course it's not snowfall. I spring out of bed and open the curtains.

There used to be a field across the road. Now, nothing remains except one lonely hillock of scruffy turf. The rest has vanished under a huge expanse of water the color—Terry Shaw was absolutely right—of under-milked tea. The distant line of willows that normally mark the riverbank are knee-deep, a wake forming round each trunk. This unstoppable mass of water must have been heading toward the village for some hours.

I haven't the remotest clue what to do. I don't know anything about floods. But it looks like an emergency to me.

I wash and throw on my clothes. I'm just pulling a sweater over my head when I hear, from downstairs, the unmistakable scuffling sound of a small beast trying to tunnel its way under the kitchen door. Great Scott! I have a dog. I've forgotten Bailey's existence overnight. In the kitchen I warm up his milk and gulp down a cup of powdered coffee standing in the doorway to the back garden while Bailey relieves himself under the hedge. When I give him his breakfast he dips his muzzle in the dish and begins inefficiently to lick up the rusk mixture, shunning my proffered spoon. This is heartening. "Good work, Bailey," I tell him. "Now pay attention. I'll be back in . . . three hours." This is a promise to myself, knowing I can't leave this creature alone for longer. "In the meantime, blanket drill for you."

He remains in his box as I leave the room. He has a rather penetrating stare, which I find unsettling in such a small dog.

The air outside is aswim with small particles, not quite rain, not quite fog, that swirl past me as I hurry toward my car in Wellingtons and a full set of waterproofs. The road looks passable for a normal car like my Vauxhall, the tarmac visible under a fast, light stream, but by the time I get to the main street the water is deeper, a rushing brook. The houses are mercifully higher than the street, the garden paths climb to the tightly shut, sandbagged front doors. There's no one to be seen.

I round the corner onto the village green. This is more serious. One half of the expanse of grass is at least a foot under, as is the road on one side.

Leaving my car on the driest corner, I start to inch along in my Wellingtons against the walls of the houses. Again, not a soul is outside. When I reach an alley named Church Walk—inappropriately so, since it's nowhere near the church—my dismay starts to mount. Built along one side of this alley are six former almshouses, inhabited now by the frailest elderly, people one faltering step from Redwood House. Each house has a front step, now perhaps two scant inches above the flood line, and there's not a sandbag in sight. The water's got muscle here: it's making the same wash around my legs as I saw with the willow trees earlier this morning. A nasty sense of humor too. The current lassoes my ankle when I set my foot to the ground, very keen to tip me onto my backside.

A face appears at a downstairs window and I make my cautious way over. It's a woman, wisps of white hair floating over her scalp, ancient, pendulous earlobes. She chirrups at me, her words muffled by the glass. "I can't open my door, Vicar. There's a flood outside." Her eyes, hooded by wrinkled lids, are cheerful.

"I know. Have you got any sandbags, Mrs. . . . ?"

"Rail. Matilda Rail. Don't worry, dear. Council are bringing them directly."

She says this in a bright, fairly forceful tone. As if she's used to jollying people along, especially those who've got no right to be miserable. Grumbling children, or men worriting about sandbags.

"Stay put, Mrs. Rail. I'll see what I can do."

"'Course I'll stay put." She gives me a beaming, slightly exasperated smile. "The lane's underwater, dear."

Toiling back toward my car I spot a telephone box on the corner. A search of my pockets produces, glory be, three two-pence coins. The door of the booth swirls the brown water as I open it. I ring the only number I've memorized so far.

"This is Upton Hall Lodge." The information is delivered with great moment, rather as the World Service announces, *This is London.* "Althea Brock speaking."

I fill her in on the situation.

"Matilda Rail told you the council had sandbags?" she barks. "She's behind the times, I'm afraid. We rang them yesterday when the village hall ran out. They've got none left."

I glance down at the slots in the wall of the booth where phone books are supposed to be kept. Both are bare.

"Lady Brock, have you a telephone directory to hand?"

"Oh Lord, I'll have to fossick around."

Her fossicking costs me another two pence but she supplies the number I need. I bid her goodbye. "Are you all right at the lodge?"

"Absolutely fine. But the school's underwater. *Huge* excitement, fire brigade, the lot. I always said to Michael his bloody house was built in the wrong place."

Soon I'm driving up out of the village onto the dry roads beyond Beacon Hill, on my way to the local army camp. I've gathered from my second phone call that the army's not at home, being occupied with exercises on Salisbury Plain, but the sentry grudgingly allowed that he *did* have sandbags. "I'm not sure I can lend you a lorry, though. You might be anyone."

"*Lorry Thief Poses as Vicar,*" I murmur, as I take the final corner with a slight skid, mentally writing the article that would follow this headline. *"He was so religious-looking,"* camp sentry Barney Barnes told *our reporter. "Just like a proper reverend."* I abandon my composition as the camp gates appear ahead of me.

The sentry muses over my driving license. Fifteen minutes must have gone by since I arrived at Church Walk. Finally he speaks.

"You're the Vicar of Upton, you say?"

"Yes."

I don't sound very convinced, even to myself.

"But it says here you live in . . . Fulbrook." He shows me my license. "Near Bristol. That's quite a long way away."

"I did live there, until very recently. I haven't got round to changing my license yet. Look, I'd be leaving my car here. And if you wanted, you could send someone with me in the lorry."

He gives my car a doubtful glance. I wonder if he's calculating its value against that of a two-ton army lorry. "There's Corporal Large," he admits. "But he's gone to bed. He's got an awful cold."

He can't yet be eighteen, this boy. His jaws are red and scraped. Taking off his first stubble with a borrowed, blunt razor, I don't doubt. I made the same hash of it at his age. He's clasping his rifle to his body as if the simple act of holding it might protect him.

"Listen, Corporal . . . what's your name?"

"Matthew Dodds."

"Matthew." I make my voice as gentle as I can in the circumstances. "There are old people in Upton whose houses will be flooded if I don't get back to them in time. I must have a lorry and the sandbags. And some paraffin stoves if you've got them. Now, can you help me?"

He shuffles from foot to foot, and then without meeting my eyes traipses back into his kiosk and returns with a set of keys.

It takes us another ten minutes to load the sandbags. I stow six paraffin stoves along with their fuel in the front of the cab and set off back to the village. It's a small flatbed lorry but still its weight drags me to the outer corner of the downward bends and I crash the gears with nearly every change. Yvette would be rolling her eyes. Soon I'm back in the village and churning once more along the flooded side of the green. There's a Land Rover in front of me. I hoot my horn and come alongside, leaning over to wind down the window.

"Morning, Vicar," says Lucy Horne from the passenger seat of the Land Rover. "Bloomin' heck."

Bloomin' heck indeed. "I wonder if you could assist?" I ask her. "Church Walk is nearly under."

The driver answers. It's a woman, her face shadowed in the interior of the vehicle. It seems she knows who I am, because she says, "We'll follow you, Reverend."

We drive down to the bottom of Church Walk. The water looks wicked here; the house at this far end is the lowest. I jump down from the cab with a splash and labor, far more gingerly now, into the middle of the road. My boots have an inch or so to spare. This is not true of the house steps. In the time I've spent to-and-froing and parlaying with the wretched Matthew Dodds, the water's now brimming at the top.

The Land Rover door is open now. The driver alights with barely a ripple and approaches me through the flood. Her stride is long and easy and seemingly in slight slow motion because of the weight of the water. The flood wouldn't dare trip her up, though. It capers tamely, cravenly around her legs—she's in denims, mostly hidden by a pair of waders that rise a long way above her knees. As she walks her blond hair starts to come loose from a bun and fall around her face. There must be too much of it to stay in the bun, or it's too smooth, or both. She shouldn't try to put her hair up in the first place. She should really let it all down.

I'm certain that she is the woman I glimpsed on that rainy day outside Lady Brock's house. Ellen Parr, widow of Selwyn Parr the miller. Fellow owner of a coal-fed kitchen stove. Calm, smiling, and about to speak, but I forestall her.

"We don't have much time."

Well done, Acton. No hint of manners or even basic friendliness. First class.

She appears not to notice. "You're right."

We're distracted by a yelp from the direction of the vehicles. Lucy is creeping through the flood toward the cab of the lorry, the water threatening to overflow her boots with every step.

"Wait, Lucy!" I lurch toward her. "Let me help." Clinging on to my arm, she leaps gamely onto the running board of the lorry.

"Get me up on the back, Mr. Acton, and I'll hand the sandbags down to you."

I make a stirrup of my hands. Lucy is light and strong. In an instant she's up on the bed of the lorry and the first sandbag is on its way. It's surprisingly heavy for its size. I carry it to the other side of the alley and surrender it to Ellen. I'm about to say, *Careful, it's heavy*, but with a bright glance—did she know what I was going to say?—she takes hold of the sandbag as if it weighs no more than a large loaf of bread and sets it down in the most endangered doorway. I start to shuttle back and forth between the two women, and soon Ellen has created three tight rows of sandbags across the first door. We fall into a rhythm, working our way back up Church Walk from one front step to the next, pausing only to reverse the vehicles at intervals. Old men and women appear at the windows as Matilda Rail did, wraithlike in the shadows of their rooms, tapping on the glass and mouthing their thanks.

"They'll be awfully cold with no power," Ellen says, taking one of the last sandbags from me. I remember this voice from before. Lively, very clear. The sort of voice that if she called you across, say, a couple of acres of pastureland, would carry without being strained or shouting.

"I have gas stoves."

I'm slightly out of breath.

Finally we're done. I glance at the empty lorry. "Let's hope that's as high as the water will go."

She shakes her head. "We can't be sure. There might be another bulge coming down the river."

I collect myself at last and put out my hand. "I'm sorry, we haven't met properly. My name is James Acton."

"Ellen Parr."

Her fingers are cold but she seems unaware of this.

"Of course," I say, as casually as I can. "Althea Brock has mentioned you. She told me you were a miller's wife. You would know about rivers."

She breaks into a delicious grin. "My late husband was always careful to say that I was a miller."

"I stand corrected."

I ought to bow my head. But her smile is causing such disarming delight to spread over me that I can't take my eyes off her. She doesn't seem to mind in the least.

"Where did you get the sandbags, Mr. Acton?" she asks as we move toward her Land Rover. "I thought they were like gold dust."

"Requisitioned from the soldiers. The camp up on the hill. I've got contacts," I add, thinking of poor Matthew Dodds.

"That's good of them."

"I don't think the quartermaster is fully aware of how generous he's been."

She lets loose a glorious, unbridled peal of laughter. Looks shocked for a moment, as if it stole up on her unawares. Then laughs again, at her own laughter, and I feel prickled all over by her pleasure, and mine, and laugh with her.

Lucy, with my help, transfers herself nimbly into the passenger seat of the Land Rover. "How's Bailey, Vicar?"

"He doesn't need his spoon anymore," I tell her, proud as any father.

I watch them travel up to the end of Church Walk. Then Ellen backs onto the village green and drives away, leaving with nothing but a swirling wake of water. A swirling wake of water and a man standing motionless in the middle of the icy flood, still smiling.

Everyone, it turns out, is grateful for paraffin stoves. My last call is on Matilda Rail at the top of the alley. She takes a while to open the door. "Oh, thank you, dear. Will you bring it upstairs for me?"

I stand the stove in the corner of her tiny bedroom, beside the chest of three narrow drawers that likely contain all her clothes. The floor is uncarpeted, a rag rug covering the bare boards by her china jug and basin. All these houses have been fitted with bathrooms, but there's a poor thin towel on a hook next to the window. She must pour water from the jug into the basin every morning to wash her face and hands. Above her bedstead hangs a Bible verse in needlework. *RE-MEMBER NOW THY CREATOR IN THE DAYS OF THY YOUTH.* In smaller script underneath, *ECCLESIASTES xii.i* and beneath that, *MATILDA PERRY AG'D 10 YRS,* and then the date *9-X-1901.*

She's climbing the stairs behind me now, a toiling figure, grappling on to both banisters.

"Shall I light it for you, Mrs. Rail?"

"Bless you, I know how to light a gas stove."

She reaches the room, pulls matches from her cardigan pocket, and does so. Then she straightens up and gives me a once-over, her eyes darting points of light beneath the brooding lids. "You were having a nice chat with Ellen Calvert, I saw."

I am reminded forcefully that I live in a village.

"Calvert, did you say?" I make sure my tone is unruffled, cheerful. "She introduced herself to me as Ellen Parr."

Matilda Rail tuts. "Parr, that's just her married name. She was Miss Calvert, that taught at Upton School when she was young."

"I didn't know she was a teacher."

Mrs. Rail makes her way over to her bed and sits down on it with a sigh. "She was never a teacher. School assistant at best. That was before the war, of course. Then she met the miller. Her luck changed then, by golly." She gives a high, clear whistle, like an urchin, from between her teeth. "But they never had kids. You got kids, Vicar?"

"One grown-up son," I reply promptly.

"Thought so. I took you for a family man."

I look back at her. She's nodding, satisfied with her own good guess. Then she holds up a forefinger. "No, hold on," she says next. "She had that little girl, didn't she, during the war."

I've lost the thread. "Who did?"

"Ellen. She had a girl who stayed with her and Mr. Parr. Who made friends with my son Bobby. Bobby was my last, I was gone forty when I had him, the little tick, he had nephews older 'n him." Mrs. Rail leans back against the wall. "Where'd she go, that child? What was she called?"

I say, "I don't know," for form's sake, and she dismisses it with a little flap of her hand, her pinpoints of eyes roaming far into the distant years.

"I should go, Mrs. Rail," I say. "Keep warm."

"Ha. 'Keep warm,' he says." Her voice is soft, nine-tenths of her mind elsewhere. "Like we ever needed telling."

I return to the camp and deliver the lorry to a relieved Matthew Dodds. "You did the right thing, Matthew."

"Maybe." He fingers his chin. "But what if you'd gone off with the lorry? What then?"

One thing is clear. Matthew Dodds is not cut out for the army.

I pass by Lady Brock, to make sure she's still above the flood line. She is, but has no power, and is dressed in boots, a trench coat bulked out with woolens underneath, and a sheepskin hat with earflaps. "The head is the most important thing," she declares. "A bare head leads to hypothermia, then derangement. Death may follow soon after, not from cold, but from fatal decisions. Leaving the main path for illusory shortcuts, for example . . . Oh!" She stops short. "But then you know that. Clive told me you were in one of those camps at the end of the war. What an ass I am, for even mentioning it. Come in for God's sake and have a whiskey."

We drink it standing in her kitchen. "No tutting, if you please," she admonishes me, when I glance at the near-empty bottle. "It's the only warming thing in the house."

I don't know how Clive came to mention that I'd been a prisoner of war. I'd far rather he hadn't.

She sets her glass down, much refreshed. "Now. Tell me about the residents of Church Walk. I'm assuming the army did their bit?"

I relate the details. "I happened to meet Ellen Parr this morning," I continue, relieved to find that I manage to say this quite normally. "With Lucy Horne. They were out in Ellen's Land Rover. The three of us, we blocked off all the doorways in Church Walk. I must say, I found Ellen to be extremely . . ." I struggle for an adjective. "Extremely practical."

What a ludicrous thing to say. Lady Brock scrutinizes me with very old eyes and the merest suspicion of a smile.

"Oh, Ellen's awfully good in floodwater. It's all that time she spent with dear Selwyn, getting logs out of millraces and leats and whatnot. She goes striding about in those—"

"In those long boots, yes." I knock back the rest of my whiskey.

"Anyway, I was thinking that, in a month or so—I'll have to do some serious cleaning beforehand—that I might have a housewarming party."

"Splendid idea! Would you like any help with the guest list?"

"Really," I say, "that would be most kind."

"Absolute pleasure," she says huskily.

As I leave she calls after me. "Oh, by the way—was it Edith's?"

"Sorry?"

"That silly scarf. Was it Edith Phelps's?"

I realize with a jolt that the scarf is still at the vicarage.

"No, and I should have given it back to you yesterday, on my way home from Redwood House. I beg your pardon, it slipped my mind. I'll drop it off before Evensong tonight."

"Ah, Evensong. Absolute *ages* since I've been."

She sounds wistful. Surely someone can bring her.

"One can only impose so much on one's friends," she says, reading my mind.

"Lady Brock—"

"Althea."

"Althea. I'll bring the scarf and pick you up for Evensong. Quarter to seven?"

I drive back to the vicarage, the single whiskey pleasantly dispersing around my chilled frame, fairly distracted by the remembered sight of Ellen taking a sandbag from me and setting it in place. She did it in the same way every time, in one single lithe turning bending motion.

Unconsciously beautifully.

Bailey squirms with joy at the sight of me, peeing by way of celebration all over the *Hampshire Chronicle* of 14th March 1969. I put him outside and clear up, then divest myself of my waterproofs.

Only then, hanging them in the hall, do I notice an envelope on the doormat bearing a muddy footprint—mine. Even before I pick it up I see my name in Tom's familiar squared-off capitals.

Along with a letter, Tom has enclosed a handful of photographs. I shuffle through them where I stand, all thoughts of a hot bath forgotten. The first picture, which is black and white, shows our tiny garden at Alver Shore. Yvette is standing by the washing line, her head on one side, giving me an admonishing pout, not remotely delighted at being photographed in her pinafore. Her hair is bound up in a checked kerchief. The second and the third are both color, taken at Fulbrook: in one she's on an autumn walk with my parents, in the other building a snowman with Tom. Both the scarves are dark and indistinct but they're definitely wintry and woolen.

The fourth photograph, I know instantly from the light, was taken in Egypt. She's sitting in the stern of a rowing boat. I'm next to her, looking at her, my eyes almost closed, and she's smiling at the camera. In this picture a thin scarf is tied jauntily around her neck with the knot at one side. In the dim light of the hall I can't make out any details on the fabric. I rummage in the pocket of my black jacket and retrieve the paper bag containing the scarf. Taking bag, letter, and photographs to the kitchen I lay out the bright-blue-and-orange silk once more on the table. The cars of the little train jumble their way through the mountains; in the meadow the farmer's wife waves beside her lowing cow. Weaving through the scene, the banner of text: *LE PETIT TRAIN DÉPARTEMENTAL.*

The photograph is black and white, so there are no colors to guide me. And it's very overexposed—a sure sign that Célia, who would be the first to say she's no photographer, was behind the camera. Apart from a couple of rumpled dark splotches and a single pencil-thin curve, the design on the scarf Yvette was wearing has been bleached out. I narrow my eyes, trying to make the blotches into the roofs of the train carriages, wondering if that bending line might be the cow's horn. But I can't fool myself. These features could just as easily be flowers. And if this scarf on the kitchen table was folded up enough times to make Yvette's appealing little necktie, the best-taken photograph in the world wouldn't have shown the design properly. The resulting band of fabric was too narrow.

Bailey, from outside the door, gives a soft woof. I let him in. I read Tom's letter while my hot bath is running.

Dear Dad,

Just thought you'd like to know I'm getting on with your jumper. I find knitting really relaxing even though Ade and Jase kill themselves every time they see me doing it. I won't share with them next year. They're not fully developed humans.

I'd like to come and visit during reading week. I can get to you Nov. 11th and stay till 18th. If that's okay?

Here are some snaps of Mum wearing scarves. You're right, it does sound rather odd. But then, you are rather odd.

Just kidding!!

Hope to see you in November.

Love, Tom.

P.S. Hope you're getting on OKAY.

"Getting on *okay*," I mutter grimly, mashing rusk into warm milk. "Hmm."

In the evening I collect Althea and give her the scarf. She puts it on, draping it with casual flair around her shoulders, where it seems to fade, become old and inconsequential. But it disturbs me all the same, seeing it on her. Resisting all offers of help, she maneuvers herself and her canes into the car.

At seven o'clock about thirty souls come tramping into the church, along with the choir, who take their positions without any cue from me. "Dearly beloved brethren," I begin in a loud voice, reciting the words I have known by heart for thirty years. *We have erred, and strayed from thy ways as lost sheep,* my congregation joins me in saying, and they know what that means, these people who have come out tonight from the hills and farms. *Oh God, make speed to save us:* as I call out, so do they vigorously respond, *Oh Lord, make haste to help us.* The service comes to a close. "The grace of our Lord Jesus Christ, and the love of God, and the fellowship of the Holy Spirit, be with us all evermore," I declaim, and I might be praying before a breaking sea, so drawn-out and reverberating is the final "Amen."

"They can do it by themselves," I remark to Althea as I run her home.

"They had to."

"Blakemore?"

"Blakemore."

We bid each other good night.

Later I go to bed and sit propped against pillows, scribbling notes for this Sunday's sermon. A paralyzed man was taken to Capernaum by his friends so that Jesus could cure him. The house where Jesus was staying was so crowded that the friends couldn't bring the man inside. So they went up on the roof of the house and removed some tiles and lowered the paralyzed man down through the hole. I picture the man, tied—he must have been tied—to some sort of raft-like bed, swaying on ropes down through the darkness, or perhaps into and out of a shaft of sunlight from the gap in the tiles, terrified. We don't know if he had faith, only that his friends did. I ponder again on Evensong. Priests come and go but it rolls on seemingly forever, as regular as the tides, this long conversation with God that is the Church of England at prayer. And I am like a pebble in the undertow, smoothed by their faith, soothed by their faith, and will I be enough for them?

I don't know.

I bet the owner of that house in Capernaum was furious. *What are you doing to my bloody roof?* My mind wanders to my own roof and the holes Tom spotted when he stowed the boxes in the attic. Yet more rain must have found its way in. Perhaps he and I could climb up and take a look, when he comes to stay.

I have erred and strayed. Left undone the things I ought to have done.

Two years after Yvette died—it was around then, because he was still a shrimp of a boy, he hadn't started to grow—Tom picked up the little cedarwood chest from the bookshelf in my bedroom and said, "What's this?"

"Sand," I told him. "Sand from Sidi Bishr. Mum's favorite beach in Alexandria."

I don't deserve Tom. I couldn't tell him the truth then, but I should have done it by now and I failed at this most recent opportunity, all these years later. I lied to my son, an adult. It was cowardly.

Something flickers at the edge of my vision. I would lift my head, curious—was that lightning over the hill?—if I didn't know this light all too well. It is an interior light, even whiter and more metallic than a magnesium flare.

I get out of bed, remove the chest from its position on the mantelpiece next to Yvette's urn, and place it on the bookshelf. When I get back into bed I can't see it at all.

❧

TEN

Yvette
21 April 1964

Alver Shore.

Sometimes my younger friends ask me, "How on earth did you do it, Yvette? You hardly knew each other!" I want to reply: For heaven's sake, nobody *knew* each other back then. We were only just adults; we didn't know *ourselves* yet. Actually, we hadn't *become* ourselves—that was what we were going to do, as husband and wife. Make each other into ourselves. I remember the couples who got married during my first year as a curate's wife, snapped like us in black and white at the top of the church steps. I saw a single wedding outfit on five different young women, the hem swirling around thin knees or thin calves (depending on the height of the girl). The bride straight-backed, often shivering, smiling fit to burst. The groom grinning, his collar gaping. The point is, we were all the same. Young. Happy. Hopeful.

"But even so," my friends remonstrate, "you came from *Alexandria!*" And all I say to that is, yes I did, and I left it behind with my childhood like everyone else leaves their childhood behind. I brought as little as possible to England. Admittedly space was at a premium, but I made sure to pack nothing more than a handful—well, maybe a small armful—of mementos. Including my *cahiers*, the school notebooks from my final year at the Lycée. I was given a prize when I left, for outstanding work, being particularly commended for the accuracy and detail of my maps and diagrams. Célia, on the other hand, left the English Girls' College with nothing more than average marks.

(I don't wish to make a great *hoo-ha* about my superior performance. But I see no reason not to mention it.)

Anyway, I brought these school notebooks to England as keepsakes, to remind me of the Alexandrian girl I once was. And now they've come in handy, full of masses of blank pages at the back to accommodate this story of mine. I have already filled up the back of *L'Histoire* with everything that happened in Egypt. I've had to move onto *La Géographie* . . .

What else did I bring? The photo album of my childhood and youth and also of that little bit of postwar time when the four of us, Peter and Célia and James and I, were still together in Egypt. Célia didn't want this album and I had rejected it as too bulky, but Maman silently squashed it into my suitcase. I also brought a silver casket my father gave me, made in Lebanon I think, a gift from his great-grandfather to his grandfather. And a miniature cedarwood chest, also from Lebanon, which I enveloped for safekeeping in an old piece of wrapping paper from Hannaux, the department store where I had bought the dreadful cloche I ended up wearing for the wedding. I used this wrapping paper as a liner for the kitchen drawer where we kept keys and bicycle lamps and so on. During those first long bewildering weeks at Alver Shore, when by the evening I was in such a daze I hardly knew my own name, I used to open the drawer and put my hand on the paper and touch the name and address of the store that was stamped, in French and Arabic, in slightly blurred sage ink on a putty background. Just to steady myself. When we moved from Alver Shore to Fulbrook I laid the paper out again in the next kitchen drawer, the one downstairs. Very soon the past got rubbed away, so that when I put my hand in for a torch battery or a dog lead or the old tin opener because I couldn't find the new one, I didn't touch my memories anymore. Maybe the word—*Alexandrie*—darted through my subconscious, a gleam too quick for me to catch but I carried on in my real life, fetching in coal or walking the dog or making spaghetti Bolognese. And so it's been ever since. Until now, of course, when I'm remembering, remembering everything.

We stayed with James's parents, Iris and Findlay, in August 1945. It was lovely to meet Iris after our letters. I had imagined a great imposing woman, I don't know why, but she was nearly as short as me. She had dark gray wavy hair, and wavy worry lines on her forehead too, that deepened when she spoke to you. But that was only because she took you seriously. By September James had been offered a curacy—a place on the Hampshire coast called Alver Shore.

I was right about the sea. At Alver Shore, my word, it *was* darker, and often the color of iron. Sometimes a greasy glint from the low sun gave it a brawny beauty but there was nothing delicate about it ever. A huge gray mole stretched out into the water like an arm but it was breached in several places and you could see the rusting rods inside and the sea roared through these broken innards and reared back and sucked and chopped against the wall. I walked down there over the pebbles, thriving on the noise and the cold salty air.

I never felt so well in my life.

Which was lucky, since I needed my strength for the confounding unfamiliarity of absolutely everything. The beets and rhubarb and the enormous cauliflower on my kitchen table, wet with rain and muddy too, a gift from a parishioner with an allotment. How to tackle them? I had no idea. The martially ordered queues at bus stop and butcher's. The cars that swished by without honking. People here weren't just mending their clothes, they were mending the mends: I had nothing shabby enough to fit in, so when I popped to the shops I buttoned my coat to the neck. It took me about a week to learn that for some people in our congregation, my usual way of greeting and making small talk was a disconcerting effusion of fuss and show—embarrassing enough with women but disgustingly flirtatious with men. (For others, people who conducted all conversation at the top of their voices, it didn't seem to matter so much.) And there was so much to get to grips with in the house. The mangle, the coal bunker, the fireplace, the floors: oh, the floors. That first autumn I was cleaning the kitchen tiles when a neighbor poked her head around the back door. "Oh, bless you, Mrs. Acton," she said. "Don't they have mops and buckets where you come from?"

Because I had my skirt hitched up, my feet bare, and I was slapping a big cloth across the floor in wide fan-shaped sweeps, the way I had seen Safa our kitchen maid do at home. "Should I explain," James said, highly entertained, "that you've never cleaned a floor in your life?"

It turned out that I did have some essential skills. Vicars' wives, we get asked how we put up with it all. Having people traipsing in and out of our living room. Never knowing who we'll find drinking tea in the kitchen. What about our private life? It still tickles me. In Alexandria the concept of a private life was unknown. My whole existence was bound up into a morass of relations and friends and acquaintances who knew my business down to the last pimple on my teenage

nose—not only did they know, they were also ready with skin preparations and dietary advice. I'd been getting lessons in tolerating people,
looking after them, making them feel welcome, since I was four years
old.

I also knew how to face them down. Once I was in the vestry hanging up James's clean surplice when I overheard a woman in the church
say, "I bet she's Jewish really. She looks Jewish."

I came out of the vestry and smiled at the woman, smiled into her
pale stare and the blushes of her friend. "If I was Jewish I'd say so."

My sleeves rolled up from housework, my forearms chilly.

"She didn't mean anything by it," said the blusher.

I picked up a duster and a tin of polish. "Shall I help you?" Because
they were cleaning the pews, and it was a lot of work. They couldn't say
no to the curate's wife. We went at it for half an hour, which I considered punishment enough, because by dint of nonstop cheerful questions and remarks I forced them to talk to me all the way through. And
then they had to thank me as I left, even though I know I did a terrible
job since it was my first try. Then, as I was going out of the door, the
pale-eyed one said, "So what are you, dear?"

I knew how to reply. My family was Catholic, I told them, but I'd
become an Anglican because it was easier all round. I said this with a
slight roll of the eyes: *These men and their churchy complications.* The
two women permitted themselves a cautious nod of approval. Their
lives had been exhausting even before the war, and now the war was
over the bloody bread was on the ration. They had a proper appreciation of things that were easier all round.

Because Alver Shore was a hard place. Men died of drink, children
of pneumonia, women of demobbed husbands who came home cruel.
James came alongside the wreckage, grabbed the outstretched hands,
and I did too. Trying to keep the bereaved families warm and fed in
the aftermath. James thrived. It seemed that all he needed was to be

home again, to be busy, to take up where he left off. Working in the service of God.

The first year was good, the second year better. The only time I thought I might fail was the winter of '46 to '47, that January and February when all the potatoes in England froze in their storehouses and could not be eaten. That nearly finished me. I swear, I couldn't have done it if I'd been any older . . .

Oh—I forgot to include my great realization. What an idiot I am. This happened right at the beginning. One morning, in the week before James was formally welcomed into his curacy, I went upstairs to find a tall black pillar in the bedroom. I shrieked and ran back down and hid in the larder. James came and stood outside the door saying, "Yvette, please come out. Please, darling." Finally I dared to open the door.

"I'm sorry," I said. "I had no warning . . ."

"I should have said."

"Take it off. I can't look at you while you're wearing it."

"You can."

"No."

"Darling, listen. I'm the same man."

I came out. A priest in a black soutane was sitting in my kitchen. I put my hands over my eyes. He started laughing.

"Yvette, if you can't bear to look at me in clerical dress . . . well, it could pose a problem."

I came to stand behind him, where I could see him but he couldn't see me, which for some reason was easier.

"I've thought about everything," I said. "You know that. It was just the sight of you in your, in your . . ."

"Cassock."

"Cassock. Of course." I had learned all the new words, but in the heat of the moment they had gone.

His head was slightly bent, his hair short—freshly barbered for his entrance into the church. The seam of the cassock was so straight along his shoulders. The collar was shaped in a gentle curve around the back of his neck.

During one of my first trips with Sébastien, before I knew very much about anything, I was at an airfield, watching a group of pilots walking out to their aircraft. There's a word in Arabic Papa taught me: *tabaghdada*. It means, "to behave like someone from Baghdad," that is, to have a swanky, swaggering air about you. That's how I thought the pilots would carry themselves. Swinging their shoulders, with a bit of braggadocio. But when they came out, it was shocking. Not only were they desperately young and slight; they also walked like schoolboys, with quick straightforward steps. They were cowled in their helmets, straps dangling as if they'd forgotten to do them up, their heads hanging so low that their goggles, pushed up onto their foreheads, caught the early morning sun. Mechanics greeted them when they reached their aircraft. Taller, burlier, their faces in shadow, the mechanics might have been the fathers and the pilots the sons. Those hanging hooded heads, those crowns of goggles: the pilots looked as if they were walking to the executioner's block.

It was all to come, my dalliance with Sébastien, the Second Alamein, and then finding James and our love bursting into being: but I remembered that small moment, how it chilled me. And only now, in my kitchen at Alver Shore, did I realize what I had failed to understand at the airfield. That for James and for so many others, it was no block the pilots were heading for. It was an altar.

What he said was true. He was the same man. Just a different kind of sacrifice.

Everything carried on outside, the dog barking next door and the men shouting and shoveling at the end of the street as they cleared the bomb damage, and the gulls crying overhead. The noises of peacetime. I stood quietly with my hand on James's shoulder.

"Is it going to be all right?" he said, without moving his head.

I said, "Of course it is."

The time ran so fast. Soon it was 1947, then 1948. We didn't want to start a family until James had finished his curacy. We couldn't even afford a dog. We protected ourselves, though it went against the grain of our desires. In the autumn of 1949 James became a vicar, took over from the previous incumbent, the elderly Mr. Jenkins, and so there was a little more money. On Boxing Day of that year we got careless, or rather we refused to be cautious, and I conceived. I was fit as a mare by then. I thrived along with the baby, jumped at every kick. When I got heavy with her we named her Catherine after Saint Catherine, who was of Alexandria, of Egypt, like me.

Don't ask me how I knew she was a girl.

Early September 1950, and I had no fear. I was making up her beds, the cot and the pram, with two different sets of sheets, the small and the smaller; the two pillowcases. I put on the bed linen and went to fetch the light baby blankets. When I reached the top of the stairs I stepped onto the landing and into a place of silence.

And I felt the backlash of the long hours of her stillness hitting me, a great slap to my mind, and I knew then, only then, that she had not moved since the previous night. Or was it earlier yet? Suddenly I could not remember when I had last felt her. I had been so busy, these past days, getting ready.

I went back downstairs without the blankets. With each step down, the darkness closed in. James was in his study, writing a letter. "I need help," I said to him.

Without turning his head he said, "Darling, I'll move the bed later. I haven't forgotten . . ."

He carried on writing. I let him finish his sentence, put a full stop. Add *yours sincerely*—I could see the letter from where I stood—and sign his name. I waited for him to do it because I wanted those last seconds before it came true, when we were still that young couple who got married in Egypt. Because the moment I spoke, I knew nothing would be the same again.

Then I said, "I can't feel Catherine anymore."

The midwife removed the stethoscope from her ears. Without speaking to us she called a doctor who repeated the task she had just performed, his eyes wide and unfocused as he strained to listen. "What do you mean, you can't find it?" said James. "Please, try again—a different place . . ." But the midwife and the doctor between them had scoped out every square inch of my silent belly. I was glad they had taken such a long time, because it prepared me for the words to come. The doctor said them softly and gently, to acknowledge that they were unhearable.

"Your baby's heart is no longer beating, Mrs. Acton."

The midwife was holding one of my hands and James the other, so that, held on to, I was led by them to the impossible truth.

They induced me later that day. It didn't matter what drugs they gave me because Catherine was beyond harm. I was too small, I think, for the volumes they administered. I floated far away on the tide, dry land not making sense anymore, being too solid and stable. Wrecked on the waves, blood and tears leaving me in streams, I pitched and rolled in time to the wringing of my contractions. When the sea flood roared in I clung sobbing to her, my treasure, but she slipped away from me to be washed out through a hole in the hull. Then I foundered, and there were hands all around me, stretching out, and they brought me to shore.

James came in. Openmouthed, his cheeks marble-pale, his eyes pouched, owl-like in grief. He sat down on the edge of my bed. He was carrying a bundle wrapped in a thin towel with a wide blue border, the blue of laundry blueing, and in this blue, picked out in white, was the word *sunlight*. Her face was in shadow where the towel was folded around her head and tight under her chin, as if to protect her from a winter day.

The advantages of having a vicar for a husband. The clerical collar pressed the medical gowns back against the walls. I was privileged. My daughter was not wrapped in newspaper nor was she left naked in the sluice. She was not buried with nine others in a mass grave. This was how it was, then—*then* being the 12th of September 1950. We cremated her and put her ashes in the small cedarwood chest my father had given me. It was good for a baby, with its chubby curved lid and squarish shape. The ashes, inside a bag, fitted in snugly. The chest was small enough to sit in my cupped hand and there it did sit, for an hour or so every day.

We went to register her death and there was no place on the certificate for her name. It said, *fetus, female.* When I got home I stuck a slip of paper over that part and wrote *Catherine*, and in my mind's eye I entered in through the high oblong doorway of St. Catherine's Cathedral in Alexandria, the lintel lifting above my head and the soft darkness within receiving me and the tiny bundled form in my arms; and all I knew of her, all I had felt of her, was the hospital towel she was wrapped in and which they gave me to take home.

Iris arrived first. I knew her well by now. She had visited regularly since our stay with her, leaving Findlay at home to feed hay to their ancient rescued horses and ponies. She had helped me cut the burned bits off my first roast dinner, joking and being kind all the while. Now she appeared with baskets of food, everything she could manage, her face graven with new and deeper lines, and as she bent her back to put the baskets on the floor and bowed her headscarved head, she could have been from any age. Women had been doing this forever, bringing sustenance to babyless mothers, and I was one in millions and millions.

James wanted to dismantle the cot and put away the pram and the clothes for me but Iris said, *No, Yvette and I will do it*. She knew I had to.

Everybody went to church in those days, and word spread fast among the kindliest and most generous. Soon it seemed the whole parish knew about us. People dropped in all the time. Those who might have brought rattles or teddies for the new baby brought flowers. All I had to do was sit and be given flowers. Elderly ladies came to visit, women I knew by sight when I saw them at the church on weekday afternoons in the shadows of the back pews, praying or just sitting, with shopping bags at their feet. They gazed speakingly into my eyes, not bothering with introducing themselves. I wished they would stay when the younger married women visited. I wished there were a wall of old women to protect me from those mothers of huge families.

Célia flew from Adelaide. My parents from Alexandria. I told them not to, but they insisted. They arrived together, my mother between my father and Célia, her arms hooked in theirs, looking tiny, caked in a terrible tan foundation and cherry lipstick, wearing a suit the same pink as a sugar mouse. "Grief has done something awful to her dress sense," I said to Célia.

Célia couldn't help a shaken laugh. "My God," she said, "I don't know how you're not in pieces."

"Because you're here," I said. "That's why." And she put her arm around me, and I realized she thought I was gaining strength from her presence whereas the opposite was true. I was only remotely coherent because they were with me, and therefore I was forced to be.

James came in with apples from the tree. Big, so big and red and swollen, so many apples the tree had, it was laden, they were crammed on every drooping branch, the lucky damned tree. I saw it every day from the bedroom window, I wanted to chop it down. Célia said, "Ah, no, James," laying her hand gently on his arm. "She won't want them."

So he took them away.

"You should have had your baby at home," Maman announced the day after her arrival, snail tracks of mascara running down her face. "You should have gone to Dr. Amenhotep Ghobrial. Everything would have been fine then."

By home, of course, she meant Alexandria. Dr. Ghobrial had delivered Célia and me and was therefore the only obstetrician to be trusted. Maman hadn't said so, but I'd seen it in every tear and wringing hand and headshake. *And now this! Look how we're battered by fate!* As if the threat of exile were not enough, another piece of trash had been thrown on the midden of her misfortunes.

Iris said, in good clear schoolgirl French, "Sometimes a baby's heart simply stops beating. Nobody knows why."

Maman affected not to understand her. *"Quoi?"* she said, raising her head as if at a mysterious noise, with a faint, delicate frown. *"Qu'est-ce qu'elle dit?"* What's she saying?

"Mais ferme-la, Maman," cried Célia, marching outside into our

small garden and lighting a cigarette. I had never heard anyone tell Maman to shut her gob before. Célia was smoking to keep herself awake, being almost exactly upside down with jet lag, and to stop herself strangling Maman.

"I'm sorry my mother's so rude," I said later to Iris. We were clearing up and Iris was drying a crystal glass with a tea towel of Belfast linen.

"She has a lot to contend with," said Iris, as the glass in her hand threw a rainbow over the wall.

Three days later my family left. How could they help me? My father did little but smoke, my mother ran through her tramadols and lost her voice from crying. Iris was right: they were already shaken. Ever since the end of the war, unrest had been swelling: Cairo burning in riots, the army on the streets of Alexandria. Everyone who was too French or Greek or Italian or Lebanese, too Orthodox or Catholic or Jewish to be counted as a proper Egyptian anymore, was packing bags, fearing that if they did not go now, they might be forced to leave everything behind. At the beginning of my pregnancy I had been replying to a letter from Maman when I happened to write *Canal Zone* (where the British troops, retreating from the country, had garrisoned themselves), and at the same moment I had a gripe of morning sickness that fused with the words, so that henceforward each time I saw *Canal Zone* written down I tasted sickness shot through with joy for the baby. I couldn't think of those letters, of the news from Egypt, without remembering that precious sick joy.

"I'm a useless old woman, I can do nothing for you," my mother whispered at me when she got into the car for the airport. "Your love is enough," I said. I wanted to go with them in the car: James was driving, and I didn't want to be left at home alone. But long journeys at that time were too inconvenient, the amount of blood I was still losing.

Célia stood in front of me clutching her suitcase, eyes hollow, nostrils flaring.

"I can't say anything, Yvette, I really can't."

"It doesn't matter."

She looked at Maman and Papa. "They're moving to Nice, you know."

"I do know." Thinking: Maman will be destroyed if she leaves Alexandria, but saying nothing, being frankly unequal to this sort of conversation.

The cedarwood chest sits on the bedroom bookshelf. Catherine rests among our novels and biographies. If I turn my head I can see her, but from James's side of the bed the chest is out of view. I watch over her, and James . . . James watches over me. We've never told Tom about her, and we make Tom himself the excuse. First he was too young to understand. Then he was older but very sensitive and impressionable. And now? Well, this is hardly the moment. But it isn't really because of Tom, it's because of James.

And I will come to that, but not now. I'm at the end of *La Géographie*. How neat my writing is. English children use ruled pages, so Tom's handwriting sprawls along the line like uncoiling springs. French squared paper is more exacting. One is compelled to put one letter in each square, join them up correctly. Tom refuses to entertain this idea, saying he's not going to squash his letters into boxes. English people, he kindly explains, like to show their individuality in their handwriting. But darling, I say to him, if I have to come and find you, to ask you what your message says, because your writing is so *individual* that you're the only person who can read it—then, we might as well be in the Stone Age.

Oh, *Mum*. He groans. Stop being so *Frenchified*.

I'm more English than he knows. Perhaps my handwriting is the only Alexandrian thing left. The words I write come from the adult woman, formed and nourished by her beloved England that welcomed her when Egypt no longer could. A woman whose heart was broken in England but is all the stronger for being broken. Tom is too young to understand what I owe to his country. To England, and to James.

ELEVEN

M r. Acton! I'm so glad to have finally caught you!"

It's eight o'clock in the morning on the second Friday in November, just over a month since the flood. The voice on the telephone is instantly recognizable.

"Good morning, Archdeacon Frobisher," I say with the smoothness of a man who has been at his desk for an hour. "What can I do for you?"

"For a start, sir, you can answer my letter." He starts to chortle in that gobbling way that I remember. "Or letters, for they have become plural, have they not?"

There are now three of them, each more adamant in his intention to visit. Why haven't I replied? I remember mentally putting him off, once because of the filth of the house, and then again during the tail end of the flood, due to the state of the roads. "I do apologize. The thing is, I—"

"Hmm." Frobisher's *hmm* is exceptionally sonorous. There's a great deal of chest for it to reverberate in. "*The thing is.* I'm not enthu-

siastic about that phrase. Too often it heralds some oversight or preter-
mission that has been left unattended to. Unremedied. Wouldn't you
say, Mr. Acton?"

I'm at fault, I know. But I don't like being browbeaten.

"You're quite right, Archdeacon," I say mildly. "In my defense, I've
been so busy that replying to your letters—well, I simply haven't got
round to it."

"Yes, that's another one, isn't it. *Got round to it.* Well, never mind.
I'm glad at least to learn you've been occupying yourself. I wish to hear
more, in person and in considerably more detail, as soon as possible.
How about . . . say, tomorrow at noon?"

Tomorrow at noon is the exact start time of my housewarming
party.

I could suggest a later time tomorrow. But how long will this shin-
dig go on, and how much clearing up will there be? I suppose I could
invite him to the party . . .

No, I could not. Apart from Blakemore's loathsome study—my
rationale being that no one will go in there—I've cleaned this place
until the paint is fairly scrubbed from the walls. I deserve a relaxed
sociable interlude getting to know my parishioners better and putting
more names to faces. Not shepherding my archdeacon about. Shuddering as his awful laugh rises above the buzz of conversation.

"I'm afraid that's not possible. Next week would be better."

"No good. My diary is full," snaps Frobisher.

"In that case, may I write to you suggesting some dates the following week?"

"Write to me?" He roars with choleric laughter. "That very much
depends, doesn't it, Mr. Acton. On whether you'll *get round to it.*"

"Archdeacon, I—"

"No, I will admit no protestations. For reasons I can't begin to
guess, you're trying to elude me, sir, and it will be in vain." His finger

wags at me down the telephone wire. "You can run as fast as you please, but you will find me at the end of the course, waiting."

He cuts the line so abruptly that I jump, as if I heard him bang his telephone receiver back in its cradle with his great hamlike hand.

I rake my fingers through my hair. I have provoked my archdeacon. What an incredibly silly thing to do. And quite unnecessary. I didn't miss his letters, they didn't slip under the doormat or get eaten by Bailey. The first inquired when he might visit. The second and third were more insistent, requesting a summary of my activities and an overview of the current situation in the parish. I ignored the lot.

I need my head examined.

Bailey, who has graduated to kibble, falls on his breakfast with appetite, strong enough now to push the metal bowl across the floor with lashes of his tongue. I steer him away from the ancient tiles Lucy Horne showed me. The pictorial hounds still leap, pale ghosts through the layers of grime. I have learned that I mustn't scrub the tiles, for fear of damage. Beyond that, I have no idea what I'm going to do about them.

I have no idea, come to that, what I'm going to do about Bailey. Is it fair, to keep a lonely dog? I'm out so much of the time. I wasn't lying to Frobisher: Curate Clive Perry and I have been busy. The pews are filling up for services, Sunday school has revived like grass after rain. Those more tender seedlings, prayer groups and Bible study, I'm cultivating with care. The Bible study evening has been a surprise, attracting people from all walks of life, standards of personal hygiene, and even sobriety (though I've instigated a rule about the latter). Clive and I bring in chairs from the kitchen, lay on refreshments, and people cram themselves into the sitting room. No less than three dauntingly thin teenage girls, sisters by the name of Chant, who come solely to gorge on custard creams and cola before stealing away into the night, bundle themselves like a family of lemurs into the rhino armchair.

Only six weeks have passed since I came to Upton but it feels as if those early days, fraught as they were with Tom's misgivings, that strange business of the scarf, were half a year ago. All that trouble long gone, drained away with the departing floodwater.

So there's absolutely no excuse for my behavior toward my archdeacon. And, unsettlingly, I'm no nearer to guessing the reason for it than Frobisher is.

The party, meanwhile, is about twenty-eight hours away. Over the weeks since I suggested it, more and more has been taken out of my hands until my only job, apart from the Herculean cleaning task, has been to fetch booze and crisps from Waltham. Lady Brock, aided by Lucy Horne, has presided over a guest list that has swelled to encompass the whole village. "Oh, they won't all come," she says, dismissing my anxiety with a flap of her hand. I've had no more control over the catering than I have over the guest list. The Sunday school children will make a nonalcoholic punch, and there will be sausage rolls. There are always sausage rolls, apparently, at the vicar's party, homemade by Deirdre Harper from the Women's Institute who, I remember being told by Lady Brock, sustains the elderly who can't cook for themselves. "Get that range of yours going nice and early on the day, if you don't mind, Reverend," Mrs. Harper told me when I took her the cash for the makings. "A good reliable fire." She gave me a sharp look. "I'm not going to all this trouble for them to be served anything but piping hot."

Therefore I am this very morning installing a new flue damper in the range. Nobody needs to tell me I'm courting disaster, leaving it so late. Luckily I've got the help of William Kennet, caretaker at Upton Hall School. He's a man apparently hewn from walnut wood, with a very old and terrible wound to his right hand. The ingrained sunburn is from his days as gardener at Upton Hall when Lady Brock still lived there. I met Mr. Kennet a fortnight ago, when Lady Brock invited me to the sheepdog trials, spending a few pleasant hours in his company as he explained to me the various challenges of the trial: the drive, the fetch, the shed. This last entails, by means of a canny dip and weave on the part of Lamp or Mist or Sweep (sheepdogs' names being of high tradition), the extraction of a single red-collared sheep from his unmarked fellows. *It's how to get a bad 'un out,* Mr. Kennet told me as we watched. *You could take a tip from Lamp, Vicar, in my opinion.* This last remark was directed at my failure to charge one Alice Goodenough with habitual pilfering from the poor box. We take weekly collections on Sundays during service and so the poor box, which hangs unobtrusively on the wall just inside the church doorway, only gets a handful of change. Since Alice Goodenough is herself poor, I see this as more of a shortcut than a theft. William doesn't approve.

True to his word, it's precisely nine o'clock when he arrives, carrying not only the flue damper but a large squashy-looking parcel. "This was on your step, Mr. Acton."

I seize it, bear it into the kitchen, and tear away the brown paper like a schoolboy on his birthday.

"Looks like you were expecting that," observes Mr. Kennet.

"It's from my son. I don't know why he's posted it. He's coming to stay on Monday." I have the train time noted down in my diary—I've *got round to* buying a modern four-foot-wide bed for the spare room (recently swabbed down) with a good deep mattress.

The parcel contains a folded sweater in dark blue wool. It's thick, close-knitted, wonderfully heavy. I admire the hem, the sleeves. I can't quite believe that Tom is so skilled. I put it on. It fits very well.

Bailey is scratching at the back door. I let him in and he scampers toward me. When I bend down to put food in his bowl, he snuffles at my sleeve with intense interest.

"Tom made this sweater, Bailey," I tell him. "Now let Mr. Kennet and me do some work."

"You'll have to take that off, Vicar. This is a sooty job."

I do as Mr. Kennet says, and between us we lift the chimney off the stove. It takes a few shrewd knocks with a hammer to dislodge it. "See if you can get that front plate loose, Vicar," William says. "That's the way. I'm not having this range defeat us. You and I, we've had to contend with mechanicals of all sorts, most of them far bigger and a damn sight deadlier. Oh, yes. Lady B told me about your doings in North Africa."

Lady B has been equally forthcoming on the subject of *his* war, and I know that the missing half of his hand was lost to shrapnel at Dammstrasse before the Battle of Messines in 1917.

"I was lucky," I tell him.

"We were both lucky." With a brief emphatic sniff, he deploys the remaining finger and thumb of his mutilated hand as pincer, grab, and hammer claw in as many seconds, retrieves the broken damper, and starts to insert the new one. I am put in my place.

"There now," he announces, after we've replaced the chimney. "Let's see how she draws. I must say, Vicar, you have cut it very fine. Mrs. Harper will be here tomorrow morning expecting this cooker to be running at full crack."

"Right you are," I say airily, putting kindling into the firebox. "I've heard there's another coal range in the village. At Parr's Mill."

"It gets a great deal of care, that one, of course." He wipes dust off the flue damper plate with deliberate strokes. "She's been baking on it since the war."

"That would be Mrs. Parr, of course."

"It would."

He bends to adjust the damper. A very promising sound, like the roar of a distant and powerful engine, issues from the chimney.

"I expect she had evacuees during the war, didn't she?"

He looks suddenly up at me, a sort of flare in his blue eyes. "Three boys," he says. "From Southampton, as I recall."

"A lot of cooking, then, I expect. Maybe more children to feed."

"Those boys were hungry all the time," he says with finality. "Now let's build up our fire, Vicar, and see if we can't get a cup of tea out of this old lady."

Over tea we talk of the machines of death we have known, specifically the calibers of various guns from the First and Second World Wars, and then he leaves for Upton Hall School with three pounds and a bottle of port. I wonder why he didn't mention the child Matilda Rail told me about, the girl who was here in the war and then gone. Maybe Matilda had got it wrong, and the girl lived with someone else. But William had spoken so firmly of three boys. Widening his eyes, a warning lamp almost. Ellen did have this girl, I think. And William will brook no intruders into her private past.

I picture her turning from her solid-fuel range and putting a loaf on the table, turning it out from the tin, and a small girl on a stool sniffing the aroma, trying to tweak off a piece of crust. *Darling, it's too hot. Oh, please, just a little bit.*

And then the child was gone.

Saturday dawns dry with bursts of mild sunshine. The party actually begins at about ten o'clock in the morning, when the extended families of the helpers, convinced the helpers won't do a good enough job on their own, start to turn up. They crowd into the kitchen, tread on each other's feet and sample the prepared foods until Mrs. Harper, purveyor of the sausage rolls, shoos them away with flicks of a tea towel. More people arrive at about eleven, bringing unasked-for but very welcome plates of sandwiches and unfamiliar bottles of drink, some half full and others dusty from long years on the highest shelf in their kitchens. By midday the house is full of people happily crunching crisps and shouting their news at each other across the already crowded rooms, so that the remaining guests arrive exclaiming, "Oh, thank God we're not the first!" and plunge into a party already in full swing. I tell the children that not a morsel of food is to pass Bailey's lips for the duration before releasing them to dart back and forth, low like swifts, offering the guests battered plastic cups of their nonalcoholic punch. It's mostly flat lemonade and blue food coloring, and mine is ladled from the bowl by one of a strikingly similar pair of young girls whose low, straggling fringes remind me of wild ponies. "I hope you don't mind me asking," I say, "but might you be twins?"

They shake their heads. "Our grandmothers are, though," volunteers one of the girls. "But *her* granny"—jerking her head at the other child—"who's my great-auntie Amy, has a chipped tooth."

"And *her* granny, who's my great-auntie Airey, doesn't," says the second girl, scooping a soggy pale pink cherry out of a tin with a teaspoon. I glance over at the makeshift bar, relieved to see that Clive my curate and Alan Sutton, father to the headstrong Meg, are serving real drinks hand over fist.

"Gosh, a cherry as well. Thank you."

The girl blinks from under her forelock. "It wouldn't be punch otherwise." She tips the cherry into my cup. "Everyone's allowed one each." She says it thoughtfully, as if to herself. "Just one."

I circulate, resplendent in my new jersey, sharing in conversations about the pros and cons of joining the common market, who the next

Dr. Who will be, and whether seat belts kill more people than they save. This is a hotly debated topic due to the recent tragic death of one Pete Molloy, a farmer from the next parish whose burned-out car was found upside down in a ditch with the hapless Pete inside, allegedly burned to a crisp, "with his charred hand clutched around the belt buckle." Which last detail is supplied by Lucy Horne and greeted with gasps of horror. I'm halfway around the room when I hear Althea Brock cry, "God, it's an absolute scrum," with evident delight. I take a deep breath. Lucy has told me that Lady Brock was being driven here by Ellen.

There they are, coming in through the doorway, Lady Brock enveloped in a scarlet shawl, Ellen standing very close behind her. Lady Brock has no canes today: she and Ellen move together toward the battered sofa, and it's only because I'm watching her so closely that I realize Ellen has her arm across Lady Brock's bowed back, her firm support concealed under the shawl. When they reach the sofa Ellen slowly bends down, chatting to another seated guest as she unobtrusively settles Lady Brock onto the cushions. It is very nicely done. Nobody would ever suspect that Lady Brock was now too lame to cross a room under her own steam.

Ellen moves away without further ado and accepts a plastic cup of children's punch. She's carrying a small package in her other hand. She is tall and smiling, her hair very elegant and shiny and pulled back. I don't understand why everyone in the room isn't looking at her. But then they've known her all her life. They must be used to her. I move through the crush toward her.

"What a nice party, Reverend," she says, holding out the package. "I hoped these might come in handy."

A housewarming present—a pair of oven gloves. How did she know I haven't got any? "Just what I needed! I keep burning my fingers."

It's true. My egg pan has a spitefully conductive metal handle.

"They're the best kind. I buy them from the Women's Institute market."

She's perfectly easy in herself, agreeable, blooming. Her eyes resting lightly on me.

"You don't come to church," I blurt, like the imbecile I've apparently become in the last six seconds.

She shakes her head, not remotely put out. "I'm afraid it would be lip service only for me, Reverend Acton."

"Please," I beg her. "Call me James."

"James. I don't mean to offend. I'm getting to be rather a pagan these days."

"Happens to a lot of women your age."

This is Frobisher's revenge, surely. I reject him in person and, using some arcane archidiaconal power, he renders me incapable of normal conversation. I fight the urge to turn on my heel, find the nearest cupboard, and get someone to lock me inside it until she's gone, that way preventing me from speaking another word to her today. This is the only way she'll ever be persuaded to talk to me again.

"Kindly explain!" she demands, eyes sparking, thoroughly amused.

Agonized, I do so, feeling hot in Tom's heavy new jersey, wishing I had something more than blue lemonade to sustain me. "Sorry. I meant that people can get to a point where . . ." Where what? "Where the received wisdoms don't satisfy them anymore. And women see more of life than men. Often they see too much. So it happens more to them."

I realize I believe every word I've said.

"Do you think so?"

"Oh, yes. Men have this great capacity for busyness. Minutiae. The behavior of machines, and so forth. They don't look up, and so they miss things."

My heart is at last slowing down somewhat, thank goodness.

"What an intriguing idea." She does look up at that point, at the ceiling—hopefully not too closely, as I swiped at it with a broom yesterday night—as she considers it. Then back at me. "Reverend, I'm assuming this story about Germans chasing you through the woods isn't just a fantasy of Althea's?"

Clive, it seems, has supplied plenty of details. "They actually trod on me one time," I tell her. "And I felt insufficiently like a pine log."

Insufficiently like a pine log. Why am I making a joke? Nothing about it was remotely funny.

"What on earth made you keep trying to escape?"

That's easier to answer. "It was my duty." I indicate her half-empty cup of children's punch. "Let me get you a proper drink."

She hands me the cup with a broad smile. "And a sausage roll, please."

I struggle through the crowd toward the drinks table, buttonholed at every turn, extricating myself again. I can feel the heat under my collar. I barge the queue with fulsome apologies and a fixed expression of congeniality that doesn't fool Clive.

"Are you okay, James?"

"Absolutely fine." I sound a little short, so I remedy it. "It's steaming-hot in here." A strange, spicy sort of smell is coming off me. I hold my sleeve to my face. Yes, it's Tom's sweater. Something half familiar, rather like Lapsang souchong tea. They smoke the tea leaves for Lapsang souchong.

"I'll open the French doors," Clive says soothingly. "What can we get you?"

I've forgotten to ask Ellen what she'd like to drink. I opt for two dry sherries, snaffle a sausage roll and a serviette, and hope for the best. By the time I reach her I'm a bit calmer.

"I was also lucky," I continue. "To get away with my life, I mean."

"Like my brother," she says. Sausage roll in hand, she recounts her brother Edward's extraordinary flight from Singapore at the very moment of its capture by the Japanese, a journey undertaken at enormous risk, to Ceylon by way of Sumatra. He was at home in the East, this brother, having sailed from England with no known destination at the age of fourteen. "Edward once told me he was a wharf rat of long standing, and that I should trust him," she concludes. "So I did."

Her eyes for a moment are far away. She's thinking of her brother, perhaps, riding those seas of Asia. Clive is opening the French doors and we both move toward them. She steps out into the garden ahead of me. Will she be cold? I hope not. She's wearing a thin woolen—I would say sweater but it's too elegant to be called that—and a swirling skirt of some velvety material. Both garments are similar in color, the top slightly more violet than gray, the skirt the other way around. Walking behind her I see why her hair is so obedient today. It's been twisted into a roll at the nape of her neck and stuck with a single long silver pin.

Some men are smoking cigars: she steers clear of them, her nose wrinkling. The Sutton boys have brought Bailey outside to sniff the air, keeping him in check by a long string attached to his collar. I hope he doesn't get tangled in the legs of guests.

"So what is your creed, then, Mrs. Parr?" I ask.

I thought Frobisher had released his hold. Clearly not, or not entirely. But it doesn't sound so bad, out here in the fresh air.

"Ellen, please."

"Ellen. Does your paganism have a hereafter?"

Her eyes widen, she represses a smile. Feeling interrogated, I can tell, but she doesn't mind. In fact—her back straightens slightly— she's going to give an account of herself.

"I believe in the beeches in Pipehouse Wood," she begins. "I can't think of anything more sensible than to worship them. And the chalk-downs flora on Beacon Hill. I believe we go into the earth and disintegrate." She pauses before continuing. "And then—how do I put this—bits of us turn into bits of other living things. A piece of moss, or a beech leaf, or an orchid. Or a raindrop. Which is as it should be, because we only come together in the first place, via a few links in the chain, from pieces of moss and beech leaves and rain. And it never stops, all through time."

"Well." I gulp down my sherry. "That's the Resurrection demolished!"

She seems very close to me, in this chilly, untended garden.

"Yes, unfortunately." Her voice is light. "But not the Life!"

But not the Life. She's beautiful. What she says is beautiful. She has floored me. I look up, helpless, seeking refuge in the sky, but the thin hazy cloud lets a lot of glare through. It's hard on the eyes.

I take too long to compose myself. Before I can speak, another party guest has presented herself at my side. She's a chum of Althea's by the name of Margaret Dennis, headmistress of Upton Hall School. "Lovely party, James. Couldn't get near you to say hello, goodbye, or how d'you do!"

I meet Margaret often at the lodge, when I'm invited for what she and Althea like to call, with a great deal of amusement, an Evening of Brahms and Liszt. They take their shoes off, serve out hefty tumblers of malt, and we pay serious, silent attention to one of Margaret's huge collection of classical records. She's a forthright, mountain-moving sort of person, thoroughly likable and just now unbelievably unwelcome.

I reply with forced cheer. "Is that what makes for a lovely party, Margaret? Hazardous overcrowding?"

"Yes, dear. One of the things, anyway. Now, may I borrow Ellen?"

As if she was mine to lend. "By all means. I've just spotted Mr. Kennet. I've been wanting to ask him about my fruit trees." I have two, a wizened cherry and a reluctant pear, but at this moment I couldn't care less about them. Ellen, who looks as taken aback as I feel, gives me an anguished glance. I sketch a wave and remove myself. With any luck Margaret will release her soon.

William is under the pear tree with Althea Brock, in conversation with a man I don't know. Lady Brock, seated on the garden bench, is next to a woman in a wheelchair who raises one hand as I approach. The gesture's familiar.

"We met at Redwood House, didn't we?" I take her hand. "How nice to see you."

"Yes," she replies, in the emphatic tone I remember. Her single expressive word.

"Hello, Vicar," says the man who was speaking to William. "You know Mum from Redwood! My name's Philip. Philip Moore."

Philip and I shake hands. He's a tall, rangy, freckled sort of man, somewhere in his forties. "How do you do." I turn to his mother. "Nice to meet you properly, Mrs. Moore."

"Yes." One side of her mouth twitches into a smile.

"Philip's a painter," says Althea Brock. "He does the most marvelous portraits. He's painted William, you know."

"Mr. Kennet, I can see you would be a great subject."

"It's hanging in the lodge." William nods, serious-faced. "Safe with Lady B. I can't have it with me at Upton Hall. I couldn't tolerate myself looking down at me. Especially in the evenings." He looks at Philip. "No offense, Philip. It's a fine quality painting."

"None taken, Mr. Kennet," Philip says. "I can't look at my own self-portraits, either. Have to turn them to the wall!"

"I'm not surprised," murmurs Althea. "Your work is, how shall I put it, very *searching*."

Philip gives me an engaging grin. "What Althea means is, I'm a bit too realistic."

I steal a glance toward the house. Mrs. Dennis is still speaking to Ellen. "Time for me to stagger inside," says Althea. "William, could you possibly?"

He gives her his arm and they set off toward the house. Ellen meets them halfway across the lawn. William transfers Althea to Ellen's care. Ellen looks toward me, waves, and mouths *Thank you*.

Wait! I nearly call out. But maybe it's better like this. I could listen to her and look at her all day long, but I have absolutely no reason to assume she feels the same. So I wave back and smile.

Philip is bending over his mother, releasing the brake of the wheelchair. Something about the back of his head and shoulder strikes me. He was the man in the doorway of Redwood House, the day before the flood. I remember his figure silhouetted, the rain glistening on his coat.

"I believe I saw you, Philip, at the nursing home, about a month ago. You were on your way in, and I passed you."

"Oh—well, I'm there every day." He doesn't remember me, not that I expect him to. "Sometimes twice. Depending where I am in a commission." He smiles again—a natural smiler, I think. "I saw you talking to Ellen Parr. Do you know, I've been away for twenty years, but she's hardly changed. Well, obviously she looks a little older. But I'm glad to see that widowhood hasn't brought her down."

"No," I say. "She looks very . . . unbowed."

"I used to see them out walking when I was young. She and Selwyn Parr, hand in hand. She was older than me, but not by much—and there she was, with that terrible old stick! I couldn't understand it. Now, of course, I realize they were soul mates. Not that Mr. Parr would have used the term!"

"Often you survive better if the marriage was happy."

Mrs. Moore lows gently. Her eyes are faded, green turning to gray, and they move rapidly, one eyebrow flickering.

"Do you agree, Mrs. Moore?"

"Yes! Yes!"

Philip laughs and puts one hand on her shoulder.

"So where have you been for those twenty years, Philip?"

"South of France. Painting. Everyone thinks of sunshine, wine, and olives. But the winters are no picnic, especially in a drafty studio."

"So I've heard. My late wife's parents moved from Alexandria to Nice." I remember Yvette's mother, complaining in her letters of the icy blasts on the Promenade des Anglais. "My mother-in-law wore her coat until June. Yvette—my late wife—used to make fun of her. Yvette herself, you see, had come from Alexandria to Alver Shore."

"Goodness," Philip says. "Alver Shore. Gosh. That really is a leap. Did you say, your *late* wife?"

"Yes. She died ten years ago."

"Yes!" It's almost a groan, and very loud. His mother is pushing herself forward in her seat, her stiff forearm lifted up as if she'd catch hold of my arm if she could.

"God," says Philip. "Oh, my God."

"Yes!" His mother bursts out again. A terrible, throaty bellow. Others in the garden turn their heads toward us and swiftly away, not wanting to stare. Philip is hunkered down beside her, and I'm bending low as well, taking her hand. She can't close her fingers around mine but her voice does all the tightening and straining. "Yes," she insists. *"Yes..."*

"What is it, Mrs. Moore? Has something happened?"

"I don't know." Philip's shaking his head, the motion is panicky.

"Are you unwell? Do you need a doctor?"

She shakes her head to one side, her face contorted.

"It must be so frustrating."

She snorts. *You have no idea.*

"Perhaps we should go home." Philip puts a hand on his mother's arm. "Would you like that, Mum? Go back to Redwood? Have a rest?" He stammers out the questions.

His mother slumps in her seat, her chin rocking up and down. Philip stands up straight. His face is so white that his freckles stand out.

I walk up the garden path with them. He blows out a shaky breath as he pushes his mother's chair. "I worry when she gets agitated," he says in a low voice. "It might lead to another—another episode."

He's talking too quietly for his mother to hear, but he still doesn't want to say the word *stroke*. She's taken up with her trouble again, re-peating "Yes, yes yes," in a broken, yearning tone. It's quite awful to hear.

We reach the house. "Shall I come and visit you, Mrs. Moore?"

"Yes, yes." Vigorous and eager.

"Philip, do you need help getting your mother's wheelchair into your car?"

"Thanks, but I left the car at Mum's."

We say goodbye and he wheels his mother carefully over the ledge of the French windows.

Nobody is left out in the garden now. I gather up a scattering of plastic cups and paper serviettes. By the time I reach the house the Moores have gone.

Of Ellen and Althea there's no sign.

The last flushed-cheeked guests depart, the bustle of clearing up begins. I dig out the presents for my helpers, boxes of chocolates and tubes of Smarties according to age, and distribute them. In the kitchen I take my place at the sink and fill it with hot soapy water. "Let battle commence," I announce, rolling up the sleeves of my new sweater as the first tray of glasses is brought in.

Finally they're all gone. I'm quite overheated now, nearly as hot as I was earlier in the day. I pull the sweater over my head and stop, stock-still, while my head is still inside it. At last I recognize the smell. It's familiar to me from the Middle East, an adjunct not of my youth but certainly of Tom's. The rich, acrid stink of hashish.

So that's what he does when he's knitting.

"Tom!" I tear off the pullover, almost shouting, with outrage, mirth, or both, I don't know. "Oh, seriously, Tom!"

That night when I close my eyes to pray, a vision of Pipehouse Wood fills my mind, the beech trunks and branches that are so limber even in great age. And the tough turf of Beacon Hill in the sunshine and under the clouds.

The Life. She held it up in front of me joyfully, this wondrous transformation that goes on and on, unfailing, abundant. How is it not everlasting? What can I say to her?

I'm a priest of the Church of England. I will be commended to Almighty God and my body committed to the ground, earth to earth, ashes to ashes, dust to dust, in sure and certain hope of the resurrection to eternal life through our Lord Jesus Christ. That is, a resurrection of the body, of all bodies. Of children, and of babies who died before they were born.

A white glare builds behind my eyelids. I let it swell and loom. Metallic, scouring the retina. My daughter's body I cannot think of, her name I cannot say. Her ashes lie in the little wooden chest on my bookshelf, unknown to everyone, even to Tom. I smuggle her through my life.

The flash recedes. Behind my eyelids, the shadows of spring leaves dance across the sunlit trunks of the beeches.

TWELVE

Yvette
16 May 1964

I will always remember Alver Shore for the kindness of the women.
In the weeks after we lost Catherine neighbors called on me,
tied on their aprons, and did the dishes. Helped me with my weekly
wash. "You're not up to it," they said firmly, whipping the handle of the
mangle around with their stringy forearms. They were right. It would
have taken me hours and hours.

"I feel useless," I said to James one evening when we were sitting
in our tiny parlor. I wasn't lamenting. It was a simple fact.

He looked tired; he stared out of the window, lost in thought.
"How long's it been?" he said at last.

"Four weeks and two days."

"Is that all? Good grief."

I was glad he was aghast at the unendingness of it. But I knew
how long it had been instinctively, and he had needed to ask.

The phone rang and he went to answer. "Yes, a stillbirth," I heard him say in the low voice he used for this subject. "Quite shattering. Yvette's doing as well as you'd expect. It's very early days."

It was extraordinary how he could even say it.

He came back and sat down again. "That was Mrs. Goodwin from the parish council. She was visiting her sister and she's only just heard the news."

"It was kind of her to ring. Would you like an omelet tonight?"

That was the sort of thing I could manage. Omelets.

"Yes, darling. That would be delicious."

I was good with powdered egg, I added mustard and chives, but of all the things the omelet might turn out to be, *delicious* was surely not one of them. I stared at him where he sat, almost lay, in the armchair, one foot crossed over the other, arms folded too. Keeping himself covered: I didn't blame him for that. *Delicious* was just another thing he felt he had to say, obviously. He had to go out and face people all day long. He'd been getting good at it, day after day. Moving through the gears.

Thinking, that, I got up from my chair.

We had a Hillman, small and very old. We thought about selling it, we used it so seldom. Some weeks all we did was turn the engine over. But petrol was off the ration now.

"I'm going for a drive," I called to James, taking the keys out of the kitchen drawer.

He appeared in the sitting room doorway, startled. "A drive? Are you sure?"

"James, I haven't forgotten how."

"Sweetheart, you're exhausted."

"I'm tired of being exhausted."

The Hillman started first time. I steered my way out to the junction and turned onto the seafront. The sea was gray under the falling dusk. Once I had driven along another promenade under a big bright moon, a giggly girl in her father's car. Scaring a fighter pilot half to death when she tried to hit a hundred. That car was sold now, and the pilot had given up his trade. The giggly girl thought she'd never laugh again.

A lorry was coming straight at me. I stamped on my brakes, he on his. We met face-to-face, the driver swearing out of a square furious mouth. I pulled straight into a parking place on the seafront, shaking. "God!" I shouted, and banged the steering wheel with my fists. "Why do we have to drive on the left?" I opened the window and in came the sea roar and the wind, blasting spittings of spray in my face. "Why?" I shouted again. "Why!"

James was so relieved to see me back. "That was very brave," he said.

"Not at all. I don't know why I didn't think of it before." I put the keys back in the drawer. "I might go out again. Every week or so, perhaps. Can we afford the petrol, do you suppose?"

"Of course we can."

"Of course we can," I echoed, desolate. "What's a few gallons of petrol compared to the cost of a child."

He closed his eyes. The lids trembled. His mouth was lipless.

I grasped him. "James, darling—"

"No, no," he said mechanically, patting my shoulder. "I'm perfectly all right."

I drew away so I could view him. "I don't think so."

"We simply need a little more time." His eyes were wide open now, fixed on a point next to me. "Then we'll be able to put it behind us."

He was referring to the tragedy, of course, when he said "it." But he still sounded as if he meant Catherine herself. That somehow we would put the baby behind us.

I could not think of her behind me. Or in any place except my arms.

The next time I got behind the wheel I made it all the way to the harbor. The driving seat was a good place to mourn, it turned out.

Then one day I went north into the countryside, found myself traveling through small towns, peaceful villages. Alver Shore could be in another country. The hills lifted me and set me down again in a valley where the river was edged by trees weeping into the water. Finally I came to a halt in a steep lane under an overhanging wall with pink daisies growing in the cracks between the stones. When I turned off the engine, the only sound was rain dripping from the daisies.

I got out of the car and walked up and down, crying for want of anything better to do.

"Are you lost, madam?"

An old man was coming toward me up the lane. His voice brusque, chirping a bit with age.

"No!" Resenting this interruption to my crying hugely. I probably glared at him.

"I wondered if that was why you were so upset."

His eyes had faded to a very light gray, so light that the irises merged into the aged, discolored whites. They strayed rheumily upward from my face—he brought them down, small black pupils lost in a sea of eye. I was still hazy about accents, but I fancied he was Irish.

"My baby died."

Hoping to send him away.

"Ah, now," he said. "That is sad."

He was carrying his hat, I noticed, his clubbed fingers folded over the brim, his hair damp on his crown. Why wasn't he wearing it? I couldn't tell.

He spoke again. "Was it your first?"

I nodded, methodically wiping the tears away.

"We lost our first too. Went on to have three more good ones, all grown up now, but I know you don't care about that."

I sniffled in the silence.

Then I said, "I'm very sorry."

"You could visit my wife. She's out most afternoons, but if you came in the morning you could sit with her, if you wanted. She'd understand. She'd be doing her chores, you see, she wouldn't get on your nerves. It would be a change of scene for you. That's all she wanted, when, you know. When it happened to us."

"You're very kind, very kind indeed, but, you see, I don't live locally. I drive around, and I was just passing through . . ."

"I see." He nodded. "Well, that's fair enough. But if you should change your mind, it's the last bungalow down the lane. Down there. Round the corner." He lifted his cane, pointed to where the lane curved away out of sight. "No obligation, my dear."

I watched him making his bowed way onward, swinging his cane.

I didn't tell James about this encounter. Not that I wanted to keep it a secret. Simply that when I got home he usually said, "Nice drive?," and I'd reply, "Yes," and before I'd even got that one little word out he'd say "Good!," and the subject was closed.

I'd seen him in fear of his life, my husband, when they made him fly ten feet off the ground; I'd seen him haunted by frozen tracks in snow. But all through that, he was still himself. Straight after we lost Catherine, he was still himself. But now, as the weeks passed, he was starting to mold himself into a new man. A competent, determinedly cheerful, solicitous consort whose every action, whether it be polishing shoes or kissing his wife, was performed with maximum efficiency and attention to detail.

One should not be misled by the superficial resemblance to the real James underneath. This performance was:

(a) Oddly overdone, in the manner of a highly trained double.
(b) More importantly, deficient in one vital respect:

> Which is that every time I mentioned our dead daughter or anything that related to her, he sidestepped or deflected or otherwise neutralized my comment.

EXAMPLE 1.

> YVETTE: "Here is this little hat we were given before she was born. Isn't it pretty?"
> JAMES: "Hats like that are very good against the sun. Now, I'm absolutely starving. Is there any cheese?"

EXAMPLE 2.

> YVETTE: "Do you remember that nice family who gave us all those flowers from their garden for the funeral? I saw them today in church."
> JAMES: "Yes, the husband is a great horticulturalist. He wins prizes for his dahlias."

In this way, time after time, he began to nudge our baby out of the conversation. Couldn't he just once join me in the moment I was obviously remembering? Give it its due debt of fond sadness? That was all I asked for.

I wrote to Célia. But I couldn't bring myself to describe James's behavior properly. I made a remark about him being a model husband, *almost too model*, but when she wrote back she didn't comment on it. She probably didn't hear me. My voice now too small and English perhaps, too wittering. Dying away in those loud broad large Australian spaces.

It was the third example that brought matters to a head.

EXAMPLE 3.

I was heating up some Camp Coffee mixed with Carnation evaporated milk.

> YVETTE: "I do hope this coffee doesn't give me heartburn. Do you remember when I was pregnant, how sweet things gave me heartburn?"
>
> JAMES: "My father suffered from heartburn until he gave up spicy food. It was a sore loss to him, after all those years in Singapore."

I took the pan off the gas and set it aside. "James," I said, "where have you gone?"

He looked genuinely puzzled.

"I'm right here with you," he said, "I always will be."

I poured the coffee into two cups. However careful I was, I always spilled a little from the pan. If only I'd brought just one cannikin with me from Alexandria, one little metal jug with a lip and a long handle, designed for sitting on the heat and making and pouring coffee. Sacrilege to fill it with this syrupy comforting pap, but still.

"You never say one word about Catherine. About the time we had with her, when I was expecting. Or about when she died. Or afterward." I wiped up the sticky slop on the stovetop. "Not one word."

"Because it makes you sad, Yvette." He spoke patiently, as if we'd had this exchange a thousand times. But I'd never said this to him before.

"It doesn't *make* me sad. I'm sad already. And I want to remember her, especially the time when she was alive." My tears were falling freely, consoling and lukewarm; a low salt content, I judged. "With every day that passes, I'm further away from her."

"Yvette, sweetheart." James's gaze was full of the most sincerely conveyed concern. "I'm sure we can find somebody for you to talk to. Mrs. Goodwin, for example. She's an awfully good listener."

I remember his face now. His brows dark above his eyes. His hair longer than it had been in the war. A student prince. (Chillingly, new James was slightly more handsome than the real one.)

"Like a pile of ironing," I said.

He moved his head a fraction sideways, to show incomprehension.

"I could take the matter of our baby, our lost baby, to this woman, the same way I could take your surplices and stoles to the laundry to be starched and pressed—"

"Darling, do you want to use the laundry? I'm sure we could afford it somehow—"

"I'm not talking about the blessed *laundry*. I'm talking about Catherine. I'm saying that such a woman would be a great convenience for you. You wouldn't have to keep trying to avoid the subject of our daughter, because I'd have no call to mention her name in this house. There would be a person I could go to, for that sort of thing."

He stood up and opened his arms. I never failed to melt when he did this, as if by touching him I could persuade myself that he hadn't changed. Leaning against his chest I felt and heard his words. "Yvette, I apologize. You've found me wanting, and I'm sorry for that. I will do better, I promise. Now let's drink up this lovely coffee while it's still hot."

I put my hand on his chest. He stepped back in surprise.

"It's not lovely, James. You know it's disgusting. You know we only drink it because it's hot and sweet and it's all we can get. We drank proper coffee together in Egypt and you call this lovely? Why are you doing this? Why are you *like* this?"

"I really don't—" he said, but I gave him no time to continue. I went and got the car keys.

"Don't ask Mrs. Goodwin," I said, putting on my coat. "It's not her I want to talk to."

If I drew a sketch map of my route out of Alver Shore, it would have nothing in common with the atlas or the motorist's map. The tracks would wander, out of scale, the turns defined pictorially—a tree here, a barn there, a scarecrow in a field. I never learned a single road number or street name. When I set out after what I would come to call the Camp Coffee incident, I wasn't even sure I'd find the place again. Luckily I came to a certain junction where the trees and verges and sky seemed a little brighter to the left, lit in some way by my memory, and I knew I was on the right road. Once more I climbed over the big bare back of the hill and came down into the village. It was the same for every following visit. I drove out of Alver Shore using a mixture of recollection and instinct. I didn't want to see the village on the map, tentacled by real roads in black or orange that led all over the county. I pretended it was in another world, and I was the only one who knew how to get there.

The place seemed so much bigger and busier than before. I passed a grocer, a baker, a saddlery, a pub. I simply hadn't noticed them the first time. Distracted, I almost overshot the turning. I parked where I had before, under the wall at the top of the lane.

The last bungalow on the left, the elderly man had said. Pointing with his cane toward the blind bend.

I set off. I was a mess of nerves, my heels slid over the wet ground, my breath was loud in my ears. I brought the umbrella low and the damped-down patter of the mild wet autumn raindrops, with their hint of saltiness, awoke an early memory, or the imagination of an early memory, of rain falling on the hood of my pram as my mother wheeled me along on a winter day in Alexandria when the air smelled of the sea.

Alexandria was still there, on the distant continent of Africa. I tried to picture the city but it seemed tiny, unreal.

By the time I got to the end of the lane the drizzle was so light it settled on my face. I wiped it away and realized I'd forgotten my lipstick. My courage was very low. The man had said, *anytime*, but I only had his word for it. He probably only thought his wife was at home all morning, when in reality she had a million and one things that took her into the village.

The house was silent, the windows dark. The latch of the small wrought-iron gate was red with rust. A piece of blue twine was hooked over the gatepost. I looked at the knots and remembered the man's blunted fingers on the rim of his hat: I didn't want to touch the string. It seemed too intimate.

I pressed down on the handle and the latch released with a startling snap. Lifting the loop of twine, I went through the gate and up the path. Outside the front door was a pot with a stalk of rosemary trying to grow, just enough for one good dinner of lamb. As if the English would ever cook lamb with rosemary, wedded as they are to their satanic mint sauce. The door itself was old wood, damp-stained at the bottom, with rippling panels of glass and a spy hole in the middle, and a snarling knocker, the head of a wolf or a dog, I couldn't tell which.

By this time I was almost certain there was no one in, and I was glad. How could I talk, about Catherine of all things, to anyone who had a door knocker like this? I was just wrapping my mac around me, about to turn for home, when a huge pink hand squashed over the inside of the glass panel, rubbing with a gray cloth that squeaked against the pane.

I gasped, "Oh!"

Whereupon the door was opened by a woman in rubber gloves, whose eyes, after a moment, became keen with understanding. When she spoke it was briskly, with the same accent as her husband, and I was sure now that it was Irish.

"Ah now, you're the girl."

She embraced me, and I could have been Catherine held in my own arms if Catherine had lived to become a squalling babe. There was nothing else to me but tears. Tears and wool, the wool of her cardiganed shoulder and her soft but nonetheless binding arms. I laid my head on her shoulder like a runaway child who lies down in the fold of the hill and makes a pillow of the turf. I cried for the scrap of my child who cried endlessly for me. The ratcheting cry of a hungry baby has nothing on the cry of a dead one sounding only in her mother's ears. I cried louder than Catherine, I drowned her out, crying on the out-breath and on the in-breath, I don't know how long for, I had no interest in knowing. The woman held firm until I went quiet, or relatively so, subsiding into a soft snuffling and sniveling, and beginning to feel a haunting, despairing thirst.

She led me to her kitchen, my eyes were swollen almost shut, and sat me down. She gave me a glass of water which I sucked down greedily, and a damp folded tea towel for my eyes.

"I heard her crying," I said.

Even saying this, I felt the sweet tingling drain of my milk letting down. Surely that was impossible all these weeks later. But no: my brassiere was damp. For a moment my breasts hurt as much as they had done on the third day after she was born when they were so engorged, with no one to suckle.

I wished to lie in bed for ever, with wool blankets folding into hills all around me.

"Do you know what the doctor said, when my milk came in?" I said next. "He said, 'You may feel a little down. It's a common side effect of the beginning of lactation.' Can you imagine."

"Sadly I can. I would have given him a piece of my mind."

I took the blindfold away. My swollen eyes had reduced a bit. She was sitting in front of me, empty hands resting on the table. She hadn't put the kettle on or done anything extraneous. I thought, a most unbustling woman. I didn't want to raise my eyes to her face in case it set me off again, so I just looked at her hands, which were solid, tanned, with wrinkles around the knuckles and wide thumbnails each with a half-moon. Very capable and slightly damp from the rubber gloves. The gloves were tossed on the edge of the sink, half inside out. She must have hugged me in them and then taken them off.

"Thank you for letting me in. I hope your husband was right, and I'm not imposing..."

After that cyclone of crying, I was talking about imposing. Ridiculous.

"We know each other very well. He wouldn't get something like that wrong."

It sounded as if she was smiling. I looked up at her and she wasn't, but it didn't matter. Some people smiled with their voices. She had a dog-lover's face, which is my private name for a certain kind of face which, I have learned, is often found in these northern parts of the world: pouchy cheeks, tanned in a country way with white sun creases around small light eyes—hers were a hazelly green—and a pudgy medium-sized unimposing nose with no attitude to it. Unlike my nose which is, let's say, the centerpiece of my face. Which makes a statement: *Here I am!* Hers was a nose simply for beneficent breathing through generous nostrils. But the most important thing about this kind of face—an expression of trust in the world. Trust in you, that you're most likely going to be reasonable, and kind.

"Sit, sit in that big chair there." She rose to her feet and held out her hand. "I'm going to finish that blessed bit of cleaning. You can look at the birds. Then I'll make some tea."

I did what she said. The chair faced a low, wide window with a deep sill. I could see out into the garden at the birds hopping around, pecking at bits of bacon rind. From time to time she came and put her hands on my shoulders without speaking, or saying just, "Weary-wearies," which was an expression I didn't know. Not that it mattered. Out of all the things strangers had said to me since I lost Catherine, "Weary-wearies" was by far the most welcome.

We had tea together looking out at this garden. Neither of us spoke for a long time. I was too drained to talk and she saw that. Of course, she didn't just see it. She knew what it was like. So the time passed freely in restful silence. Not only didn't I talk, I don't even think I thought.

Eventually she broke into my nonthinking.

"I hope you don't mind me asking. But might you be a Copt, my dear?"

What a delightful question. She must have seen the icons painted by the original Christians of Egypt. The Blessed Virgin and the female saints all had the same face: oval, with dark eyes and bow-shaped eyebrows and—of course—long noses. It was such a good guess, such an intelligent guess, I almost wished I was, so she could be right.

"No, but I am Egyptian, like the Copts. My family is Melkite— Catholic, that is to say, and originally from Lebanon—but I'm Church of England now. My husband's a vicar."

She nodded, comprehending. "I learned about the Copts and the Maronites and the Melkites at school. We took our religious instruction seriously in Ireland! And where did you meet your husband?"

"In Alexandria during the war. We came to England, to Alver Shore, down on the coast, it must be . . . five years ago."

Was that all? Sometimes, especially now, I felt I'd been here all my life. And Alexandria was a dream or a shadow of a previous existence.

She was shaking her head and smiling. "My Lord. From Alexandria to Alver Shore, and in 1945 to boot! You poor, poor girl. How did you survive the cold? And the food, or lack of?"

"Oh . . . I didn't really mind."

"Get away with you."

"Well." I managed to smile back. "That part was hellish. But I'd have gone through it ten times, if it meant that my child lived."

"I know, I know."

Finally I got up to leave. She followed me into the hall. Pictures of her children ascended the staircase in merry leaps, tumbles, and bounds, imps sawing at my innards with serrated knives. She stroked my arm, knowing. Then pointed upward to a watercolor of stillness high on the stairs but visible in the shadow. "There he is," she said. "My first-born son."

He was a dim little form under a blanket. I couldn't really make him out, and I didn't want to climb the stairs to see him. I didn't know what it would do to me.

"We called him Gerard, after my father," she said.

Gerard. A nice name, but rather solemn for such a little swaddled hump. A name to be grown into.

"I am sorrowing for you," I said. "Do you say that in English?"

Because sorrowing was how I felt for her. Something more active than simply describing myself as sorry.

"Not generally. But we ought to."

"Please," I said, "please can I come back and see you again?"

Because at that moment I couldn't face my life without her.

Nice drive?"

"Yes—"

"Good."

I found a knife and an onion and began to chop. Our meal was to be liver and onions, with yesterday's mash and cabbage fried up. "Heavens, this onion is strong."

He came toward me. "Yvie, you've still got your coat on."

I put down the knife and let him slide the coat off my shoulders. He hung it up and came back to me and touched my face where the tears fell. I put my hand over his. Let him be quiet, I thought. Let me find him again in this gesture.

But he said, "I'm glad they're just onion tears! Now, I've got some minutes of a meeting to read through. Please would you call me when you need the table laid?"

"Of course."

I fried the onions and the liver, mixed together the potatoes and the cabbage and fried that too. I remembered the winter of '47, the pair of us in the kitchen in our overcoats. I had been stirring soup while James was opening a bag of coal. At that time, coal was sometimes sold short, the bag filled up with a makeweight of useless stones. I heard a shout of rage and looked up to see James pulling out an enormous chunk of slate. "Look at it!" he bellowed. "It must weigh five pounds!" He went outside and threw the slate on the ground, and when it broke he stamped separately on every single broken piece, swearing so loudly that our neighbor opened his window and called down, "Mr. Acton. I have not heard such language since the Battle of Bréville. Shame on you, sir, as a man of the cloth." We had embraced there in the garden, trembling with cold and with silent laughter.

How precious that moment seemed now.

The onions were browning. I took the pan off the heat.

We ate our supper and afterward sat in the parlor. James read a book while I sat leaning my head against the wing of the armchair. I glanced sideways at the title of his book as the fire crackled. *The Shaking of the Foundations.*

"What's your book about?"

He put it down. "It's a collection of sermons by Paul Tillich. I'm reading one about hope." He quoted. *"For we are saved by hope: but hope for that which is seen is not hope: for what a man seeth, why doth he yet hope for? But if we hope for that we see not, then do we with patience wait for it.* That's the Bible. Romans 8, verses 24–25."

"And what does Tillich say about this?"

"I don't know yet. Do you want to listen to the gramophone, darling? Some piano? I could put on the William Kapell."

"It's true, isn't it," I said. "You can't hope for something you can already see coming. True hope, truly patient waiting, is for things that aren't there yet. That might never be there."

He got up and pulled the Kapell from its sleeve. I watched him place the disc on the turntable, then crouch down in order to settle the needle onto the disk. When he did normal things like this it was worse because he moved exactly like his old self.

I might hope that James would come to be himself again. There was no evidence of that happening, of course. But that was why it was true hope.

"I've found a woman to talk to. She lost her son at birth. She's very nice."

He turned his head, the relief plain on his face. "Oh, I'm so pleased. Do I know her?"

"No. I hardly know her myself."

His eyes dropped to the gramophone needle between his thumb and forefinger. Without a tremor he let it down onto the disc. He went back to his chair and picked up his book, and the Prokofiev concerto began to fill the room. I got up and bent over the back of his chair and put my arms around him. He leaned his head back against my breast with his eyes shut. I didn't speak. I was coming to learn that when I spoke, it was always new James who answered. And I imagined that old James might be there underneath. I wanted him to be sure I was here and I loved him. New James might be keeping him in the dark.

Presently he took his head away and began reading once more. I sat back down. When Kapell moved on to the Khachaturian I went upstairs to bed and left him reading.

❦

THIRTEEN

I can see a woman in a tree," says Tom.

We're on the roof of the vicarage, in the valley between the twin gables, mending the holes. The attic ladder leans against one side of the valley, and Tom is perched near the top, one hand on the ridge of the roof and the other holding my binoculars.

William Kennet is below, squinting up at us against the sun. Aghast at the thought of me on the roof, he's come to supervise operations. I assured him it was only a few missing tiles, and I wouldn't be clambering around the eaves and guttering. But Mr. Kennet shook his head. The long ladder, the one we've used to get up here, is the property of Upton Hall School. Therefore he, being the school caretaker, is obliged to stay. That's his reasoning.

"Mr. Kennet," I had protested, "do I look like the sort of idiot who would stumble off the edge of a roof?"

"No," came his measured reply. "But you might be expecting the angels to catch you on the way down."

Of course, Tom is here, but Tom isn't good enough reason for Mr.

Kennet to desert his post. I've sensed by his brief greeting that he's rather wary of Tom. I don't entirely blame him. Tom's dark brown curls brush his shoulders, his sideburns reach his jawline, or almost, and he's currently in a grubby sweatshirt and jeans gaping at the knees.

As it turns out, it's not just a matter of filling in the gaps. A great many tiles are old and cracked, so we're replacing them too. A local builder, Stan Rail—one of the many sons of the estimable Matilda Rail, whose front door I had sandbagged on the day of the flood—has supplied the tiles. "If the job gets too much for you, Vicar," he told me, "give us a ring."

"I'm sure it won't be."

Mr. Rail, a large imperturbable man, had pressed a business card into my hand. "Just in case."

The weather on this mid-November day is fine and dry. The sun's warming my face as I lever out a crumbling slab of tile, more lichen and moss than clay. I tut at the exposed batten, pull out a penknife with foreboding. But the batten is sound and dry and so is the rafter underneath.

"A woman in a what?" I lent Tom the binoculars so he could view Beacon Hill. Not spy on our neighbors.

"In a tree."

I straighten up. "What's she doing?"

"Picking apples. You'd better not look, Dad. Think about it. 'Vicar in rooftop ogling incident. I was only replacing my tiles, protested the Rev. Jim Aitken, 78—'"

"Really, Tom. It's a tree, not a bathroom window."

"And it came to pass in an eveningtide," recites my atheist son, *"that David arose from off his bed—"*

"And walked upon the roof of the king's house." I take up the verse. *"And from the roof he saw a woman bathing, and the woman was—"*

"—very beautiful to look upon."

The last five words we speak in unison. The second book of Samuel, chapter 11. I'm glad he hasn't forgotten. "*Is* she beautiful?"

He shades his hand. "Can't see. Long hair, though."

"What color?"

"Blond. The tree's near a huge square building. At the end of a track."

He hands me the binoculars and gets back to work. After a second I sling them around my neck and climb the attic ladder. Carefully I point them in the other direction, admire the rampart of downland that I now know as Beacon Hill. It is bald and sere under the autumn sunshine, the recumbent flank of a lion. But then I find myself swooping northward over a dizzying rush of hedgerow, pull up sharply to rise above a meadow bordered by woodland. There's the track. It leads me over the rough grass to a high-walled block of a building. It's Parr's Mill, of course. My heart thumps. Next to the mill is a cottage, a garden, an apple tree. I let the lens swing over the crown of the tree and down. A flurry of leaves, a blurred mist of hair; a figure leaps down from the lowest branch. It's a burly young man with a long strawberry-blond mane and a sack of apples carried on a shoulder strap.

"This woman of yours, Tom? It's Colin Bowyer. He manages the mill with his father. His hair's even longer than yours."

Tom finds this very funny. But my pulse is racing with shame. Supposing it *had* been Ellen? I'd have been . . . I'd have been ogling her, just as Tom said. I've been thinking of her all week, wishing Margaret Dennis hadn't buttonholed her. Reliving the encounter: her extraordinary creed, her smile.

Friends have set me up, over the years, with a succession of kind, friendly, attractive women. The earlier encounters were excruciating, later ones less so. None of them anything more than pleasant. I don't know why this is different. All I know is that I want to advance, arm out like a traffic policeman, stopping a phalanx of Margaret Dennises in their tracks. I want to know everything about Ellen, softly pelt her with questions. An importunate, impetuous vicar: I can't imagine anyone less likely to appeal to her.

"Earth to Dad. Any chance of you getting off that ladder?"

I stammer an apology and climb down. He drags the ladder along the gully and begins to pull away rotten tiles. "How is Florence?" I ask, taking the tiles from him and setting them down.

Tom's gaze rises away from mine into the sky, an apostle with dark brown eyes lit from within by the inner flame of love—not, in his case, for the divine. His passion is wholly earthly.

"She's fine. Oh, she's fantastic, Dad."

The pair of us. My heart dips a little. He and Florence are very young, and with five hundred miles between them, how will they manage? I start handing up new tiles, each one the size of my forearm and weighing a good ten pounds.

"It's a shame you're so far apart."

That makes him laugh. "Who proposed to Mum from a prison camp? After, what, two meetings?"

I grin up at him. "True enough . . . I'm glad you're here, Tom."

"Me too." He pushes his hair out of his eyes. "I'm sorry for what I said last time. About the furniture being tragic."

"No, you were right. In fact—"

"Ahoy!" William calls from below. "Ahoy up there!" Always authoritative, his voice now sounds urgent.

I take careful steps, one foot in front of the other, along the gully. I left William seated on the garden bench with his tin of tobacco and a ham sandwich made by Tom. Now he's standing at the foot of the ladder, clasping the uprights with a staring grimace on his face.

"What is it, Mr. Kennet?"

"There's a bloke out front!" I realize he's trying to make himself heard while keeping his voice down. The result is a quiet screech. "Looking into all the windows!"

"What?"

"Big bloke, dressed in black! With a dog collar!"

I'm mystified, but only for a moment. Then I put my finger to my lips and gesture toward the bench. Deadpan, he winks at me and returns to his seat. I shuffle backward from the edge of the roof and kneel up.

Tom is approaching along the gully. "What's going on?"

"Shh." I rise to my feet, squeeze past him toward the front of the house. Dropping once more to a crawl, I ease my head over the gutter to hear an imperious bang-bang, good and loud, a bailiff's knock if ever there was one, from a man practiced at summoning people from the depths of large, cold houses with many internal doors.

If only it were a bailiff.

With dismay I stare down at the bald crown that's presented to me. The portly body steps back from the front door and the face begins to lift—I duck backward away from the edge of the roof and shuffle in reverse along the gulley. Tom is waiting, agog.

"It's a man called Frobisher," I murmur. "He's my archdeacon."

"You didn't say anyone was coming."

"I didn't know."

"Weird," Tom whispers. "Or is it weird? Is that what they do? Just turn up with no warning, like inspectors?"

"Ha," I say grimly. "No. I'm supposed to have written him a letter, a sort of report, really. On what I've been up to. And I still haven't done it, although he's asked me three times. And now here he is."

Tom is a picture of astonished glee. "Dad, that's *heavy*. What are you going to say? Bailey ate your homework?"

Voices float up from below. Frobisher's come around to the back of the house. I can hear him in parley with William. William's saying, "...couldn't exactly say," his tone grudging, uncomfortable. I shouldn't be putting him in this position. Frobisher responds with a hectoring sentence ending in "...the roof?" Seconds later, to the audible remonstrations of William, footsteps begin to clang up the ladder.

"He'll kill himself," I murmur. "He's not built for climbing." Once more I go toward the back of the house. "Archdeacon Frobisher," I call. "Please wait for me to come down..."

I'm too late. He's already halfway up by the time I get to the edge of the roof. He's climbing with disconcerting strength and agility, bald head swinging from side to side, like a torpedo finning its way up from the depths. William's holding the bottom of the ladder. He doesn't look up.

Frobisher reaches the top, waves away my helping hand. "No, no. No need." He hauls his black-clad bulk over the top rung. "My word," he continues, lunging into an upright position, tugging a handkerchief from his breast pocket. "This *is* a crow's nest, is it not. And you the pirate!" He sets about rubbing down his face, head, and neck with a circular buffing motion, as if burnishing brass work. "Pirates, I should say!" he adds, catching sight of Tom. All of this in the voice that I'd been so struck by before, the same hampered waffling sound. "Good gracious, Mr. Acton. This is a pretty pass. A clergyman repairing his own roof. Are diocesan funds really this hard to come by?"

I recollect myself—I'm so intrigued by the burnishing, the way it actually has made his head shinier—and glance down at my clothes. A paint-stained pair of dark blue canvas trousers, an ancient rugby shirt that has long forgotten its better days. And Tom in his dilapidated denim. "Forgive us, Archdeacon! We're dressed for the occasion. And it's only a few patches of tiling, so I took matters into my own hands." I move to one side so that Tom can come forward. "Tom, this is Archdeacon Frobisher. Archdeacon, my son, Tom."

Tom leans past me and extends his hand. "Pleased to meet you, Archdeacon."

"Likewise, likewise, I'm sure." Frobisher's eyes bustle over Tom. "Are you down, Tom?"

Tom stares. "Down?"

"From varsity." Frobisher sounds impatient.

"Oh. Yes." Tom allows himself a single wild flicker of eyes toward me. "Yes. Down from varsity."

"And what is your area of study?"

Tom produces a huge grin. "Sex change in flatfish."

"Archdeacon, shall we descend?" I try to usher him back the way he came. "I'd have joined you below, you know, if I'd known you were here . . ."

Frobisher gives me a sharp glance from his pale thick-lidded eyes. It's the look of an intelligent pig. "I don't mind a climb. I scurried up and down a fair few ladders, I can tell you, when the Germans attacked us in the middle of the Atlantic." A jovial smile stretches his lips, unnervingly simultaneous with a drilling stare for Tom. "But a glass of water would be most welcome."

"I'm sure we can do better than that . . ." This may not be true. I think of the calcified inch of instant coffee in the jar and the single custard cream at the bottom of the biscuit tin. Tom's eaten constantly since he arrived and we haven't been shopping yet.

Three most unjolly Jack-tars make their way down the rocking ladder. I'm the first, and William gravely steps aside for me. I apologize to him in an undertone, for the embarrassment. He pulls his hat lower, the better to speak privately. "Don't you worry about that, Vicar. I'll be off back to the school. I can see now, you're in safe hands with Tom."

When Tom reaches the bottom I say quietly, "You don't need to stay with us, you know. Feel free to go and study."

Tom looks horrified. "Not likely. He might eat you."

We stare up at the descending Frobisher. A man never looks his best coming down a ladder. Frobisher is no exception.

In the kitchen Tom shows the ancient floor tiles to our guest. "Good heavens," says Frobisher, bending and peering at the dim shapes. "Stabbed Wessex, if I'm not mistaken. Late twelve or early thirteen hundreds. What a find."

"I've been told they were taken from Waltham Priory."

"Well. If not in the floor of a religious building, their place is in a museum."

My heart sinks. "I was thinking about somewhere local. Where people could view them without having to travel."

"We'll see." He's not so keen on that idea.

I assemble mugs and tea bags. The milk, subjected to a searching sniff, passes muster. "Would you care for a piece of toast, Archdeacon?" Tom asks. A vicar's son when he wants to be.

"No, thank you."

"We've got chocolate spread," Tom coaxes.

Frobisher feigns not to hear this, plants himself on a kitchen chair, legs apart, black-socked ankles, rather swollen, on view. Bailey, who has taken to sunning himself in the sitting room, saunters in. I'm about to scoop the dog up and put him outside—Bailey has discovered the joy of shoelaces—but Frobisher is leaning forward, extending his hand toward the dog, and saying, "Now who is this? Who is this, now?" Before I can say anything, my archdeacon gets down off his chair and lowers himself into a kneeling position. Bailey hurries toward him and plants his front paws on the twin boulders of Frobisher's knees.

"Are you a hound pup, by any chance?" murmurs Frobisher. "I think you are." He begins to stroke the dog briskly, his hand enveloping the small body entirely, and Bailey climbs right up onto his lap, legs splayed foursquare as he squirms in bliss under Frobisher's heavy palm. Frobisher's slablike cheeks and doughty chin are softening, softening and almost . . . trembling? Can they be? But they are, almost imperceptibly, like a blancmange might tremble on a plate when a heavy lorry goes by on the road outside. "There, there," he's saying to the dog, who is gazing up at him with naked, greedy adoration. "There, there."

Tom is standing immobile, knife in the air, halfway through troweling chocolate spread onto toast.

"He's called Bailey," I say softly. "He was given to me by a parishioner."

My voice brings the archdeacon to his senses. His face solidifies into its tougher, more familiar mien. He sets Bailey onto the floor. "That's enough of that, little chap." He clambers up off his knees and resumes his seat on the kitchen chair. Tom takes a bite out of his toast and, with a final wide-eyed stare at me, sidles to the door.

"I think I'll go and hit veg ecology," he says, or something like it—the toast makes it hard to be sure—and disappears.

I put a cup of tea in front of Frobisher, who is once more polishing his head. With another man I might suggest he make himself at home, take his jacket off at least, but just as he's not a chocolate-spread man, he's not a jacket-removing man either. I try to think of something to say.

"So you spent the war in the navy, I gather, Archdeacon."

"Yes, indeed I did. But it's not germane. Not germane." He returns his handkerchief with a flourish to his breast pocket. "Your news, or lack of, is the subject at hand. I'm sure you know, Mr. Acton, that I didn't expect a *screed*. I can't abide pages of blither. Who more likely than we who have borne arms to abhor manila folders and red tape, hmm? Those desk johnnies with their chits and dockets." He gives me a fat, chummy smile.

I can't bear the phrase *borne arms*, but that doesn't matter. I launch into a sincerely meant apology complete with a formal mode of address. "My archdeacon, I'm sorry for being so impolite and so derelict in my duty that I've brought about this ridiculous state of affairs," I begin, "whereby you're forced to come to my house and—"

"Climb your confounded ladder. Yes. You knew I was down there, didn't you. But you . . . shall we say, you were rather backward in coming forward?"

I bow my head. I don't think I've ever been so embarrassed in my professional capacity.

He lets me wallow, bending toward the briefcase at his feet. I've managed not to focus on this briefcase but I know he picked it up from the grass by the bottom of the ladder, where he'd left it prior to his climb. It's dark dull black with a gold-colored hasp and, where one might find initials, a gold cross. In a doctor's hand this sort of bag is an instrument of comfort, but there's no comfort here. "Ah. Here we are." Out of the briefcase comes something unpleasantly similar to the manila folder he has so recently derided. He hands it to me and I open it to find a single sheet of paper bearing, in fresh black typescript, a list of three items spaced at wide intervals down the page.

1. *Pastoral Ministry*
2. *Organization/Administration*
3. *Mission*

I place the list on the table. "What is this?"

"It's a prompt, dear boy. When you write your report, simply group your responses under these headings." Frobisher leans forward, parks his heavy arms on the table. "Look, Acton. I'll be candid. I can see how this happened. It's a new post, you have a hundred calls on your time, and there's that blessed blank page staring up at you. Anyone can suffer a bout of writer's block."

I pour milk into my cup of tea. In the short interval since I served Frobisher, the milk has turned and it splits into tiny white worms. Like the milk, my thoughts curdle and spin. Frobisher continues, unperturbed by my lack of response.

"I've had very good news of you, both from your curate Clive Perry and from your Parish Council. Administratively you are *diligent*. In your pastoral ministry, again, *impressive and energetic*." He leans slightly on the adjectives to indicate that they're Clive's choice and not his.

"That's very kind of Clive," I manage to say before Frobisher grinds on.

"Turning now to this last element . . ." His forefinger squashes down on the word *Mission*. "Mr. Perry has pointed out, very reasonably, that no one would expect leaps and bounds on this front. But what I do expect of you, at this juncture, now that you've got the measure of the place, is some *views*. Some ideas on how this *gathering-in* might be accomplished. I need not remind you that you are, of course, not simply priest of a congregation but vicar to the parish."

"That's true. The whole parish, whether they come to church or not."

"Exactly. That is why we reach out, after all. To bring people into a community which draws its strength, its life, from communal worship and fellowship in the Lord. To seek out those who have strayed from His ways like lost sheep."

In the long silence that follows I look out through the open back door into the garden. The sunshine is very strong just now, shining hard on the path and the unkempt grass.

"I don't want to be rounding people up like a sheepdog. If sheepdogs grip they get disqualified."

Frobisher is puzzled. "What, pray, is gripping?"

"When the dog bites a sheep."

He's looking at me gravely, his head low. At close quarters I have no choice but to stare straight into his small penetrating eyes, behind which I sense the thorough and powerful workings of his brain.

"You're not a sheepdog, Mr. Acton. You are a shepherd." He snaps his briefcase shut and looks down. "Come now, little man. That is not your bed."

Bailey is lying with his head on Frobisher's right foot.

"Did you get a hundred lines?" Tom asks, when Frobisher is gone and we are driving to Waltham for food. "Or did Bailey melt his heart?"

"A mixture of both." I tell Tom about the Mission part of my brief, Frobisher's urgings.

"But you're meant to round them up, aren't you? You did at Fulbrook."

And at Alver Shore before Fulbrook. But during the last few years at Fulbrook the gaps in pews were larger, the faces older. Upton is still well-attended but how much of that is due to novelty? How much longer can I supply the impressive energy that Clive, bless him, had talked about?

"Tom, if I tried to round you up, what would you do?"

"I've got no business in church, Dad, you know that. I don't believe in God."

"True."

"I can't help it. I just don't."

We park near the main square. Tom immediately spots a shop called Waltham Health Foods, a place I've never noticed, and heads for it, leaving me with his list. I cross the cobbles of the square, which on this brisk sunny day looks rather beautiful, the clean windows of the town hall catching the sunlight. In the supermarket I load my basket with milk, vegetables, and other sundries, and then make my way toward the frozen food section at the back. Tom has asked for haddock.

There, standing by one of the tall freezer cabinets, is Ellen.

She's looking at herself in the glass door of the cabinet. As I watch she lifts her hands up to her hair, touches it where it is caught into a bun. She moves her head to one side, catches a stray lock between two fingers and makes a scissoring motion. She's deciding whether to have it cut.

Oh, let her not cut her hair.

I should do something. Cough, so that I catch her eye, and make sure I'm inspecting the ice creams when she spots me. But I carry on standing there. And it came to pass in morningtide that James arose from his bed and walked upon the roof of the vicar's house. And from the roof he saw a man, which greatly disappointed him, but later that same morning he saw the woman privately looking at her reflection in a freezer cabinet, and she was *beautiful to*—

"Good morning, Ellen," I blurt out.

She turns around. "Good morning!" Her cheeks go pink, and that's my fault. Nonetheless she's smiling. "I was just thinking about my hair . . ."

"You're permitted," I say. "I was thinking only about supper. I was after some fish."

"And I'm standing in your way." She steps back from the freezer cabinet. "I'm getting a few things for a young girl I'm looking after. She likes food in packets."

She looks fondly at the contents of her basket, as if the young girl is contained in the things.

"So do I. My son gives me frequent tellings-off."

She looks up. "You have a son?"

"He's studying environmental sciences at the University of East Anglia. He's against packets, on the whole. He's staying with me just now, so I'm getting a large piece of haddock."

"Excellent." Smiling, she glances toward the door of the supermarket. I'm keeping her. She needs to get back to her young girl. I should say goodbye and release her but I can't just yet.

Go on, Acton. Speak your mind.

"Ellen—perhaps you'd join me one evening next week for a glass of sherry? Tuesday, say? Parishioners permitting."

I've done my best. A steady voice, a warm smile, and—I'm hoping—a relaxed, friendly look in my eyes. If she declines, so be it.

She blinks rapidly. The very becoming pale pink appears once more in her cheeks. "That would be lovely." She opens her bag. "I haven't got your phone number . . ."

"Ask Althea," I suggest, my heart singing.

"Do you know, I'd rather not." She looks up—her eyes sparkle. "Sometimes I'm glad my friends are so attentive and caring. But not all the time."

She writes my number on a slip of paper. We leave the shop together and go out into the sunny square. She swings herself up into her Land Rover and drives off with a wave.

Tom lopes up, bearing a bulging carrier bag. He nods at my purchases.

"Did you get the fish?"

I slap my hand to my head. "I completely forgot."

He grins. "Chrissake, Dad."

I give him a level stare. "Enough of the 'Chrissake.' Have some respect."

He falls silent, walks by my side back into the supermarket, selects the fish. In the checkout queue he says, "Sorry."

"It's all right. Now to the off-license. I've got a guest coming on Tuesday evening for a drink. The only booze we've got is dire leftovers from my party."

"Don't I know it . . . What kind of guest?"

"A friend. Someone I hope will become a friend."

Tom gives me a sidelong glance. Says nothing.

That night I roll at twelve thousand feet, light and agile. I have no weapons on my wings. My armorer took my cannons away before I left. "It's your last day," he said. "So you won't need them."

So I turn over and over, the still point, the axis of the gimbal. The blue dome of sky and white dome of desert slip round and round me. The midday sun sets and rises, sets and rises.

The 109s have no difficulty in finding me. Eight, nine, ten of them, they come out of the sun like bees from a hive.

They hit me again and again. The flames are so transparent in the brilliant sunshine that I'm not even sure they're real. I feel for the lever that releases the emergency exit panel. But my hand can't find it. When I turn my head to look, there's no lever. With a yell of rage I punch a hole in the side of the cockpit and crawl out.

It's a hard landing on desert stones, but I still don't wake. The white parachute canopy envelops me, binding itself against my face. The harder I struggle, the tighter it winds around me. I can't seem to—

"Get free," I say aloud, thrashing my way out of the bedsheet.

"Dad?" Tom's in the doorway.

"What?"

"You were shouting."

"What's the time?"

"Quarter to five."

"Sorry, Tom. Just a dream."

He lingers for a moment, a tall shadow, and then goes back to bed.

FOURTEEN

❦

Yvette
5 June 1964

*L*a *Géographie* is full up, so here I am, starting today on the back pages of *La Biologie.* I've just been admiring my truly staggering diagram of the human circulatory system. Gazing with envy on those bright cushions of red blood cells—labeled, with curving arrows, *les érythrocytes*—bouncing along a cross section of the artery that loops and twists—*wheee!*—from lung to heart to aorta. I bought a special ink to color those erythrocytes, a Sennelier carmine, and over twenty years later the result is still spectacular . . .

Yes, I gaze with envy on them because my blood tests have revealed that my own erythrocytes are not flourishing as they should under my drug regime. My condition is *refractory,* that is to say, it is not responding to treatment. The word sounds like a mixture of *recalcitrant* and *fractious.* As if the disease is folding its arms and stamping away to sulk in a corner. The best thing you can do with a small boy in this mood is to put on the wireless and carry on with your tasks, humming along to the melodies and pausing occasionally to give the boy a kiss (growlingly shaken off) or a stroke of the hair (angry little head ducks away). But I do not know what blandishments I can offer my leukemia. This being the case, I will, for the time being, ignore it.

The kind woman's husband had been right. He'd said that it would be "a change of scene for you," and so it was. It was soothing to be in a house I'd never been pregnant in. To look at a garden where I'd never imagined Catherine playing.

I started to visit about once every month or so. I never saw the husband on any of these occasions. I sat at ease with his wife, sobbed, and spoke and it might be sobbing or speech that was preponderant but you could hardly tell, they were so intermingled. It didn't matter. Gradually the speech outwon the sobs and in the end I stumbled onto the subject of James. I had to talk to *someone*, and I didn't dare confide in anyone at Alver Shore, not even the nicest of women. I couldn't start unburdening myself to these friendly souls about the vicar of their parish.

I began with the Camp Coffee incident that had originally brought me to her door.

"It was when he promised to do better," I said. "Do better in talking about Catherine. You see, the old James would never have needed to *promise* to talk about Catherine. The idea would have been absurd, that she would be a special chore he had to remember."

"He must be protecting himself." Her tone was speculative.

"Yes. Like a crab. I know he's somewhere inside," I concluded, heaving a great sigh. "Too sad to come out. Or maybe too angry. How was your husband, Bridie, after it happened to you?"

We had been on first-name terms for a while.

"Ah! Pat, now." Bridie thought about it while she blanket-stitched a duster, her busy hands sunbrowned even in winter. She must spend so much time outdoors. "Pat didn't know how to . . . carry himself. It was most odd. He'd go lurching out of the room, I thought he was about to bash someone, the way his fists were swinging by his sides, but he was just on his way to work. He drove buses for South Down. It wasn't *worrying*, his behavior. The bus company, they knew him well, they understood." She leaned back in her chair, reflecting. "He chopped a lot of wood that winter. I used to watch him from the kitchen window, the ax right up above his head and then he'd bring it down, bang! And the two halves of the log would jump in the air!"

We both laughed. We'd earned the right.

"And then we had another baby," she went on, "and everything started again. It will for you too."

I couldn't imagine it, and sighed again, to say so. Bridie chuckled.

"You're not the most patient girl, are you. How long's it been?"

The afternoon was fading outside. We were in January now, 1951. I don't know how I had got through Christmas. Well, I do. There was no way *around* Christmas, so I had to. To look at James on Christmas Day, a shining, impervious, smiling vicar, you'd think nothing had happened at all. Iris rang me often. "He's being very . . . strong," I told her one time, and she said, "Oh, *men*," in a way that made me feel she might understand, but I couldn't elaborate. I remembered the deep relief in her voice when he recovered after the war. I didn't have the courage to go back on everything and say: *Iris, everything's wrong. James is—wrong.* Because what could Iris do, anyway?

"Oh, five months," I said to Bridie, "and . . . eight days."

"You'll need to let the year go round."

What a lovely thing to hear. Life was so exhausting that the idea of *letting* something happen, instead of having to *make* it happen, was balm. Time would take me onward until I'd no longer be thinking, *This time last year I was this big with Catherine, and then this big* . . .

As I was looking gratefully at Bridie my eye was caught by the picture on the wall behind her. It was the baby I'd glimpsed at the top of the stairs, her first and stillborn whose name was Gerard. "Oh, look." I felt a rush of tenderness. "Gerard's come down to us."

"Indeed he has. Since meeting you, I've been reminded."

"Oh, Bridie, I hope I haven't made you sad."

This was honestly the first time the thought had crossed my mind.

"No, I didn't mean that." She got up and unhooked the picture from the wall and handed it to me. "I haven't paid him as much attention as I should, these past years. That's all."

He was a shut-eyed light-haired baby, mouth closed, one loose little fist raised above the hem of a blanket.

"That was how he lay in the hospital cot," said Bridie, sitting down again. "With his hand like that. Not that I saw him. Pat did. Father O'Neill was with us and he insisted Pat be allowed." She sighed. "But I wasn't. They thought it would be too upsetting."

"I'm sorry you never got to hold him."

"And I'm sorry you never saw Catherine, my dear. If she took after you she was a pretty girl."

I was silent, looking down at my hands. They had held my daughter like a pair of scale pans, one palm under her bottom and the other under her head. That wrapped-up baby, hooded as she was by her towel: the state I must have been in, not to pull that towel away from her face. What they must have injected me with . . .

"Bridie." Only now did the question occur to me. "How did you get to have this beautiful drawing? It can't have been done in the hospital, surely?"

Bridie put one hand on her chest, just below her neck. A gesture she made sometimes, to show mild remorse. "Goodness, I haven't explained. My grown-up son drew it from my husband's memory of Gerard. Pat hadn't forgotten a single detail, not one, of that little baby's body. Down to fingernails. Earlobes. That's the fine copy, with a little color added, as you see."

Just a little color, yes. On the tiny sandy locks of hair. On the rosy hue inside curling fingers, and the blue-violet shadow of a fold of the blanket. I couldn't imagine what kind of baby Catherine had been. All I had was a strange vision of a miniature girl with long hair, much longer than a baby's hair ever is, radiating out from her head as if she were underwater or as if the air were thicker than normal air. So that she could be suspended in it like an angel.

"Your son's a good artist."

"He's the baby I mentioned, the one who came after Gerard. I love my girls desperately, of course, but the rainbow child, the one who comes at the end of the storm, is always a bit special."

I looked at Bridie, and she gazed back at me. Her manner of speaking had been so matter-of-fact and steady. I'd never be like her. I didn't have her trusting uplands of eyes, that mild light hazel green that was home to mountain thyme and blooming heather and griefs salved and healed over and knitted up. My eyes were still swamps with tracks of mascara leading out.

"I wish I had a picture of Catherine. Even if it was imaginary."

"Let me see." Bridie paused. "My son will be here next Saturday. Pat's found him some work in the village. Half a day, puttying windows into a greenhouse at Upton Hall. He's never in funds." She patted my arm. "Lord, I didn't mean to imply you had to pay him."

"Of course I'd pay him," I said. "Not that we're ever in funds, but—"

"No, he'd be delighted to do it for nothing—"

"I'm sure that for this we could manage a reasonable sum—"

"Dear Yvette," Bridie said, "he would do it as a favor for a friend of mine."

I swear, I had merely been musing aloud over the possibility. But now she was saying it . . .

"If you could ask him, Bridie," I said, "I would be grateful."

James was writing a sermon when I got home. I could tell from the rhythm of his typing. Rippling out fast, then stopping, then another rush. If it had been a letter or a memorandum the rap of the keys would be more regular, following a precomposed train of thought. Sermons on the other hand were fits and starts of inspiration and used a lot of paper. I heard the ping of the carriage return and then, to my surprise, a long sigh. He never sighed in front of me these days. It was something new James never seemed to do, expressing as it did dejection or at the very least fatigue. The sigh told me he hadn't heard me come in.

I slipped my feet out of my shoes but one heel dropped onto the linoleum and his voice came immediately. "Yvette? Darling, is that you?"

Cheerful, composed, with a new and quite dreadfully annoying musical note. I strode directly into the study where he sat bolt upright behind his typewriter in black bib and white clerical collar and black jacket and trousers and white teeth and shining black hair, every inch a vicar. It was just impossible. Nobody was really every inch a vicar. Every real priest had a corner or cranny of anger or weakness or ennui.

"Why did you sigh?"

"What?" He frowned a light quizzical frown.

"Just now. I heard you sigh when I came in."

He smiled. "Perhaps it was a sigh of satisfaction. I've done awfully well this afternoon. Now, are we to have herrings for supper?"

I gave a high shriek, whirled my handbag around my head, and slung it at him.

No, of course I didn't. But the idea was exquisite.

That night we made love.

I have described our bed episode in Aunt Monique's flat in Cairo. That tender disaster was not repeated. On those cold nights after the war we went to bed early. There was a great deal to do, we found, before we went to sleep.

I should not complain about new James in bed. It is spoiled and unkind of me. I should be grateful that even then at his darkest time, James was trying in his own way to be close to me. But I cannot deny that the adjective that suited him most as a lover was . . .

Efficient.

So efficient, in fact, that he left me—how shall I put this—he left me feeling somewhat *redundant*. There were times I longed for Cairo, because we'd been closer then.

Actually, do you know what I missed most of all? I missed the touches of marriage. Living together as we did in a small house, we never seemed to be more than a couple of yards apart. When I was washing up, James would stroke my back in passing. I would put my arm across his shoulders if he called me to read a letter from Peter with him. He put his hands on my hips if I was tired going upstairs, giving me very gentle pushes. When we were out in the car, he used to take his hand from the gear stick and put it on my knee. Or I would put my hand on his knee. Or rest my head on his shoulder when we read in bed or listened to music in the parlor. I worried at first: I had been told about Englishmen, how they disliked being smothered. But, as with two countries after centuries of peace, the boundaries between us all but disappeared. We know, we who are lucky enough to experience this, that these touches are almost unconscious, as natural as any other movement; and when they are taken away, the body starves.

These days, when I reached out, new James suffered me to touch him, waited patiently until I had finished, and then moved away.

Anyway, we made love. Afterward I sat up against my pillows.

"James. You know when you held Catherine?"

His eyes darted toward me in the gloom of the bedroom.

"Yes?"

A low, cautious yes, but good enough. No prevarication or protest at the subject. I'd half expected him to say, *Darling, you mustn't dwell on these things*.

"You didn't . . . see any bit of her?"

"She was wrapped in a shawl."

"It was a towel."

"Well, then, you remember how it was." He sat up too. "Can't you love her without knowing what she looked like?"

He sounded slightly irritated. As if I might have a defect, an incapability.

"My love for my daughter is not in question," I said softly. "I asked you about her appearance."

"Yvie, I'm sorry. I didn't mean it to come out like that." He put his arm around me. "The midwife didn't even want me to take her in to you. But I insisted that at least you should be able to hold her."

I sat a while longer reveling in the rare clasp of his arm, even when it began to weigh heavily on my shoulders. I didn't want to move in case he thought I was shrugging him off.

We sat there quietly until we got cold, and then we both lay down.

At Bridie's front door I knocked as usual with the dog-wolf knocker that had so daunted me the first time. Its fierceness, I had learned, was only a guard against strangers, and I was no longer a stranger. This time the door swung inward against the pressure of my hand. I pushed it all the way open. Bridie was in the kitchen: I could see her framed in the doorway of the hall, sitting with her hands resting on the table. She was wearing her pink rubber gloves.

"Yvette?" she said without moving her head. "Come in, won't you, dear."

I walked into the kitchen pulling off my coat, my hair wild from the wind. I had taken to bringing small gifts on my visits. This time it was a tub of cockles fresh that morning from my fishmonger, she and Pat being partial to shellfish, so I went straight to her refrigerator and put them in, saying, "The gale today! I nearly got blown off the causeway!" And it was only then, turning around, that I saw the young man on the other side of the kitchen table.

I gave a small gasp. I didn't know he'd be there this early. I needed time to talk to Bridie, make some uncertain prevaricating noises about the plan, tell her I didn't really know how to go about describing my imaginary vision. But here he was, leaning over a big piece of paper clipped to a board and making great strokes across it with a piece of charcoal, brushing away a lock of curly reddish-fair hair that was falling over his forehead.

"This is Philip," said Bridie calmly.

He looked about twenty years old. I should have realized he might be young. I knew Bridie and Pat had started their family late in life.

"How do you do, Philip." He didn't reply.

"Ah, you won't get much from him till he's finished," said Bridie.

"He doesn't mean to be rude. Sit down—here, on this side, with me. He won't be long, he's drawing fairly lively."

"Sorry," murmured Philip, working at his deep strokes that involved his whole arm—a thin arm I noticed, the elbow sharp under a checked shirt that I could see through a hole in his threadbare chestnut woolen jersey. "Be done in a jiffy . . ."

I sat down gingerly beside Bridie and listened to the schuss of the charcoal across the paper.

"We're not to mind him," said Bridie. "We can talk. It's all supposed to be natural, you see, as if he's caught me doing chores. That's why I'm in my rubber gloves. I am in essence a housewife, you see."

We had kept to such sad subjects, Bridie and I, up to now, that this peppery humor was a delightful discovery.

"Wait, Mother," said the artist, who had put down his charcoal on the table and was now swiftly smearing the paper with his fingers. "God, they're tremendous to draw."

"You were wearing these gloves when I met you," I said, grinning.

"So I was."

She was a good sitter. Probably used to it. Philip glanced up at her, a practical, appraising gaze, and down at his paper again. His face was thin, his jaw angular. Nose, quite beaky. Freckled. Green in his eyes like his mother, but more flecks of hazel. He moved his mouth as he drew, small tweaks of his thin lips. And his hair bounced away from his parting in curls. Much too long, I felt, but then longer hair was the rage now, among these young bohemian types. It actually brushed his collar.

Finally he stopped, frowned with his head on one side, and turned the board around. There was Bridie, her compact, comfortable body, her brisk short graying hair, her blouse collar buttoned straightly just above the neckline of her sweater. The gloves, however, were enormous, twice normal size, clutching each other, deep folds in the fingers and a dull wet rubbery sheen. They were funny, incongruous, but she was in on the joke. Her eyes were crinkled, perspicacious, knowing only too well what the artist was up to.

"Phil!" His mother gave a cry of appreciation. "It's marvelous, dear. Will you look at those gloves! Am I working on the trawlers?" She playfully buffed his arm.

I was captivated. "They've got a life of their own!"

"Not a Housewife?" Philip suggested, as a title.

"No," his mother said. *"The Housewife.* Let the viewer work it out." She pulled the gloves off and got to her feet. "Now then. I'm up to the shop for a couple of ounces of tea and a few odds and ends."

In an instant, or so it seemed to me, she was opening the front door with her coat on and her basket in her hand. I didn't want her to go at all. But the door closed on her, and then it was just me and Philip, sitting opposite each other or nearly, and my heart was skipping about in trepidation.

"Mrs. Acton, please accept my condolences for your baby girl. Ma told me what happened, of course. I wasn't born when my parents had Gerard, but I know they suffered, and I'm sorry you did too."

I had not expected such a properly expressed, dignified speech of sympathy from this gangling, untidy young man, and it moved me.

"That's very kind of you, Philip." I tried to gather my thoughts. "Now, the problem with the drawing is that we—my husband and I..."

I clutched my hands together on the tabletop. I wished Bridie was here.

"You and your husband...," he prompted.

"We each held her, him first and then me. But she was swathed in a towel." I liked using the word *swathed,* which I had recently learned.

The poetry of it gave me a sense of control over the situation. "I thought my husband might have remembered something since, caught some glimpses before I held her, but he hadn't. So neither of us really saw her. We couldn't even really make out her face. So I don't know how you can go about making a drawing of her."

He nodded to himself and said nothing. Which was good.

"I'm sorry too," I added, "that you had a brother you never knew."

"Not many people say that. Thank you." He picked up a pencil that was lying on the table, twirled it in his fingers. "What was her name, your daughter?"

"Catherine. She's the saint of the city of Alexandria, where I come from."

He clipped another piece of paper to his board. His fingers were very long, the knuckles big. I had a feeling when he stood up that he would be tall.

"Cat*rine*," he echoed uncertainly. It was obvious he didn't speak French.

"*Cath*-rin." I pronounced it the English way this time. "I imagine she might look like me. Although more babyish, of course, and with a snub nose."

Snub, another word recently acquired.

Eyes lowered, Philip was making tiny scuffing strokes with his pencil. "Tell me more, if you can, Mrs. Acton."

"Please call me Yvette."

"Yvette."

I told him about my vision of a suspended baby with the radiating hair. His eyes lit up. "*That's* more like it," he exclaimed, and with great alacrity began to make a variety of swirling and slanting strokes on the paper. I sat silently watching. He was rendering my dead child on the page and yet he exuded this joyful, organic energy. It stabbed my heart.

The child he drew was lighter than air, her body in an angel's robe, arms spread out and feet together. Her face, a sun with dark rays. Her eyes and mouth mine, her expression solemn. Her fingers and toes individually and carefully drawn. "I have probably given her Gerard's fingers and toes," Philip said. "I hope you don't mind."

"I don't mind at all."

"It's you, really, this picture," he said. "I mean, your love for her."

"Yes."

But I was not sure. He had captured my vision, but this small stately suspended girl didn't feel like her, or me, or my love for her. But Philip couldn't have done any more.

The front door rattled open and Bridie appeared. "I've bought a Swiss roll," she announced. "Philip, I hope you've got time for some tea?"

Philip looked at his watch. "I'd better go. I must get up to the school by eleven. I'm putting new panes into a greenhouse," he told me.

Bridie said, "No, you'll both have tea with me. Yvette can run you up to the school afterward. It'll only take five minutes. You don't mind, do you, dear?"

"No, of course not."

We showed her the picture and she cried out, "Look, an angel!" And she put her arm around me without saying anything more. Perhaps she sensed my disappointment.

While we drank our tea, Philip produced a sketchbook and started drawing the teapot. I thought we'd have to be quiet again but Bridie said no, only when he was embarked on a big drawing, a portrait. "Not while he's idly sketching. If that was true, I'd never get a word out."

"I do nothing idly, mother."

"I know." She smiled. "I just wish—"

"She just wishes I was making a bit of money by now."

"You weren't meant to come out of it poor!" Bridie turned to me. "That art school. Like a palace, and those clever, gifted professors teaching him for nothing, the child of a couple like us, a bus driver and a—"

"Housewife," Philip groaned. "I *know*."

"I'm serious, my dear. That huge chance you were given, and now we want to see you prosper!"

"In a minute," he tells me, "she's going to say how my father went to school on a donkey. And he was *lucky* to do so. So as not to wear out his *boots from walking*. What happened to the donkey while he was at school, I wonder? Was he tethered outside?"

I remembered a trip to Rosetta, seeing two boys riding a donkey along the dusty paths by the irrigation channels of the countryside beyond the town. The donkey's iron hooves stirring up the dust, its tripping indefatigable trot. The two children jolted along in and out of the shadow of date palms, one dressed for school, his face washed and hair combed, the other small, tousle-haired, tunicked, barefoot.

"He might have taken a little brother or sister along, to ride it back. That donkey would have work to do during the day."

"She's right," said Bridie.

"Oh, of course," Philip said. "I mean, for you, being from Egypt, it would be an everyday occurrence . . ."

"Oh, yes."

"I didn't mean to imply there's anything *wrong* with traveling that way. Far from it. I should imagine you all just . . ."

"Hop on a donkey," I said, "without giving it a second thought. Absolutely."

He cleared his throat, drew for a bit, while his forehead turned slightly pink. Then he scratched his head. "I'm an ignorant cuss, aren't I," he said finally.

"I confess, Philip. I went to school by tram."

"Oh, you wicked woman." He sat back, eyes gleaming, marvelously entertained. "To make fun of a simple artist who knows nothing about foreign lands, whose education has been all paint and perspective and figure drawing."

When I had finished laughing at his expense I said, "Tell me about these things, then. How did you start out?"

"Drawing casts in the Ashmolean Museum in Oxford. Greek and Roman statues, torsos, busts. The Slade—my art school—was evacuated to Oxford during the war, you see, and it was years before they returned to London. I was in my second year by the time we got back to Holborn. And there we drew the male nude for a year and a half. The male nude, the male nude, nothing but the—"

"Enough of that, Phil," Bridie said. "It's a respectable girl we've got here, a vicar's wife. She doesn't want to hear about men in the nip."

I stared. "In the *nip*?"

"Irish for naked." Philip sighed. "Oh, dear. That sounds worse. I'm sure Ma thinks *naked* is even ruder than *nude*. Don't you, Ma?"

"I refuse to be drawn further into the subject," said his mother, folding her hands.

When the time came for him to leave, we got into my car. He was so lanky, his knees came high up in the passenger seat. His trousers were baggy on him, a big leather belt holding them up. His sweater hung loose from his shoulders. I'm making his thinness sound unusual: I don't mean to. A lot of men were thin in those days. Women too, come to that. But the loose clothes emphasized it, perhaps. Gave him a famished look.

He guided me along the narrow lanes of the village. "Will I ever find my way back to the main road?" I wondered.

"Where do you live?"

"Alver Shore."

He whistled through his teeth. "Oh, no, no, no. I can't direct you to Alver Shore. Turn right here, please."

"Why not?" I did as he said, finding myself on a tree-shaded drive that was none too well paved.

"You're far too beautiful and chic to live there. Get your vicar man to find another church. The one here in the village, for example. Then I could come down from London and paint you every weekend. Clothed, obviously. I've got no experience with the female form. Trained as I am in depicting only—"

"Men in the *nip*!"

The drive opened out into the forecourt of a huge brick house. I came to a halt. A man in a broad-brimmed hat was loading sheets of glass onto a handcart with immense care.

"Oh, Mr. Kennet's already started. Listen, Yvette. Could you sit for me at Ma and Pa's? So I can do a portrait? Ma won't mind in the least. Please say you'll do it."

"How old are you?" I asked him.

"Twenty-two. Why?"

Only five years younger than me, but because of those five years he had fought no battles, he mourned no one, he had nothing to atone for. He was freshly made for this new world we lived in. The gap between us made me dizzy.

"Look," he said, when I didn't reply. "I must get puttying. But please think about it. I don't need paying. I'm desperate for subjects."

"I don't know . . ." I shifted my hands on the wheel. "I mean, yes, I would like to. At least, I think so."

He nodded, smiling with his lips closed. They curved up at the corners. "You're allowed to think about it. You think a lot about everything."

"I have a lot to think about."

"I know."

He said it lightly, already turning his head, opening the car door, so that if I wanted to, I could pretend I hadn't heard him.

"Thank you—" I blurted as he got out, and he waved his hand. I watched him hurry toward the man in the hat, shrugging his shoulders, tilting his head at the car, no doubt saying, *I got a lift, but honestly, she went so slowly . . .*

"Ha!" I cried, at the cheek of him, and turned the car with a skid of tires on the gravel, and shot off down the drive, jinking past a pothole or two, very pleased by their astonished faces in the rearview mirror. I found the main road and drove at a clip all the way back, fifty miles an hour and hang the fuel. When I got to Alver Shore I parked on the seafront and picked my way down over the pebble beach. The winter sun was setting. The sun was often so weak at this time of year, I used to wonder how it managed to trudge on westward over the ocean. But today it was strong enough to light the whole of America.

FIFTEEN

⚜

S he eats meat, doesn't she? Your friend?"

Tom's feeding himself porridge as he talks, using the largest spoon in the house.

"I expect so," I reply, bewildered. "Why?"

"I'll need to know what to cook." This comes out indistinctly between one enormous mouthful and the next.

"It's just a drink, Tom. She's not staying for supper."

Tom puts down his bowl and spoon. "Dad, of course we invite her to supper. You expect her to trek out to this awful barn for a packet of pork scratchings? That's inhumane."

"I'd hardly offer her pork scratchings!"

"What, then?"

"I've got some peanuts and crisps."

"He's got some peanuts and crisps," Tom intones, lifting his eyes to the ceiling.

He's right, of course. I wonder if I'm getting used to the awfulness of this place. Blakemore's study being a case in point: I should have done it before the party, but now that motivation is gone. I only go in there to fetch floor coverings for Bailey, and that increasingly seldom as Bailey becomes more continent.

"Oh, yes. She had a sausage roll at the party."

"Aha. Fairly definitive evidence of meat eating." He starts to scoop up the last of his porridge. "Keep going. I want all the details. Name, looks, the lot."

"Really, Tom, you are brutal."

"It's the only way, with you. It's like dealing with a—who are those monks who never talk?"

"Trappists." I relent. "She's called Ellen Parr. She's a widow, and she's lived in Upton all her life. Her late husband—I mean, she and her late husband—used to run the water mill on the edge of the village. She's tall, with blond hair and blue eyes."

"I suppose you met her at some wild church-related bun-fight?"

"No, actually. She's not a churchgoer. She helped me sandbag some elderly people's doorways during the flood. She was in waders, being a miller, and very competent."

"Age?"

"Astonishingly, I haven't asked her."

"You must have some idea."

"Late forties? Early fifties, perhaps. Really Tom, I've got no . . . I've got no designs."

His grin shows nearly all his teeth. "You meet a tall, single, golden-haired woman in thigh-boots, and you don't have designs. You must be off your nut."

"I doubt she'll consider me for a minute." I bring the tea mugs to the sink. "Not only does she not go to church, she doesn't believe in God at all."

Tom starts the washing up. "Does that bother you?"

"I'm saying, it'll bother *her*."

"But she said yes to your invitation." There's a pause while he scrubs the porridge pan. When he speaks again it is very steadily, his gaze directed firmly down at the washing-up bowl. "I'm glad she's tall and English-looking. No chance of being spooked. You know, when she turns up on the doorstep."

He flicks me a glance, his eyes fiery.

"Oh, Tom."

I want to embrace him but he's attacking the porridge pan again, so I must hug his back. Which he lets me do.

Redwood House is lit up yellow and welcoming when I arrive. Terry Shaw is in the dayroom. "I'm glad you're here, I was going to ring you," she says. "It's Bridget. She's desperate to see you."

"Bridget?"

"Bridget Moore." Her face is tight with anxiety. "I can't work out what the matter is, and neither can Philip. We've only just realized it's *you* she wants. It's not good for her, to get so het up. She's stopped eating. I know you have so many calls on your time . . ."

"Terry, this is my job," I tell her. "I can't stay all day, admittedly, but long enough."

Her face brightens in relief. "I'm so glad you said that. Only Mr. Blakemore was always so impatient . . ."

Bridget Moore is sitting in a large armchair. She's become visibly frailer in the week that's elapsed since the party, her wrists poking bonily from the sleeves of her cardigan, her skin papery.

"Lost your appetite, have you, Mrs. Moore?"

I expect her, as before, to say yes in reply to my remark, imbuing the word with her chosen meaning. But instead I'm jolted by her deep dark glare. Is it anger? No, urgency. She opens her mouth and her voice rattles out like water over pebbles. I lean forward, straining all my powers of comprehension but I can't distinguish any consonants let alone intelligible words.

"Bridie, do try and calm down," pleads Terry.

"Bridie, that's a nickname from Ireland," I remark. "Are you Irish, Mrs. Moore?"

"Yes," says Bridie, with half a grudging smile.

"Have you ever played the yes-no game?"

She lifts one shoulder. *I care little for games.*

"Suppose we try it? If your answer is yes, say yes. If it's no, make a sign. What sign do you want to make?"

She lifts her good hand and lets it fall in a gentle slap onto her knee.

"Okay. Now, may I call you Bridie?"

"Yes."

"And do you want to play the yes-no game?"

She wags her head. This time the yes is more conditional.

I glance up at Terry and nod. With a murmur, she leaves us.

"Let's start," I say to Bridie Moore. "The thing you want to tell me. Is it about a person?"

"Yes."

"Is the person here in Upton?"

A long pause before she simultaneously says, "Yes," and slaps her knee.

"Yes and no?"

She points at me and then to a space beside me, and then she touches her chest. And says, "Yes."

I'm at a loss. "I'm sorry, Mrs. Moore, I'm very slow on the uptake."

She snorts. *Telling me.*

Then she makes a sort of rubbing-out motion in the air. I recognize it instantly as the gesture people make when playing charades. *Forget that*, it means. *I'm trying another tack.* This time she drags a pointing finger across her lap.

"A line?"

A reproving slap, this time, and a hiss. *Hold your horses.* She starts again.

The finger repeats the line, comes to a halt. I keep my mouth shut. Then it tracks backward toward her body, then sideways, and then, with a great deal of wavering, back to the start of the first line. She repeats the whole operation, this time trying to follow the tartan pattern on her skirt, as an aid to make all four sides equal.

"A square?"

A bold, triumphant, "Yes!"

She makes it once again, to ingrain it in my mind. After all, I *am* slow on the uptake. Then she pats the square, as if to say: *There it is.* She's much calmer now, looking down at her creation with a certain amount of satisfaction.

"Hello, Mr. Acton."

Philip has arrived bearing a tea tray. He sets it down and takes a seat next to his mother before offering her a child's cup, the kind with a plastic lid and a teat, supporting her hand as she brings it to her mouth. She drinks eagerly.

"Your mother's doing my brain a great deal of good, Philip," I say. "Making it work so hard." I address his mother again. "So there is someone beside me, and something to do with my chest. And now there's a square."

"A square?" Philip frowns.

"Your mother drew it for me."

Mrs. Moore's stare tells me this is no time to chat. She hasn't finished. I watch her lever her good hand to her mouth, purse her lips and expel a puff of air. Enough air, it seems, to blow her hand away, because it falls down onto her lap. She repeats the gesture, raising her hand to her mouth: "Pfff," she goes, as her hand flies down.

"Pfff," I say. "Is that a word?"

A ridiculous idea, upsettingly wrong. She swings her head from side to side and flaps her good arm at her son. "Oh, oh," she says.

"I'm sorry I'm so hopeless, Bridie."

She groans again, this time with an almighty glare at Philip.

"Oh, Mum." He sighs. "You'd feel so much better if you had some-thing to eat."

I pour out two cups of tea. We all drink in various kinds of silence—mine remorseful, Bridie's frankly grumpy. Philip's silence is tense, his eyes shifting around the room.

"For a while, when I was a young man, I had no appetite at all," I tell Bridie after a while. "People put food in front of me, and I couldn't imagine getting it inside me, there was so much. It was like asking me to eat a mountain."

She gives me a quizzing glance.

"My strategy was to concentrate on the foothills. Take it from the edge of the plate. It was much easier when I had a tiny helping on a saucer, like this one." I glance at Philip for confirmation of this idea, and he nods. "And perhaps a teaspoon." I put both items on the table. "Do you think you could tackle a snack this size?"

I watch her considering the idea. Half of her forehead frowns. Is it curiosity?

"I'll think about everything you've told me," I continue, "and I'll come back, let me see, tomorrow afternoon, if that would suit you. And we can talk again."

She leans her head back against the chair, emitting a single ex-hausted, "Yes."

I leave her with her son and rejoin Terry Shaw, who hands me this week's *Hampshire Chronicle* and directs me to read out the prices for animal fodder to a skeletal lady in a hairnet and dark glasses. "Mildred Chant farmed sheep on her own for fifty years," Mrs. Shaw tells me, nodding toward the lady. "Until she got too blind to see them at dusk."

"I know some girls called Chant," I say. "They come to Bible study."

"You're joking." Terry is highly amused. "The Chant sisters?"

"They don't stay long," I say with a grin.

Miss Chant tuts when I read out the price of hay. "You'd think it was spun gold," she booms from her tiny, hollow chest. She deplores the way Beacon Hill has been plowed halfway up its lovely side. "They did it in the war, you know, when we needed the arable. But they never put it back to grass. Spoils the look of the hill."

I say goodbye and she thanks me absentmindedly, perhaps still musing on the view she can now see only in her mind's eye.

Philip Moore follows me as I make my way down the corridor toward the front door. I notice how pale he looks, his mouth open but unspeaking.

"How are you, Philip?"

"Fine. Worried about Mum, that's all."

He speaks tonelessly, his shoulders slumped. We reach the entrance to the building and I pull open the heavy door. He gathers himself. "Thank you for encouraging her to eat, James. How come you couldn't, by the way? Eat, I mean."

"I was a POW in Germany. We were permanently hungry. It was quite overwhelming. In one of the compounds the men mobbed the soup cauldron, so the sergeant turned it over in front of them. Bang went their supper, all across the floor."

Philip winced. "I've heard the guards could be terribly savage."

"No, he was their own sergeant. A British airman. He had to do it, you see, to keep them in line henceforward. Anyway, I used to imagine all the enormous meals I'd have when it was all over—we all did. But when I went back to Alexandria straight after the war, I literally couldn't stomach a proper plateful. So my wife's mother made me little dishes to nibble at in my own time. She was very kind."

He looks utterly blank, as if a wash of gray has passed over his face. "I didn't know that," he says slowly.

"There's no reason why you should."

He blinks a few times, nods.

"I'll see you soon," I say, stepping out into the air.

Without a word he closes the door.

When I get home I find Tom upstairs. He has brought the table and chair from his room out onto the landing, placed the chair on the table, and is now standing on the chair directly underneath the hatch to the attic.

"What on earth's going on?"

"The roof's been creaking."

I listen.

"I can't hear anything."

"Obviously it's not doing it right *now*." He pushes up the hatch, and the chair teeters on the table.

I make a grab for the chair legs. "You could have fetched the attic ladder."

"No way. I'm not going up on that roof again." Grunting, he hauls himself into the attic. "Can't see anything wrong," he reports, his voice muffled. Then comes a shifting, bumping sound. "I'm bringing these boxes out. The ones with all your papers in. Everything will get ruined up here."

"I'm sure they'll be fine."

"Better safe than sorry."

So we manhandle several dirty, dusty boxes out of the attic and onto the landing, and he scrambles down. His face is sweaty, drawn, his eyes flat. I've seen this look many times in my life. It's that of a young man who has just been thoroughly frightened.

"That creak must have been pretty impressive, Tom."

"There were two separate creaks. They both went, UH-UH-UH. Really loud. Like in a Hammer horror. I thought the house was going to fall down."

"Well, if it does, the creaks will warn us. Hopefully. Do you think they'll be loud enough to wake us up?"

"Ah, seriously, Dad."

"I'll report them to Stan Rail. He gave me his business card."

Stan, however, is unavailable. Tom, after a restorative cheese sandwich, seems to be putting the episode from his mind. He does some dinner preparation while I plan confirmation classes with Clive Perry and catch up on my correspondence. Enticing smells issue from the kitchen, but when I go in there the room is empty, a pot simmering on the range.

I find Tom upstairs, lying on his bed. One of the boxes from the attic is on the floor, its contents scattered about, among which is a pile of notebooks bound in blue paper. I pick one up. The label on the front reads *Yvette Haddad. La Géographie.* "These are Mum's homework books," I tell Tom, "from her last year at the Lycée. She won a prize, you know."

She showed them to me, rather embarrassed, as she was packing in Alexandria. I remember turning the pages, very moved both by the exquisite results of her labor and by her pride in her work.

"I'm into the Bombardment of Alexandria," Tom murmurs.

So he is. I hadn't noticed, but he's got *L'Histoire* open in his hands.

"This was in 1882," he continues. "Brits and French propping up the regime against the locals, surprise." He abandons his reading and gets up off the bed. "Time to take Bailey for a quick stroll."

I look at my watch. It's already a quarter to seven. "Blast, I didn't put the wine in the fridge."

"Don't worry, I did." He looks at my face, and grins. *"Courage, mon vieux."*

His accent is impeccable. So it should be. He's been taught by two francophone women who love him.

I shave, follow it with aftershave. The smell is repellent—polecat. Can aftershave go off? I wash it from my face, inadvertently drenching my shirt collar. While I'm changing my shirt I hear voices in the hall. Tom, and Ellen. They must have met in the lane and come back together. Hastily I button my dry shirt and pull on a sweater. Thanks to Tom's kind gift, all the sweaters in my drawer now smell faintly of hashish. I catch sight of myself in the mirror: an unkempt fellow with the expression of a startled burglar stares back. "Get a grip, Acton," I murmur, brushing my hair.

I come downstairs to an unimaginable wonder. Ellen is inside my house, not only here but clearly happy to be here, chatting to my son and bearing gifts in the form of a multicolored bunch of dahlias from her garden and a large Kilner jar. "Nothing more exciting than stewed apple, I'm afraid," she says. "Lucy and I went mad this year. We had a bumper crop and couldn't bear to waste it. So nobody escapes!"

Her cheeks have taken color from the walk, and she smells of fresh air.

"Brilliant!" Tom says. "I'll make some apple turnovers for pud." He takes the jar and the flowers into the kitchen.

She accepts the offer of white wine and I show her into the sitting room. When I return with two glasses of Chablis, she's seated on the sofa with Bailey curled in her lap. "How he's grown." She looks up. "I saw him when he was at the kennels, a tiny grub of a creature. I fed him from a little bottle."

I set her glass on the coffee table in front of her and sit down in the rhino-like leather armchair. "He was on rusks by the time he came here," I tell her. "When Lucy foisted him on me."

"She's quite ruthless," Ellen agrees. "But she'll be so pleased with his progress." She leans forward for her glass. "To your good health, James."

"And yours."

For the first time I look at her properly. She's in a long dress of some soft woolly material, the color a deep blue. Flat leather boots, elegant yet suitable for the lanes. Her hair is put up as usual but this time cunningly braided in on itself somehow, to make a fascinatingly complicated woven bun high on the back of her head. The overall effect is both feminine and disciplined. She might be a member of some exclusive order of women—not religious, not necessarily spiritual at all, but dedicated all the same to a selfless cause. Rescuing men, perhaps. Seeking out the terrible knots we get ourselves into and untying them, gently and practically, without condescension. I wonder what I must look like to her, in my clean but aged clothes, against my backdrop of tumbledown furniture. Should I apologize for the state of the place? I'm pretty sure, from the way she's bending her head to stroke Bailey, that she's taking care not to show she's noticed it. I break the silence.

"Have you got a dog, Ellen?"

She shakes her head. "Dogs can't help it, but they do startle the birds. And when I'm walking I like to see yellowhammers in the hedgerows. And the flocks of plovers in the fields under Beacon Hill, in the winter. You walk by and they lift and fall in a wave." She mimics the wave with her hand. "If I'm out with Althea Brock and her blessed Stuart, they scatter entirely."

I remember my encounter with Stuart outside Althea Brock's house. How long ago it seems, that day when Ellen came upon me in the shrubbery. Shall I tell her? No, not now. Not while she's looking at me like this, her face friendly and open, her eyes full of the lively, seeking interest that I remember from the party.

"Your son has learned to cook, it seems!" she says next.

"Luckily for us. Although supper may feature chickpeas."

She ponders. "I don't believe I've eaten chickpeas. Though I've never met an ingredient I didn't like."

"They're from the health food shop in Waltham."

"I haven't been in there." She sounds rueful. "How unadventurous of me."

I tell her about the creaking roof, and Stan Rail's insistence on giving me his card. "Maybe he knows something I don't."

"I've never trusted this house, James. Do talk to him, and be careful." She puts Bailey down on the floor. "When I was an assistant at the village school I gave lessons to Stan Rail. And his brother Ernest. Ernest was a scrap of a child. Clever. I remember trying to explain algebra. If $2a$ equals 10, what is a?" She clasps her knees, "My example featured twin lambs, together weighing ten pounds. What then does a single lamb weigh? Only Ernest got it. He's a shipping accountant now, lives in Alver Shore. It's a place down on the coast . . ."

"I know Alver Shore. It was my first parish, in 1946."

"Good heavens. And there was I thinking you were a stranger from afar! Have you been back?"

"No . . . no, it hasn't even occurred to me."

I remember what I said to Frobisher. *A far cry.*

"Too long ago, perhaps."

"Yes."

"It still has that brutal seawall, which I rather like. Anyway, Stan's just as sharp as Ernest now when it comes to figures. Doing very well for himself by all accounts!"

I look at her graceful interlaced fingers. The only ring is on her right hand, a dark blue stone set in silver.

"Matilda Rail is their mother, of course."

"Yes."

"I met her on the day of the flood, when we sandbagged Church Walk. She told me about your school assistant post."

"So she saw us from her window." Ellen fails to smother a grin. "I bet she called me Calvert."

"Ha. Yes, she did."

"Matilda, goodness. She had so many children that her youngest was still at school during the war. Long after my days as teaching assistant."

"Yes," I say. "Bobby."

Something has tightened in her face. She looks younger, but not happier.

"So she told you about Pamela, then. The girl I had in the war."

"Yes."

I shouldn't have mentioned Bobby. I'm about to apologize when she starts talking, turning away from me to look out of the window where darkness has fallen.

"Pamela and Bobby used to draw hopscotches in the road with lumps of chalk they brought back from the railway embankment. Precious few cars back then. They spent hours and hours hopscotching. Sometimes they stole away up the hill to the anti-aircraft battery. This was toward the end of the war, when there was nothing left of the battery but barbed wire, but all the same it was expressly forbidden . . ." She looks back at me. "I should have expected someone to come for her in the end."

It is easy, in the immense quiet that seems to have fallen in this room, to imagine the streets of Upton in wartime. A child playing, beloved, and then gone.

"Who came?"

"Her father. He was wounded at sea. He found Pamela with us and took her to his sister in Ireland."

She says *Ireland* with great finality, as if it were some distant alien land, barred by mountains and violent seas.

"You didn't keep in touch?"

She shakes her head. "This sister, who Pamela went to live with— she thought it best if we cut off all contact. Gave her a new start in life. And her father agreed. Even Selwyn could see why they did it. But nobody asked Pamela."

"And nobody asked you."

"I didn't count. I really didn't. Only Pamela mattered."

I am silenced by this awesome cruelty.

"Yes, I know," she says, catching my expression. "But things were different then. It was such a long time ago. I don't suppose Matilda even remembered her name."

I remember Matilda's wonderings, her distant, wrinkled little eyes. *Where'd she go, that child? What was she called?*

"It's ready!" Tom calls from next door.

I study my clasped hands, clear my throat.

"I would wager," I say slowly, "that the people who care about you, William, and Althea, and Lucy, remember Pamela. I bet they haven't forgotten a thing. Her looks, her games. Her favorite foods."

"And her extremely annoying habits." Ellen laughs loudly, her eyes suddenly wet. "You're right. Of course they remember her." She gazes at me. "I like hearing you say *Pamela*. That's all I need, I realize. For people to say her—"

"Dad, for goodness' sake," calls Tom from the kitchen. "Come and let me feed your guest!"

SIXTEEN

A ll the rooms are equally awful," Tom explains as we sit down to eat in the kitchen. "But this one is slightly warmer. Anyway, you're dressed for the vicarage, Ellen."

The range, bolstered up with coal, is doing its best. Ellen glances down at her warm dress. "Don't worry, I've been here before."

Tom smiles and takes the lid off the pot in the middle of the table, liberating a smell so delicious that I could be satisfied with it alone.

"Mr. Blakemore always held a tea party with carols to mark the beginning of Advent," Ellen continues. "We all vied with each other to hand around the mince pies. Treading on each other's feet, jabbing each other in the ribs. Lucy had the sharpest elbows, so she usually won."

"Was it a great honor?" I ask.

Ellen shakes her head, highly amused. "It was so we could sneak a few into our pockets." She turns to Tom. "This dish is lovely, Tom."

Chunks of sausage are mixed in with the chickpeas. The result is delicious. "I think you'd better start sending me recipes," I tell him.

"Left to himself," Tom tells Ellen, "he will buy tinned potatoes."

I let them both decry this awful habit. A terrible waste of money (Tom). Not even nice potatoes, always very small (Ellen). Can't he manage to peel a potato? (Tom). Horrid texture, and quite tasteless (Ellen). They continue in this vein for quite some time.

Watching and listening to them I feel a sudden, intense happiness.

"I could take the rest to Mrs. Moore," I say, when we've finished both the main course and the apple turnovers (with fresh custard, of course) that Tom has made. "She won't eat, or can't bring herself to, and this is so tasty. Do you know Bridie Moore, Ellen?"

I am relaxed. We all are. A bare half inch of wine remains in the bottle.

"I certainly do know Bridie, and I feel guilty about not visiting her." She sighs. "She used to make soda bread for the Women's Institute. I like her a great deal. She's always taken the time to listen to people properly."

"I went to see her this afternoon. She's got some kind of message for me, something I must know. Philip can't imagine what it might be, and neither can Terry Shaw." I shrug helplessly. "Bridget was very inventive, with noises and gestures and so on, but I was too much of a duffer to work it out."

"You could show us," says Tom, bringing coffee pot and cups to the table.

"Show you?"

"What she did. The movements. And the sounds."

"That's a good idea." I reflect for a moment. "The first part went like this. She was trying to describe a particular person." I look at Tom, and then point at a space beside him before bringing my hand to my chest. He looks in the direction I'm pointing.

"Someone far away?" he queries.

I pour the coffee. "No, I think it was closer than that."

"Someone beside you," Ellen says.

"Connected in some way to his chest," says Tom to Ellen.

"His *heart*," says Ellen to Tom.

"Before that, when I asked her if the person was in Upton, she said yes and no at the same time. It was obvious I didn't understand at all, so she started again." I pass the milk jug and sugar bowl. "Okay. Now what's this?"

I draw a square on the table.

"A square," they both say.

"And this?" I make the final gesture, putting my fingertips to my lips and then puffing them away so that my hand flies down onto the table.

Ellen sips her coffee, pondering. Tom says, "Do it again."

I repeat the movement.

"Perhaps those are words," Ellen says, "falling from her mouth. Perhaps she's saying, *I can't talk.*"

"A smoker," suggests Tom. "Trying to give up. Taking one puff and throwing it away. There's the cigarette packet on the table."

"Where?"

"The square," Ellen and Tom reply in unison. "Look, it's still there, where you drew it," Ellen adds.

"Did she smoke?" Tom asks. "Perhaps she's dying for one."

"No, wait. It's not a cigarette packet," Ellen says to him. "That would be oblong."

"True," I agree. "Bridget was quite particular about it being a square."

The conversation revolves around square things for a moment or two—picture, house, window, field, two apple turnovers back-to-back—before Ellen turns to Tom. She learns about Florence, her cleverness and beauty, about the University of East Anglia, and about the emission of carbon dioxide into the atmosphere. "The coal in that range was laid down in the Jurassic era," Tom is telling her when I leave the table to take Bailey out for his evening stroll. "We send it up the chimney and whoosh, we add Jurassic carbon dioxide to our present-day atmosphere. Carbon dioxide traps heat, which is good, otherwise we'd all be in the deep freeze. But with more and more CO_2 up there from all the coal and oil, our nice warm blanket is going to get way too hot. We're already at 330 parts per million, and . . ."

There doesn't seem to be much sign of a heated atmosphere to-night. The sky is low, the air chilly, restless. I glance toward the kitchen and see Tom's hand gesticulating, a pointed finger going around and around as he draws an unending circle. Then he makes a square and I hear them both laugh.

Of Ellen I can see only the side of her face. Her cheek, that is, and a portion of her neck visible through the slit in her high collar.

I imagine walking with her in mild dry winter sunshine, some-where high. Returning at the day's end, still talking, perhaps more freely in the twilight.

"How about a tramp to Beacon Hill?" I suggest as I help her into her coat. "While this weather holds? No Bailey," I add, for the sake of the birds.

"It would be *much* too far for him," says Tom admonishingly.

We agree on the day after tomorrow. "Thank you, both," she says. "I feel quite restored."

Her eyes are bright. She kisses us in turn, without any awkward-ness. Her lips on my cheek are warm, fleeting. And then she's gone, striding out to the road, the beam of her torch lighting the way ahead of her.

Neither Tom nor I say a word as we clear up. As he passes me a glass or a dish to wash, I catch his eye, but I can't read his expression. When it's all done, and I'm wiping the table, he clears his throat.

"Well. She listened to every word of my CO_2 lecture. That's never happened before."

I carry on cleaning the table.

"She might just be crazy about atmospheric chemistry, of course," he continues.

"In Upton and Barrow End," I say, still wiping, "we speak of little else."

He makes a sort of gurgling sound and leaves the room.

The sky is low, heavy, thundery. Ellen is holding a child against her hip, dancing around and around. The child's small cardiganed arms stick out sideways, her chubby chin is lowered. Her shoes are brown. Girls' shoes, covering the toes only, with a strap at the ankle. Between toes and strap the top of her plump little foot, covered in white lacy sock, bulges slightly. Ellen turns back toward me but it's Yvette, singing, bouncing the child who has got smaller, who is now two, three. The child's hair has gone curly and dark. I reach out. I want to take hold of this little foot and kiss the bulging part.

All I need is for people to—

What are you saying? I can't hear you above the thunder.

Yvette shakes her head and bears the child away. The back of the small dark curly head recedes, the air rumbles. Yvette's hurrying now, she must take her in before the rain falls.

All I need is for you to say her name.

"Dad? Wake up! Dad?"

The rumble bursts out of my dream. I leap out of bed. A worried

Tom is just outside my bedroom door, looking up at the hatch to the loft. The noise is much louder on the landing. Tom grabs my arm just as a series of gigantic, tumbling bangs shakes the house. We both shout with fright and leap into my bedroom, where we wait, our eyes fixed on the ceiling, until the bangs stop.

Tom is clutching my arm. "Holy shit, the roof's come down."

"So much for the warning creaks." I head out across the landing to his room.

"What are you doing?"

"Getting your table and chair." I drag the table out onto the landing.

"Dad, that's crazy."

"I can't not look."

I fetch the chair and position it on the table before climbing up. The hatch won't budge at first. It must be weighed down with bits of roof. I bend forward to get the back of my head and my shoulders against it. Heavy things slide off as I push the hatch upward. "That's very bad for your neck," says Tom.

"I don't care."

I heave myself into the attic. Dust hangs thick in the air. A hole has appeared in the side of the gable, a snaggletoothed rent five yards by two and roughly the shape of a whale. It starts about halfway along the roof and almost reaches the gable end. On the floor beneath it lies a long mound of broken timber and tile. The upper rafters and the ridgepole seem to be intact. I call back down to Tom.

"The top of the roof's okay. The hole is in the side. Can you fetch me my penknife? It's on the chest of drawers in my room."

"No, I bloody can't. You need to come down, Dad, you're freaking me out. Can't you see it's dangerous?"

"Only comparatively."

"Fetch your own penknife. I'm going to make breakfast. When you've stopped being a berk, you can come and join me."

He stomps off. I clamber down, fetch my own penknife, and heave myself back up again. Crawling forward on forearms and knees—I want to spread my weight—I reach the pile of debris and drag out a broken rafter. The mound slides and topples. Even this minor collapse makes the most tremendous din.

My blade goes into the wood like butter. I pick up a second fragment. The surface feels strangely thready. When I hold it up to the light from the hole, I see that the wood is laced with white tendrils.

The only timbers I checked were those we uncovered when we were out on the roof. I should have come up here first. Examined every single batten and rafter and beam from the inside. Through the hole, the clouds sail indifferently by.

"Bloody shambles," I whisper.

By the time I get clean and respectable, Tom has fried four eggs and made toast. He dishes up two plates and hands me a mug of milky instant coffee.

"I'm sorry about earlier, Tom. You're right, I shouldn't have gone up there."

"Oh, why not?" he says with his mouth full. "After all, it was *only comparatively* dangerous. Don't come running to me when you've *only comparatively* broken your neck."

"I wouldn't be able to, would I."

He growls with exasperation. I tuck into my eggs.

Stan Rail is still unavailable. I ring Frobisher, who is also absent, but tell his secretary about these unexpected alterations to the architecture of Upton Vicarage. Tom spends the morning sitting by the range with Bailey on his lap, thereby availing himself of the only two sources of heat in the house. A further fruitless call to Stan Rail makes me wonder if I should try someone else farther afield. I trust Stan, though, and want to give the work to him.

I have a terrible suspicion that my roof is full of dry rot.

In the late afternoon, after some steady hours at my typewriter, I track Tom down in his bedroom. He's sitting on the floor with Bailey, reading another of Yvette's notebooks. *La Géographie* this time.

"Have you seen her maps of the climates of Egypt?" I ask him. "Arid, semi-arid, and tropical? Wonderful drawings of plants and wild animals."

He's silent. There's a distance in his eyes that I've seen many times before, when he's sunk in deep thought.

"Did Mum ever mention someone called Sébastien?" he says suddenly.

"Doesn't ring a bell. Why?"

He says nothing.

"Tom?"

"Oh . . . I was looking at the photo albums a while back. You know, when you asked me about Mum wearing a scarf. I guess I wanted to sort out all those people."

The Haddad clan dressed properly even on the beach: grown-ups in suits or dresses, hats for both men and women, teenage boys sweltering in trousers and blazers. Crowds of people in each shot, with their names crammed in underneath the photograph. Tiny block capitals in white ink on the black page of the album, so close together that it's a job to tell who was who. *Maurice, Anatole, Alphonse.* There's bound to be a Sébastien somewhere among them.

"Probably one of the uncles, or the cousins. You haven't brought any of the albums, have you?"

"No."

He strokes the dog. His bare feet, I notice, are propped on a book entitled *Aims and Methods of Vegetation Ecology*.

I nod at the book. "Is the information going in through your heels?"

He looks up, brows raised. "All vegetation ecology is studied this way."

"Honestly, Tom."

"I'm surprised you didn't know."

"Anyway, I'm off to Redwood House," I say, smiling at him. "I promised Bridget Moore I'd see her again. I'll be back by suppertime."

He might be a teenager: we might be back in Fulbrook, in the vicarage there, in the warm burrow of our home. Him upstairs with a record playing, me setting off, not knowing exactly when I'll be back. It's happened enough times. A vicar's son, he's used to it.

I drop in at the church on my way to Mrs. Moore, going no farther than the noticeboard in the porch where I pin up an announcement about the special service on the last Sunday of Advent. I only have three tacks so I scavenge one from another message, redundant now, scrawled with my own handwriting. *Found in church: one silk headsquare. Please apply to the vicarage.* I shove this slip of paper into my pocket and set off for Redwood House.

One silk headsquare. I turn over the word in my mind as I drive. *Headsquare* sounds old-fashioned. People say *headscarf* much more often. Yvette had to learn to tie hers in the English fashion under her chin for warmth. She abjured any clothing that gave her an exotic or wealthy air. She needed plain English plumage, she said.

And that scarf was so brightly colored.

Suddenly, on this overcast afternoon, I remember the day of the photograph in the boat.

It was summer 1945, just after the war, and we were bobbing on the small choppy waves off Glymenopoulo beach. Célia, Peter, Yvette, and I in the sunshine and wind, the salty spray cool on our faces. And Yvette said . . .

Yvette said, *"Sha'ri zayy leefah,"* to her sister, untying her scarf from around her neck.

"Leefah?" I echoed, that being the only word I could make out.

Célia told me. "She said my hair is like a loofah. Rough and dry—"

Yvette laughed. "Oh, thank you, Célia." She let the bright-blue-and-orange silk flap on the breeze. I caught hold of it and with tender fingers retied it around her neck—the wrong way. "James, I was going to put it over my hair. And now you've made me into a Boy Scout. *Un scoot.*" She whipped it off again but the breeze was now too strong to tame either her hair or the scarf. She held it like a flag. At that moment my eye took a snapshot of her thin young face, her olive tan, her parted smiling lips and white teeth, the sun-warmed skin of her neck. She was so beautiful, you see, and so gracious to Peter, that I forgot all about what happened next.

Peter, with his one eye, was bad at judging depth. He dug the oar into the water, caught a crab, and sent the bow of the boat into the wind. Sparks streamed from the tip of his cigarette and—no!—too late, they flew onto the scarf and speckled it with burn holes. Peter, aghast, dashed the cigarette into the water. Yvette dabbed at the silk saying, "Darling Peter, it was an accident, it doesn't matter, look, I hardly ever wear it anyway." Folding up the ruined scarf, slipping it into her bag. Then she made a motion with her hand, a little scrub of the air, to obliterate the incident. "Peter, seriously. *Ma'alesh, tant pis, never mind!*"

Ma'alesh, tant pis, never mind. All meaning the same thing.

Mrs. Moore used that gesture yesterday. The wiping-out movement. Because I'd been slow on the uptake, she had to try another tack.

So she drew the square. And put her fingers to her mouth. *Pfff.* Like a smoker, Tom said. And then her hand flew down, onto the square. As I drive I picture her doing it again. Smoking her cigarette in mime. Letting imaginary sparks fly down onto the headsquare.

The car is rolling to a halt, and I have no idea why. Some moments later I realize it's because I've lifted my foot entirely from the accelerator.

With great care I turn the car around in the lane, and head for Upton Hall Lodge.

Lady Brock's house is surrounded by gravel. I have managed to get here by dint of going very slowly indeed. The stones grind and pop one by one under the tires. I apply the hand brake. The pawl clicks over each tooth of the ratchet, counting down into silence.

All my energy has gone to my mind, which is trying to shift an idea into play but the idea is a mighty great stone, almost immovable. I get out of the car. As I walk to Althea's door I make a misstep or two. The ground seems farther away than it should. When I stagger, the idea rocks in my mind.

The sun's gone down. A glow of lamps in the window, music from the gramophone.

Althea exclaims with surprise and pleasure, admits me. Margaret Dennis, who's sitting by the electric fire, a chunky tumbler in her hand, gives a similar hail of welcome.

"I'm sorry to disturb you," I say, and find I can get no further.

Althea pauses for a second and then says, "Parish business, is it? We'll adjourn to the study. Margaret, my dear, excuse us for a moment."

"My dear James. You look . . . what's the expression? As if a harrow has run over your soul."

"The scarf," I manage to say. "The one you left in the church. It turns out it belonged to Bridie Moore. I need to give it back to her."

"What, this instant?"

"If you don't mind."

She gives me a narrow, sidelong look, sniffs, and leaves the room.

An untidy desk, two paintings looking down at her. Sir Michael Brock in uniform, a hollowed face, a medaled, waterlogged chest. And Philip Moore's painting of William. A fleck of scarlet at the corner of his eye makes the blue blaze. The majestic ruin of his hand, the nub of a missing finger and the truncated half palm, a silvered braid of scar tissue. Philip, I think distantly, is uncommonly good.

Lady Brock has returned. "Here it is. I'm glad we found the rightful owner. A few memories there, I don't doubt."

I hold it up against the lamp. I can hardly see them, they weave into the fabric like small clouds or spots on your retina as you gaze into blue sky.

"I know," says Lady Brock. "*Masses* of little darns. Cigarettes, for certain. When I was young you couldn't go to a party without your finery getting singed to absolute lace by the blasted smokers . . . James, you look quite odd."

"I need to go to Redwood House."

"For heaven's sake, what's the rush?" She's following me down the hall. "Stay for a drink at least! James, honestly," she cries, as I open her front door. "I hope to hear, eventually, what on *earth* you're up to!"

An awkward Anglepoise is shining straight at the side of Bridie Moore's face. She doesn't like it, the light's going in her eye. I twist the lamp's head and raise it so that it illuminates the wall and sends a gentler glow into her bedroom. She's sitting up in bed against a mound of pillows. She hasn't felt very well today, Terry Shaw has informed me. I mustn't stay long. It's so quiet that the room itself, the carpet and drawn curtains, seem to be breathing.

The silk is crushed in the embrace of my hands. I hold it to my face and breathe in, close my eyes and feel my way over the fabric. Here is a darn, and here and here. The mends are finer than my own fingerprints, each one a scar almost healed. I can believe that if they're left long enough, the new threads will merge indistinguishably with the old.

I put the edge of the scarf into Bridie's hand. Her eyes are sharp. She's already understood. She can't rub it between fingers and thumb, that action has been forgotten, but she nods all the same. I only ever caught a glimpse of the scarf, that day on the water in Egypt. But Bridie knew it so well that she recognized the design instantly, the day I brought it to Redwood House. The scarf had disappointed her that day, looking so undamaged and new. Now she feels the repairs. It is, after all, the scarf she remembered. The one that had been full of little holes.

"Somebody must have mended it," I say. "Before it went in the jumble sale."

Her eyes widen. *Obviously.*

She had listened while I spoke to Philip. A desultory, inconsequential conversation at the end of a party. *My late wife,* she heard, and *Alexandria,* and *Yvette.* And she was galvanized into a mighty groan.

She tried to tell me, the only way she knew how.

"So Yvette came to your house?" I ask her.

"Yes."

"Why?"

Bridie sighs, rocks her head back. Working out how to explain. In the end she lifts her hand, points to a picture on the wall. I get up to look at it. A watercolor of an infant. *Gerard,* it says underneath. And there is a date, and before the date, a sign of the cross.

"Oh, Bridie. I'm so sorry."

An indeterminate amount of time has passed. Bridie has made no sound. I'm sitting on the edge of her bed now.

"She told me she'd found someone to talk to. And that was all. She never told me who. Not that I blame her. I couldn't speak about it. About . . ." I close my eyes for a moment, as whiteness flares on the insides of my eyelids. "I couldn't help Yvette, you see, Bridie. I've always regretted that. How badly I let her down."

She reaches out, lets her hand fall gently onto mine. Of course, she knows all this. Yvette told her.

Outside the wind is gusting hard enough to move the hem of the curtain even though the window's closed. It must be late. I should leave. I put the scarf on Bridie's bedside cabinet. This makes her cluck and wag her head in annoyance.

"Didn't she give it to you? She left it by mistake?"

"Yes," says Bridget.

"I don't even understand why she had it with her. She never wore it."

Her lips press together.

"What did she do with it, then?"

The mobile side of her mouth turns down. She says, "Ohh, ahh, ohh."

An imitation of someone crying.

A knock at the door. Bridie says, "Yes."

Terry Shaw puts her head around. "Oh! James. I didn't know who on earth it could be, at this time . . ."

"I know, it's very late. I must go. Bridie, let's talk again about Yvette."

She rocks her head up and down.

Terry sees me to the front door.

"Terry, are you ever off duty?"

She smiles. "I went to Jersey three years ago. A delightful island. Have you solved the mystery, by the way?"

"Yes. That's why I'm here. The most extraordinary thing—Bridie knew my late wife. We lived at Alver Shore back then, you see, and they—they met by chance. Now I know why Bridie got so upset at my party when I mentioned Yvette, my wife. She was desperate that I should know and of course she couldn't say anything. Philip was so worried . . ."

I come to a standstill in the doorway.

"James?"

"Oh . . . yes. Bridie was very kind to her . . . thanks, Terry, I'll see you soon . . ."

"I'm glad!" Terry calls after me.

The house seems very still when I return.

"Tom? Where are you?" My voice echoes in the empty stairwell.

Bailey's in his basket. Apart from a token wag of the tail he doesn't move. "Tom?" I go into the sitting room. His textbooks and files have been removed. Searching upstairs, I find his bedroom empty of everything except the box from the attic and a sock, kicked under the bed.

Finally I go into my own bedroom. On the mantelpiece, next to Yvette's urn, there's a note.

Dad. Gone back to uni.

Need to be on my own for a while.

I've been reading a story. I don't think Mum ever meant me to see it. I don't know who it was for. Certainly not you. I felt like I was prying, even though it was lovely seeing her handwriting again.

Whether she wanted to or not, she told me the truth. Something you've never bothered to do. In fact, you decided to lie. You didn't think about me, what I needed to know, what was right, and just, and how I would feel if I found out by accident that I'd been kept in the dark.

Anyway you'll notice I've taken the "sand." My sister needs to spend some time in the company of someone who honors her existence.

T. A.

I had put the little cedarwood chest on the bookshelf. When I go to look, I find that it has gone.

On my bed, carefully laid out, are three of Yvette's notebooks. I pick up the one farthest to the left, *L'Histoire*, turn it over in my hands. A segment of the paper cover is a lighter blue, faded by a long-ago

Egyptian sun. The shock has made me stupid. I riffle through the pages. Suddenly the language changes to English. The writing goes all the way to the end. I search the next notebook and the next. All of the leftover pages at the back are full, full with lines and lines of English prose in blue ink, in black, in Biro, and in felt pen. Underlinings. Stars. Tom has put the books in the right order: each passage is dated, all the dates in the first half of 1964.

She died in July of that year.

I open *L'Histoire* again and find my way back to the first English line.

He held my hand in the dust. That was the first time he touched me.

I lift my head, remembering her last July. The pale yellow sky, the boundless evening light. I have just broken into a private room, a small place wholly hers, still hers, no matter how long she's been gone. Tom needn't feel guilty. It wasn't him she was hiding it from.

I turn once more to the page.

SEVENTEEN

Yvette
29 June 1964

"Well now," said Bridie, as I unwrapped a small bright-blue-and-yellow can with a screw top. "I don't know that I've ever cooked with olive oil."

She didn't even like the idea of eating it, I could tell. She'd probably only seen it in the chemist's. But this was one of six cans my mother had sent me from Nice, produce of the Alziari mill in Provence, wrapped in copies of *Le Figaro*. "Try some on a slice of this delicious bread of yours, Bridie, with a little salt and pepper. You won't regret it."

The bread was warm from the oven. Bridie had made it with bicarbonate instead of yeast and it was a revelation to me.

Philip had put down his small drawing notebook and pencil and done as I suggested. "I'm transported," he said with his mouth full.

He didn't appear to have brushed his hair since we last met, and the brindled chestnut sweater had a row of small dark oily stains along the hem, each with a smudge of a different color in the center. He cleaned his brushes on his clothes. How profligate. Such good quality wool, and he'd wrecked it. I shook my head in sorrow. He followed my eyes and grinned.

"I know. I'm a disgrace."

"Why don't you wear a . . ." *Une blouse,* what did they call it. "A tunic for painting?"

"A smock? Like a proper artist, you mean?" He popped another piece of bread into his mouth.

"Aren't you a proper artist?" I said, smiling.

"Not yet."

"When will you be?" asked his mother.

He leaned back in his chair and stretched his arms. "When I do something I still like after a year. Maybe then."

The house was tranquil. The only noise that penetrated was that made by tractors as they passed on their way to the fields. The crumpled pages of *Le Figaro,* scarred with black headlines about the French fighting in Vietnam, belonged in a sorrier, darker realm.

"And how is your mother getting used to Nice, my dear?" Bridie asked.

"Quite well, considering." I poured some of the green-gold oil onto my piece of bread. "They took every stick of furniture with them, so when she closes the blinds she can pretty much pretend she's still in Alexandria. Even when she opens them she sees a promenade with palm trees." The oil was good: it should satisfy Maman. "She's been complaining about the sun, of course," I went on. "It goes down on the right now, you see, instead of the left. She can't get used to it. But since she's found a hairdresser who *understands* her hair, she hasn't mentioned the sun. So all is well."

"Goodness, she's lucky!" Bridie patted her own brisk upstanding crop. "I doubt I've ever found a hairdresser who understood *my* hair!" She pushed her chair back and got to her feet. "Well, I'm for the bus. It's market day in Waltham. Now don't make her sit for too long,

Philip," she said, buttoning her coat. "It's surprisingly tiring," she told me. "And he gets lost in what he's doing. I'll see you later, if you haven't gone."

We both said, "Okay." Like young people.

The front door closed behind her and there was a moment of silence. I screwed the cap back onto the olive oil. The can really was beautiful, the bright blue blazing against the yellow label.

"Did it make you homesick?" Philip asked. He had his arms folded on the table, he was leaning forward.

"What?"

"The oil."

I smiled. "My home is Alver Shore."

"Ah yes, the dreaded Alver Shore."

"Don't call it dreaded. Parts of it are very nice." I peered over at his notebook. "Can I see what you were drawing? Or is it private?"

He showed me the pages. Hands cupping cups, clasping cup handles. Bridie's fingers curled at rest, her knuckles lovingly wrinkled. My fingers dashed off in quick thin lines, splayed out on the edge of the tabletop, all the detail concentrated on my rings, which he had enlarged into a bloated diamond that sat glittering next to a fat shiny nugget of a wedding ring.

"*The Wife*," I exclaimed.

That made him laugh. "I promise that your rings will be normal size in the painting."

"You're an artist, you have complete license."

"Come, to work." He got up and went to the low window that faced the garden. "The light's best here. Try this easy chair."

I sat down. In front of me and slightly to one side was a low easel with a backless wooden seat attached to it. "This is my donkey," Philip said, bestriding the seat. "I hardly dare name it after your mischievous teasing. The art school donkeys were all designed for normal mortals, they gave me cramp in the knees, so I constructed this one myself. Make yourself comfortable, Yvette. Move when you need to. I'll make lots of drawings. If you want to stop, tell me."

He sounded calm, and older. Working at his profession.

This was the same chair I'd sat in on my first visit. When I arrived out of the blue, or almost, and unloaded a shocking cataract of tears all over a kind woman who'd answered the door to a stranger in the middle of her morning chores. I'd watched the birds hop and cheep and peck. The chair was just as enclosing and comforting as before. I thought of Bridie, how she had turned my unfeeling mockery of Maman into a joke against herself. She had no quarrel with the world. And neither did Philip. How contentedly she gazed at him, her oldest, second child, the joy of her life. She loved all her children but Philip was special, the first after Gerard.

Would I ever come to gaze at *my* second child? Waiting for this baby was like looking into the sea mist off Alver Shore, straining your eyes for the light of an approaching boat. You could lose your wits staring into the fog. Supposing there wasn't any boat? I simply had to hope. *Hope for that which is seen is not hope.*

Was I starting to give up hope? Not just for a baby, but for the man I had married in Egypt and loved in Alver Shore during those years before Catherine? To lose him as well as Catherine, to live forever with this lookalike, trying every day to forget how he used to be—how could I ever be strong enough for that?

"Would you like to look up now, at the view?" Philip said. "You can lean your head back against the chair."

I let my eyes wander upward beyond the garden. The distant summit of a long hill rose above the trees. I drove over this hill on my way to the village, but it looked so different from here. It seemed to have no solidity today, as if it and the blue sky and the pink-tinged clouds were all painted flat upon a screen.

"That's Beacon Hill," said Philip. "A nice place to walk."

I imagined us up there, two diminutive painted figures, one with a leaping stride, the other trotting behind. "I'd never keep up with you."

"But you were imagining it, at least. Going for a walk with me." He let his drawing arm drop, the soft pencil loose in his hand, and pushed his hair out of his eyes. The sweater fell from his shoulders like the smock he didn't want to wear. "I won't leave you behind, I promise. And I'll carry the picnic."

"So we're having a picnic now."

"It's a long way, there and back. And the slightest exercise makes me starving."

That was true of me too. I smiled. "What shall we take?"

"The olive oil, for starters. Some bread. Swiss chocolate."

"*Swiss* chocolate? I'd have to sell my great big diamond."

"You've got time. We won't go till the weather's warmer."

A quiet descended, broken by intakes of breath, sighs, the hushing sound made by bodies moving in winter clothing. The scrape of a shoe on the floor. The occasional muttering of a young man deep in thought, a tutting followed by urgent shading-in. Sheets of paper rustling as he took them off the board and let them fall to the floor. The sun came out and everything loomed into brightness.

"Oh," I said, as if I'd just been woken.

He got up without a word and went to put the kettle on.

I knelt on the floor in a patch of sunlight and leafed through the drawings he'd made. The first Yvette was very correct, shoulders back and knees together, a shine on her neat hair. Thoughtful, a bit pent-up. "*Train Passenger*," I called over to Philip. "No, wait: *The Dentist's Waiting Room.*"

"Ha!" he said, splashing water into the teapot.

The next Yvette was only half alive, pinned to the back of the chair by an invisible spike. Her eyes were foundering in sadness, her hands hauntingly empty in her lap. The third Yvette burst on me in mid-sentence, her lips in motion, a glimmer in her eyes.

Philip came and knelt down next to me, setting two saucerless cups on the floor.

"This one"—I pushed the sad drawing toward him—"is terribly good. Keep it. But I never want to see it again."

"I'm sorry." He laid it aside. "I went too far."

"As I said, you have license. You must draw what you see." I held up the last picture. "*This* is me. How I used to be, anyway, before the baby."

The glimmer, I saw, was a square of light—the window, reflected in my eyes.

"Oh, that girl is here," he said. "I believe I met her last week."

"Really?"

"Mmm. She said, 'men in the *nip*'!"

I looked up at him. Everything about him, his comical nose, his narrowed hazelish eyes, his curling thin lips, mischievous and playful. So easy to let my own smile widen, to meet those eyes. Then I sniffed.

"Philip, what do you call that spirit, the liquid for cleaning paintbrushes?"

"Turps," he said.

"Teups?" Some English words, you simply couldn't get them on the first try.

"Turpentine." He gave a gentle laugh. "You're telling me I smell of turpentine."

"Don't worry. It's not unpleasant."

We drank our tea and looked at the drawing. "Color," Philip said. "I want to surround you with color and light and heat." He touched the drawing, swept his hand around my head and down my side. Then, with the back of his forefinger, the back of the tip of his forefinger, he stroked my face. My face in the drawing.

"My clothes are all rather drab, I'm afraid," I heard myself say.

His finger was still stroking the sketch girl's face. The sketch girl turned toward his hand until his palm cupped her cheek, and she closed her eyes. Because his hand was so warm and gentle and tender—

"Philip," I blurted. "I don't know."

"You don't know about the clothes?"

I couldn't find any words. The silence extended hideously.

"You mean, you don't know if you'll sit for me again," he said at last. "I see. Well, it's entirely up to you."

"It's a question of time, you see. I have so many things—"

"Things to do at home, of course you have. You're a vicar's wife, after all."

"Yes."

"Vicar's wives are generally quite involved with the parish, I've heard."

He sounded desolate.

"We are."

"Helping your husbands."

We were still kneeling on the floor, side by side.

"You've become very serious." I was almost whispering. I couldn't believe what I was saying.

"I *feel* serious." He moved closer. "Yvette, I'm not stupid. I know there's absolutely no hope at all. But I want to see you. Not for the painting, though I do want to paint you. I like talking to you. I like . . . I like being with you."

I didn't move. I didn't even lift my head for fear of what he'd see in my eyes.

"Now you've made it worse," I said in despair. "It can't be like this."

"Yes, it can—"

"No. I'll bring James to meet your mother. You could meet him too. It would be nice." I was gabbling now. "There's no reason why we can't all be friends."

"I don't want us all to be friends—"

"We *must* be, if I'm to ever come back!"

I spoke vehemently because I had to.

We got up off the floor. He was so much taller than me. He would have to bend to kiss me, and I would have to stand on tiptoe. I would have to, if I ever allowed myself to be gathered into his arms.

I turned on my heel and left.

Our house was empty when I got back, so I went straight to the church. James would be there, it was a Wednesday, and Evensong was imminent.

He was in the vestry putting on his cassock, he didn't see me as I approached the doorway. I seldom came on him unawares and, like the time when I heard him sigh, I profited from this moment by staying quiet and immobile. He buttoned his cassock to the collar and took a white surplice out of the cupboard and pulled it over his head. It seemed to get stuck: he struggled inside it and I nearly hurried forward to help him, pull it down over his shoulders but the urge to stay hidden and spying was too strong. Eventually he got his head free. He was breathing hard, I noticed, and when he had tugged the white folds down over his cassock he went to place his elbows on the high ledge of the vestry window and bury his head in his hands.

I watched his shoulders rise and fall as he sighed once and again. Then I heard a whisper. "Dear God, Almighty God . . ." and then the whisper died away. His eyes were squeezed shut. His lips moved silently against his hands, which were now clasped in front of his mouth as if he didn't want the words to come out but he couldn't stop saying them.

I went into the vestry and put my hand on his arm.

He jumped. "Yvette! You gave me a fright!" New James was armoring himself rapidly. "How are you, darling? Have you been out?"

"What were you praying for?"

"World peace." He shook his head. "I can't believe people are fighting again."

I thought of my glimpse of *Le Figaro*, the news from Vietnam. To give him his due, he looked haunted by the outbreak of new wars, as well he might. But I knew all the same that his answer was a flat lie.

"It is almost inconceivable," I said.

He went to fetch his stole from the high hook where it hung to avoid getting creased, to spare me, because ironing stoles was my least favorite job. I didn't mind a surplice; it was a huge long pleated garment. You could have fun with a surplice. But stoles, though they were comparatively undemanding, being a single four-inch-wide length of patterned silk, went on and on. There was something depressing about a stole. Most vicars' wives, I had discovered, took the opposite view. I knew I was unusual in liking ironing. It reminded me of our years of happiness when we first came to England.

"This woman I've been seeing," I said. "She's helped me a great deal. She's older than me, you see, and her other children are grown up. So we've had time to talk."

"Excellent!" He turned to me. "I'm terribly pleased, darling, it all sounds so positive. She must be a thoroughly good sort of person, to have survived her own tragedy. No, more than that, surmounted it to the extent that she can reach out to younger bereaved mothers."

New James was dictating this, as if for a pamphlet.

Now was the moment to bring it all out in the open. Mark out my private land with names and places, neutralize the sunlit silences. The tenderness which I had felt in the gentle things Philip had said to me. His forwardness, his mischief, his frankness. Above all, his frankness. The sheer joy at being with someone who said what he thought.

"Would you come with me?" I asked James.

"What?" He was busy adjusting the stole.

"I wondered if you'd come with me one day. We needn't talk about the baby at all. It would simply be nice for you to meet—"

"I don't think so, darling." He tugged the stole a meticulous half inch down on one side. "When would I get the time? And I do think it's *your* activity, don't you? I can't be poking my nose in everywhere!"

He gave me such a white, handsome smile that I went straightaway and embraced him. Then I put my palms one on each side of his face. "Oh, my darling, I love you so much. How can I help you?"

I searched his eyes. I was so close to him that I could look from one to the other. There was an instant of anguish and then, as if he'd flicked a switch, his eyes filled with a warm, faultlessly attentive concern.

"I don't need help, darling."

"That's not true. You know what I'm talking about, I saw you a second ago. Darling, you've been like this ever since Catherine, now *please*—"

He put his hands on my shoulders, assumed a bewildered yet affectionate expression—slight frown, warm eyes, head on one side. "I haven't *been like* anything. I'm always the same. You know me."

The concern was still flowing, unstinted. I was a skilled assayer by this time: I judged it to be very acceptable, good quality. If you'd never known anything different, you could take it at face value. It made my gorge rise.

"Aren't you hurt by what I said?" My voice began to shake with misery. "Isn't it upsetting, at the very least, to be accused of having changed? Changed so much that your wife is *begging* you to go back to how you were?"

"I'm not upset."

"You should be!"

"Well, I'm sorry I'm not." He looked at his watch. "And I must get on."

I slept badly that week. On the Friday night, the night before I was supposed to go back and see Philip, I got out of bed in the small hours and went downstairs and sat in the kitchen. My handbag rested on the countertop. I remembered the angel Philip had drawn. I felt guilty forgetting her. She had been rejected, folded, almost crumpled, in my handbag. I got up and took her out.

There were big creases in the paper but I smoothed them as best I could. The only thing that pleased me was her hair—that, and the way she was suspended in the air. Not flying like a fairy but hanging, beautifully, as if she had achieved her natural level of buoyancy in this thick, almost but not quite aqueous, atmosphere. It was dignified and not at all childlike.

I stroked her face as Philip had stroked me on the paper. The picture where I had the glimmer in my eyes. What had amused me? Oh, yes. Selling a fictitious diamond for a hypothetical bar of Swiss chocolate to take on a completely imaginary walk up a painted hillside. All this playful nonsense swept away by one touch of my face, of his drawing of my face.

I could not feel anything of Catherine beneath my fingers.

They had meant well, they had drugged me to seal off the pain, but my mind had been sealed off as well. My own quick wits. James came in with our bundled baby and I took hold of her obediently, one hand for her head, one hand for her bottom. And afterward I came to understand how lucky I'd been to even touch her. How lucky that James, with his authority, had persuaded the midwife to let him bring her in to me. I'd heard him next door talking to the midwife. He had said, *Can you wrap her up? Please let my wife hold her,* and it seemed very spoiled of me to insist on anything more. I mean, I'd held her, I knew her weight, she was real. I would have that knowledge forever. Most women, their stillborn children disappeared without trace. They lay awake at night wondering if they'd ever had a baby at all.

I sat still, in the electric light, the winter sky dark outside. Pondering and meandering and wondering against the black square of the window and the custard-colored light. His words turning like tea leaves running away down the sink, each revolution not only smaller but spinning faster and faster and faster until they swirled away with a gulp.

"God have mercy," I said aloud.

The only thing that kept me going, the night I labored with Catherine, was a light glowing at me from the distance. A deep, warm yellow glow, far away and high up. I went through my drugged convulsions on the bed and endured the loud encouragement from the midwife to pant or push. *Pant!* she cried, then *Push!* The words came out without any brake on them, any modulation, any acknowledgment that the child she was delivering was dead: *Pant! Push!,* she cajoled me, as if there were a life at stake. This midwife had wanted me to lie with my feet in the stirrups but I refused. I sat up and she planted a heavy hand in the middle of my chest and pushed me down. I slapped her hand away and got up onto my knees, and she knew she was beaten.

I knew, from the light's deep, warm yellowness, that it represented James's love for me, and as long as I kept my eyes on it I would survive. And so I did, washed up into daylight. I realized then that I'd been staring at the light in the corridor outside the labor room, which I could see through a panel of glass above the door. But that didn't mean it wasn't James's glowing love, the love that was now all I had.

The pain had continued identical for hours. A circle tightening as it widened, and biting as it tightened, and widening even as it bit. There was no end to it except in silence, and that silence came when my growls of agony stopped as Catherine was released from my body. Silence as the midwife shut her urgent mouth, and silence from a baby who did not cry. Operating according to her instructions the midwife took Catherine away the moment the cord was clamped and cut. As I was on all fours I didn't see her.

Catherine's birth, I think, was at sunrise.

A cold early morning light, a lot of new noises. Clangs and rattles—hospital trolleys. A man whistling. Everything seemed to echo.

James had been outside the room all night and now I heard him next door. I heard the midwife say, "Vicar," and James said, 'Please let my wife hold her.'

But before that, he had said, "Can you wrap her up?"

I went upstairs, deeply chilled from all that sitting in the cold. James was lying on his front, eyes closed. I got into bed and he stirred and felt for me. "Yvie, you're icy," he mumbled when he touched my arm, and slept again.

"Why didn't you tell me?" I whispered. "All I wanted was to know."

When I first remembered his voice I could have erupted in rage as the hairs rose on my neck—*you liar*—but what had enveloped me instead was a patient, lenient, yearning. I lay by his side and spoke to him as he drifted through a half sleep. "You said you didn't see her, but I heard you ask the midwife to wrap her up. You were there when she was naked. You must have seen her." I waited as his breathing became shallower, less rhythmic, as he sighed his way into consciousness. Then he rolled onto his back, his eyes open and vacant.

"I'm not asking you to tell me now. But you have to know that *I* know that you've been pretending all this while. Pretending that you didn't see her. Pretending with everything else."

He blinked rapidly, squeezed his eyes shut.

"I don't know what you mean," he said.

I stroked his forehead, then his eyelids. Men's eyelids are very soft. "My love," I said, "that's not true."

I've put everything into these notebooks. They contain me and yet I burst out of their academic categories. There is only one subject now, and that's me. A forty-year-old woman, two thousand miles from the city where I was born. History birthed me; geography gave me a new home to love. Biology broke my heart long ago with Catherine and now I'm at its mercy again, being ill, being drugged once more but still writing, writing. Not to excuse or blame myself, but to bear witness to my life, the gifts I've been given, the people I've loved, before the light fails. I must go on, I will go on, until the end. And only then will I write *FIN*.

Bridie was in her garden, digging in a square bed. "This will be for my early spuds. Time to wake up the earth." She looked ruddier and squarer in the open air. "Philip's up on Beacon Hill." She pointed to the high humpback line in the distance. "He told me he'd be back in an hour. You can wait for him, or you can drive to the track and climb up yourself. Go past Pipehouse Wood and turn right."

"Pipehouse Wood?"

"The high beech wood beside the road. You'll have the hill in your sight all the time, you won't miss it."

She was right, the track up to the hill was easy to find. I parked at the end, just off the road, and started to walk. The track was dry, chalky, wide enough for four people to walk abreast. Then a fence and a stile and beyond that, a steep incline of turf. The slope was rutted with little paths that zigzagged across the face of the hill, but I went straight up.

At the top I found myself standing on a grassy bank that went all the way around the summit. In the middle there were round hillocks and hollows in sun and shadow.

Philip was sitting on the bank on the other side of the summit, facing outward over the land below. He had his back to me and I could tell by the way he was leaning forward, intent, that he was drawing.

My footsteps were noiseless on the grass but I was breathing hard from the climb. He heard me and turned around. Said nothing, simply looked mildly up at me. His notebook was open, the black hatchings of the distant city skyline laid out across two pages under the fire of the declining sun. He put a finger on his sketch and then pointed toward the coast.

"I was thinking of you down by the sea. And yet here you are."

I sat down beside him. "You don't seem at all surprised to see me."

"No." He glanced behind me at the edge of the rampart. "Did you bring your husband?"

I gazed down at the fields spread out below. His mother's house was visible among the trees on the edge of the village, a white oblong against the young, acid spring green. I didn't know if she was still outside in her garden. She was too small to see from here.

"No." I turned to him. "I did not."

He looked back at me with a question in his eyes. I must have answered it because he put his hand on my shoulder.

He said, "Yvette," and took me into his arms. I pushed his hair out of his eyes and kissed him on his smiling lips, betraying my husband, the love of my life. The turf smelled of spring.

EIGHTEEN

In March of 1943 I returned to the Libyan desert to find that the scorched wasteland I had fought over on previous summers was gone. Instead I appeared to be flying above the hillocks and dales of a fertile meadow where sheep and goats ran at dawn, and where the dry riverbeds were filled with the tiny white, yellow, and violet stars of wildflowers that thrived among thorns and dry thickets. I wished I could pick some and send them to the girl waiting for me in Alexandria. Last year I had sheltered from an air raid holding hands with this girl: it was my first raid, I mean my first as a sitting duck rather than a combatant, and I couldn't tell whose grip was tighter. I fell hard for this girl and afterward wished I'd made my feelings plainer.

Now I knew her better, I was able to see how the flowers suited her, being arrestingly dainty and beautiful and tough. I had no idea back then what she would have to endure nor how beautiful she would become.

We camped at Castel Benito, a temporary camp because the next day we would move up to the battle lines. It rained, and some of my

companions pitched their tents in an orchard but I chose to sleep under my plane. I lay there in the dusk looking up at the scarred under-
carriage and the battered air filter and at my twin cannons looming in
their gondolas above me, each one longer than I was tall, the barrel
alone longer than she was tall. I was in 6 Squadron now, and I had just
seen Yvette for the second time. I had declared my love and so had she.
When I admitted I thought of my cannons day and night, she didn't try
to distract me, or tell me not to be afraid, or any of that type of tosh.
She was happy that they weighed so heavily on my mind. That way, she
understood, I might survive.

The following morning we left Castel Benito in the rain and flew
to the war, the squalls harrying us all the way. When we reached our
destination south of the Mareth Line we had to wait on the ground for
orders, watching Bostons and Baltimores fly overhead on their way to
the German lines while our landing ground turned to mud around us.
Then the barrage finally opened and we fought and waited and fought.
In April I met my match in the form of a 109 that stitched bullets along
my fuselage and ruptured my oil line. The engine seized, caught fire,
and I bailed out as the cockpit filled with smoke.

I tripped over on landing, knocking myself out on a stone. That
did for me, that and the windless weather. The air was so still that my
'chute canopy settled right on top of me. By the time I came to and
tried to struggle free, a small party of Germans was approaching, all
badly sunburned as I recall, looking about sixteen. One of them
pointed a gun at me. Somewhere out of sight my Hurricane exploded
with a big boom and the young German was so startled he nearly
shot me.

A captive, I was taken north to Germany. The journey was long
and increasingly cold. I had time to reflect on the end of my war, and
I found that I was glad I'd killed no one on that last flight and there-

fore not added to my bloodstained tally of the previous days and indeed years.

S he walks toward me over the sand and small stones of the desert at Amiriya. It is just after the war, I have come from England and we don't immediately recognize each other. I am still a ghost of myself, she a uniformed silhouette in the heat haze.

She gets closer, becomes clearer, the light strikes her face under the peak of her cap. I can't see her eyes but her lips are parted as if at any moment she will speak.

"So you kissed him?" I ask her. "And what then? What happened?"

She shakes her head, she's too young to know. She holds out her arms.

The light strengthens, dims the bare bulb hanging from my bedroom ceiling. The notebook falls from my hand. *Yvette Haddad. La Biologie.*

The book is filled to the last page.

The other two notebooks lie on the floor in front of me. I have searched everywhere, swept my room and Tom's, upended the packing boxes and rummaged through the heaps of contents. But there are no more books to be found, nothing more to be read. In the spring of 1951 she climbed up a chalk hill in the south of England, a hill I can see for myself should I go up to the roof of my house, and there she kissed another man. That is all I know.

That alone is impossible to think about.

I tug the counterpane off the bed, pull it over me, lie down on the floor on my side and close my eyes so that this new merciless day doesn't begin yet. So I can lie awhile longer and think of that other green and flowering Libyan spring, when I was young and lay under my plane and listened to the rain patter on the wings, and thought of my guns and my impending battle, and most of all of my true love, of her, of her.

Downstairs a small dog is barking. A dog who's starting to get the hang of waiting until he's allowed outside. Who, on the occasions that he disgraces himself, is almost inconsolable. The barks are muffled but his desperation is clear.

I pull off my covering and make my way down to the kitchen.

Bailey hurries out to the hedge. Returns to find his food bowl unfilled. He noses it across the floor to me. I know he needs feeding but it takes a while to enlist my muscles for the task. Eventually I serve him his dole of kibble thinking that my shock is somehow unmerited since nothing has changed. It's been real and true all this time.

I go into the dining room. I thought I was steady but as I pick up the telephone receiver my left hand begins to shake—big, pulsing quakes like someone afflicted with a disease of the nerves. I manage to hook the forefinger of my right hand into the "zero" hole of the rotary dial of the telephone: 0603 for Norwich. I drag the dial down to the stop, take my finger out of the hole, the dial purrs its way back again. Entering the whole number takes a long time. The connection is made, the phone in Norwich rings and rings.

Tom asked me if I'd known about anyone called Sébastien. He must have been sounding me out, trying to gauge what I knew. Calculating exactly how secret it was, the story cached inside those schoolgirlish blue covers. No, she never said anything about him to me. I wouldn't have cared about this Sébastien if she *had* told me. She didn't betray anyone with him.

"Yep?"

A breathy voice, not my son's. Must be Ade or Jase.

"H-hello. May I speak to Tom, please? This is his father—"

"He's not here."

"It's seven a.m.," I plead to Jase or Ade. "He must be."

"He's not, sorry."

The line is cut. I replace the receiver.

Time passes.

I'm in the kitchen again, and Bailey's making revolutions around the table, clockwise, anticlockwise, stopping by my feet on each turn and then moving on. He doesn't understand why I'm not talking to him. I've made some tea, it appears, but it sits in front of me, cold in the mug. A skin has formed.

I didn't go to bed at all last night. After I got to the end of *Biologie*, when she kissed Philip, I stayed sitting on the floor until dawn. Leaning against the wall. Dozing, waking, picking up a notebook, rereading, re-rereading. Holding the pages to my face, to try to feel her. Putting her handwriting against my cheek.

Even the last page, where his name is written, I held against my face.

Next door the telephone rings. Tom. I hurry to answer, a pit yawning inside me.

But the caller is Clive. "James, we're about to start." His voice is cheerful, raised against the noise of a busy classroom. "Are you on your way?"

The school. I'm supposed to be there with Clive, telling the children about Advent, which is fast approaching.

"No, I'm . . . I'm unwell. I'm terribly sorry, Clive. I can't come."

"Okey-doke. Not to worry!" He must be surrounded by teachers, curious children. Before he cuts the line I hear him say, "Oh dear, Mr. Acton's tied up, so let's make one *big* group . . ."

I feel no consternation or guilt. The school, Clive, the children: they all seem, to my mind, to be in a distant country.

Early afternoon, I think, judging by the light outside. I'm wearing my coat and Wellingtons, searching my pockets for the dog lead.

"Stand by, Bailey. We will shortly be going on a trek."

It's too far for him, he'll probably peg out halfway, but I don't want to leave him here. I don't know how long I'll be gone. Once we are outside the house I spend some time on the doorstep rubbing my face with my hands, rubbing my head, as if to clean some matter off me, some cobwebs perhaps or clinging dust.

She remembered the apples at Alver Shore. The ones I brought into the house after we came back from the hospital, hoping she would like them. She turned her face away. Something childlike about the gesture, as if along with her baby she'd been robbed of all her adult comportment. Célia said, "She doesn't want them, James," and I straightaway took the apples back outside. Early the next morning I stripped the branches and gave the fruit away in boxes to all comers.

Her face in repose became a mask of tragedy, eyes and mouth yanked down at the corners. I saw this expression whenever she didn't know I was looking at her.

Oddly overdone, she wrote about me. *Like a highly trained double.* I can almost hear her voice. It would be funny if it wasn't me she was talking about.

I did my best but my best was lamentable. What she actually

needed, I couldn't give her. And now I'm being punished at last for my failure, for my confusion, for not being enough for her. For giving her a facsimile of myself while the real one struggled in darkness or rather in blinding light. Overwhelmed by cataclysm.

Philip Moore is living at his mother's house in Ash Lane, a cut in the hillside off the main street of Upton, so deep and steep that there's a high stone retaining wall at the top. The house is around the corner, the last bungalow on the left. He hasn't given me this information but luckily I can follow the directions supplied by my dead wife, who not only told me the name of the man she kissed but the exact location of his home.

The latch of the gate is stiff, the wolf's-head door knocker snarls at me. She wondered if it might be a dog, but I don't think so.

Bailey barks before I can knock, making me start, because a silence seems to have descended everywhere. No living thing is here, not even a singing bird. And no sound comes from inside the house. I hush Bailey but he barks again. Now a shape appears, a darker shadow in the shade of the hallway. A lock rattles and the door is opened.

He's barefoot, his hair tousled, a tall rangy figure in a creased shirt. As if my discovery has sent him back to the bohemian dishevelment of his youth. He pushes back his hair. Those long fingers stroked my wife's arm no doubt, her shoulder, her neck perhaps, for in kissing people come close, they touch. Even if nothing else happened, he touched her.

"Philip," I say, recalling from a distant yesterday that we were on first-name terms. "I'm sorry if I've disturbed you."

How disingenuous. I've come expressly to disturb him.

"Is it about Mum?" He looks worried. "I was having a nap, I might have missed the phone . . ."

"No. I mean, I've heard nothing from Redwood House."

"Maybe I should ring and check . . ."

He loiters, lost in anxiety.

"I wonder if I could come in?" I say after a moment. "I can leave my dog outside if you prefer."

"No, bring it in. I mean, do come in. How rude of me."

Bailey crosses the tiles of the kitchen floor, his claws clicking. "If you don't mind, I'll ring Redwood," Philip says, and disappears into another room. Soon I hear his voice on the phone, an indistinct up-and-down murmur.

The low-silled window, the one with a garden view, is filled with a jungle of pot plants. No armchair in front of it anymore: I'm glad. I don't have to imagine her sitting in it.

"Everything's fine," he says, returning to the room. "Can I get you something? Coffee?"

"Yes, please. And some water for the dog, if you don't mind."

The mug is almost too hot to hold but I wrap my fingers around it anyway and the mild scalding focuses my mind. "Thank you. This is very welcome. I'm sorry"—nodding at Bailey, who is lashing droplets of water in a wide circle over the floor. "He's not a tidy drinker."

"They told me you visited Mum yesterday evening, and she seems much calmer today." He gives a tentative smile. "Thank you. I don't know what you said to her!"

"Oh, it's simple. I realized at last what she was trying to tell me."

The smile stiffens on his face. "Oh yes?"

That is all he can say, this man who knew this very thing all along, who had stood and watched his stricken mother try in vain to tell me.

"It's the most extraordinary thing," I continue. "She knew my late wife, Yvette. Yvette used to come and visit her. I think I mentioned Yvette to you at my party."

"Did you? I can't remember." He starts to blink rapidly, so rapidly that his eyes are hardly open at all. "Gosh, so Mum and—your wife, they knew each other. You're right, that *is* rather extraordinary . . ."

So he's going to lie to the end. All of a sudden I feel terribly tired. I squandered a great deal of strength in my youth, fighting, killing, escaping, hungering, marching. Used up an awful lot in my middle age too, working, loving, mourning, fathering, and I've got precious little left over. Will I have to carry him, a deadweight now, over the line? He's got to help me or I'll never get there.

"Did you ever paint her, after doing those drawings?"

"Paint who? I—I'm sorry, I don't follow—"

"Philip." I lean forward in my chair. "Please."

He turns his head away, and I see the tears filming his eyes.

In the north light she laughs at us. No, not at us. She laughs and we watch her. She's sitting on the floor cross-legged, I don't know where. Perhaps a room of his imagination. In one hand she holds a can of olive oil, in the other a piece of bread.

The canvas is framed, leaning against a wall.

"When did she die?" Philip's voice is gluey. I think he might be weeping.

"July 1964. Leukemia." I supply this extra detail in a tone of voice that I hope will shut him up. I'm trying not to take much notice of him, preferring to remember instead those cans of olive oil from Moulin Alziari. We were given some more Alziari olive oil when we finally had the money to take Tom to France. An epic journey with the Hillman and a tent, a stay with Maman and Papa in Nice. A sea that didn't reduce Tom to a shivering, purple-lipped waif. And ice cream for him every day in a little cut-glass dish served to him by his grandmother with a silver spoon, and every day I prayed he wouldn't drop the dish. His grandfather showed him photographs by Félix Bonfils of the temples and tombs of ancient Egypt, and drawings by Georges Bénédite, the books he had set out for me in his study in Alexandria, after the war, to help me escape from my thoughts. His daughter once wished aloud that I could borrow the Bénédite. I didn't speak my mind on that occasion. I should have told her that because I was a pilot I had no expectations, but she should know all the same that I thought she was quite lovely.

Never mind. I found her in the end.

And here she is, laughing.

"I can't understand," Philip says, sniffling. "I didn't think you knew..."

"I've only just found out."

I don't explain. Instead I make a gesture at the painting. "I didn't imagine in my wildest dreams that anyone could cheer her up back then. But it seems you cast quite a spell on her. A woman who'd almost taken leave of her senses from grief. Did you think of that, when you began your affair? That she might not have known what she was doing?"

He flinches at my level tone. I can see it's far worse for him than shouting. It's worse for me too, as the pain of the idea burns only inward and fixes like bright-blue-and-yellow enamel on tin. *Moulin Alziari*: there is the can in her hand, her slim small hand as she beams at her lover, tainting that holiday in Provence, one of our happiest times, indelibly.

He's shaking his head now, his eyes small with distress, his lips dry. "No, it wasn't an affair. Honestly, nothing happened—"

"Why should I believe you? You've lied and lied." The anger, I find, is feeding me. I gather strength. "You've covered everything up, all along. If you're so innocent, why were you so worried your mother would speak out of turn and betray you? So worried you wouldn't even help her say she knew Yvette? Did she know about your affair?"

"No. I mean, we didn't have an affair—"

"Please don't keep saying that." I lift the painting up by its frame and, taking great care, turn it to the wall. "And please don't show this work. Even though she's got her clothes on. I should be thankful for that, I suppose."

I had wanted to crush him but it cost too much. When he bows his head, his hand over his eyes, I'm eviscerated all over again.

As I close the gate he calls to me from the doorway. "James!" A hopeless cry. "Wait."

Bailey's tugging. I force myself to turn around. He looks stronger to me: he's mastered himself somehow, his face is more firmly set.

"I loved her, you know!" he bursts out.

"You *loved* her?" I speak very soft, winded by anger. "I doubt you knew the first thing about her."

When I'm almost at the end of the lane, he shouts something after me but I close my ears.

We take the track up to the top of Beacon Hill. Bailey runs ahead, he has no idea he'll have to walk all the way back again. The hawthorn hedges straggle to nothing as the hill rises, the fields on both sides salt-and-peppered with chalk. The cloud cover is unbroken to the horizon, motionless and iron-gray.

What would she have been wearing on her feet? She had a pair of pumps she slid on for driving, black, a bit like dancing shoes. They wouldn't have shielded her from rough tussocks of wet grass, the slippery bare chalk. But then she was walking in the spring. It was dry. She picked her way up here without a second thought for her shoes, nimbly, like one of those deer who live on high peaks. Did she step here, or there? Her stride was shorter than mine but now and again my wet tramping boots must be crushing her footprints.

She delighted in his youth, his lanky charm, the words that came out of his mouth. Every single one of them real and true, without dissimulation. Not the polished phrases of a hollow man.

I climb the last few yards and it is how she described it, a strange flattish ramparted summit edged all around by humps and dips. Bailey hurries over the ground, tail up. At the southern edge I look out over the distant sea. The refinery's visible on the coast, the chimneys very clear as is often the case with this kind of still overcast, as if each outline has been inked in. Inked in by Philip perhaps. Perhaps I'm looking back in time and all this, the chimneys, the tall blocks of the city, and the dark stain of the brick terraces of Alver Shore, is his vision. Perhaps they were sitting here a moment ago and I've just missed them, missed the last seconds before he kissed her.

She'd already known this kiss was coming. She'd seen his hand stroke her cheek on the paper. Imagined her skin under his caressing fingers. They had spoken: she had understood him. She was already gone when she climbed this hill to find him.

"Please. Yvie, tell me."

The sky is quiet.

"This isn't right. My sweetheart, no . . ."

The distant water is dull and flat as lead.

"Please, Yvette, it can't be true. Tell me, Yvie. Yvie?"

The shoreline swings away as I turn inland, ninety, one-eighty, three-sixty degrees—have I turned a full circle? I don't know anymore. I've lost my compass bearing. I've lost my heading, my easting, my northing, my darling, my darling, my darling. Yvie, tell me you didn't. Sweetheart, tell me it's not so.

The trees are beginning to lose their shapes, become one frieze of darkness. Bailey's lagging at last, weaving on exhausted legs, his head hanging. I lift him up and button him into my coat, curling one arm around him. There may not be enough light to last us all the way home but I can walk in the dark.

Headlights throw a long shadow down the lane in front of me, a man seemingly one-armed, very long-legged. My shadow dwindles fast, the roar of an engine mounts behind me, and I step aside onto the verge.

The vehicle slows and comes to a halt. The headlights make it impossible to see anything else. A voice I know calls, "James! I thought it was you!"

I can see the shine of her eyes and the outline of her face, that's all.

"Hello, Ellen," I say.

"Do you want a lift? It's getting rather dark."

I'm seized momentarily with the urge to laugh a laugh of despair. "It certainly is," I agree.

When I climb into the vehicle she sees the dog's head poking out from the open collar of my coat. "Oh, poor Bailey! Is he exhausted?"

"Yes."

I pull on the seat belt, expecting her to turn the key in the ignition but instead she says, "James, your face . . . what's happened?"

"A terrible thing."

"Oh, dear."

When I say nothing else, she restarts the engine. We travel for two, three minutes before I manage to speak again.

"It actually happened a long time ago, this thing. But I didn't know until now."

"Do you want to tell me what it is?"

"I can't, I'm sorry. I can't really bear to think about it, let alone talk."

"I see."

She continues to drive. I risk a glance at her. She's wearing what looks like a very old coat. She nods, thinking about what I've said, but choosing not to press me with questions. The silence becomes calm.

"I wonder sometimes if I could drive these roads with my eyes shut," she says after a while. "I know them so well."

"I fell asleep once in my Hurricane. Only for about half a minute. I'd lost a thousand feet, but otherwise all was well."

"My goodness," she says wonderingly. "You must have been very tired."

"I expect so. Ellen, I enjoyed our evening together so much. I want you to know that. I wish I could go back to it. I wish we could sit around the table again."

She smiles. "Tom and I were very mean to you."

"Were you? I don't remember."

"About the tinned potatoes."

The sorrow engulfs me, so much so that I only realize we're coming up to the vicarage when she pulls onto the side of the road and switches her indicator on. She's not going to turn into the drive.

"You wouldn't believe," I tell her, "how happy that made me."

"And you can't be happy now?"

I turn and look at her. She is lit on one side by the interior light, the planes of her face carved out of the gloom. She watches me, steady and solemn. I feel as if I've seen her properly for the first time.

"I don't know if I can, Ellen. Not at the moment. So much happened, long ago, and it's forcing me to question everything, even myself. I'm sorry for babbling on . . ."

"You have nothing to apologize for."

I climb out carefully, holding Bailey, and look back at Ellen. Her hair is down, tucked into the collar of the coat. Now I can see from the wide shoulders that it's a man's coat: it envelops her, the cuffs go down over her wrists. I deduce that her husband had been tall.

"You know," she says to me, "things can change. Even if they lie in the distant past. Even if they are shocking, ugly. It's a matter of seeing them in a new light." She gives me a sudden, startling smile, and puts her vehicle into gear. "Look after yourself, James. Look after Bailey."

I close the passenger door, and she drives away.

In my bedroom I undertake another fruitless search through the notebooks to see if I could possibly have missed anything. I examine every page, the schoolwork pages included, for a scribble in the margin, for anything that might indicate where the rest of the story is.

Maybe that was all she wanted to say. Maybe she felt too ill to write any more.

No. She was going on until the end. She wouldn't give up.

I know perfectly well why I felt that pit in my stomach when I rang Tom this morning. I've known it all day. I need to ask him if he took the last book, or books, away with him.

For the second time I call his number. Once again Ade, or Jase, informs me that Tom is out. "He really is out this time," he adds, which tells me all I need to know.

Wait. Perhaps there is still another place to look. I packed up so haphazardly, I can't even remember how many boxes I filled. Tom might not have got them all down from the attic. The creaks had scared him: maybe he was too hasty. The end of the story might be up there, above my head, waiting to be unpacked.

I fetch Tom's table and chair out onto the landing, set the chair on the table, and climb up to the hatch. This time, as I haul myself into the attic, I manage to kick the chair off the table. Too bad. I'll just have to jump down.

One star is visible through the fissure in the roof, but no light floods in. The night is moonless. No matter. I can see enough. Is that a pile of boxes there in the middle of the floor? Or is it the fallen tiles? As I approach the uncertain shape it assumes an odd flatness, like a large water stain.

I step forward and my foot plunges down into nothing.

It happens so fast that I don't even cry out. I make a grab at the darkness, get a purchase on a splintered beam, nearly wrench my arm out of its socket. Immediately the pain in my shoulder becomes so agonizing that I let go and drop down onto my bedroom floor. I land heavily and pitch forward onto the shattered roof tiles. They must have made the hole, weighing the rotten planking down until it gave way.

"Jesus Christ!" I bellow, brought to profanity by the pain in my shoulder and my knees.

Above me, as if in response, comes a colossal bang, a knock of doom. Then another and another, each one following more quickly on the heels of the last.

What did they use to say in air raids? In the event of a direct hit, an iron bedstead offers the best shelter. Best get under the bed.

Quick, get under—get under the bed—

NINETEEN

I did not know about the appreciation of beauty.

I did not know that if the body is in immense pain the mind can still revel in the morning light. The slowness with which it builds in the north. Its clarity in winter.

All those separate aspects of the light, slow, winter, morning, enchanting me as individual nails of pain are hammered into different sites of my body.

The snow looms into visibility as the light builds. Creamy, gorgeous. Edible. Many things remind us of food.

Why would I not strain toward this loveliness? The track we're traveling down is hideous, compacted to ice, mud, filth. Half of the lads have been eating cabbage stalks stolen from frozen fields, thereby griping their guts. In the last village a guard kicked over a bucket of clean water given to us by an old woman. In the village before that, another guard shot a dog. The dog was yapping, it irritated him. We pile into barns, packed close for warmth but even so I woke up this morning with my companions Flying Officer William Barratt and

Squadron Leader Meynard Hill frozen to death on either side of me, having given me the greatest gift of all, that of their body heat.

Why should I march any longer down this track when beside us this beautiful white expanse of snow spreads away over the hill? Tucked in the valley is a farmhouse, with firelight glinting in the windows and soup on the stove. A trestle table in the kitchen laid out with bowls and spoons and big tureens, and the soup will be full of butter and stock and chunks of fresh vegetables and meat, things I haven't tasted for nearly two years. *Come on,* I urge my companions. *It's that way. And they've got soup.* Nobody can see the sense of this, people are hanging on to my arms, pulling me back, they want to go on down this frozen track into the face of the blizzard. A hoarse female voice barks, *Hypothermia, then derangement. Death may follow soon after.*

Damn it, I say, *you're all fools.*

Alastair Pearce appears in front of me, dressed for the desert in an airman's jersey and shorts and his tanned knees strike me as very comical. *Hahaha, Pearce, look at your knees,* I say, but he takes no notice, points out over the field, shouting to me on shortwave, crackling and buzzing, *Come on, Acton, no time to lose.* For a dead man he has the liveliest eyes, they wink and blink as he speaks. Then he gives me a thumbs-up and puts on his goggles. *Follow me,* he buzzes, and takes off, his legs together and straight out behind him, his arms spread wide. Like a black moth under the low white cloud.

The sky fills with moths.

My eyes are as wide open as possible and still the moths ripple and surge and coalesce. Perhaps I was wrong and they're not moths but starlings. The way starlings reel and swarm in the sky, it's called something, can't remember what.

Can't see worth a damn, anyway.

Terrible fit of coughing. Oh, agony. Broken a rib for certain. More than one. Head's excruciating too. But I can move my arms, legs, so my back's not broken. Good. Hopefully broken rib won't puncture a lung. Do not cough. Do *not* cough.

Ah, oh, more agony.

I fell down a hole, a hole in the attic floor, and it's done me no good at all. Feeling awfully sleepy, ought to get into bed. Bed must be somewhere nearby, all ready for me, sheets and blankets in order, sheet folded over top of blanket and well tucked in. Pity they don't have competitions. *Always a gifted bedmaker, James Acton reached the semifinals on account of his impeccable hospital corners.* Oh, oh, the agony. Maybe if I get my head up I'll see better. Here we go.

More moths, this time pulsing in time with my heart, and an awful grating inside my head, sick-making noise. Ah for the love, for the love of all that's holy. What is holy? The beeches in Pipehouse Wood, and the flowers in the turf on Beacon Hill. Don't think of Beacon Hill. Lay head down again, grating noise, do *not* be sick. There's a name for this kind of fracture too. Can't remember it either.

Marching? It is not marching, not in this blizzard. A wincing limping from foot to foot with the foot frozen to the sock frozen to the boot. Day upon day upon day. We come to Luckenwalde, followed in time by others from camps farther east and south. These other men are far, far thinner than us, their eyes wild or utterly blank. There are not as many as there should be: they feel this, searching around for their companions, waiting for a rearguard that never comes. In the spring the Germans flee before the Russian advance. When the Russians arrive, they are not overly keen to liberate us—they make us wait with nothing to eat but heels of stale bread. In the end they relinquish us. We cross the bridge to the Americans.

Uh-uh-uh. Strange deep hollow wooden juddering noise, coming from above me, the rattle of a giant's cough in his coffin.

Aha. The creak that *freaked* Tom *out.*

When I was small I had a bedroom door that juddered when it was closed, wooden hinges, you see. The noise reminded me of a lion, a hungry one, growling in a thicket. I didn't want a lion for a door, so my mother said, *This is your friendly lion, he's letting you know he's here to guard you from bad dreams and terrors.*

This is a big piece of timber. Moving. That ought not to be moving.

Urgent desire to move out of its way.

Turn head with scrupulous care, avoid grating noise. Spread out hands, surrounding surface is smooth, whitish, crisscrossed with strands of fibrous material, perhaps straw. Straw from the barns blowing over snow. Push with one hand, pull with the other, oh, mercy me, my ribs. Engage feet in enterprise. Struggle like upturned beetle. Very sweaty now and vision totally clouded.

No use. Passing out.

Water's falling. Icicles melting at Luckenwalde. Spring, warm sunshine, the friendly iron grip of Russians. A dog, barking and barking. Somebody stop that dog barking.

"Acton. Acton. Can you hear me? Open your eyes if you can."

Voice is familiar, I can't place it.

"Make Bailey shut up," I croak. "Or the guard will kill him."

"Bailey is safe in my car. No guards. Open your eyes."

I drag my eyelids apart and see a large, rather sweaty but imperturbable face above me.

In croaking incredulity: "Archdeacon Frobisher?"

The very same," he announces. "I've telephoned the emergency services." He's speaking with great calm. "Can you move?"

"Been trying. Didn't get far. Broke ribs, I think. Broke my head. Ah, no, I beg you, don't do that." My skull is being searched by sturdy fingers.

"Found it." Great satisfaction. "A crepitating fracture. If I'm not mistaken. I shall take extreme care—"

He is silenced by a series of distant echoing reports. Gunfire, maybe, or the beginning of a thunderstorm on the coast. We know it's neither of those things. Immediately he seizes me under the arms and heaves. The grating of my skull makes me retch, my ribs poke nastily at my lungs. "Frobisher, let go," I gasp. "Get out of here." I shut my eyes, the snowfield envelops me.

"Imbecile." He starts to drag me. "Nearly there—"

"Push off, I tell you—"

A terrible crash batters my eardrums. We both cry out as bricks start smashing down outside the room. "Don't move!" shouts Frobisher.

As if I could.

The bricks fall by the hundreds in mortared chunks, exactly as if they're being unloaded from a giant shovel somewhere up in the chimney tops. I shut my eyes against the noise and dust. When I open them again it's much darker. A click, and Frobisher's face appears unflatteringly lit from below by torchlight.

"Now we're entirely trapped, I'm afraid." His voice seems much louder now in the enclosed space. "I believe the front of the house has

.fallen in. At any rate, that large piece of wall has stopped up the door to this room."

I peer in the gloom. He's right. Our exit is blocked as efficiently as if it had been bricked up.

"Thank heavens for your torch."

"I always keep one in the glove compartment of my motorcar," Frobisher booms. "I would not enter a damaged building without a source of light. I must say, it's lucky you were behaving like such a ninny. Had you been a little more enthusiastic about your egress, less inclined to tell me to *push off*, we'd have both been flattened out there. Oh, the depth of the riches of the wisdom and knowledge of God! How unsearchable his judgments and his paths beyond tracing out!" He pauses, a huge thick-lipped grin on his face. "Now. Ambulance and fire brigade will take some time, I'm afraid. Explosion at the refinery. So we must work. We have some resources, including . . ." He shuffles away, taking the light with him. "This iron bed." A prolonged episode of clanking ensues, over which he has to raise his voice. "The fall from your bedroom has broken it apart but the pieces may serve very well. Yes, indeed."

The fall from my bedroom? What does he mean? The torchlight spins around the room again, this time revealing—what? They look like stalagmites. Whitish, ghostly, some up to waist height, others squatter. More like pillars, in fact, than stalagmites. Squared-off pillars. My eyes strain to interpret them. They're newspapers. I'm lying on bales of newspapers, and tall stacks of newspapers are surrounding me, tied up with string, dating from the 1950s to the present day.

I'm in Blakemore's study.

My head swims. In the flickering of the torch I can now see a long rent down the middle of the ceiling, an extruded stuffing of broken rafters, floorboards, plaster. I, along with my bed, must have come down through this gap.

"Good God," I croak.

"Indeed He is." Frobisher has rolled up his sleeves now the better to haul some mighty object across the floor.

Haltingly I explain how I started my journey in the attic. "I've come down two floors. Why aren't I bashed to pieces?"

"You are fairly bashed, if I may say so."

It drifts into my mind that it must be the next day. "What's the time?"

"About ten in the morning."

"I've been here for . . . sixteen hours."

He darts me a look. "As long as that? Not good, not good at all. However, nothing can be done. Now, this mahogany desk"—he shunts it into position beside me—"will serve as one of our two walls. There is much to be said for a bit of well-joined hardwood. Had it been your modern desk, your plywood gimcrackery, it would be a very different story." He pauses to throw aside some bales of newspaper, his arms and shoulders moving like a trawlerman's. "And on the other side a table, what good fortune, in the same material." He drags, puffs, pushes. "Not as strong as the desk. We can but hope. Finally, your iron bed. Conveniently dismantled, as I said, into three pieces." Frobisher takes hold of the largest piece, the frame on which the mattress lay— where the mattress is, I have no idea—and heaves it into position across the two walls he has created out of desk and table. He follows with the headboard and the footboard. The result is an iron roof, more or less flat.

Uh-uh-uh. Here comes the gigantic juddering creak again. Surprisingly nimbly, Frobisher ducks down and shuffles into the makeshift cabin. I struggle into a semi-sitting position, lean my shoulder against a ledge of newspapers. It's much more painful but I must make room for him.

"That noise is probably your main beam," he says. "Wedged against a bulkhead, but slipping. Not yet weighting down those unsupported rafters above our heads, but that will happen, and the rafters will fall. Along with the beam and most of the roof, I should imagine." He turns the torch up to the ravaged ceiling. "It's only a matter of time before the rest follows." He sighs. "Dry rot, I'll be bound. In addition to neglect, apathy, scarcity of funds. A near-lethal combination in which the diocese has played its sorry part, in which I, therefore, have a measure of culpability, and I can only apologize to you, Acton, for endangering your life."

"But you are saving my life now," I say, aghast to find my voice is unsteady. "Archdeacon, I hope you don't mind my saying, but you are astonishing me."

He shifts position, glances down. We're both sitting on a bed of newspaper. "And you've created a bit of luck for yourself too," he observes. "It appears one of the things you never *got round to* is clearing up this study. I'm assuming this hoard of old newspapers belonged to Charles Blakemore. So your fall was broken by"—he peers—"the *Hampshire Chronicle*, no less." He lifts a finger, entranced. "I say, Acton. You should write in! *But for the H.C. I'd have been a goner.* It would make a remarkably diverting piece." His shoulders begin to shake. "Hum hum hum. Probably earn you a lifelong subscription!"

I screw my eyes up tight. I can put up with anything except this chortling.

"Am I irritating you?" He sounds genuinely taken aback. "Awfully sorry. I can be irritating, I know."

"Please don't think twice about it—"

He doesn't, and neither do I, because at that moment the thunder starts right above us. Unable to look away, I see the ceiling bulge, the gap widen. Here they come: roof tiles, first singly, then in hammering cloudbursts, clanging and crashing down on the bed frame a foot above our heads. I've got my hands over my head but Frobisher has spread his arms to grip hold of the desk and the table. I force myself to do likewise. The action makes me nauseated. Our wooden walls shake with each crash.

I can't imagine the main beam falling on us. How we'd ever survive it.

Then the downpour stops. The only sound now is our paroxysms of coughing. Each spasm pushes a white-hot lance into my side. Frobisher's great shoulders are heaving, his glasses covered in red dust. This doesn't stop him from crawling out of the shelter and removing debris from our roof. "Quite a lot of brick," he manages to gasp as he works, "as well as the roof tiles. I imagine the bricks to come from your inner bedroom walls. Perhaps the one with the fireplace." He shoves his way back under the bed frame, looking more squashed than ever.

For the first time I think of Yvette. "My wife's ashes."

Those of my daughter are safe, of course, with her brother.

"Where are they?"

"On my bedroom mantelpiece, above the grate."

"I'm sorry. You will have to hope."

That is simple for Frobisher. He's full of hope. Not me. I think I will walk off the track and into the snow, make my last landfall. The snow is so warm. Why didn't anyone tell me how warm snow is? Yvette will cry, but she will marry someone else in the end and have other children. I shut my eyes, cradled in this firm yet yielding softness.

"Acton." He's slapping his heavy fingers against my cheek. "Wake up."

"That hurts, you know."

"Fall asleep and I'll do it again."

"You have a remarkable range of skills," I tell him, on a painful breath.

"I worked in a mine once."

He lowers his head, removes his glasses, and cleans them on the front hem of his shirt. That is what we've come to. Frobisher's shirt is untucked. His eyes are pouches, red-rimmed. He appears to be absorbed in his task. I have to ask. If he doesn't want to tell me, he can always say, *It's not germane.*

"Where was the mine, Archdeacon?"

He looks up from his polishing, but just for an instant.

"Sosnitza," he says after a moment. "Poland." He replaces his glasses. "I was captured in '42."

He says nothing more. I remain still, trying not to breathe too deep in case I cough. A long, quiet while goes by. I ponder on Frobisher.

"Is that where you found God?" I ask him a while later. "In the mine?"

Frobisher shakes his head. "No. I was converted on the march. But you know about marching in the snow. Sagan, was it? The details of your file are somewhat misty."

And yet he had the right camp, nonetheless. "Yes."

Frobisher's gaze is distant. "I walked two hundred miles. Yes. Two hundred, before I fell by the wayside. Those who went all the way to Luckenwalde, double that."

I had marched fifty.

In April 1942 Frobisher's ship was two days out from Trinidad when a German warship attacked. "We were terribly outgunned," he says. "We landed perhaps one blow on the enemy before we began to sink. By that time all our decks were on fire. The German captain sent his lifeboats. All of ours were burned."

Many died in the battle and the sinking. The rest, the captain took on board his vessel. They were sent to the camp at Lamsdorf; from there they went out in *Arbeitskommando*, working parties, to the fields and factories. In the summer of '43 Frobisher was sent eighty miles from Lamsdorf to the mine.

"More men died in the mine, of course."

I am silent. In the summer of 1943, many of us at Sagan had passed the time playing golf.

Like us, Frobisher and his fellows had been marched out of the camp ahead of the Russian advance. Streaming out in long, straggling columns, the guards frightened, the men rapidly beginning to freeze and starve to death. Some tried a route via the mountains. Four hundred died out of a thousand.

"And then, oh, there came a day when I couldn't walk any farther. I was stripped to the bone." Frobisher looks down at his bulk. "Hard to imagine now, of course. So the Germans left me for dead in a schoolhouse. Try as I might I can't remember the name of the village."

He has erased it, I think, from his mind.

"But I was still alive a week later when the Americans came. Barely alive, but they saved me." He turns his gaze on me, a sudden fire in his eyes. "God be thanked for the Americans, without whom all our suffering would have been in vain."

"Amen," I whisper, in sincere accord.

"Now. A most important point. At this stage in my life I was not an atheist, by no means. I felt reasonably certain there was a deity, certainly a deity real enough for me to pray to Him to preserve my life. But I did not do that. No." Frobisher's jowls tremble. "Instead it came to me that I must freely surrender myself to Him, that He might deal with me as He wished. And so I did. I gave myself up to God. I prayed: Let me die or live according to your wish, Oh Lord. And I survived. All these years, Acton, I've lived by His grace. And when He wishes to take me, I will know that it will be because I've fulfilled His purpose."

A whispering, shifting noise above us makes me look up. Brick dust is falling, a thin cataract. The smallest breeze presages the tempest.

The beam strikes our iron roof with a bang like ball lightning. The table is dashed onto its side and the bed frame slams down, leaving us roofless. Rafters, lath, and plaster descend in a solid rain. Roaring, Frobisher seizes the iron headboard and throws it over us, propping it with the frame. I fold myself at an excruciating acute angle, giving him all the room I can. No air left, only dust. In the cacophony I feel Yvette's hand, the very first touch, but before I can close my fingers on hers, she slips away.

The curtain of dust thins, parts. The beam lies a couple of yards away, leaning against the wall of the study. Frobisher is gazing upward, weeping brown tears. The dust has irritated his eyes. A gray light gleams on the top of his head. "I can see the sky," he announces, and I understand that it is daylight shining on his crown. Does that mean that there is nothing else to fall? Presently Frobisher sighs and puts his glasses back on, the movement so everyday and businesslike that he could be about to speak at a meeting of the bishop's staff.

"It seems God can spare you for a bit longer," I say.

"Ha!" He claps his hands, gives me his usual bumptious grin. "Enough about me," he says, jollily. "What about your vocation, Acton?"

I tell him about the padre I met at Sagan, who gave me the usual spiel about a just war. I replied that this idea was one thing in a book, quite

another in life and, begging his pardon, I did not believe he had ever
borne down on an armored column and found himself strafing an
open lorryload of German troops, all of them too young to have voted
for any leader however evil.

"It was my wife, my future wife, who helped me out," I continue.
"She wrote to me at Sagan. Said, under the circumstances, there was
nothing else for it."

"Tsk-tsk." He shakes his head. The grin's still there, but there's an
awful lot more purpose behind it.

"What do you mean, *tsk-tsk*?"

"I don't mean how you *confirmed* your vocation."

"What, then?"

"How it has all come undone. How you lost your faith."

"What—what did you say?"

"Your faith, dear boy. You have lost it, haven't you?"

He holds me in his sights. A big, cumbrous, lonely man. Dogged,
and clever, and unfoolable. I've always known that.

I am a man fallen sick in Capernaum, tied against my will to a pallet
and lowered through broken tiles which let a shaft of light down
into the house: I swing into this searing light and out again into bot-
tomless dark. I am powerless, tied as I am to my raft of a bed. I cannot
imagine what lies below, I have no belief in this healing:

I have no belief.

I still call on God, even if my call is almost without hope, like the
call of a man at his back door for a dog who has long since run away:
the man peers through the veil of rain caught in the light from his
kitchen but he can see nothing beyond it except the blackness of night.

I have found a way to live in my ministry, prayed with my congre-
gations who answer *Amen* with the reverberating power of a breaking

sea: their faith holds me even when I'm swept into the undertow. By hospital beds and biers I have supported them and in return they throw me a rope, again and again they throw me the rope of their trust. It is a slender line, it does not bear too much weight, but it has held. All these years it has held.

Until now.

I watch Frobisher, kneeling with the faint pallor of daylight on his scalp. Will he ever understand me, this man for whom God's mighty hand is ready to lift him at any moment into the Life Eternal? How can he? How can he know how long I have kept watch? Day after week after month after year, switching on the airstrip lights at dusk, waiting for that glint on the horizon, for that distant drone to rise to a joyous roar, for that glorious touchdown? Will it make any difference to Frobisher, how hard I tried?

The daylight strengthens, briefly haloes him, then fades once more. Clouds must be passing overhead.

"How did you know?"

"Ah." He breathes noisily. "You're not the first. You all share a certain haunted look, you know, when you're forced to come anywhere near the big questions. Spreading the word of the Lord, for example. In your case, I was struck by your extreme reluctance to communicate with me. I must say, you're the only one who's actually tried to hide from me on top of a roof. Ha! Hum. I don't suppose you'd care to tell me how long it's been?"

The question almost makes me laugh. I don't even dare tell myself. "I would not."

"Well, all in good time." His magnificence only slightly diminished by his busy licking of a tiny pencil wedged between his stumpy fingers, Frobisher is making notes in the small black leather-bound diary in his other hand. "There are things that need to be done. Clearly a furlough is in order. And you will need temporary accommodation. There are some clergymen's rooms near the cathedral . . ."

"No—no—please, not that. I'll find something local."

Frobisher snorts. "As you like. You won't be able to do much anyway, with your head and your ribs stove in."

We look at each other silently for some moments. Beside him I feel brutish, unbroken, a stranger to harness.

"James. Put your trust in me. I am on your side."

He's never used my first name before. I shake my head, my ribs stabbing my heart. "Archdeacon, you don't know what's happened— you don't know—"

But he's stopping me with a raised hand, cocking his head. "Listen."

Thinly, and then gathering volume, comes the rumble of large, many-wheeled machines. Not long after that, questing shouts.

Two hours later, after a fair bit of scaffolding and much work with shovels, they stretcher me out and lay me on the grass. The ambulance is on its way. Frobisher kneels beside me. I can tell his knees are stiff, he is tired. Bailey's barking from his car.

"Let him loose, Archdeacon. He can't wait very long."

Bailey hops down, sniffs the air, trots away to relieve himself under a tree before following Frobisher back to me. Frobisher kneels down once more and strokes him. The dog noses his hand, nearly tipped off his feet by the wagging of his own tail.

The ambulance arrives. I am surrounded by medical people. In the last few minutes my lungs have begun to fill with what feels like sand, leaving only a few cubic inches for breath.

"Archdeacon—do you want Bailey?"

He beams. "I'd be very happy to look after him," he says. "Until you're on your feet again."

"No—I mean—keep him . . ."

"Really?" He looks at me, startled. "Are you sure?"

"No time for a dog—he's fond of you—and you—of him . . ."

"Why, yes." Frobisher is flushing with happiness. "That is certainly true. How very kind, very kind indeed, Acton. I accept with the greatest pleasure."

An oxygen mask is clamped on my face. I wanted to say how glad I was to be able to give Frobisher something in return for saving my life. I make a few gestures as I am loaded into the ambulance, trying to convey these sentiments. But Frobisher is no longer looking at me. He's still kneeling on the grass, filthy and shirtsleeved, murmuring endearments to the dog in his arms.

TWENTY

It's a farmhouse out beyond Barrow End. Belongs to Harvey Corey but Harvey's selling, he's got too old to cope with it now. He's in a nice comfy bungalow in Upton, and when the land sale goes through, he's going to turn the house into a B&B, which his daughter will run. But that won't be for yonks. So you can have it in the meantime. The farmhouse. For a bit of rent. James, are you listening?"

Althea Brock peers down at me. I'm lying on a hospital bed with a pipe coming out of my chest. One of my three broken ribs has poked through the membrane surrounding my left lung, and the interstice between membrane and lung is vengefully leaking fluid. This is the fifth, or possibly the sixth day I've spent in this condition, and each one has dawned without any noticeable improvement.

I make an encouraging motion with my hand.

"No heating, of course," she continues, "gas lamps in the bedrooms, and no running water either. Harvey says the pump's in the kitchen and the bath is a tin tub. Cooking's on a propane stove and the cylinder's full." She spreads her hands. "What else? Oh, yes. Miles from anywhere and no telephone. Just what you wanted, you silly fool."

I give her a thumbs-up. "Perfect," I whisper. "Thank you."

She shrugs her bony shoulders. "Oh, I'm only following instructions from Clive Perry. He told me to obey your every wish and whim. I asked him why on *earth* you wanted to be in the back of beyond when there are a number of willing hosts in Upton, every one of them with *extensive* private quarters for guests. But he said he was only the curate, and my guess was as good as his. A likely story." She sips from a plastic cup and eyes it with wonderment. "Heavens, this coffee is filthy. Now"—leaning forward—"what about Tom? Still adamant, are you, that he should be kept in the dark?"

Althea has been very kind, offering to telephone Tom or take a letter at my dictation, but the offer is becoming rather insistent. Tom and I don't need to talk about this stupid accident. We have a much bigger and more dreadful subject to address, and that won't happen until he's ready. "Yes, I am." I take as deep a breath as I dare. "Althea, may we consider the subject of Tom closed for now?"

"As you wish." She flops backward in her chair. "It's your funeral. And, my goodness, it very nearly was. What about that archdeacon of yours! An absolute revelation. I hope he's given you six weeks off. The very minimum, in the circs."

I move my head toward the bedside cabinet. "Would you like to read his letter? It came yesterday."

"Ah, a copperplate hand," she murmurs, holding the stiff white pages at arm's length and squinting at them. "And a high style. *Heretofore. Whence.* Blah . . . blah . . . Sick leave . . . Blah . . . Retreat? . . . Sabbatical?" She puts the letter down. "James, have I got this right? You're off duty until March next year?"

We will speak soon, the letter concludes. *There is much to discuss.* His swirling strokes of black ink make the sentiment all the more threatening. I know perfectly well what he has in mind. He'll knock some God into James Acton, just see if he won't.

He's got his work cut out, is all I can say.

The pause that Althea expects me to bring to an end lengthens. She leans once more toward me, superlatively craggy. "James, whatever it *is* . . . " She widens her old, veined eyes. "Whatever it is, remember. I'm tight as a clam."

"No mystery. Just going into dry dock. For a refit. Vicars do that, you know, as well as ships."

"Hmm."

A period of quiet follows.

"Ellen," she says suddenly. "She's dreadfully worried. She wants to come—"

"No. No, Althea, please. She's not going to see me like this."

"Oh!" She gives a derisive squawk. "You young people and your *vanity*."

It takes a fortnight in all, but finally the lung membrane seals its leak. The skull bones knit. The ribs still rage, but I'm discharged armed with pills. Clive Perry comes to collect me. I approach him with wariness. Another Upton vicar keels over—what must he be thinking? Mercifully he's technical. I hear about the house: only the back half is left standing, the front lying in ruins. The diocese, eventually, will pay for a total demolition. As for my belongings, those that are salvageable have been packed up and taken to Harvey Corey's farmhouse. "Everything's a bit battered, but you've got some clothes and books and so on. I'm afraid your record collection's done for. And . . . your wife's ashes. Archdeacon Frobisher asked the team to comb through the rubble, but they haven't found the urn yet."

"Thank you, Clive, for everything you've done."

We're on the road to Upton from Southampton—the road Tom and I took together two months ago. We go through small village after small village: the brick-and-flint walls spin by, the dripping thatch. Prosperity scraped up over centuries out of lamb upon lamb, thin harvest on thin harvest. Above a certain height, the soil's nothing but chalk crumb. My wife walked up those heights and kissed her lover.

Philip Moore. Lying in my hospital bed I revisited our encounter many times and each time he became shiftier, his lying more barefaced, more ominous. Oh, Yvie. She can't have. And yet, supposing she did? A fortnight ago I risked my life trying to get to the truth, but now I'm not sure I've got the courage to find out. What it is to be both suspicious and cowardly. Thinking the worst of my wife, and yet too afraid to do anything about it.

Did I ever catch a glimpse, a spark in the daylight, there and then gone? Did she ever mention the village by name, then, or afterward, so that when I saw it, *Upton*, so many years later in my widowhood, in the candle flame in my study at Fulbrook, it caught alight all over again? I don't know. I had no call, until now, to consider the way she used to be, Yvette, when she came back from her trips in the car. Coming back with her eyes lively from a drive in the country.

We reach Barrow End. The hamlet has a single road leading up and out. The farmhouse has the hill at its back. Clive knows the way: he's already brought all my things here. As we enter the farmyard I see my car parked in a tractor shed.

"I'm sorry I've let you down, Clive."

Clive shakes his head, he doesn't want that. "We haven't had that drink," he says. "And we should. Good beer. No talking shop. Whenever you like."

Downstairs my kitchen things are on the table, along with a supermarket bag of groceries. I try out the water pump, gingerly: the handle requires a downward push. Take a torch to the privy.

Tomato soup and toast. Reminded again of Tom. Unpack the groceries. Find a bottle of Glenlivet and, at the bottom of the bag, a tin of potatoes.

The rest of my things are stacked in the parlor, still boxed and bundled. The totality of my possessions. Even if he were in the mood to do so, Tom needn't worry anymore about the state of the furniture. It is all smashed and gone. The rhino chair is no more.

I can't do what Frobisher is asking of me. There will be no refit. I can't retreat, meditate, take spiritual instruction. This is a fitting point to end this pretense. When I'm healed I will find a self-drive van similar to the one I hired in Fulbrook, and take these last few things away. Where to, I have no idea. The speed of the collapse is making my head spin.

What will I do? Fifty-five-year-old man seeks employment. Skills: Baptizing unruly toddlers, extremely low flying. Can walk a long way in snow. Quite a long way. Not as far as some.

Upstairs I find that my bed is made. The kindness of that simple act nearly overwhelms me. The bedroom is peaceful, with a sloping floor. I light the gas lamp on the night table and sit down on the bed.

It is Advent, I realize. I hope the winter will come quickly, bring that bitter snap in the air, a sniff of frost, and the Christ Child coming. *Veni, veni, Emmanuel,* O come, O come, Emmanuel. Thou Rod of Jesse, thou Dayspring, thou Key of David. I've been in one long Advent for years and years. I stand up, preparing to get into bed without praying but I can't. I haven't done that since I've been able to talk. So I get cautiously down onto my knees and pray, *O come, O come,* into the darkness of my closed eyes.

I climb into bed, arrange myself to the advantage of my injured side. The sheets aren't mine. These are white and crisp and scented with lavender. My eye is caught by a jug on the chest of drawers. In the jug, some tall white dahlias.

In the morning the sunlight is gentle, the silence broken only by the occasional bleating of sheep. Mr. Corey's, I assume. I lie in bed, as passive as I was on my return to England after the war and my mother brought me chicken broth.

From Luckenwalde to Leipzig, from Leipzig to Halle and then to Brussels. We had time for our freedom to fall on us gradually. I remember the last flight: one quick hour and we landed in England. A young WAAF fed us in an aircraft hangar: I tackled a mammoth plateful of food with three companions but we had to push it away, it was beyond us. When she brought us three more plates we realized that the first plate had been a single helping. Then they loaded us onto a Forces train and we chugged through Shropshire toward an RAF base. The hills rose and fell under a haze of warmth and the trees were in full leaf. I went to sleep immediately and so did many others. It was shock, or disbelief: yes, a sleep of disbelief. Shropshire, hills, trees, liberty: none of it could possibly be real.

I feel like this now, lying in this bed, in this room I do not know. Half of me is still asking: What on earth has happened?

At the RAF base we had a medical and a debrief. Like many others I was diagnosed with emaciation and strain, neither of those being actual diseases I would say, more like two different types of emptiness. The first I could try to fill, the second not. As for God, they were neither able nor unable to diagnose His presence in me, not having the correct instruments, but He was there. Still there all through the war.

Then home, to my mother and broth.

As soon as I could—I wanted to escape the broth—I flew to Egypt, landing at Amiriya where Yvette found me again. We didn't recognize each other, she in her uniform, me I don't know how many pounds lighter. Still unable to eat very much, or talk very much, or be capable of anything that might be called courting.

But she was practical: she got to work on me.

In England she had nothing to sustain her except my love and her courage but she had plenty of both. Her English was strongly accented in those days and very, very French in construction but she relished her mistakes. She befriended everyone.

Once I overheard my mother tell Tom, when Tom was in disgrace after some frightful infraction of our parental rules, "We'll love you forever, Grandpa and I, whatever you do."

Yvie. I'll love you forever whatever you did.

But I must know.

I am summoned downstairs by a knock at the door. It's a fire officer, and he's holding a plastic bag. He hands it over. "I'm sorry about this nasty bag," he says. "I couldn't find anything better for her." Inside the bag is Yvette's urn. A slight scratch at the shoulder the only damage.

I like the way he used both hands to give me the bag, the way he bowed his head slightly as he apologized for it, and the way he spoke of "her."

"I'm very grateful," I say. I am.

After breakfast I sit down and write to Tom. I begin by giving him the Corey farmhouse address and telling him about the collapse of the vicarage, my injury and rescue. Keeping strictly to the physical aspects. I'm not about to start on the spiritual. *The God situation*, as Tom might very well call it. I continue:

> *It is true that I lied about the little chest.*
> *I hope that one day I shall be able to tell you why.*

In the small hours, while Yvette labored to bring forth the daughter who had already died, God was still with me. I had no idea that He was to steal away at dawn like a deserter from the camp. No use raising the alarm. By the time we left the hospital, He was long gone. This was the 12th September 1950.

A date I will go to great lengths to keep from Frobisher.

Yvette needed me so much, I had to give her something. The man she called New James was the best I could do by way of fabrication. My real self, the blundering, Godforsaken soul inside him, would have been worse than useless to her. While she begged me for the truth I shut my doors on her; even when the bleaching light seared the interiors of my closed eyelids I did not admit her.

Only later did I bring myself to tell her the truth. *I know I did see her, but the shock of her death was so great that the memory has been erased from my mind. I am so sorry.* That was the beginning of the end for my assumed, false personality. I don't remember exactly when I struggled out from under New James. I was very glad to. He was absolutely exhausting.

Yvette was there waiting for me. She could talk to me now. She understood that, even if I couldn't always reply, I was listening and taking her words to heart.

On the last evening before Tom was born, Yvette was so round, so burdened, that she tackled the stairs like they were a mountain face, her eyes shining coins of love. "I can't take much more of this," she said, and laughed, knowing that she could. That night in the small hours the bedside lamp lit her grin of pain and her fingers clenched in mine as I dialed the doctor's number with my free hand. The doctor arrived with his pajama legs poking out from under his trousers. "Try to breathe, Mrs. Acton," he implored her, but she had no time for breathing, only for strident dry-eyed cries as Tom appeared, his fast transit congesting her face, his little red bloody body sliding into the world. We knew him the moment he arrived. Of course he was Tom, there could be no other baby. He knew we were waiting for him. His howls told us so. *Here I am! Here I am at last!*

I held Yvette in my arms in bed as she fed him. While he suckled he clung on to her little finger, opening just a slit of one eye to give me a beady look. *She's mine now, and don't you forget it.* My arms were around her forming a perimeter defense in which she could cradle him. She moved in bed and hissed at the pain, cursed. *Not since the Battle of Bréville.* A dam and her cub, and my job was to feed her and thereby feed him. I did so; she wanted porridge, so we both had some. A midwife came early in the morning and tutted. Mrs. Acton had not bathed the baby.

"She hasn't bathed him *yet*," I said.

"Mr. Acton, please compose yourself and take away those dishes," said the midwife. "Your wife and I have business together."

I had thought that I was composed but on my way downstairs I touched my face and it was wet with tears that had brimmed over.

I cross out the previous lines about the little cedarwood chest. I'm not going to send this letter, it's such a sorry effort, but I write down the question anyway.

Dear Tom,

Is there another notebook?
Do you know what happened?

A familiar sound outside. The squeak of brake blocks on the rim of a wheel. I put down my pen, peer out of the window. A child on a bicycle is pedaling round and round in the farmyard. The rider, in gumboots and an anorak with the hood up, is trying to make the circle smaller with each revolution. That will only work up to a certain point. Beyond that, your machine will stall. There we go, momentum lost: the rider skids on one foot over the concrete yard, parks the bike against the rusty gate, which is always propped open. Saunters up to the kitchen door. Rat-a-tat-tat.

What can this young person want?

She begins to sing, her voice high and mournful. A certain Major Tom, I gather, is not responding to Ground Control. Is this a message for me? If it is, I haven't got the right codes.

"Come in," I call. "It's open."

The door opens, the child pulls back the hood, reveals short tufts of hair. A girl of about eleven or twelve. "Hello. Are you Mr. Acton? I'm Penny Lacey. How do you do."

"How do you do, Penny Lacey."

She grins, bends sideways like a reed in the wind for no discernible reason, straightens up again. "Ellen wants to know if you're up to visitors. She says that if not it doesn't matter, we'll go straight on by. The last thing we want to be is *de trop*. That means 'too much.' She thinks we might be too much for you. Because of your accident, I'm guessing, but she didn't say so."

She waits, this startling visitor, beaming and expectant. I review the local conditions. The dishes are dried and put away. I'm washed and brushed, my clothes clean. My first tablet of the day is having its usual marvelous effect on my breakages. It probably won't get any better than this.

"Please tell Ellen," I say, "that you would not be *de trop*."

"Okay! If she sees my bike at the gate, she'll come straight in. She won't be long but obviously she lags behind on the hills. Being so much *older*. Is that a water pump? May I have a go?"

"By all means." I've worked out the least distressing way to push the handle down, but it's still a trial. "Would you mind filling a couple of jugs for me?"

She sets to work, coaxing a higher and more rhythmic squeak out of the pump than I've yet managed, talking nineteen to the dozen all the while. "Ellen told me your house fell down while you were inside it, and an arch*bishop* saved your life! Gosh, what a turn-up. There, that's the jugs. Can I fill up anything else? Saucepans? Great. I wish Upton Hall School would fall down. While it was empty, of course. The girls are a nest of vipers and vixens but I wouldn't want to kill them. What about those plastic bowls? You can't have too much water. My dad's away in the army, you know. And my mum's at the Laurels, so I go to Ellen's when we're allowed out. Did you know Ellen rescued me from the flood? Were you here in the flood? It was fantastic, the whole school was underwater. Anyway, she took me to her house. It's lovely there. So warm, you can't believe, and we had shepherd's pie . . ."

I become distracted by my growing unease. I've got no idea what

I can say to Ellen. It had been almost impossible to refuse Penny, but perhaps I should have. There's nothing I can give Ellen.

". . . And I bet you can't guess where!" Penny lets go of the pump handle at last and beams at me.

"I'm sorry, Penny, what were you saying?"

"Ellen's going somewhere, and I bet you can't guess!"

"You're right. I have no idea."

"Singapore!" She claps her hands. "I know! I'll miss her to death but isn't it groovy?" Her eyes dart to the window. "Look, there she is, coming now."

Singapore? Before I can say anything, Penny hurries out into the yard where, I can see from the window, Ellen is parking her bike. After a brief exchange Penny goes into the barn. Ellen's dressed for cycling, in jeans and a jersey the color of her eyes. Roses in her cheeks: it was a long pull up the hill out of Barrow End, and her jacket is tied by the sleeves around her waist. Her hair is drawn up in a bun, but the wind has half destroyed it. She lifts up her hands and pulls it loose, the tresses swirl around her face, and her lips move, *Oh, bother.* She turns into the wind, side-on to me, and corrals it into a heavy plait which she pins up behind her head. I can tell by the way she rams in the hairpins that she wants to make her bun again, but it's impossible in this wind.

Tall, springy as a beech bough, and just now fairly annoyed. I watch her avidly.

"Penny's fetching some hay for Harvey's sheep," she tells me as I let her in. "He's kept a dozen of his favorites. She's to spend a long time checking them over, to see if any are limping. Foot rot is a pest. How are you?"

She steps over the threshold—no she doesn't step, she makes a small leap, all whipped up as she is by the wind and the sunlight.

"Free of foot rot, at least," I manage to say, through the dazzlement.

"I'm glad to hear it." She gives me a long, penetrating gaze, one I don't feel remotely ready for. "You look very well, considering. Very . . . I don't know. Very upright."

"It's the bandage round my chest."

"Oh, James." Her eyes start to glisten. "When Althea told me what had happened, goodness me. I could *kiss* your archdeacon Frobisher. Give him a great smacker on the cheek!"

"Please," I implore her, "don't make me laugh."

"Forgive me. I didn't mean to!"

The pain is enormous, not that I care in the least.

"Would you like some coffee? Or water?" I indicate the filled containers on the countertop. "As you can see, I've got plenty. Your splendid young friend doesn't do things by halves, does she."

"No, and I heard all about it in the yard. I'd love a cup of coffee, thank you." Ellen unwraps her jacket from her waist, hangs it on the back of a chair. "We've been up since the crack of dawn."

"Penny said you rescued her during the flood."

"She was stuck in the middle of a drowned field. Without a friend in the world. Her mother's been having a breakdown, one involving an awful lot of gin."

"Ah. The Laurels."

"She's doing better now, I think, and so is Penny."

"Thanks to you, no doubt."

"Perhaps." She glances around the kitchen, her eyes warm. "I used to come up here as a girl, with Lucy Horne, to visit Daniel, Harvey Corey's son. Lucy and Dan weren't fitted for school; it was cruel to keep them there, year after year, trying in vain to spell *archipelago*. So I used to do their homework for them. I remember Dan making that egg rack." She moves to the dresser and picks it up, a miniature wooden table with a dozen circles cut out of the top. "See these smaller holes? They're for bantam eggs. Dan wanted to make me one, to say thank you for the homework." She lifts it higher, blows away dust. "But Mother and I never had more than two eggs in the house at a time, so instead he made me a tiny rack for my thimbles. It was very useful. I did a great deal of patching and darning in those days."

She sits down when I set the coffee on the table. Suddenly it's too quiet in here, too still, and the tension builds.

I break the silence. "Thank you for the dahlias."

She glances up at the ceiling. I know instantly that she's thinking of the bedroom, where the flowers are. The bedroom and the bed, the sheets, their crispness, their scent of lavender. So am I, of course. The flush that has been fading from her cheeks builds again. She adds milk to her coffee, paying close attention to the task.

"You needed something nice," she says in a small voice.

"I did," I tell her. "I do."

Her embarrassment vanishes. The look she gives me now is watchful, almost stern. I remember our last conversation in the dark of the lane. Well might she be wary.

"Singapore," I burst out, seizing on another subject. "Penny told me. Are you going to see your brother?"

She'd told me about him at the party. His adventurous wartime escape from the invasion.

"Yes." She relaxes. "All these years, and I've never been! And Edward must have come here a dozen times."

"He went back there after the war, then?"

"Oh, yes. It's his home." Sipping her coffee.

"When are you going?"

"In . . ." She looks at her watch. "Thirty-two hours. I've had a great many jabs. Edward and I will spend some time in Singapore, then we'll go up through the Malay Peninsula to Penang. Then he'll let me loose.

I'll make for Thailand, I think. Apparently the food is excellent. I probably won't be back until February."

"Good heavens!"

"I know. Here I am, a middle-aged woman, and I've led such a sheltered life. How on earth will I manage?"

"Honestly, I didn't mean that—"

"No, you're right to be amazed. The idea's ridiculous, really."

Her lip curls, she's quite merciless.

"Go easy on me," I beg her. "I'm just a man. Ouch. A man who can't even laugh."

"Just as well. This is no laughing matter."

"I meant . . ."

"I know what you meant, James. You meant, it's a long time. So long, in fact, that you may not be here when I come back."

I didn't expect such a direct hit. The sad shame compresses my chest. I try hard to breathe out so I can breathe in again.

"How did you know?"

"I wouldn't say I knew, exactly. More a case of impressions. Your extreme despair when I gave you a lift—you practically apologized for knowing me. And then Althea's been so incredibly cagey and mournful. Like a raven—occasionally cawing enigmatically, giving off this air of doom. Of something being *afoot*. And the look on your face now, of course. I made a guess. A good guess, as it turned out . . . James, are you all right?"

"Sorry. It's the ribs. Too long sitting. Can't get my breath."

She rises to her feet, holds out her hand. "You need air."

I take hold. Her fingers are slim, strong.

TWENTY-ONE

The sky is active, clouds bound across it, the wind swirls around us. A front is coming. We pass the barn and enter a rough field that rises sharply to a fence. On the other side of the fence Penny stands waist-deep in sheep, tugging handfuls off a bale of hay. Beyond her, the sloping skyline.

Ellen walks close by me.

"It's not inhalation that's the problem, it's exhalation," I tell her. "Getting rid of the carbon dioxide. Makes me think of Tom, saying that. Haha."

An agonizing sadness. I remember looking at the kitchen window from the darkness of the garden. Seeing Ellen's neck, her updrawn hair.

"How is Tom? He must be awfully shocked at what's happened."

Awfully shocked at what's happened. He certainly is. Another spasm. It can't be called laughing, to be honest. More a kind of internal wringing. I come to a halt, my hand on my left side.

"James, do you want to go back?"

"No, not at all—"

"I'm walking on the wrong side, on your bad side," Ellen exclaims, and comes around to my right. "Would it be easier if you gave me your arm?"

"It would."

She links her arm into mine. She's wearing no coat and her body radiates warmth. My lungs fill up properly with fresh air. Our strides are the same length and we walk in step. I'm glad she's beside me, setting a course across this field, or I wouldn't know which direction to take.

"What a terrible old crock I am."

"I was thinking that very thing. I mean, a few paltry broken ribs, a punctured lung, a skull fracture, concussion, and it's not even as if the *whole* house fell down on you. Now look at you, all you can manage after these piffling injuries is a brisk walk up a steep slope."

"Ha—no, really. I've been falling down too. And Frobisher's found out, you see. Very sagacious man, Ronald Frobisher. Very shrewd. Ellen, I'm not the man you think I am."

Her mouth falls open. "James, how preposterous!"

"No, I mean it. I'm a fraud."

"That's a very strong word."

"What else would you call a vicar who doesn't believe in God?"

She comes to a halt, moves in front of me, her eyes narrowed against the breeze that is blustering in my ears, scrambling my wits. I cling on to pieces of myself but it's a losing battle. The many men I've been, the pilot, the prisoner, the priest, are thinning down to transparency, tearing off, whipping away in the wind. I don't know what's left.

"I haven't forgotten what you told me at your party," she says. "When I said I was getting pagan in my old age. About women seeing things. I realized then that you were a good vicar. You always have been."

"How can you know?"

"I know you," she replies, unperturbed.

"Ha. I wish I did . . ."

She takes my arm again and we walk on. Oh, that we could travel the hills and valleys together. Oh, that I didn't have a spear in my side, stabbing all the way to my heart.

"Archdeacon Frobisher's hatched a plan," I tell her. "After my sick leave, I'm supposed to take a sabbatical. I expect he'll find spiritual counsel for me. Possibly a retreat. We haven't discussed the details, but I can imagine it." Polished staircases, reading rooms, reflective conversations. Bright faces at communal breakfasts.

"But you don't want to."

"I can't think of anything more excruciating or pointless."

"So you want to stop looking for God now."

"Mm. Tired of it."

We've reached the fence. Beyond us, the sheep field, and Penny striding in the distance.

"Which is why," Ellen says, "you might be gone by February."

I think back to that evening with Bridie at Redwood House when I brought her the scarf. I held the silk in my hands and felt her again, my girl in the grain. Even if I had asked Bridie no further questions I wouldn't have been spared the truth. At that same moment Tom had been reading his way toward Philip Moore.

I risk a look at Ellen. Her profile is fine-cut, like a face on a coin. Even in repose she has a questing, outward look. She's waiting for me to speak, of course, because if ever a statement required confirmation or denial, it was hers.

"I discovered . . ." I drag my eyes from her and look away at the hill. "I discovered that Upton has always been too close to Alver Shore."

"So." She releases my arm with a gentle pat. "Well, I can't argue with geography." She moves away from me, grasps the top rail of the fence, and climbs over. I watch her stride over the grass in the direction of the sheep and Penny. After a moment she stops, turns around, and comes back to face me. "Actually, James, I'm not entirely sure you've got the right."

"The right to what?"

"To give up on us all, with no warning or explanation." She folds her arms, expecting me to respond to this challenge.

"I'm not sure I know what you mean," I say weakly.

"You made a promise to us, didn't you? To the people of Upton? To serve us?"

"Yes, but that promise was false. It was contingent on my having faith, and I—"

"Faith." Her face tells me what she thinks of that. "Let me tell you about Daniel Corey, Harvey's son."

"The boy who made your thimble holder."

"Yes. He died in Italy, in August 1944, fighting on the Gothic Line. A hard, bloody battlefront as I'm sure you know, killing thousands and thousands."

"Ellen, I'm so sorry . . ."

"John Blunden, Dan's friend, was with him all through the war. When John came home, he told Dan's sister it should have been him, John, instead, and he packed up and left for Southampton. He couldn't bring himself to stay here, bumping into the Coreys every day. So we don't see John anymore. William Kennet nearly fell off his feet when I told him the news. All he could say was, 'Not Daniel, not Daniel.'"

"Poor William . . ."

"Dan got married in 1939," she continues, holding up her hand. "A week before Selwyn and me. Marcy, his widow, has never looked at another man. His mother, old Mrs. Corey, she's made of some sort of granite, I think, she struggles on. Another old lady still fighting the war. As for Harvey, Dan's father, he's broken. He's never got over it and neither, for that matter, has Lucy. Dan was her oldest friend. He was a good friend to me as well during my hardest times. So even now, thirty years later, when I look at Dan's picture and think of all this waste and damage, I get quite breathless with anger."

Her tone is gentle, conversational. It makes her words all the more devastating.

"I'm telling you this," she continues, "because Harvey Corey and his wife, and Lucy, and William, along with all the others who lost Daniel, and everyone else who comes to that church week after week, with other equally terrible holes in their lives—they expect you to be there. *I* expect you to be there, to help them keep going. You know all about keeping going. This is not the time to give up, James. Do you understand? This is not the time."

A patch of sunshine races up the field, strafes us, flies on over the brow of the hill. Penny lollops toward us on long legs.

I'm off to East Anglia," I tell Ellen in the farmyard. Penny has said goodbye and is speeding off down the hill to Barrow End, standing on the pedals. "I must see my son."

"Today?"

"Yes."

Now that I've said it, I have to go. This can't wait any longer.

"It's an awfully long way. Can you drive, with your ribs?" She looks up at me, shielding her eyes from the sun. "I don't know why I'm even asking. You've made up your mind."

"Yes." I try to find a reassuring expression, like a man who knows what he's doing. "*Bon voyage,* Ellen. Good luck on your great adventure. Please send me a postcard. Send me a lot of postcards."

"Where to?" Her eyes suddenly blaze. "Corey's Farm? Or somewhere else?"

Penny calls from a few hundred yards away, wheeling in the road.

"Ellen, please come *on*, I'm *starving . . .*" Ellen turns away from me toward her bicycle. "Goodbye, James," she says, pushing it past the gateway. "Good luck."

She can't just leave like this. Yes, she can. She's going to. I hurry after her.

"Please," I beg her. "Please give me time . . ."

"You've *got* time, James. You have to decide what to do with it."

Astride her bike, she leans over and kisses me on the cheek. "That's for Archdeacon Frobisher," she whispers.

I shout with aghast laughter. "Am I to pass it on?"

"Goodbye, James!" she calls, and cycles off, fast, after Penny. I watch them until they reach a point where the road gets a lot steeper and they plunge out of sight. Two long, thrilled screams fade into silence. I stand with my hand on my cheek, listening, but there's nothing else to hear.

Now that I've decided to make the trip today, I'm overtaken by haste. A thermos of tea, a cobbled-together sandwich. I pencil out the route in my road atlas: the journey will take hours and hours. I pack a bag of necessities, lock all the doors. It's now eleven in the morning.

Turning left is much worse than turning right. The pain focuses my mind on the driving, to the exclusion of all else.

Four and a half hours later I reach Unthank Road in heavy rain. Tom's street is on the left—naturally—and number 23 is halfway up. Parking is a trial, getting out of the car is perfect agony. I rap on the door, rain pours over my head and mackintoshed shoulders. Nobody comes. With immense weariness I make my way back down the steps, preparing to fold myself back into the car and wait.

A drenched figure is loping up the street. Wet hair in his eyes, a bag of groceries swinging from one hand. No raincoat, just a soaked denim jacket and flared trousers with a tidemark of damp approaching his knees. He's slowing now, squeezing one hand into a tight pocket for his house key. Mildly muttering, probably at the rain. I move into his line of sight.

"Oh, God Almighty," he says.

I don't reply. Silently he lets us in. He squelches into the kitchen and I follow him. He takes off his jacket and spreads it over a vast radiator. Then he hands me a dishcloth: "For your hair." He's far wetter than I am, but it doesn't seem to bother him at all. The cloth is dry, though, smells of nothing more offensive than baked beans. Tom lights a match under the kettle, glances at me again.

"Sit down, Dad."

"I'd rather stand, if it's all the same."

"Suit yourself." He sighs. "I'm sorry I left without saying goodbye. But I was so . . . What's the word for a mixture of rage, disgust, and grief?"

"Do you need a single word? Those three convey your meaning perfectly well."

I take hold of the back of a kitchen chair and try to laugh in a way that will hurt me the least. The resulting noise is a strange panting exhalation, like a man entering an Arctic sea.

"Dad. Are you having a heart attack?"

The young. It's the first thing they think of.

"No, I'm fine. Oh. Ah."

"Come on. You're clutching your left side." Red-faced with worry, he rushes past me out of the room. "I'm calling an ambulance."

I follow him. "Tom"—catching up with him in the hall, putting a hand on his shoulder as he picks up the receiver. "It's okay," I gasp. "I've broken a couple of ribs, that's all."

"What the hell?" He hangs up the phone. "How did you do that? Don't tell me—mucking about in the attic. Am I right?"

"Mm-hm."

He shakes his head in despair. "I don't know what on earth's going on," he says, raking both hands through his hair. "I'm just trying to lead my life, you know? But now there's all this . . . stuff, about Mum, and my sister . . ." He turns around and I'm shaken by the look he gives me, one I've never seen before, a fully grown adult glare. "And that *man*. You ought to know that I blame *you* for that. The way you *behaved*."

"Indeed." At last I feel some mettle. "Philip Moore had nothing to do with it?"

The glare diminishes, but he's still hot-eyed; he pushes at his fringe. "Yeah, well, obviously a bit."

"I couldn't have told you about Philip. Your mother never said a word. I don't know any more than you. Possibly less than you, if there's another notebook." I take my courage in my hands. "Is there another notebook, Tom?"

He says, "Yes, it's upstairs."

I shut my eyes and breathe in, my hands flat over my mouth.

"I haven't read it," I hear him saying. "I couldn't, in the end. I thought you should be first."

He takes my arm. "Come on. This way." I open my eyes again; he ushers me to the foot of the stairs. "Do I need to, sort of, shunt you up there?"

"I beg you, no shunting."

"Did you fall off the chair when you got down?" he says as we ascend. "I bet you did. Trust you to try and mend the hole by yourself."

"Wasn't mending the hole." Climbing makes me short of breath.

"What, then?"

I signal that I can't talk anymore. He shows me the bathroom, points toward another door: "That's my room," and goes back down-stairs to make tea.

The bathroom is medically clean. His room spotless, tidy. Rush mat-ting on the floor, a lowered blind, beanbags. My gaze runs over posters of sweating guitar-harnessed men, snake-haired women, a striking im-age of a beam of light refracted through a triangular prism. A crammed bookshelf made of planks on bricks. A chest of drawers, on the bare wooden top a circle made out of small pebbles and seashells. Both pebbles and shells are striped with white and a multitude of grays, the stones smooth and seamed with quartz, the shells perfect ribbed fans. They alternate, pebble and shell, touching edge to edge like the beads of a necklace.

In the middle of this circle is the cedarwood chest.

"There she is. Safe with her brother."

Tom's standing behind me with two mugs of tea. He nods toward the pebbles and shells. "That was Florence's idea," he continues. "So I went with my mates to Holkham and Cromer, to the beaches."

"Beautiful."

He shrugs. *It is what it is.* "Which is better for you? Sitting or lying down?"

"Lying down."

He pushes a low table toward the bed with one foot and puts one of the mugs on it. The bed is almost on the floor, a king-size mattress on a pallet. I kneel down by the mattress and, gritting my teeth, roll onto it. After I've lain there panting for a minute or so, I say, "I was in the attic because I was looking for the blasted notebook."

I tell him about the hole in the attic, my fall, the collapse of the house, Frobisher's role in saving me, my injuries and hospitalization.

I omit all talk of God. It's a brief account, calmly related, but by the time I've finished his face has frozen.

"Bloody hell," he breathes. "If I hadn't taken the book . . ."

"No, no. The roof could have gone any time. I might have died in my bed."

"Dad, don't talk like that. So you've been in hospital and I didn't know?" He passes a hand over his mouth. "Why didn't you *tell* me!"

"What, you mean, rung you up?"

"All right, all right." His eyes are hot.

"It was a good job you took the little chest," I say after a pause. "Mum's urn survived with a scratch, but the chest might not have been so lucky."

"Yes. Especially when you remember that I only knew of her existence because Mum wrote about Catherine in her book. Listen to you. *The chest*. Not, *Catherine's ashes*. Can't you even say her name?"

I push myself up onto the pillows so that my head is high enough for me to drink tea. In my own time, I take hold of the mug and sip for a while. I'm very thirsty, I find.

"No, Tom, I can't."

That floors him. He lowers his eyes.

"Mum suffered."

"Yes, she did."

"And you were . . . nowhere."

"True. I let her down. And I let you down by lying to you about the baby, and for that I am sincerely sorry."

He still looks implacably angry. I expected to feel anguish, guilt, but I can't summon any emotion at all. Maybe it's the effect of the pills—I took one in the bathroom—or maybe I'm too tired. Or maybe I just can't bring myself to plead for forgiveness. Maybe, after everything else, that is beyond me.

The bed is actually quite comfortable. I can contemplate turning onto my side.

"I've met Philip Moore, you know. He's in Upton, looking after his mother. Bridie, who was so kind. She's had a stroke, she can't speak properly. I went to see him after I found out about—about him."

"What did he say?"

"It doesn't matter. He had already lied to me about knowing Mum, you see. He let me assume they'd never met. So I can't be sure of anything he says. He did a painting of Mum."

"What's it like?"

"Good. A good likeness. Do you remember when we went to Nice, to visit Mamie and Papie?"

"I remember the ice cream." His eyes are misty. "And the sea. And Papie's books about the Pyramids."

"Well, the painting reminds me of the South of France. There's sunshine, and an olive tree. And she's smiling."

"But not at you," Tom says after a moment.

"No."

He nods, absorbing this. A grown-up now, perhaps. Able to contemplate his mother as a woman, lonely, bereaved, seeking consolation.

"Oh, but Mum would never, ever do that!" he bursts out. "I can't believe you'd even think so!"

Inwardly I smile. Maybe not so grown-up after all.

"Anyway." I shift position. "I think I'm ready now."

Tom gets to his feet, opens the top drawer of the chest, brings out a notebook covered, like all the others, in dark blue paper. He hands it to me. "I'm going to cook," he says, but then hangs in the doorway for a moment. "Archdeacon Frobisher . . . I mean, *wow*."

"I've given him Bailey."

His eyes soften. "Ah, way cool, Dad. They were made for each other."

He leaves the room. The dread expands inside me.

I hold the notebook in my hands. On the front, in impeccable handwriting, the title *La Zoologie*. On the first page, a drawing of a chameleon. Once again the nerves surge through me. I carry on turning the pages. The snouts of the crocodile, alligator, caiman, gharial compared. A blank page, and then there she is with no warning.

TWENTY-TWO

Yvette
9 July 1964

Greenish-blue irises, rimmed by a crinkly circle of hazel flecks that the light turned gold. Pupils small in the sun, whites clear.

It had been a gentle, closed, dry-lipped kiss. When it ended he said that was all he wanted, one kiss.

"Am I supposed to believe you?"

Scrutinizing those interesting irises.

He said, "Does it matter, as long as I behave?"

A pragmatic approach.

We walked down the hill together. He held my hand when I climbed over the stiles. Making it slightly more difficult. I didn't tell him so. He was playing a part already. We didn't talk very much. The important thing was, we knew that we could if we wanted to. We knew that we could say anything we liked to each other. There was no pretense.

Bridie was still in the garden when we got back. She waved at us through the window as if nothing had happened.

I sat straight down and he made a few sketches. But there wasn't really enough time left, what with the walking and the kiss, and so we talked about him. He lived in Holborn, in a flat with three friends. The bath was in the kitchen. When they wanted to cook, they put a board over the bath and chopped up their potatoes and onions on it. Holborn was still pretty bomb-damaged, he said.

"So is Alver Shore."

"Yes."

He put down his pencil and leaned forward and kissed me on the cheek.

Later that evening James said, "Will you come to Evensong, Yvette?" I said, "Of course." We went to the church and I sat near the door so I could encourage latecomers inside. It was comforting to pray surrounded by others, our lips moving, our voices indistinguishable one from the other. I could shut my eyes and imagine myself in a cathedral, a vast metropolitan congregation where I knew no one, where I was subsumed into a nameless crowd. Perhaps I could find a Catholic church, a place where I was not known. Perhaps I'd even go to Confession. I hadn't missed Confession at all since I'd joined the Church of England. I'd never got on very well with it. Try as I might, I could never think of myself as particularly sinful, especially after being told that this very idea was a sin and therefore worthy of confession. It was not a sense of sin that called me to Confession, rather, a longing to speak from my heart into a comforting darkness.

The following week Philip met me at the top of the lane and took my hand.

"Philip, we'll be seen!"

"Nobody knows you."

"They'll say to your mother, I saw Philip with his new lady friend. They seemed very taken with each other."

Quickly Philip released my hand. He had no aptitude for subterfuge.

Hollandaise-yellow dollops of sunshine. A violet shadow of a mountain, heated rock, and parched thyme. Ruby glimmers on the belly of a carafe of wine. Olive-green olives and olive-green olive leaves, and in the middle an olive-skinned girl, cross-legged in a buttermilk blouse and dark blue sailor trousers. I told Philip the trousers were made out of my mother-in-law's tablecloth. "She hated it, so she was glad to see it cut up." I'd spent weeks on these trousers, laying the pieces out over chairs, letting tacking threads trail onto the floor, sticking pins into the arms of the sofa. James, pulling a pair of pinking shears from under a cushion, had implored Saint Anne, patron saint of seamstresses, to come to my aid before he suffered grave injury. This was a long time before Catherine.

"These colors," Philip said. "I'm trying to give you back the Mediterranean."

I was touched, but I had to explain that this Provençal, artist's Mediterranean would have been as foreign to my straitlaced, bourgeois, industrious family as it was to him. "Our house was never flooded with light. The upholstery, for one thing. Maman would never have allowed it to fade." For months of the year the blinds and curtains were closed through the broiling afternoons and then the electric lights put on for dinner, when we ate off good china and listened to my father, tired from a day in his office, try to defend himself from my mother's complaining. I remembered the weddings, funerals, Sunday visits where the talk was all of clothes and babies and illnesses, and the men would go on for hours about the price of silk or salt or soap. "It was suffocating,"

I said. "But we loved each other. And Célia and I were lucky. We were allowed to go swimming, meet selected friends on the beach."

"Yes, what about the sea? Surely that was romantic?"

"To me, yes. Not to the fishermen. I used to go with Maman sometimes—there was a league of charitable ladies—and feed their children when the catch was poor." I remembered the children's big eyes fixed on the rib-sticking bowls of *foul* beans we set down in front of them. The stacks of round flatbreads went down so fast, you'd think it was by magic.

"Well, *this* Mediterranean is romantic," Philip said. "It's about light and color and shapes. And troubadours singing." He began to do so from behind the easel. *"Alas my lo-ove you doo me wrong to cast me o-off discourteouslee..."*

I laughed out loud. "I could never be discourteous to you!"

"Oh, but you've got to, eventually. Hard-heartedly banish me. Not yet, of course. At least wait till this is finished. Now, I need something blue. To conjure up the Mediterranean sky."

We pondered. Such a blue couldn't be found for six hundred miles. I knew the color he needed. Hard, bright, heated like enamel...

"Moulin Alziari! The olive oil can!"

"Perfect."

"And some bread, please. I'm starving."

He was singing again under his breath. To the tune of "Greensleeves." *"My love, she fashioned her trousers new—from a tableclo-oth of navy hue..."*

The painting took six weeks. I went to Upton on the same day at the same time. New James never asked where I was going. Once, when I was putting my coat on, he held the door open for me. I thought: he's waiting for me to leave.

"What do you do when I'm out, James?"

He raised his eyebrows. "It's a visiting afternoon. I thought you knew."

Parish rounds. "Of course."

"That's why it's so convenient." He gave me a forbearing look. "What did you think I was up to?"

"Let me think. Wandering round the house, maybe. Or lying on the bed, staring at the ceiling."

A faint flush appeared on his cheeks. "Why would I waste my time in that fashion?"

I gave the suggestion of a shrug only. Kept my eyes trained on his, which were wide, shining, affronted.

"I have no idea. But you wouldn't tell me anyway. So there's no point speculating."

Bridie used to come home from the market half an hour before I was due to leave. So we all viewed the painting together and watched me take on form and depth, seat myself in the folds of the rug on the armchair, begin smiling with my eyes, let the smile spread to my mouth. Offer the viewer a crust of bread on which I was pouring olive oil. The entirety of my body framed by the flank of a mountain, dappled by the shade from olive branches, under the volumes of sunshine. Because Bridie was with us, Philip and I could delude ourselves into thinking we were safe, that we had not created a private world where we alone existed.

No, that's not right. I knew all too well what we were doing.

On the last day we finished early. All he needed to do now was work on the background, he said. I unwound from my pose, stretched one leg out. "My foot's cramping."

Philip, who had dismounted from his wooden donkey, knelt in front of me. "Thank you for being a good model, Yvette." He took hold of my extended foot and began to stroke the sole. "A model model, in fact."

"Thank you for my Mediterranean."

His thumb pressed into my arch, working its way along my instep. "I thought you said it wasn't yours."

"It is, now. I take ownership."

He let go of my foot and knelt up so that he was between my knees. I closed my eyes. He kissed me. This time his lips were parted, rubbing over mine.

I slid down off the chair so that I was kneeling in front of him. I put my hand at the back of his head, laced my fingers in his curls. His fingers grazed my breast, he gasped into my mouth. We pulled each other close. He was breathing nearly as fast as his heart was beating. A sudden, golden, streaming silence.

Can you do it, Yvette?

That was Célia's voice. Asking me if I was strong enough for James. Imagine if she and Peter could see me now. Darling Peter, watching me betray his friend and comrade. God, the hope I'd had, watching the parachutes plump open, taking James in my arms after everything he'd gone through. Oh, Célia, my sister, help me. I've tried and tried. I'm sorry.

Philip was stroking my back, his cheek against mine.

"Kiss me," I said. "Kiss me again, and I'll stop crying."

"I can't kiss a woman who's crying," he said. "I've never done that."

"Honestly, I'll stop if you kiss me. Please, Philip."

He released me. "No. I want to make you happy, and—"

I put my arms around his neck. "Who cares about being bloody *happy*."

"Oh, Yvette," he said. "If you aren't happy, then neither am I."

At that moment the front door opened. We both leaped to our feet. I scurried out to the lavatory, buried my face in a towel. My insides convulsed with suppressed sobs. When I was able, I turned on the cold tap and rinsed my face, panting, each breath shaken by the pulse beating in my throat. I dried my face and looked in the mirror. My hair was on end as if I'd been electrified. I tidied it but couldn't do anything about my red eyes.

I could hear them talking in the kitchen. "I've bought a lardy cake, dear. Where's Yvette? Oh—have you finished?"

"Pretty much, Ma. She's in the whatnot."

"Shall I heat this a little?"

"Mmm, yes, do."

Their voices, back and forth, mother and son. He would fly free and live his life but he and his Ma would always be the same, whenever they met. Peaceful. Wanting to be happy.

I came out and ate the lardy cake and drank a cup of tea. Lardy cake is a fatty dough studded with dry currants and crystals of sugar, the outside caramelized almost black. Only when you've tried and failed to light a fire with damp coal in an English coastal town in February—only then, do you appreciate the insulating power of lardy cake. It's also good to eat, I found, straight after you've cried your eyes out.

I couldn't hide from Bridie. "What's upset you?" she exclaimed. "Not Philip!"

"No, no, he's been very kind—"

"Yvette's rather fed up," said Philip. "I'm afraid I've been reminding her of sunshine, and lots of other things she misses."

Bridie glanced down. "That poor pretty hankie," she said next, as I wiped my eyes. "How many tears have you shed into it?"

I spread it out. It wasn't actually a hankie, it was an old scarf my mother had given me, a Hermès. It had the daftest picture on it, a train and a cow and a farmer's wife. Maman had said, *Now take care of it, Yvette,* and what had I done? Taken it out on the boat and Peter, bless him, had ruined it with cigarette burns. "Look." I spread it out so she could see the little holes. "Look how spoiled and charred it is. It's good for nothing but crying into."

"You're a brave girl, and no doubt," said Bridie. "You might cry from time to time, but you'll never lose heart. You won't lose heart, will you, Yvette?"

Her eyes with a sudden speaking light in them.

Philip gathered up his brushes and went out to the scullery. Bridie took my hand, preparing to say something, but I forestalled her.

"Bridie, I may not come back again."

She closed her mouth. Whatever she had been preparing to tell me, it was no longer necessary.

"It's been a very great pleasure knowing you, Yvette," she said after a pause. "I shall miss you."

"And I you. But I must . . ."

"You must get on with life. Your husband will need you."

"He thinks he doesn't—"

Her fingers squeezed mine. "He needs you."

Philip walked with me to the wall full of pink daisies where I always parked the car. He picked some and handed them to me. They were only just in flower.

"You've got roots there, and some soil. Plant them in a dry stony place, like this wall."

"I hope it will turn out to be a good painting."

"I think it will." He grinned, and then the grin vanished. "You could come back and view it . . ."

"No, I can't."

"Well, I won't sell it," he said. "So if you change your mind. Perhaps in twenty years' time. You might look me up. Remind yourself how beautiful you were."

"Goodness, yes, I'll need to. I'll be forty-seven, after all."

"My God, Yvette," he said shakily. "I could spend the rest of my life looking at you, painting you. Talking to you. Loving you. We could live together, you and I, somewhere in the South. France, maybe. On a mountain, with blue sky, and sunshine, and—"

"And an olive grove to wander in."

Such a young, freckled face. It crumpled so badly when he was sad. "You think I'm joking."

"I think you're kind and clever and talented and loving," I said. "But I'm married to—"

"A man who makes you cry."

"Go to France, darling Philip, if you can."

I kissed him for the last time, on the cheek, and we bade each other goodbye. As I drove away I saw him in my rearview mirror, running. Not toward me but away. His long legs carrying him fast and far.

When I got home I opened the kitchen drawer. The paper had been crumpled up and smoothed out but the creases were still there, touchable. *Hannaux,* it said in French, in Arabic هانو. Reminding me of perfume and Maman and being fitted for my first brassiere. I considered the olive branch design. The leaves were tiny, stodged into one solid fringe, the olives themselves mere blobs. The best olives and oils were expensive in Egypt, they came from Greece and Spain. So this design was suitable for Hannaux, being a stamp and symbol of imported luxury.

Philip's olive leaves shed light and shadows that moved over my face.

I put the car keys down on the paper and closed the drawer.

The change was not sudden. I don't know if I was responsible in any way for it. I simply became aware that new James was peeling away scrap by scrap like birchbark, leaving a soft tender patch underneath. I watched this happen, treading carefully, fearing at any moment he might re-armor himself. But he continued to emerge. He was quieter than before, less obviously energetic. I was changing too, becoming more hesitant, thoughtful. In this state I was able to look back at a whole piece of time, one that stretched from my arrival in England all the way to a full year after Catherine's death, and see it as a single storm of joy and love and excitement and terrible grief. A storm that had now passed. I was in a new, empty territory where the shadows fell differently in the streets, the daily business of life was slightly more daunting. We took evening strolls arm in arm. We shared crossword clues. We were able to give each other our full attention, as childless couples do.

I don't have any kind of singing voice but I began to sing in the house. I switched on the wireless for *Housewives' Choice*, a program whose jaunty, noodling introductory melody stuck in my head all day and poured out of my mouth every evening until one night when we were undressing for bed, James began to laugh. "Stop this torture, I beg you. I promise I'll tell you everything I know."

Standing there in my slip, I began to smile. "The secret submarine bases?"

"Yes. And the signal codes."

"What else?"

"The name of my pet rabbit."

"You had a rabbit?"

"Yes. A Dutch rabbit. I got him when I was six." He pulled off his shirt and collar, frowning in mock indignation. "Why is that so unlikely?"

I stepped out of my slip. "So what *was* it called, this pet rabbit?"

"He. Gordon."

I marveled at this hitherto unknown creature. "Why did you never tell me?"

"The subject never came up, I suppose."

"What was he like?"

"Half black and half white. Right round his middle. It was like having two rabbits for the price of one. He was awfully good fun. He liked obstacle courses. Yvette, I'm so sorry. You were right."

By now I was sitting at my dressing table brushing my hair. I looked up at his reflection, he was standing behind me.

"About what?"

I was genuinely at a loss. Still thinking about Gordon.

"I did see her."

My back prickled all over. I turned around to look at his real face.

"I saw her but . . ." He sat down on the bed so that he was more on a level with me. "I think the shock somehow erased her image from my mind. This is the absolute truth, Yvette. The shock lasted a long time. It knocked me for six. I should have told you at the time instead of pretending that nothing was wrong. I know you tried to help me. I apologize. And I'm sorry, I still can't remember her. I don't know if I ever will."

He said all this quickly and smoothly so that it came out all of a piece without a gap for me to interrupt into. I tried to absorb it all.

"You had all that love for her," he was saying now. "And love left over for me, to help me. I refused to let you. I gave you nothing in return."

I held out my arms. He came and embraced me. It was awkward with me sitting but that didn't bother us. His stubble scraped my cheek and my hands felt the warmth of his back.

"But you have," I murmured. "You have given me so much."

That day, I moved Catherine's little chest from its place on my dressing table to the bedroom bookshelf so that James could not see it from where he lay in bed. When we moved I did the same in this house too. I know he loves her. I don't ask anything more of him.

One day we had some time to ourselves, we drove westward down the coast to Dorset, climbed the Golden Cap. It was grand on top of the headland, the great scalloping bays unrolling to the east and the sea a holidaymaker's blue. I lay back on the grass.

I said, "I don't think I'll have another baby—"

"No, darling!" His face appeared above me, eyes so wide the whites showed all the way around. "We must keep hoping for another baby! We must! You can't give up! I'll do anything—"

"You know there's only one thing you need to do." I started to smile. "Or keep doing. James, I was going to say, 'I don't think I'll have another baby until we move.' I have a feeling it won't happen while we're at Alver Shore. So actually there is another thing you need to do. Find another post, somewhere else. Darling, we need to start again."

He was smiling too, the sea wind ruffling his hair. At his temple, a single strand of gray among the black. He was thirty-two and I was nearly twenty-eight. There was so much still to happen, so much happiness to come. The tears came to my eyes. I rummaged in my pocket for the old ruined scarf I used as a handkerchief, the one I'd shown

Bridie, but it wasn't there. I'd left it at Bridie's house. Never mind. She'd use it as a duster, if I knew her at all. And I did know her, I knew her well, and I was glad to have known her.

I haven't got much time. I'm backed up into a corner in three jerseys and woolen stockings, on a lambskin rug, and I weigh five stone. Where's the rest of me gone? At the end of last winter Tom pointed at our shrinking snowman and asked James, "Where's the rest of him gone?" because there was no puddle of meltwater. James told him that the crystals in the snow had sublimed: they'd gone straight from solid to gas without passing through the liquid stage. Maybe that's what I'm doing, subliming. It sounds nice—if cold. I was worried I'd scare Tom when I started to dwindle. But he didn't seem to notice. Perhaps he was choosing not to see me as I am now.

He's been told, now. We thought it was for the best. He's very angry with me—he doesn't want to say good night to me or good morning. If he comes into the bedroom it is to stand looking down at me, hands in pockets, with burning scorn. Well he might. All I can do is thank God for his father. If I know anything in this world, I know that James will not fail him.

I'm very thirsty now and water doesn't quench it, or only for a second or two. As if I'm full of dry dust. I crave the drinks of my childhood, carob juice, guava juice, foaming in glasses from a street seller or juice bar. Hibiscus in a jug full of ice. Licorice root, apricot, mango. James got some mango juice sent from London. It came in tiny tins and tasted of the tin.

Lemon granita.

It is the evening. Soon James will come and sit beside the bed and read aloud—at the moment it's *Le Petit Prince*, a book I used to read to Tom. James loves Saint-Exupéry too, for his writing and for his bravery as a fellow airman of the desert. Soon my strong medicine begins to tinge the small innocent words with brilliance so that each one falls like a raindrop, wobbling and plunging through low light, and my comprehension of the story is lost in a drugged wonder and then I fall into the strangest dreams. Last night I dreamed with certainty that babies grow up in the afterlife and that therefore Catherine was fourteen now, living in the Alexandria of my youth, a foundling. Nobody knew who she belonged to, but a family I didn't know had taken her in. All she knew was that she lived in Cleopatra with her *tante* and *oncle*.

She wasn't remotely pleased to see me. She tossed her head and flounced off. I called after her, *"P'tite sauvage!,"* which is what Maman used to say to me.

I could never imagine Catherine at twelve or eight or three. Tom came after, so he was always too late in his rolling, crawling, rhyming, counting, he was always showing me how she might have been four years previous. I'm glad we had a boy afterward. Think of leaving a ten-year-old girl behind, using my last breaths to tell her about sanitary towels and diaphragms and what men *do*, all jumbled into a basket for the jolting journey to come.

Catherine won't be fourteen. That was just a dream. She'll still be a baby, I know, one of those hundreds of thousands of early babies who come flocking into the afterlife before their mothers. Who lie waiting just as babies wait in a nursery at the end of the day for their mothers to come from the factories or fields and take them in their arms and hold them to their faces and smell them. The thought of all those babies is daunting. I'm sure there will be people to help me find her, help all the other mothers like me, who never saw their children.

Hard to push the pen along. Great unwieldy thing. Letters sprawling outside the squares. *Mais quel gribouillis, Yvette!*

James, I'm sorry. Don't let Philip spoil everything else. Like when you
open an ink bottle underwater in a clear pool
    Don't let the pollution funnel up and color everything. Remember
the apple blossom raining from the tree
    Tom butting my breast like a lamb, nine days old,
    and you laughing
    Don't lose this, James, don't let his little face be shadowed by what
I did. Please don't lose
    Don't lose the best of us

Take my ashes and Catherine's
    Put them together but
    Do not mix them
    She is she and I am I
    Disperse-les au milieu des primevères
    Do you remember where
    Le chapeau que tu n'as jamais vu
    La même couleur
    La même
    couleur

*T*ake *my ashes and . . . scatter them among the . . .* what's *prime-vères,* Dad?"

"Primroses."

It's late the next morning. I survived the night on Tom's bed, he on his sofa downstairs. Now he's sitting on the bedroom floor, the notebook open in his hand. "Okay. *Among the primroses. He will know where. The hat he never saw. The same color, the same color.*" He wipes his eyes. "What's she saying?"

"There was a hat I never saw, that was the same color as the primroses."

He stares at the ceiling. "I skipped through a couple of paragraphs with Philip Moore. Same with that guy, Sébastien. I mean, my mother. There's some info I really don't need."

I'm standing up, and at this point I turn to face the window. Terrace houses and back gardens being easier to look at.

"But you've gathered enough."

"Yeah. She didn't . . ."

"No."

I press the heels of my hands into my eyes; Tom has kept up a quiet steady snivel throughout his reading. Two Englishmen, utterly failing to keep their composure. Though I'm not being fair. We did the clinging together and the racking sobs ten years ago, a little boy and his daddy. We're just not up to it today. My ribs, for one thing.

For another, Tom's got no interest in hugging me at the moment.

Even when she wanted Philip, kissing him made her too sad to carry on. Suddenly Célia and Peter came to her mind. She'd sat in that cellar after the bombs came down, sat with Célia's head in her lap. Afraid for her. She was loyal. She gripped on to all of us together.

"I shouldn't have doubted her."

"Well, *I* never did." Tom's sending me a dark look. I can feel it landing between my shoulder blades.

"And you'd have forgiven her if she had. So would I, as it happens."

That takes him aback. When he speaks again, after some nose-blowing, it's in a more mollified tone. "I remember now. She wrote about that hat. It was bombed, right? And she was reminded of it when you were walking down the lane by the playground. At Fulbrook. Because the primroses were the same color . . ." His eyes widen as it dawns on him. "Oh. She was talking about being scattered there. With Catherine."

"Looks like it," I say.

All that stuff she wrote about you." Tom lifts his brimming pint to his lips, takes off about a third in one gulp. "The cannons. The prison camp. I never knew. I mean, I knew the facts. But not really what *happened* to you."

One arched loom of desert light, when he speaks, and then back to the comfortable, sound-deadening dimness of the pub. We're at a corner table in the Black Horse, coming up to midday. Only a half for me: I'm starting to think of my drive home.

"It's fairly hard to convey."

"And your friend Alastair . . . I never thought about *any* of it, not really. All these people your age. *My* age. You went screaming through the air plugging Germans with machine-gun bullets—"

"Italians too. Don't forget the Italians."

"And then you came home and, I don't know, got to be vicars, or sold cars like Uncle Peter. Played Ping-Pong with your kids. Ate plowman's lunches. I don't know how you did it." A flurry of blinking. "I could do with a plowman's right now."

It's been a bare two hours since his breakfast of egg and beans on toast. "I'll get you one as long as we change the subject. Have you heard from Florence?"

Happiness breaks out over his face. "I'm going to Bordeaux at Christmas. Florence can't wait. Me neither."

It must be costing him a fortune. I bet he's saving money on food. I buy him a plowman's and write him a check, to be spent on groceries.

"I don't want to let go of Catherine yet. I've only just found her."

We're back on his street, coming up to the house. My things are in my car, ready for me to leave.

"We wouldn't do it before the spring, Tom. Doesn't even have to be *this* spring."

"I suppose not . . . I feel sorry for Mum, though. She's waited awhile."

I ponder saying: *Time doesn't exist where she is.* Decide against it.

"Mum wouldn't want you to rush."

Tom nods to himself, loping along beside me. Hair falling

forward. I can't see his face. "So anyway, Dad," he says, in his invisibility. "Catherine."

I thrust my hands deep into my pockets, search the sky. It's low, gray, a reliable refuge, useful to plunge into, to shake off a pursuer. If only I was up there, jinking every three seconds. I'd soon leave him behind.

"What about her, particularly?"

"Why couldn't you see her?"

The lightest drizzle is breathing over us, condensing in beads on Tom's hair. He stands back, arms across his body, the closed fingers of one hand against his mouth. Scared of what he might say? Of what he might hear? He has endurance but it's so different from mine. Mine is a fueled engine, it powers onward. His is more of a bending, incompressible entity, like water. No point throwing up defenses. He'll just go around.

"I couldn't bring my mind's eye to bear on her," I say. "I still can't. Each time I try there's a sort of flash, like a flare. It's always been the same."

"Why?"

"I can only assume it's shock. The kind that lasts a long time."

He doesn't move or speak.

"I should get going, Tom."

"Where are you living now?" he manages to ask, after a long moment staring within himself.

I explain about the farmhouse, the lack of telephone, and fumble for my diary and pen. "Here, I'll give you the address."

"How's Ellen, by the way? She must have been really worried."

"She has been." I strive to keep my handwriting neat as I reply. "She's off to Singapore, actually. Today, in fact. Won't be back for ages."

"Singapore!"

I recall Ellen's amusement, her teasing. How merciless she was. That makes me feel better.

"Her brother lives there." I tear out the slip of paper and hand it to him. "I can't say how long I'll be at this address. But I'll keep in touch."

He gives a tentative smile. "I bet you've got some time off, now, haven't you. What with the accident."

"I certainly have."

We embrace carefully and I get into the car. His face appears at the window. "I hope you don't mind me going to Bordeaux for Christmas. I feel guilty, after everything that's happened to you."

"Tom, you don't have to pay me duty visits. Not yet, anyway."

He grins with relief. Then he says, "I wish you *could* tell me. So I could picture her myself. Maybe the flash will kind of wear off. You could try some meditation, Dad."

"I could."

"It would be good for you anyway, I think. Deep breathing and all that."

"Thanks for the advice. Bye, Tom. Cook yourself a steak. Write to me."

"Bye, Dad."

In the rearview mirror I see him bound up the steps to his front door.

The farmhouse looks different when I get back. Solid in low sunshine, more welcoming, less of a bolt-hole. I let myself in, pour a glass of water from one of my many receptacles. Imagine Ellen traveling into a short night, meeting the sun coming around the other way. She and her brother, they'll have a rare adventure.

This is not the time to give up, Ellen said to me, out on the hill. *This is not the time.*

I stand in the kitchen, in the peace of the still air and the fading afternoon light. Nothing to hear but a gull crying in the field. Ellen doesn't know what she's asking. How can I pick up that burden again?

I take a pill. Shortly afterward, judging that I missed one when I was driving, I take another. Then I trudge upstairs, lie down on the bed, and fall heavily asleep.

When I wake up it's dark. I reach for the matches, light the gas lamp. The glow rises and spreads into the corners of the room, and falls on Yvette, who is sitting on my bed.

Mouth dry, I push myself up against the pillow.

These ructions don't seem to disturb her. She continues to sit neatly at the end of the bed, knees together, face averted, hands folded in her lap. She doesn't make much of an indentation in the bedcover, but then she never weighed a great deal. She looks as she did the year before she died, a small slender woman of nearly forty, dressed casually in trousers and jersey, curly hair tucked behind her ear so I can see her cheek and jawline. She's at least as real as I am.

"Yvie?" It comes out as a hoarse whisper.

She turns as naturally as if we're at home together in the bedroom at Fulbrook. "I was wondering when you were going to wake up," she says.

"I'm awake!" I'm panting with fear. "Darling . . ."

She smiles. "You've been looking in the wrong place. All this while."

"Where should I look?" I don't know exactly what she means, but maybe it's the same for ghosts as it is for sleepwalkers. Keep them talking.

She casts her eyes to the ceiling. The gesture—*Lord, men can be obtuse*—is so familiar. "Honestly, James," she says, and gets up off the bed and leaves the room. The door swings shut behind her with a clatter from the wooden latch that makes every hair on my head rise up.

About an hour later, I dare to go downstairs.

Women. They push and prod me, they don't leave me to my own laggardly pace. As if they aren't bossy enough, two days later—days in which I stroll in the fields, lie reading on the bed, and scare away ghosts however beloved with wireless programs—I get a postcard from Tom. On the front is a photograph of a monument to one Henry Blogg, hero of the Cromer Lifeboat, a sou'westered captain cast in bronze. On the back, a message. The capital letters are so big that they collide into each other on the right-hand side. The handwriting, and the message, make me think Tom wrote this late of an evening in the Black Horse.

Henry Blogg, his plaque informs me, was THE BRAVEST MAN WHO EVER LIVED.

Tom's message is one word.

DEBATABLE.

Later that morning I set out on foot. A long walk ahead, but I have absolutely no desire to get behind the wheel of a car. The day is clear, dry. A thin light wind chills my head and ears. Emerging as I do from the house, harrowed by my visit to Tom and recently ghosted, I feel like a sheep tipped out into the yard after shearing, shivering in an unfamiliar breeze, curiously underweight.

The road runs along the far side of Beacon Hill. Here the land doesn't plunge down to make a rampart as it does on the Upton side. Instead the hill falls away gently and then levels into a wide plateau of plowed land. I walk between fields so wide I can't see the other side, the shallow soil fading to white where the chalk has worn through. There's no break from the wind; the boundaries are marked only by thin wire fences. Birds lift into the air as I pass, alighting again behind me, churring. I don't know what they are. I'm no expert on birds.

Yvette was utterly herself. Nothing mysterious or portentous about her. As if she'd got up early and was popping in to see me on her way out. She'd started learning sign language before she fell ill, the better to communicate with two new deaf children, brothers, at Sunday school. She might have been on her way to her sign language class. Yes, slightly impatient with me, as if I was holding her up with my foolishness. She might have been chiding me for looking for socks in the larder, or writing paper in the coal bunker. I hear her voice, echoing up the stairs to Tom, who had lost his shoes for the thousandth time. *They're your shoes, darling. Think! Where did you take them off?*

A useful function of ghosts. Giving the searchers a good kick up the bottom. *You've jolly well got to find it yourself.*

My route drops down to the river valley and I emerge onto a road I know, the one that runs along under the beech wood. I would like to walk among the trees but the paths have a lot of slippery, jolting ups-and-downs, and besides, I'm nearly there. The urgency gathers in me and I pick up my pace. If he's out, I'll simply wait until he comes back.

The wall bulges, too late in the season for rock daisies to flower. She used to park the Hillman here, under the wall where the road widens. Almost twenty-five years ago now. A long time.

I pass on down the lane.

As before, the canine wolf greets me with his silent snarl. I try to make my knocking neighborly but the knocker slips from my numb fingers and bangs down hard on the plate. A pulse beats at my throat.

Footsteps, and then the door is opened.

He pales at the sight of me. Dreadful, that I have this effect on another human being.

"I've come to apologize."

He looks utterly bewildered.

"Philip. I should have taken you at your word."

He takes his time replying, so long that I wonder if he's going to send me away.

"I've behaved very badly," he says in the end.

"The point is, what you actually said was true."

He considers that. "Er, would you like to come in? You look awfully cold."

I wasn't planning to. I'd pictured myself making my request on the doorstep. That way, he'd find it easier to refuse if he wanted to. But I see now that it was a terrible idea and I should leave with *No, thank you, I won't disturb you. I simply came to apologize.* A sudden fit of shivering seizes me.

He opens the door wide. "Come in, James," he says.

He sloshes Scotch into my coffee without asking, doses his own cup liberally. "I did fall in love, James, I really did. You need to know that."

I'm not at all sure I do, especially since I believe him this time. But we both gulp at our mugs, and the Scotch and the silence work away at me.

"So at least you cared for her, you mean," I say finally.

He looks down, addresses the knots in the pine table. "It took me a long time to forget her. No, not forget her. I never did that." He looks up, almost accusingly. "That day at your party. Suddenly there you were talking about Yvette, your late wife. And I thought, he's *that* Mr. Acton, and then I realized, oh, my God, she's *dead* . . ."

I remember him kneeling white-faced by his mother's wheelchair. "I'm sorry. It must have been a blow."

His laugh is sad and almost soundless. "You're extremely for-bearing."

"I don't know about that. A better man would thank you for being kind to her, appreciating her. Making her laugh. I was doing a very bad job of all that, you see, at the time. And when . . . when it came to it, you didn't take advantage of her unhappiness."

"But *you're* not going to thank me."

"Nope." I toss back the remains of my drink. "I'm not a bloody saint, Philip."

That makes him smile. "James, it's entirely inappropriate for me to say so . . ." He pauses, his eyes shining. "But you were a lucky man."

"Obviously you're the talk of Upton," he tells me a short while later, after we've refilled our mugs. "Rumor has it that a beam hit you on the head and you can't speak. Which is why you're holed up in Harvey Corey's farmhouse. What happened to your dog? Some people are say-ing he died in the accident. I do hope that's not true."

"No, thank goodness . . ."

"The other story is that he was dog-napped. William Kennet saw him being driven out of the village by a huge criminal-looking type dressed as a vicar."

"Ha! That's the man who rescued me!" I explain about Bailey's new master.

"An archdeacon." Philip whistles. "And he saved your life. We should make sure to tell Mr. Kennet. He thought the vicar disguise was very low."

I'm on my feet, this being more comfortable, looking out of the window at Beacon Hill. "I saw Yvette last night."

"What? You mean, you had a dream?"

"No. I'd just driven back from Norwich, I was in pain, and I took two tablets instead of one." I turn back to Philip. "I woke up and there she was, sitting at the end of the bed. She was mightily real. She talked to me, and when she left she even managed to rattle the latch on the door."

"Good grief. How incredibly unnerving!"

"Yes, it was."

"How was she?" He reddens. "What a stupid thing to say."

"No, not at all." I find myself smiling. "It was exactly like that. As if she'd just dropped in. She seemed fine. Very much her usual self."

When he speaks next it is idly, in a friendly way, his cheeks still flushed. I'm not ready for what he says, but I have to accept I'll never be ready.

He asks me, "What did she say?"

One summer evening I put a match to a candle, began to compose a sermon. Became distracted by a small white shape on the edge of my vision that grew sharper and brighter as I wrote: the corner of a page of the *Church Times* lying within the pool of light. *Rural parish, Hampshire.* A signal flare, telling me, *You have some way to go.*

It's only fifteen miles from Alver Shore to Upton. Three minutes' flight in a Hurricane, half an hour's driving on country lanes, but it took me years and years. I made a wrong turn, you see. Yvette asked me if I would come with her, to meet her kind woman friend, and I refused. Ended up going the long way round. I've been a terribly stubborn case, needed such a lot of pushing. Althea Brock, Tom, Frobisher, Ellen. Even Yvette had to come and help. And now I'm nearly there, with Philip before me.

At my bidding, Philip is telling me what it was like when he drew his stillborn older brother. I can't see any other way of approaching the subject.

"It was a struggle," he's saying. "Not for me so much as for my father. I was young. I was terribly sad that Gerard had died, and I loved my ma and pa, but I didn't remotely understand what they went through. And Pa wasn't a wordy man." He bites his lip, remembering. "But each time I got something right, he pounced on it. *That's the boy, that's my little man.* He only got to see the baby because Father O'Neill was there and he insisted. But they wouldn't let Ma." He sighs. "So cruel. They feared it would upset her, for crying out loud. How? He was beautiful."

There is a short pause. I'm aware of my hands gripping each other, the clench of my fingers. Not much else.

"Yvette didn't see our daughter either," I tell him. "She held her, but the baby was wrapped up. Yvette couldn't even see her face. Sometime later, she asked me what the baby looked like. Probably when Bridie suggested to Yvette that you make a picture of her."

"So you saw the baby, like Pa?"

"I saw her by accident. They didn't mean to show me."

"Oh, I see." Philip looks puzzled. "Yvette said—"

"Yvette didn't know I'd seen the baby. I couldn't tell her."

"Why not?"

"Because the baby . . ."

She was not a sight. She was not. She was not a sight to be seen. I can't say this. I don't know if that is true or right. The flash blooms, flares, blinds.

Silence for a long time. I don't move. The light is actually deafening me. Distantly I hear Philip's footsteps retreat and return. Then, penetrating the glare, the sweep of large sheets of paper over the table. I open my eyes to see Philip gathering charcoal from a glass jar, soft pencils, squashy stubs of eraser.

"After we got home I couldn't see her anymore. My mind wouldn't let me. I had nothing to say to Yvette. I could give her nothing."

Philip shifts his chair, sits down, positions a drawing board so it's leaning against the edge of the table. "Ready when you are."

"But I—I can't. I don't know . . ."

"James." He regards me over the top of his board. His expression is really quite stern. "Isn't this why you're here?"

The light has a basis in reality. The day it happened was very bright and the room had tall windows. A clean place, naturally, a reek of disinfectant. The people in the room were cheerful, their voices loud and sharp against the swabbed tiled walls and white sinks. The clinking of medical instruments equally so. There was absolutely no shadow, and the structure of everything was revealed.

The people in the room were occupied with their tasks, so they didn't see me enter.

I only came in because I was looking for Yvette. She had been moved to another place during the night and I wanted to ask somebody where I should go. That's how I knew that I had fallen into a doze, because I didn't see them move her.

There was a table made of metal, probably steel, and it was shining and clean except for a towel laid out upon it. The towel bore a few blotches of blood, the blood rose-pink, spreading, as if it had been diluted with another fluid. On the towel a tiny baby girl lay on her back, naked, arms flung out, legs akimbo, her head rolled slightly to one side so that her chin pointed down toward her collarbone.

Her skull was a shape I had not seen before, her forehead sloping back into a shallow cone. The hair on her head, slicked into furrows of small regular curls, reminded me of the fleece of a newborn lamb. Her mouth was open in an *O*, her lips the dark red of early blackberries. The color was sharp-cut against the gray of her face. In the side of her chest was a large soft-looking depression as if a rubber ball the size of a grapefruit had been pressed against her ribs. Her umbilicus was dark, swollen, clamped. Shallow, wrinkled blisters, varying in size from a sixpence to an egg and filled with a watery ochre fluid, covered her forehead, chest and the tops of her legs. Her entire body was smothered with streaks of viscous bloody material and also with a strange greenish-brown liquor. Her hands lay palm-up, the fingers slightly curled. Her fingernails were the same color as her lips. Her feet were the only part of her that resembled any other human being I had seen. They were narrow, the toes neat, Yvette's in miniature.

Although it takes a moment or two to describe, I saw all of her very quickly. Really, in an instant.

At the far end of the table, two midwives were standing over her. The older midwife was talking to the younger. "This is Baby Acton," she was saying. "Died in the womb and mother didn't realize." She put a hand on the younger midwife's arm. "Take a good look, dear, you want to be prepared. You can see by the state of her skin that the waters broke some time ago. Happened in the bath, I expect, or her mother might have noticed. Oh, dear, quite a dent on her side, she probably got that coming out. The bones are so soft. You can see by the head. Already engaged, that's why the peculiar shape."

"She looks like she's wearing lipstick," murmured the younger midwife, now whey-faced.

"They're often like that, the stillborns. The blood, pooling. Same with the nails." The older midwife looked up. "Oh, goodness. Vicar, I'm afraid I must shoo you out. We're bidding farewell to this poor little scrap."

I said, "Mrs. Acton is my wife."

That got their attention.

"Oh dear God," said the older midwife.

"Please . . . can you clean her? Can you wrap her up, so that my wife can hold her?"

"Absolutely not. We never allow the mothers to see the babies, especially—"

"Wrap a cloth around her. Around her face too. Please. Let my wife hold her."

When they were ready, I followed the midwives to Yvette's new room, the baby in my arms. They had put a hat on her head in case the new white towel slipped, but I made sure that she was tightly scarved so that her gray face and stark near-black red lips were deeply shadowed. There was sunlight everywhere, a very intense slanting light that as good as blinded me. I delivered her to Yvette who looked up at me with disbelieving eyes. She held her daughter obediently, blinking. She made no sound when they took the baby away.

I sat with Yvette until the medication wore off. They pronounced her healthy, of all things. By which we understood that she was free to go.

I waited while she washed and dressed, and then we left. We went for a short drive before heading for home, a route that weaved along the coast, so that she could sit in peace in the car and watch the shoreline, the marshes and inlets and stretches of pebble beach. Then she said she was bleeding and needed to go home. When I reached our street and got out of the car I couldn't work out if it was morning or evening. I realized I was in a different world now, a world of human love and tears and laughter. Of fields and cities and sunshine and seas. Where the earth was revolving, revolving, the sun was casting light on us all and would do so until the end of its lifespan as a star. And there was no God anywhere.

Philip is still occupied with drawing. A noisy artist, full of sighs and grunts and long strokes over the paper, murmurs of rubbing out.

"I gave you no warning," I say. "I'm sorry."

Philip makes a noncommittal sigh. He's not listening. I sit quietly, attentive only to the heaving in my chest.

Eventually he finishes his work and turns to stare, not at me, but out of the window behind me. He looks older, heavy-eyed. "What I do . . . ," he says, "it can't be prettified, or made-up. It must be faithful. Otherwise it's no good. And you're the only person who can judge that." He unclips the paper from the board and lays it on the table. Then he stands up, stretches his arms and hands. "I'm going for a stroll in the garden."

Philip's house is quiet. Yvette is long gone from it. I wonder what it's like, where she is now. I sense that they're all busy. A lot of busy women. She was in a bit of a hurry, after all, when she came to visit me.

I get up onto my feet and go and look at the drawing.

I thought I had learned something about fighting, in my youth. But I know nothing compared to my daughter.

Now that Philip has brought her back into her flesh, I can see that she fought harder for life than I ever did. Her blemishes are her battle honors.

She is not alive. But she is nonetheless powerfully existent.

She is not to be pitied.

I gather her up in her clean white towel. Her head lies in the crook of my arm and her body rests against my chest. All the time I've been away, she has been held for me by another father who has carried her in his arms until I am ready. What is she if not the embodiment of His love? What is He, if not love?

"Catherine," I say.

Knowing that I am speaking to God.

"Catherine."

TWENTY-FOUR

It was one thing to find a couple of stones in a bag of coal, but a great chunk of slate? That was going too far. So I took the slate outside and chucked it on the ground. And I was busy stamping all over it, cursing away at the top of my voice, when the bedroom window went up next door and Brigadier Stott put his head out and said, 'Mr. Acton. I have not heard such language since the Battle of Bréville. Shame on you, sir, as a man of the cloth.'

"So now you know," I conclude, with a glance at Tom.

"At last," he says, deeply satisfied. "*Shame on you, sir, as a man of the cloth.* I like that bit too. Oh, take that left turn. The one to Yoxter."

"Are you sure?"

We're trying a scenic route from Southampton, where I picked Tom up from the station, to Fulbrook. It's turned out to be rather eventful, so far featuring a one-in-eight climb, a river ford, and a grass-grown hollow lane that entailed a long reverse in the face of a tractor towing a slurry tank. I'm mildly regretting the pub lunch that we've missed entirely, meandering as we now are through the Mendip Hills under the early spring sunshine. Not at all regretting being here with Tom, whom I haven't seen since the day we parted in Norwich three months ago.

He checks his competently folded map. "Yoxter. Hundred percent sure. Did you ever take a photo of Bailey, Dad? Florence wants to see him."

"A photo of Bailey? What an idea."

"Why not?"

"Waste film on that scrap of a dog? Never."

"You miss him, really."

"I do not. I saw him when I had my appointment with Archdeacon Frobisher. He was very dismissive of me."

Bailey had given me a single sniff and put his nose in the air—oh, yes, *that* man—before trotting back to sit at his new master's feet. This was back in January, and Bailey was sleek and bouncing. Frobisher appeared to be thriving too. Less slablike of face, somewhat trimmer. Still given to finger-wagging. "Oh no, Mr. Acton, not so fast. I'm not having you back in harness without a thorough spiritual overhaul." So I've been put through a series of vigorous examinations of my soul, including the retreat I so dreaded.

I tried not to be too bright at breakfast time. Tried not to be too springy. But it's hard not to be since that December day at Philip Moore's house. Sometimes it feels almost violent, the onslaught of joy. Like being power-hosed with one part icy water to three parts glory of God.

Frobisher. His finger-wagging will always be intensely annoying, but nonetheless he is . . .

"Tom, how would you describe Archdeacon Frobisher?"

Tom has asked for an extended version of the terse account I gave him in Norwich of my accident. So he's now fully aware of my archdeacon's qualities: the strength of his shoulders, his unshakable trust in his Maker, and his proven endurance of extreme suffering.

"Redoubtable, I think," Tom says. "Yes. Redoubtable. Look, there's Fulbrook."

The hills have parted and the town lies spread out below us. We begin our descent.

Yvette's and Célia's parents departed this life in 1962, within months of each other. Their father's funeral had turned into a memorial for them both. After the service Peter and I had loitered on the edge of a teeming gathering at Henri Negresco's hotel in Nice while our children careened about on the promenade and Yvette and Célia entangled themselves blissfully in a net of old, old friends and long-missed cousins who had come from an alphabet of cities—Beirut, Adelaide, Montreal, Paris—to bid her parents farewell. The second purpose of their journeys being, of course, to catch up on years of news, at top speed and high volume, in the turbulent mixture of Alexandrian French and Egyptian Arabic that was the language of their youth. "My goodness," said Yvette afterward, fanning her face, "it was lovely but I do remember why I was sometimes so desperate to be on my own."

Maman had been sixty-eight, Papa seventy-two. Papa had smoked all his life and Maman always ate far too many cakes. Yvette was the first to say so. But she felt all the same that her parents' lives had been shortened by exile.

I was glad for them, that they hadn't outlived their daughter.

Tom and I have been for a nose around our old home, had a cuppa with the beaming, rock-climbing vicar I welcomed to the parish five months ago. He was well bedded in, he told us. "But there's always a surprise around the corner," he added cheerfully. "How about you? Enjoying the rural peace?"

Now Tom and I are walking along the path behind the school playground. Soon the lane widens and the trees grow tall. On a bank beneath the trees, in shade and sun, the primroses are flowering.

"What's the time?" Tom asks.

I glance at my watch. "Ten to three."

"I can't believe it. After all that chugging through the Mendips, we're still early."

Picking her way along the lane from the opposite direction, huddled in a long black coat, is a woman of stunning beauty. Her black hair—rigorously black, these days—falls to her shoulders and she's wearing enormous dark glasses. She doesn't see us; she's busy negotiating a puddle. Not a drop of water must touch the high platform soles of her shiny black boots.

"Look, Tom." I start to smile. "So is she."

Tom doesn't need telling twice. He bounds forward with a delighted shout, he might be twelve years old. "Auntie Célia!"

Célia gives a scream of astonished joy. "Tom! Look at you!" He envelops her, his head bending to hers. I've always thought of Célia as tall, but for the first time I realize she was simply taller than Yvette. A different thing altogether.

She turns to me. "Darling James."

"Dearest Célia." We embrace tightly. She smells deliciously expensive. Peter is doing very well indeed. Her cheek is wet with tears.

"Oh, damn, waterworks already," she says in pure Australian.

Célia has flown to Bristol from Paris, and will return this evening to continue her stay with some cousins in the 16th arrondissement. "You couldn't keep me away," she says, taking off the sunglasses and dabbing at her face. "Don't tell me," she goes on, catching my eye and smiling. "I'm the spitting image of Aunt Monique now. My cousins can't get over it."

Her face, softened and shadowed and elaborately made-up, is almost identical to the glamorous creature who had whisked herself discreetly out of her flat in Cairo during the war, so that Yvette and I could be together alone.

"Célia, you are incomparable."

We all turn to look at the bank of primroses. The trees are still bare but they lean out over us, so that we, as well as the flowers, are caught in the moving shadows of their branches.

"Right," says Tom, and opens his rucksack.

The funeral had been a hideous blur in which our only concern, mine and Célia's, was to get Tom through the day with minimal addition to his suffering. Ten years ago, or almost. Now the air is fresh, the sun shining. We're all older. We've all learned how to do that seemingly impossible thing, namely, to live without Yvette.

"I don't want to speak English," Célia says. "It won't sound right."

"Don't, then," I say softly.

"L'Eternel est mon berger: je ne manquerai de rien," Célia begins in her old, Alexandrian voice, the one she had when I met her. *"Il me fait reposer dans de verts pâturages, il me dirige près des eaux paisibles ..."*

The Lord is my shepherd: I shall not want. He maketh me to lie down in green pastures: he leadeth me beside the still waters. I picture Yvette coming into the hall at Fulbrook vicarage in her mac, pushing the hood back and shaking the rain from her umbrella. *The heavens have opened!* she would announce with a dazzling smile. She loved all the English expressions for heavy rain—*cloudburst, downpour, cats and dogs*—and would use them triumphantly after a wet walk. She loved English rain, English greenness. She loved England, full stop.

Tom, to my surprise, has chosen part of Ben Jonson's ode about the lily that lived such a little time. *Although it fall and die that night, it was the plant and flower of light.* He reads very solemnly and sounds unlike himself. "It's for Catherine obviously," he says when he's finished, in a more normal voice. "But also for Mum, who died before she was ready. Certainly before *I* was ready."

Passing the urn and then the cedarwood chest from hand to hand, we pour out the ashes. We are careful to let them fall in small heaps next to each other without mixing, as Yvette specified, but a portion of finer ash drifts like smoke from each deposition and the two small clouds mingle in the air before settling. Tom and Célia pick some primroses and scatter them over the ashes. Then, as if by common consent, they start to walk away down the lane, leaving me to say my words alone.

The breeze rises. The primroses flutter into the light as the shadows move; into the light and out of it again. Yvette and Catherine can hear me. No one else.

Célia gives us letters—one from Peter to me, and two from her sons to Tom. We hand her ours in return, and all embrace once more. Célia's tears return in torrents. "I plan to cry all the way to Paris. Bloody Yvette. I still miss her so much. Goodbye, darlings." She goes straight to her taxi, which has been waiting all this time. She won't look back.

Tom whistles softly as the taxi departs. "She came from Bristol airport in that cab. Jeez. They must have some *dough*."

The university spring holiday has begun and Tom is staying with me for a few days at Corey's Farm. We make our way, at a markedly increased pace, back to Upton. Driving fast on busy main roads has a powerfully restorative effect on me. The sun is setting as we reach Waltham and the supermarket is closed, so we stop for fish and chips. We park in the square and the car fills with the comforting smell of vinegar and hot newspaper as we devour our food.

"I feel surprisingly okay now," says Tom, through a mouthful of crispy cod. "You know, considering."

I've barely made a dent in my mountainous helping. "Do you want some of my chips, Tom?"

"Go on, then."

The windows are misting up. I'm seized by my usual urge to swipe a chammy leather back and forth until the glass is clear again. But the car is stationary, I tell myself, and we're parked safely in a small town in the south of England, in peacetime. There is nothing to fear from any quarter.

That night I sleep dreamlessly and wake late. Probably for the first time in our lives, Tom is up before me. I find him at the kitchen table writing a shopping list. "If we go soon," he says, "we'll miss the crowds."

I stare at him. "Crowds? In Waltham?"

"At the health food shop. They've got fresh yeast today."

"How on earth do you know?"

"I asked them the last time I was here. Saturdays, they said. I'm going to make some wholemeal bread. Shall we pass by the House of Usher on the way? I'm crazy to see it."

As we approach the vicarage I notice that the daylight seems oddly bright through the trees ahead of us. Sky is appearing where it shouldn't. By the time I pull in between the gate posts, all is shockingly clear.

"Oh, no, Tom. You've missed it."

The back of the house has finally been taken down. Nothing remains except a low mountain range, a series of foothills really, of broken brickwork and timbers, mangled piping, and pulverized glass and ceramic. A roaring digger is at work, scooping the debris into a waiting skip, and a couple of mattock-wielding men are levering up the planking of the floors. Gone is the pitched silhouette, always so dark against the sky. Long shadows will no longer frown over the lawn. All in all, it's a substantial improvement to the local area.

We get out of the car and make our way toward the site. "Look, Dad!" says Tom, raising his voice over the digger. "Your bath is in the garden."

So it is, lying in solitary state, tapless, under the first few white blossoms of the cherry tree.

"Wouldn't it be jolly, to have a bath under a cherry tree."

I glance back at the men with mattocks. One of them has moved toward the kitchen. The range has long gone, vanished from the scene one night over Christmas. Everyone was mystified. Well, claiming to be mystified. Whoever stole it had a job of work, anyway, manhandling that tonnage of iron in the small hours. I notice that the lad working in the kitchen is using a sledgehammer, not a mattock. As I watch, he brings it down onto the clay tiles with a crack.

The hounds. I've forgotten all about the hounds.

With a cry of alarm, I dash over to him. "Stop! Stop!" I scramble over heaps of rubble, my feet sliding in my haste. "The tiles!" I'm shouting against the three-liter diesel engine of the excavator. "You can't smash the tiles!"

The young man, startled, lets the hammer drop by his feet. The digger driver, equally put out, responds to my frantic arm-waving with a soundless volley of invective. Tom is hurrying over, followed by an older man, clearly director of works. I recognize Stan Rail.

"They're breaking up the floor!" I call to Mr. Rail. "But I've got to get the tiles out!"

The excavator's bucket swings past our heads and I can't help ducking. This building could still kill me if it had a mind. The boss makes a slicing gesture along his neck and the driver kills the engine.

"They're medieval," I plead in the merciful quiet. "I can't let them be destroyed."

Stan Rail gives me a daunting stare. Even without a hard hat, he's a man to be reckoned with; helmeted, he's a centurion. "Nobody said anything about rescuing tiles to me. Site clearance is what it says on the docket. So site clearance it is."

"We'll do it, then. My son and I. Please could you lend us some tools? We'll only need an hour or so."

"I'm paying four men today, Mr. Acton. They can't stop while you scurry here and there, chipping out bits and pieces of—"

"I'll give you five pounds."

Stan fingers his chin. "Ten," he declares.

"Mr. Rail, I can't remember the last time I had ten pounds on me. You'll have to wait until I can get to the bank. But I promise I'll pay you."

Stan takes a moment to think it through. "I'll take the lads to Elston's," he says with a sigh.

"Thank you."

Elston's is a mobile café by the main road, and Elston himself makes the best sausage sandwiches in the county. Stan rustles up a couple of small chisels and hammers before loading the men into his minivan. "One hour," he says as he gets behind the wheel, and I hand him thirty pence for a sandwich for Tom.

"With or without ketchup," he asks with a face of stone.

"With, please," says Tom meekly.

The van departs and I return to the precious floor. The range's rectangular footprint gives me my bearings and I pace out the distance to the ancient tiles. The hounds are there, pale ghosts in the daylight through a blizzard of dirt. All the others are hidden. Tom sloshes a bucket of rainwater over the floor, which contributes greatly to the overall filth without uncovering any more patterns, as I point out to him with a degree of acerbity.

"Well, sorr-*ee*."

"I did mop the floor when I lived here, you know. If they were that easy to find, I'd have—"

"Okay, okay."

"See if you can't extricate some of these hounds. Chip along the grouting, look."

"How old are they?" he asks, grunting as he wields a hammer and chisel.

"About seven hundred years."

The grouting, it transpires, is harder than granite. After twenty minutes Tom and I have extracted two tiles. Just when I'm sitting back on my heels, nearly defeated, a heavy engine growls in the lane. I look up to see a Land Rover pulling into the driveway. I scramble to my feet, my heart in my mouth.

The Land Rover comes to a halt. The driver's door opens. Out gets William Kennet, and he's alone.

"I passed Stan Rail in the road, Vicar," he says as I approach. "He told me what was up, *and* how he's got a tenner off you." He gives me a blue glare. "That man can be a right object. But never fear. I've been and fetched a few implements from the hall."

We go to the back of the Land Rover and unload, in short order, a lump hammer, a bolster, spikes, another chisel, and a crowbar. "These belonged to Sir Michael. Lady B's hung on to them for fifty years, give or take. Quality, you see. Now, our best bet is to chip out a big square, dig underneath, and lever 'em out in lumps. One or two may crack, but we'll save the most part."

"A splendid idea," I tell him. "But we mustn't harm the hounds. They're for Lucy Horne, if she wants them." I glance at the vehicle. "I see Ellen's lent you her Land Rover . . ."

"Yup. Always does when she's away. Or if I need it for a special journey. I fetched her back on Monday from the airport, but she says I can keep it till tomorrow. Lucky for you."

Monday. That's six days ago. She's been home for nearly a week and not a word.

"Lucky for the tiles!" I say brightly. "I can't thank you enough, William."

By the time Stan Rail comes back we've liberated nigh on fifty tiles in several sizable chunks that fit into my car with the back seat folded down. What I will do with them, I don't know. There are other things on my mind.

William gets ready to depart. I accompany him to the Land Rover. "So." I clear my throat. "How's—how's Ellen? Did she enjoy her trip?"

"Mightily. She's nut-brown and thin as a lath. And taking to her bed at three in the afternoon!" He tuts. "I hope she's quite well."

That makes me smile. "I'm sure it's only jet lag."

William harrumphs. "That girl has never been one for lying in bed."

I get into the car with Tom, who has gratefully accepted his sausage sandwich from Stan. "That Elston," he says as we pull away. "When it comes to a sausage sarnie, he's the man."

Six days she's been back. Admittedly I haven't got a telephone. Maybe that's it. If I did have a phone, she'd have rung me. But she doesn't want to toil up to the farmhouse. I might be out, after all.

"Dad?"

"Oh—yes . . . he's renowned . . ."

I drive into Waltham and we go to the supermarket. I shop tersely. When Tom puts two jars of jam in the trolley I snap at him that I'm not made of money. He stalks off to the health food shop. The journey home is passed in silence.

"Well," says Tom, when we arrive back at Corey's Farm. "I think I'll make some bread. What are you up to, Dad?"

"I'm going for a walk."

"I hope it puts you in a better mood."

"There's nothing wrong with my mood."

"If you say so."

Tom can be extremely irritating sometimes.

I stride along the tops of the fields thinking constantly of our walk together, of her arm in mine. Her nearness. Six entire days! She'll have seen Althea, for certain. She'll have learned that I'm still here at the farmhouse. There's only one possible explanation.

"She's met someone else in Singapore," I burst out as I enter the kitchen.

A loaf of bread is cooling on a wire rack. Tom turns from a pot on the stove, mouth open. "What are you talking about?"

"Ellen's met someone else while she was away. What other explanation can there be? She's been home for six days. Six days, Tom. She knows where I am, so it's obvious she doesn't want to see me, and that's why. I'm too late. I missed my chance. Please stop laughing, it's very unkind."

"Go and see her," he says, when he's got the breath.

"I can't just *go and see her.*"

"For heaven's sake." He puts his hands to his head. "Go now! And take her something nice!"

"I haven't got anything nice!" I bellow.

"Well, think of something!"

I cast wildly around the room. The loaf of bread is beautifully browned and giving off the most heavenly smell. I seize it in my hands and run out of the house, heedless of my son's cries of outrage.

No reply when I knock. I can hardly hear the knocker over the pounding in my ears. Twice, three times. Absurdly dashed, I take a few steps back down the path. My hand is on the gate when I hear the muffled rapping of knuckles on glass. As I turn around, an upper window opens and a slight, golden-looking person puts her head out, yawning, eyes half shut.

"You're very persistent," she says.

"I woke you up," I say, unnecessarily. "I'm very sorry." I hold out the bread. "I wanted you to have this while it was still fresh."

She considers it. "It looks homemade. Not by you, surely?"

"No, by Tom . . ."

She looks at me silently, as if she knows me for the hardened bread thief I am. A man so ruthless he will rob his own son of a wholemeal loaf. Then the window shuts again.

Nothing can calm the storm of agitation inside me.

She opens her front door, ushering me past her into a shadowed hallway ornamented only with a prayer chair, the kind with a tall back and a low seat to be knelt on. When she closes the door, what little light there was disappears and she's almost hidden in the darkness. I can only see the shape of her face and her hair falling over her shoulders and her hand, held out to take my coat. I put the bread down on the prayer chair and divest myself with a lot of rustling and loud breathing and general barbarism.

She picks up the loaf, which still smells lovely. "Thank you," she says, brushing past me. "Come this way."

"Ellen, if I'm disturbing you, please say."

She doesn't answer, so all I can do is follow her. This reserve, this quiet voice, is terribly unnerving.

She leads me into her sitting room—"Do sit down"—and goes on through the next door. As it opens I glimpse a kitchen clock on the wall. One of the kind known as railway clocks.

Logs are burning in the grate and heat comes in a wave from the nearest radiator. I pull off the thick sweater Tom made for me, attempt to smooth my hair and my shirt. I feel crumpled and untidy, even more so because the room is so peaceful and modestly furnished. There's a piano, but no music on it. A couple of silver cigarette boxes on the mantelpiece. A beaten copper coal scuttle by the fire.

"Your blood has thinned," I say, when she comes back in with a tray of buttered slices of bread.

She sets out the plates with slender golden-brown hands, gives me another of these polite responsive smiles I'm beginning, heart-sinkingly, to get used to. "I have to stoke up the heating when Edward comes to stay. Now I know why. I suppose I might stop shivering by the summer solstice."

"I hope so." My laugh is forced.

"I'm sorry, you must be far too hot."

"I'm not."

"You are." Her eyes gleam. "You're living up at Corey's Farm. You must be sweltering in here."

"Yes, I am hot. And I'm also very, very glad to see you. Ellen, I—"

Next door, the boiling kettle emits a keening whistle. She leaps up and disappears into the kitchen.

"Very good," she pronounces, chewing. "Is this Tom's first go?"

"No." I sip my tea. "He started during the bread strike."

"There's been a bread strike?"

"Yes, back in December. Shortly after you left for the Far East."

"I've certainly missed some major events." She looks up at me thoughtfully. "You, for instance. Something's happened to you, I can see now. Something wondrous."

"The best of all possible things."

"God?"

"Yes."

"Good." She gives me a genuine, delighted smile. "I'm very glad."

I can't think what more to say about God to her, so I join her in a piece of bread. I'm glad I brought her food. The act of eating seems to be banishing the terrifyingly courteous, flitting sort of creature who greeted me at the door. Replacing her with someone more familiar.

"Well," she says next. "You're still here, I see."

I swallow painfully. "Yes."

"So does that mean you're staying?"

"Of course!"

Her eyes widen. "There's no 'of course' about it, James. For a start, Alver Shore, and whatever it was that happened there, has not moved."

"Moved?"

"You said it was too close to Upton."

What a troubled man I was that day. So plagued by the past, so faithless. Ellen kissed me, she actually kissed me, even if it was intended for another, rather more formidable personage. And all I had for her was a bleating, *I need time*. The shame is intense.

She's getting to her feet.

"Oh, Ellen," I cry, "what can I say to you?"

"I'm not showing you the door!" She's blushing, half laughing. "I thought we might go for a walk."

The afternoon is turning blustery. March is coming in like a lion, with rough patches of bright blue sky. We set a fine pace, feeling the wind after hothousing in her sitting room, and soon we are climbing up into Pipehouse Wood. The trees are still leafless and will remain so for a month at least.

"Do you play the piano?" I ask her.

"No. My husband—Selwyn—he was very good. He could turn his hand to all sorts of things. Chopin, carols, Irish airs. What about you?"

"I used to play when I was young."

"And then what happened?"

"Well, I practiced and practiced, and I never seemed to get any better. In fact . . ."

Long ago a young woman laughed at me under a bomber's moon. That moon is small and distant today, a crescent fragile as ash in the blue sky, and the laughter can't be heard anymore. I look up into the beech trees, whose bareness is almost human.

"In fact you got worse?" Ellen says.

I glance at her in surprise. "How did you know?"

"Selwyn used to talk about it. It happens if you practice too much, too intensely. James, the thing is, I loved Selwyn very much."

"Of course you did."

"He was such a good, brave man. He gave me everything he could."

And no one can replace him. Here it comes, the hammer blow. Everything has been leading up to this. I actually close my eyes.

"But the Great War . . . ," I hear her say. "The Great War . . . James, I can't speak to you with your eyes shut."

I open my eyes, chastened. She's looking steadily up at me.

"When I was young . . ." She pauses. "When I was young, and Selwyn was in love with me, Lady Brock asked me if I knew what a *marriage blanc* was. I thought it was a white wedding. But Althea corrected me. She said that, like many men whose nerves were damaged in the Great War, Selwyn would never be able to give me children. Then he told me so himself, and pleaded with me to forget him. I brushed all that aside. I wanted him, not his offspring. We were intensely happy for over thirty years. If ours was not a marriage, then the word has no meaning. But . . ."

"Ellen, you don't have to say—"

"The flights were very long, you see. I had too much time to think. For all I knew you'd be gone when I returned. So by the time I landed in England, well, I had talked myself out of you. Out of the idea of you."

"Yes, I see—"

"I forgot I was a grown woman, a confident person, somebody open to new experiences—"

"Ellen, really, I understand—"

"Especially those experiences which everybody seems to agree are very, very enjoyable indeed. And now I see you I can't—can't believe I nearly missed you—"

I hold out my arms. She enters my embrace willingly, and I feel a few warm breaths against my shoulder.

"James." Her voice is muffled. "I'm absolutely terrified."

I bind my arms tightly around her.

"Whatever you wish us to be," I say, "we will be. I promise you. Ellen. All will be well."

We walk on, eventually. We don't want to leave each other, and we don't want to be inside. Ellen isn't the slightest bit cold now. She needed to be moving through her own landscape, I think. Feeling the woodland floor and the turf beneath her feet. She belongs here. I hope I will too.

We're on the track leading up to Beacon Hill. It is bordered on each side by the thin fields where gray clods, cut by the blade of the plow, shine in the flashes of sun. The humped outline rises in front of me and I feel my breath coming short. I gesture at the skyline. "This hill must have been quite daunting to ancient people."

Ellen doesn't immediately reply. I listen to the wind buffeting my ears, the peal of a gull overhead. Our boots tramping over the dry ground.

"Why do I have the feeling," she says, "that it is you who are daunted?"

I'm already picturing the hillocks and dips of the summit, the soft short nibbled turf, the rampart facing south. "I have ghosts to lay to rest."

"Oh, so did I." She speaks as if it's the most normal thing in the world. "I've cried so many tears on top of this blessed hill, you can't imagine. But it's a beautiful place, and I didn't want to be banished from it, so I kept coming up here until the tears were gone. It was the only way. Come, I'd like to show you one of my favorite wildflowers. It's called buckhorn plantain. It grows very close to the ground and you can eat it if you're hungry."

"Buckhorn plantain. I could learn a lot from you."

She throws her head back, laughing. "I've got many enthusiasms, I admit. But I swear I won't bore you with them."

Her hand and mine seek each other out. She turns her face to me. Her lips are warm on mine. I kiss her very gently, like the civilized, well-mannered man I strive to be. She draws away with a most glorious smile. We walk on, our fingers still interlinked.

"Tell me more about your enthusiasms, Ellen. Books? Music? Baking?"

She laughs. "All those things. I like making clothes, too. And sometimes I do fine repairs for the jumble sales. If we get some lovely piece that's a bit worse for wear, I smarten it up. You should be glad I do. A lot of the money goes toward the church roof."

We are walking easily up the steep side of the hill, taking slow steps as if going upstairs. I'm listening, but so absorbed in her, in the fact that her hand is in mine, that I don't immediately register what she's just said.

"Do you remember a scarf with a train on it, and a cow?"

"Yes," she says immediately. "Althea bought it. Silk, it was. My mother taught me how to darn silk when I was six years old. Back when we had silk clothes to darn. Why?"

The wind is singing about my head, filling me with an enormous energy.

"It belonged to Bridie Moore. It had gone in the jumble sale by mistake when she moved to Redwood House."

"Goodness, Bridie Moore . . . Did you ever solve her riddle, by the way?"

"Yes, in the end."

"What was the answer? . . . Oh!" She clutches my arm. "It was about the scarf, wasn't it! Smoking, and the square! That's what she was trying to tell you! She wanted her scarf back! Well, it's in much better shape now. I remember each and every one of those tiny burn holes, they took me hours . . . That scarf must have meant a great deal to Bridie."

"Yes. It belonged to her dear friend."

We're at the summit now. The sun is settling on the sea. Ellen looks up at me. "It's not often that a man notices the design of a woman's scarf."

The sea is calm, shining, deep blue. It lifts, and falls. A gentle swell, no more.

I say, "My late wife had one just like it."

TWENTY-FIVE

M y darling—
       As Sébastien once said to me, I say to you:

Au revoir, mon chéri, et bonne chance
Goodbye, darling, and good luck

Pense à moi (pas trop souvent)
Think of me (not too often)

Souviens-toi de moi à Amiriya
Remember me at Amiriya

J'avais quelque chose dans l'oeil   Peut-être un grain de sable
I had something in my eye   Maybe a grain of sand

Peut-être pas
Maybe not

A NOTE ON PLACE

Unlike the village of Upton in Hampshire, the Upton of *Think of Me* is an imaginary place, as are the towns of Waltham and Alver Shore and the hamlet of Barrow End. The Egyptian city of Alexandria, of course, is real, as are the events described as part of the North African Campaign of the Second World War. With the exception of some well-known generals, Alexandrian musical figures, and one gifted eye surgeon, the people depicted in this novel are entirely fictional.

My maternal grandmother had a brother who married a Cairene émigré. Jacqueline was beautiful, *soignée*, charming. She deftly and kindly fielded my enthusiastic, ignorant questions about Egypt. When I myself went to Egypt, I translated a novel, *City of Saffron*, by the renowned Egyptian modernist Edwar al-Kharrat. The world of *City of Saffron* is the Alexandria of the 1930s, '40s and '50s. Only then did I properly understand what Jacqueline had experienced. That the cities that she had known as a child, Cairo and Alexandria, were so utterly changed as to have almost disappeared. That you can be exiled from the places of your heart, not only by distance but also by time.

A great many families left Alexandria in the 1950s. Many were of Lebanese, Italian, or Greek heritage; of Orthodox, Catholic, or Jewish faith. They were mostly French-speaking—at least, they chose French out of a multitude of familiar tongues as their common currency. They had to start again in new lands; to become American, Canadian, Australian, English. They strove for prosperity, brought up children, and—so important—enjoyed life. They had the courage to say: That was then, and this is now. We will not think about our birthplace, the wondrous, incomparable, vanished Alexandria—or, at least, not too often.

The Second World War took both my grandfathers to Egypt. My paternal grandfather, who had command of the 6th Royal Tank

Regiment at the time, was attacked in error by an RAF "tin opener," a Hurricane fighter aircraft loaded with anti-tank cannon. Having failed to hit my grandfather's tank on his first attempt, the Hurricane pilot fired a second pair of shells. Luckily, he missed again. My other grandfather, who was in the RAF (though not a pilot), remembered the jasmine which grew at Boulaq Bridge in Cairo. As an elderly man he told me to smell the jasmine for him when I left his house, aged twenty-two, to begin my own journey to Egypt. I didn't see him again, and the jasmine had long gone from Boulaq Bridge, but I never forgot his words.

So I decided to make my protagonist James Acton into a Hurricane pilot, armed with anti-tank cannon, who had breathed in the scent of the jasmine at Boulaq Bridge. And to make him fall in love, in the middle of the war, with Yvette, a young, vivacious Alexandrian woman, who was brave enough to leave her home behind and make a new life with James in England.

The England of my childhood has also changed, but I am luckier than Yvette. I can still walk in the beech woods and over the chalk hills; I can still visit the church where I sang hymns as a child. Like Yvette, I lost a child, and I took refuge in the trees and hills simply because, when it seemed that everything was lost, they endured. This landscape turned into the fictional village of Upton, where James, now a priest and a widower, arrives to begin a new ministry. He does not suspect what else he will find: a startling reexamination of his past with Yvette, and an even more unexpected promise of love to come.

This is a novel about starting again after losing. It might be a country, a beloved spouse, a child, a faith. From the grave Yvette wishes her grieving husband luck, sending him onward into hope, into a new life. *Au revoir mon chéri et bonne chance. Goodbye, my darling, and good luck. Pense à moi (pas trop souvent).*

Think of me (not too often.)

ACKNOWLEDGMENTS

I am more grateful than I can say . . .

To my friends, the writers Alison Clink, Nikki Lloyd, and Crysse Morrison. For forensic critiques, delicious snacks, and encouragement over the years.

To my husband, Robert, first reader and cook, who called me down for dinner at 7 p.m. on the dot during the last long months of writing this book.

To my agents, Deborah Schneider in the United States and Jo Unwin in the UK, and to my editors, Tara Singh Carlson at G. P. Putnam's Sons and Helen Garnons-Williams and Anna Kelly at 4th Estate. I could not have been better agented, edited, and supported.

Merci à Patricia Seixas for checking the written French. Any remaining errors are my responsibility alone. (Particular thanks for *gribouillis*.)

And finally to Rachel and Jo, midwives at the Royal United Hospital, Bath, on duty in the small hours of 12 September 2005. My angels.

SOURCES

The following works represent the tip of the tip of the iceberg—a highly selective list of the most pertinent, vivid, and enjoyable items I came across as I researched *Think of Me*.

JAMES'S WAR—THE NORTH AFRICAN CAMPAIGN

Viewed as controversial by some, *The Desert Generals* by Corelli Barnett (W. Kimber, 1960) nonetheless gives a strong sense of the terrible to-and-fro of the fighting across North Africa. *A History of the Mediterranean Air War* by Christopher Shores and Giovanni Massimello (Grub Street, 2016, Vol. 2) is the a painstakingly accurate account of the day-by-day progress of the air campaign. For James's squadrons I referred to the National Archives, where 274 Squadron's Operations Record Books for 1941 and 1942 can be found under AIR-27-1558 to 1559. For 6 Squadron, follow AIR-27-73 to 76. Every detail, from dogfights against Me 109s down to a lost lavatory seat, is preserved here by the squadrons' adjutants who kept typing, often on fading typewriter ribbons, through battles, dust storms, and airfield bombings, for all the years of the campaign. I also admired *6 Squadron* by Peter Moulding (Bashall Eaves, 1972), himself a wartime 6 Squadron pilot.

HURRICANES

Hawker Hurricane: Owners Workshop Manual by Paul Blackah, Malcolm V. Lowe, and Louise Blackah (Haynes, 2010). Indispensable, and kindly loaned to me by my nephew Billy Parker. For the big canon of the Hurricane IID (the aircraft of 6 Squadron), I am grateful to the 6 Squadron website webmaster for *A Squadron in Service* by Jim Fox, a technical account of the armory of 6 Squadron in 1942–1943. For flying a Hurricane against the Messerschmitt 109, see an interview with Stewart "Bomb" Finney, 1 Squadron SAAF, https://www.youtube.com/watch?v=AWyY78s8L3w.

The diary of pilot C. D. C. Dunsford Wood paints a vivid picture of his anti-tank training with 6 Squadron at https://storyofwar.com/2012/11/30/november-30th-1942-cairo/. Pilot Roy Veal crashed during this training: his story is in the BBC *WW2 People's War* archive, https://www.bbc.co.uk/history/ww2peopleswar/stories/61/a3293561.shtml.

Deaths during anti-tank training are recorded in the National Archives, Air-27-75, details above.

Finally, an extract from a letter to my grandmother from my grandfather Henry Maughan "Bill" Liardet. Bill had command of the 6th Royal Tank Regiment during the retreat in June 1942 before the First Battle of El-Alamein. "*I got taken on by one of our own Tank Busters, a Hurricane, who did two attacks . . . but luckily missed each time.*" A lesson on tank recognition had been given to 6 Squadron on 1 May 1942 (AIR 27-75), so it is likely that dusk, and a large dust cloud, caused the eager Hurricane pilot to mistake his target on that day in June—and, happily, twice fail to hit it!

ALEXANDRIA

For context, *Levant: Splendour and Catastrophe on the Mediterranean* by Philip Mansel (John Murray, 2010). For a literary and social portrait of Alexandria 1900 to 1950, *Alexandria: City of Memory* by Michael Haag (Yale University Press, 2004). See p. 277 for M. de Menasce's musical afternoons featuring the pianist Gina Bachauer—and cakes!

Personal memories include *Out of Egypt: A Memoir*, by André Aciman (Picador, 1994). This foremost writer on exile describes the exploits of three generations of his Jewish family from their arrival in Alexandria to their sad departure. *Les Cahiers AAHA* (Amicale Alexandrie Hier et Aujourd'hui, http://www.aaha.ch) are a rich resource of history and debate on all aspects of Alexandria and her communities, from history, politics, and culture to food, drink, and beachside cafés. I am grateful to the collection of interviews *Voices from Cosmopolitan Alexandria* (eds. M. Awad and S. Hamouda, Biblioteca Alexandrina, 2006) for a certain venerable lady's recollection that during the war, people used to remark that only the ugly girls married RAF pilots . . .

For air raids on Alexandria, https://www.britishpathe.com /video/alexandria-bombed/query/Precautions will take you to a Pathé newsreel of the aftermath of a bombing. Individual raids in the spring of 1942 are listed in Shores and Massimello (see above). The novel *No One Sleeps in Alexandria* (see below) gives details of bombings, air-raid shelters, and Egyptian casualties.

For Yvette's blue-jacketed Lycée notebooks: *In the Afternoon Sun,* a memoir by Julie Hill (Bookbaby, 2017).

I also drew on fictional works. Robert Solé's *Birds of Passage* (translated by John Brownjohn, Harvill Press, 2000) is an enchanting novel, grounded in the author's family history, about several generations of a Greek Catholic, Syrian Alexandrian family. It was my privilege to translate two novels by a master of modernist literature, Edwar al-Kharrat: *City of Saffron* and *Girls of Alexandria* (Quartet, 1989 and 1993). Al-Kharrat was born in 1926 into a Coptic family in Alexandria, and his novels intertwine stories of love and family life from the 1930s and 1940s with the city's eternal myths. *No One Sleeps in Alexandria*, a novel by Ibrahim Abdel Meguid (translated by Farouk Abdel Wahab, AUC Press, 1996, mentioned above), vividly describes the wartime tribulations of ordinary Alexandrians.

Out of the thousands of photographic archives available online, the historic fragments and memorabilia of the Cohen family, including sketches by the artist Sidney Arrobus, can be viewed at https://www.flickr.com/photos/cam37/sets/72157601540771110/. This collection includes a wrinkled scrap of wrapping paper from Hannaux Department Store in Alexandria, too small, I think, to line a kitchen drawer. Yvette's must surely have been bigger.

The Women's Auxiliary Air Force (WAAF) in Egypt

The WAAF at War by John F. Turner (Pen and Sword Aviation, 2011) and *Sand in My Shoes* by Joan Rice (Harper Perennial, 2007) address the topic from different angles.

"Joining the W.A.A.F. aka W.A.A.F. Recruiting in the Middle East" (britishpathe.com) shows recruits exchanging their pretty shoes for sturdy lace-ups as they enroll in the force. For a photograph of some of these new WAAFS learning how to pack parachutes at an operational station in Egypt, go to https://www.iwm.org.uk/collections/item/object/205216431; for local WAAF recruits "dressing up" a line, see CM5166.jpg—Wikimedia Commons. One young woman's story is related by a family member: "Ginette Shama, daughter of Ezra Shama (a cotton classifier), was born in October 1917 at Alexandria.

Gina joined the WAAF in 1942 and was based in Alexandria, she was Aircraft Woman 1st class. In 1944 Ginette married . . . Frederick Charles Rounsley, a British serviceman, at St. Mark's Church, Alexandria" (https://www.rootschat.com/forum/index.php?topic= 659584.0)

On the subject of marriage, another union celebrated at St. Mark's was between an ex-member of 6 Squadron, Flying Officer M. A. Mac-Donald, and Mlle. Nadia Khayyat, at 3 p.m. on 1 February 1943. "A large party of officers of the Squadron attended the wedding" (AIR 27-76-3).

Peter Ingram's Injury, His Hospital, and His Treatment

Peter's injury was inspired by the pilot Gordon "Mouse" Cleaver, whose experience is recorded in detail in *Speed Kings* by Andy Bull (Penguin Random House, 2015, pp. 346, 356). Cleaver was injured during the Battle of Britain and treated in England, but it was up to an eye surgeon in Cairo to save Peter's sight—Hyla Stallard, based at the 15th Scottish General Hospital in Agouza. For more on this talented man, see "Henry [Hyla] Stallard" by John D. Bullock in *Doctors of Another Calling* (Rowman and Littlefield, 2013). Nurse Selina "Pam" Dunnett of the Queen Alexandra's Imperial Nursing Service recalls her time at the 15th Scottish General and her admiration of Mr. Stallard in an Imperial War Museum recording, https://www.iwm.org.uk/collections/item/object/80017831. For the hospital's splendidly attired Sudanese waiters, see Part 7 of "Else happened and I was in uniform" by Geoffrey Dent at https://www.bbc.co.uk/history/ww2peopleswar/stories/56/a4585656.shtml.

The Second World War's *Services Guide to Cairo* (warlinks.com) gives details of Willcocks' croquet ground and much more.

James and Archdeacon Frobisher: Their Capture, Imprisonment, and Marches to Liberation

John Carson Wilson's capture (https://www.iwm.org.uk/collections /item/object/80014876) along with the final flight of Paul Brickhill, who was shot down in Tunisia in 1943, gave me ideas for James's final minutes of combat and ensuing capture. Frobisher's sea battle is modeled on the encounter between the German cruiser *Thor* and HMS *Voltaire*; for details, see *Sailors in Cages* by R. V. Coward (TBS, 1967). Prisoners from the *Voltaire* were sent to Lamsdorf and then out into factories and mines: Frobisher's work party can be found among the lists on this website: https://www.prisonersofwarmuseum.com/lams-dorf-working-parties.html.

For hunger, and the tipped-over dinner cauldron, see Trevor Keeling in the People's War archive at https://www.bbc.co.uk/history /ww2peopleswar/stories/44/a2974944.shtml.

Frobisher's and James's marches are described at https://www .lamsdorflongmarch.com/ and https://www.stalagluft3.com/long -march/. I beg forgiveness for transposing two small incidents, concerning a bucket of water and a dog, from Joseph Fusniak's account of the march from Lamsdorf—the ordeal undertaken by Ronald Frobisher—to James's shorter journey from Belaria to Luckenwalde (https://www.bbc.co.uk/history/ww2peopleswar/stories/38 /a1317638.shtml).

Stillbirth

As Yvette says, she was lucky even to hold her stillborn child in 1950. Parish records and widely reported anecdotal evidence tell of babies being immediately removed from the mother and treated as Yvette attests (https://www.bbc.co.uk/news/education-51271977). More on baby loss past and present in the UK can be found at https://www.sands.org.uk/.

Times had changed by 2005 when I lost my own daughter at birth, and I cannot fault the care given to me, my daughter, and her father. All the same, no research was needed to create Yvette and James's beloved Catherine and her hard journey into the world.

THE CHURCH OF ENGLAND FROM THE POSTWAR PERIOD UNTIL THE 1970s

Although James was ordained before the war, his era was indeed a time when many young men went straight into the Church after demobilization. *The Testing of Vocation* by Robert Reiss (Church House Publishing, 2013) describes the wave of postwar ordinations into the Church of England that Ronald Frobisher alludes to in the opening pages of *Think of Me.* Christopher Campling, who served in the wartime navy before entering the Church, writes atmospherically in his autobiography *I Was Glad* (Janus, 2007) about his religious training with all its burdens and austerities. Like James Acton, Prebendary Austen Williams, already a military chaplain, was captured by the Germans in 1940. He commented later that his world-famous ministry at the church of St. Martin-in-the Fields in the 1970s, with its Sunday soup kitchen and scores of homeless sheltering in the crypt, was not unlike an internment camp: "There are people who smell in some way or don't use the right language. They are a threat and a bore and a mess. But you can't exclude them. You live with, you get fed up with— and you live with getting fed up with—them, and you just go on. There is no getting away" (Beeson, p. 149, see below). The experiences of these young priests gave me an insight into James as curate and vicar to the people of Alver Shore. Alver Shore is not Gosport, Hampshire, but this photo archive gives a feel for the wartime south coast: https://www.gosportsociety.co.uk/GosportSociety_the_war_years.html.

Trevor Beeson's *Around the Church in Fifty Years* (SCM Press, 2007, mentioned above) gives a lively overview of the main trends in the Church from the 1950s to the 1990s. We know that in 1950 James, as a man searching for a God who had seemingly abandoned him, was reading Paul Tillich's sermons (*The Shaking of the Foundations*, Scribner, 1948); I like to think that he also read John A. T. Robinson's *Honest to God* (SCM Press, 1963) during the 1960s, and that perhaps, after he found his Maker again, *Yes to God* by Alan Ecclestone (Darton, Longman and Todd, 1975) later in the 1970s. But that lies in his happy future, beyond the end of *Think of Me*.

—FRANCES LIARDET, MAY 2021